Void Of Endings

Hillary Raymer

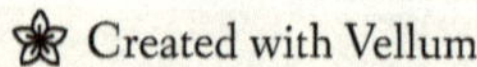 Created with Vellum

*For my readers...to the end of the world
and back again.*

Trigger Warnings

- Graphic violence
- Sexually explicit content
- Death
- Blood & torture
- Emotional abuse/trauma
- Adult language
- Loss of family member

Brackroth
Dragon Riders
Suvarese
Rainbow River
Lismore
Marin
Wenfyre
Fleet

utumn
egion
Winter
Legion
Summer
Legion
Pass
of
Veils

"Pulse of my heart, it beats only for thee,
Through dreams, and realms, and centuries.
Bound to you through night, and the in between.
Soul of my soul, our lives entwined by fate,
For each breath, each sigh, I will always wait.
My once now and forever faerie queen."

~Tiernan Velless, High King of the Summer Court

Chapter One

Maeve's blood burned, hot and acidic, like all the fires from the innermost circle of hell. Every breath was sharp, a piercing inhale that left her lungs raw and scalded her throat. Magic coursed through her veins, filling her with the desire to seek, defend, and destroy. Impatience gnawed at her, scraping the corners of her mind.

Only hours had passed since her return to Faeven, but she could no longer stand on this balcony and be idle.

She had to do something. She had to save him.

Tiernan Velless. The High King of Summer. Her *sirra*.

Lir had told her as much, tried his damnedest to remind her of who she was, of her life before the Ether. But Lir was only one person, a glimpse of her past, and the stories he told weren't enough to revive the memories lost to her.

But Tiernan...he lived in her soul. She could feel him, she could hear his voice throughout her dreams and every waking hour, calling to her. Asking her to remember. His face was a blur, a smear of colors washed away by spilled ink.

Her hands coiled around the smooth stone railing, tightening until her knuckles were white, and her fingers ached. She glanced down, her gaze snagging on the ring she wore. The round stone shone back at her, twinkling in the sunlight, reflecting the deepest shades of blue and violet. Mounted in a setting shaped like the sun, its dazzling beauty was a harsh reminder of all she stood to lose.

Maeve took a breath, inhaling the sweet scent of plumeria surrounding her.

But something was missing.

He was missing.

The witch thread on her wrist, the mark of twin mountain peaks with a star bursting between them, scalded her skin. Aching. She clamped her hand over it, then squeezed her eyes shut.

Harsh, tormenting images entered her mind's eye with ruthless clarity.

She saw them. Tiernan and the one named Merrick. Dark splotches of crimson muddled their filthy clothing. Hair matted with dried blood clung to their swollen and bruised faces. Both of them were on their knees, their limbs chained in the metal teeth of iron. A gathering of trooping fae stood around them, and one in particular captured Maeve's attention. He was eerily tall. Gangly. Unsightly. The leader.

He was speaking to Tiernan and Merrick, but his words were too distorted for Maeve to understand, the distance between them making it nearly impossible to interpret.

The leader jerked his head and another fae stalked up. He swung his leg back, then kicked Merrick hard in the chest. He toppled over, unable to catch himself with his wrists bound behind his back. The cracking of his ribs echoed off the mountains sloping up behind them.

Maeve ignited. Her magic churned, combusting with an all-consuming rage that threatened to sear through her like an inferno.

The image only intensified as the one she thought to be the leader loomed over Tiernan.

No.

The leader's boot collided with the underside of Tiernan's jaw. His head snapped back, blood spilling from his mouth, splattering over the sodden ground. He rocked backward, but regained his balance, and glared up at the bastard who struck him with a pair of piercing twilight eyes.

Maeve hissed. She seethed. She roared.

In a fury, her wings tore from her back, the dense scent of magic coating the air. So thick it was almost suffocating. Her power swelled in a riot of flames. She would aim for the western mountains, where the land seemed covered in a haze of fog, obscured from the light of day. She would follow the witch thread to him, to them both, and she would destroy anyone who stood in her way.

Spreading her wings, she prepared to launch into the skies.

"Maeve!" a familiar male voice called from behind her.

She spun, chest heaving, and found Lir bursting through the door behind her. He hesitated, one hand lifting as though to reach for her, the other holding on tightly to the door.

He watched her. Gauged her. "Wait."

"I have waited long enough. I have waited while everything was stolen from me. My memories. My life. The very air I need to breathe." Her mate, but those words were a whisper through her heart. "I am going to take back what is *mine.* I will not rest until he is returned to me."

This time, Lir moved toward her. "My lady, you cannot—"

"I can." She spread her arms wide. "And I will."

Glamour coated her as aubergine leather armor embellished

with rose gold stitching in the form of vine-like roses fused to her body. Fastened to her thigh, her Aurastone glowed like the brightest dawn. Wind billowed around her, pulling her hair back and plaiting it into a braid held in place by ribbon. She opened one hand and a sword appeared. The hilt was gold, comfortable against her palm. Its blade was incandescent, engulfed by radiant beams of sunlight. The weapon was familiar to her, a part of her, one she'd wielded multiple times over. Not once had it failed her.

She turned away from him then, ignoring the cacophony of feminine voices echoing from the corridor. More names she didn't know, more faces she couldn't recall. All of them calling out to her.

But right now, she would waste no more time.

Without another word, Maeve darted upward, following the tug on her wrist, the pain of her soulmate. She flew through the clouds, heading toward the silvery mist shrouding the west. She soared through the sky, passing over a lush green forest just north of the Summer Court. Between the fluttering of jade leaves and the stretch of long branches, she caught the glimpse of a faerie pool. A glistening waterfall rushed over the edge of a small mountain, causing the surface of the pool to ripple, reflecting dozens of tiny rainbows. There was a smooth bank where the soft blades of grass sprouted like a cushiony blanket, ready to offer a reprieve from the sun beneath the shade of towering trees. A tiny prickle tingled along the back of Maeve's neck. She'd been there before, she was sure of it. But she would worry about her lost memories later.

Right now, there was only one thing she wanted to do.

Destroy the ones responsible for harming those she loved.

With her sword in hand, she barreled toward the majestic twin mountain peaks, cutting through the space between them like a blazing, bursting star.

Her gaze scanned the base of the mountains where she'd

seen Tiernan and Merrick through the bond of witch thread. A path curved off to her left, a pass cloaked in shade from the rising mountains looming over it. Sparse trees with pale green leaves dotted the mountain pass, leading to a space where the veil of heavy mist shifted, creating a narrow opening to whatever lay beyond.

The scent hit her first.

The metallic tang of blood. The curdling stench of sullied magic. The reek of cold iron.

She spied them a second later. Merrick was still on his side, struggling to sit up. Tiernan bared his teeth like a feral beast ready to attack.

Maeve tucked in her wings, plummeting toward the ring of trooping fae surrounding them. Her boots slammed into the ground so hard the earth shuddered and the mountains trembled beneath her power.

Slowly, she raised her head.

Her braid fell over one shoulder and she flicked her wrist, twirling her sword.

The trooping fae scattered. Some of them ran to seek refuge behind the cover of trees, but five of them gathered their weapons, preparing to fight. The dubious leader stood among them, his arms far longer than was natural, and a freakishly wide grin plastered on his gaunt face.

Maeve lifted her sword and pointed it directly at him.

"You stole something of mine." Fire erupted around her in currents of incendiary waves. They swirled, licking the sky and singeing the earth. She nodded to where Tiernan and Merrick were held captive. "Release them...and I'll spare your life."

She almost smiled.

Part of her wanted the wretched male to defy her, to refuse to heed her warning. She would gladly show him and his companions no mercy for the suffering they inflicted. Her blood thrummed with malice, silently daring him to challenge her.

The gangly fae sneered, taking a single step closer. "And if I don't?"

This time, Maeve smirked.

"Then I'll kill you." Her magic pulsed through her, ready to break free. "And anyone who stands in my way."

He cackled. A hoarse, grating sound.

From her right, one of the trooping fae spat, his face twisted in disgust. "We're not afraid of you."

"You should be." It was another male who spoke. His tone was light, amused even, but there was an underlying bite of sarcasm. One she nearly recognized.

Her gaze slid to the far left, and Merrick's cerulean eyes found hers. They were filled with knowing vengeance. His lips were upturned in a bloody smile, his dimples winking.

Maeve didn't dare look at the male who was next to him. She couldn't...not yet.

The leader of the trooping fae hoisted his weapon and called out, "Teach this fae bitch a lesson."

As though they didn't have minds of their own, the fools advanced on her. That was their first mistake.

Four of them circled her, their swords at the ready. Moving as one unit, they attacked from all sides. She ducked low, avoiding the swipe of an angry blade as it cut through the air across her head. Leaning back, Maeve braced herself on her left hand and kicked her leg out, hooking it around the fae standing in front of her. She took his legs out from under him, then arced her sword of sunlight high into the air, slicing down the fae who came at her on the right. His agonizing scream pierced the air but she paid him no mind.

His death would not seek refuge in her conscience.

Maeve shoved up from the ground, stretched her wings,

beating them in rapid procession. She knocked back the male and female who moved in on her with their axes raised high.

These fae were not warriors. They were not battle-hardened or trained to fight. They knew nothing of combat or the ways of war. She almost pitied them, for they were simply following the orders of a common fae, and she could practically guarantee they never thought he would be a good enough reason to die.

Unfortunately for them, they'd chosen to fight on the wrong side.

Against *her*.

Maeve rose up on her toes and spun, the flares of her sword taking them down in one clean swipe. Their charred bodies dropped to the ground, the resounding thud rumbling up into the face of the mountains.

Three down. Two to go.

The other trooping fae before her scrambled to his feet, his yellow gaze focused on her. His face was drawn, furrowed with loathing. No doubt he'd seen the mess she'd made of his companions.

Stepping toward him, she offered a ruthless smile. "Are you afraid now?"

"I'll kill you for what you've done to them!" he shouted, spittle clinging to the scruff of his filthy face. He rushed her with his sword and she parried.

"Not if I kill you first."

Maeve didn't even give him a chance to retaliate. She summoned the creation, the lifeblood of magic flowing inside of her. A well of power poured from her, its magnitude enough to bring down the heavens. She channeled it into the earth, and a tremor rumbled beneath the trooping fae's feet. His eyes went wide, his skin turned the color of ash. The soil cracked, fracturing into a dozen different directions as fissures took form, shooting debris into the air. The ground he stood upon crumbled, giving way at Maeve's command. There was a brief look of horror on his face before he fell into oblivion and the earth swallowed him whole.

Gradually, the land repaired itself, sealing every crevice. A cool breeze filtered down from the mountaintops, dusting away the footprints, erasing every last trace of the trooping fae.

Maeve turned to face the so-called leader and the blood in her veins ran cold.

He stood behind Tiernan, flashing her that same hideous smile. His gnarled hand was fisted into her mate's hair, yanking his head back and exposing the length of the bronze neck. Positioned at the base of his throat was a jagged blade.

One wrong move, and the bastard would plunge it into Tiernan, killing him.

"Release him," she warned.

"Drop your weapon." The leader angled the blade deeper, so beads of red slid down Tiernan's neck. His veins bulged, and even from a few feet away, Maeve could see the severe clench of his jaw.

He was furious.

But she hadn't come all the way back from the Ether only to watch him die.

Maeve opened her hand, and the sword of sunlight vanished.

The fae blinked. "Who are you?"

"I am Maeve Ruhdneah. High Princess of the Autumn Court. Goddess-blessed. The Dawnbringer. Queen of the Furies." Maeve took one calculating step forward, and for the first time since her arrival, she met her mate's empowering gaze. "And I show mercy to no one."

Dawn exploded around them.

Maeve grabbed her Aurastone, and just as the blinding aurora ebbed, she flung it right into the trooping fae's throat.

The blade of the Aurastone never missed its mark.

She stalked over to the fallen fae and pulled her dagger from his neck. The sucking sound it made caused her gut to seize. Wiping away the sticky blood, she sheathed it, then finally faced the two fae males who each held a different piece of her heart. One, her family. The other, her soul.

Time seemed to halt completely. An eternity could have passed and she wouldn't even have noticed. Merrick stood there, his face discolored from bruising, his lip busted and bleeding. His snow-white hair with a streak of shocking pink fell in his face, covering one bright blue eye. Carefully, so not to hurt him, she reached out and gingerly smoothed the pieces back from his face.

His smile gutted her.

Whatever moments they shared, whatever time they spent together, was lost to her.

Merrick bowed slowly, and winced. "Looking good, my lady."

A shaky breath escaped her and her gaze fell upon Tiernan. *Mine.*

Maeve stared at the male before her with eyes reminiscent of the twilight hour—both blue and violet, and devastating. He'd been beaten severely, they both had, and blood still pooled from the wound near his mouth. She expected something, anything, but only emptiness found her. The ache was soul deep. The weight of loss crushed her. She ran her thumb along the underside of the ring she wore, and he tracked the movement. No matter how desperately she reached for her memories, there was nothing, an expansive void of a life she couldn't remember. All she had was the witch thread marking her wrist. A binding promise, a declaration that told her she should know him, that she should love him. That this male, this High King, belonged to her.

"*Astora.*" His voice was hoarse, as though he'd suffered an agony far greater than torture.

Awareness crawled along her spine and she stole a hasty glance over her shoulder to the remaining trooping fae still cowering in the woods.

"Leave," she demanded, the singular word holding a vow to end them all if they refused to obey. "Now."

They darted through the trees, heading east, disappearing behind a wall of overgrowth and low-hanging vines. Only once she was certain they were gone did she turn back to Tiernan and Merrick.

Their wounds were numerous. There was no way of knowing how much blood they'd lost, or how long they'd gone without food or water. Overhead, clouds rolled across the sky, gray and ominous. The wind picked up, gusting down through the mountain pass, carrying with it a distinctive chill and the threat of...something else.

Maeve shuddered, shaking off the strange sensation. She approached Merrick, her gaze fastened to the iron cuffs clamped on his wrists and ankles. Tilting her head, she looked up at him. "Let's get you out of these, shall we?"

"Be careful, my lady." He pulled away when she reached for him. "It's iron."

The corner of her mouth curved into a smile. "Don't worry, my lord. I won't hurt you."

Maeve held out her hand, channeling her magic, focusing on the imprisoning metal. She melded it, warped it, warmed it until the iron softened like ribbons of silver. Her blood hummed, strengthening, and the cuffs fell away. She repeated the same process on Tiernan, relief easing the ache in her heart when they were finally free of the iron.

A rush of energy spiraled around Tiernan and Merrick, their power finally unleashed. Maeve staggered back as the overwhelming scent of orange blossom and cedarwood ruptured between them, filling the small clearing with immeasurable force, a wave of intensity she could barely withstand. The air crackled, her wings fluttered, and her braid lifted from her shoulder at the sheer magnitude of the Archfae standing in front of her.

Their magic was wondrous.

Breathtaking.

Tiernan stepped toward her, but the mountains rumbled. The sound of it reminded Maeve of a low growl, like a beast awakening from a long slumber. Bits of rock tumbled down the mountain face, and the mist to the west started to shift as though it was taking on a life of its own. Maeve swallowed a gasp as the world shimmered.

"Glamour," she breathed.

Merrick inhaled, the blue of his eyes darkening. "We have to get out of here."

Another gust of wind slammed into them, more vicious than before.

Tiernan was by her side a second later. "Can you *fade?*"

She blinked, staring at him.

An earth-shattering crack sent her careening into his arms as the ground rumbled in anger.

"Go!" Merrick shouted.

Tiernan crushed Maeve to him, grabbed Merrick by the arm, and together, they *faded.*

Chapter Two

The swell of magic surrounding Maeve eased and when she finally caught her breath, she found herself standing in a courtyard, the warm caress of Summer welcoming her home.

She was still in Tiernan's arms, the strength of him supporting her, holding her steady. Palm trees swayed in the comforting breeze, their long fronds sifting against one another, creating a soothing melody. Sparkling streams of turquoise wound their way through the enclosure and fountains gurgled to life as sunlight caught their sprays, showering the courtyard in tiny rainbows. On a breath, the tantalizing scent of sun-drenched palms, sandalwood, and the faintest hint of plumeria filled her.

Tiernan.

This was where she belonged.

His grip on her waist tightened, and she was so close to leaning into him, to tilting her head up and pressing a small kiss to the underside of his bruised jaw, when a symphony of voices echoed off the glistening white stone walls.

Maeve reared back as three females raced toward her. One with springy, burgundy curls. Another with hair the color of moonlight. And the third, whose tresses reminded her of the sun. Two of them were fae, one was decidedly mortal. They darted toward her in a flurry of gowns and armor, their faces full of elation. Maeve braced herself for the onslaught of questions she couldn't answer, for the disappointment that would follow when they realized she'd lost part of herself.

"Maeve!"

"You found them! Oh, Maeve, you found them!"

The one with silver hair reached her first, but Lir was faster. He stepped in front of Maeve like a barrier and held up one hand.

"Stop." The grim somberness of his tone set Maeve's teeth on edge. Silence befell the courtyard. "She does not remember us."

At his words, Tiernan's hand fell and he stepped back, away from her. "How is this possible?"

Cold seeped into Maeve's bones at the loss of him.

Lir faced his High King, bowing. "Her time in the Ether stole her memories. She has nothing from before her arrival there, no recollection of the life she lived before she was taken from us. Until her memories are restored, we are strangers to her."

"Maeve." The one with a braid of silver stepped forward, the lines of her face etched with puzzlement and hurt. "Is this true?"

She nodded, solemn, wishing she could make them understand.

"I know in my heart that I love each of you. That you're my friends. My family." Her nose tingled and she sniffled, willing away the urge to cry. "But your faces are indistinct in my mind. Your names...erased."

Lir shifted to the side, and the female with golden blonde hair moved closer. There was a swell of magic, a calming repose that mended the growing ache inside Maeve's heart. She clasped her hands in front of her, golden flower tattoos crawling up her arms. Her gown of blush rippled in the breeze and when she smiled, a distant memory fluttered just beyond Maeve's reach.

"My name is Ceridwen Velless, High Princess of the Summer Court. Sister to Tiernan." Her eyes, the same shade as her twin brother's, glowed with kindness. "And I'm one of your closest friends."

Merrick moved into her line of sight, his injuries slowly healing.

"Merrick Solasta. Famed hunter of the Summer Legion." He winked and fisted a hand over his heart. "Devoted champion to High King Tiernan Velless, and to you, my lady."

The other fae female grinned, rolling a toothpick between her teeth. She wore a belt of daggers slung around her waist and Maeve couldn't be sure, but she could've sworn the female's eyes changed colors from gold to bright green.

"Brynn Banlisch." She inclined her head. "Healer. Warrior. Friend."

Maeve faced the mortal female then, the one whose face was wrought with agony and disbelief, as though she was trying to will Maeve to remember every moment they spent together. She plucked the pale pink rose out from behind her ear and tucked it neatly into Maeve's braid.

"I am Saoirse Doran. I have known you since we were children. I stood with you in Kells and I stand with you now." Her voice cracked. She pressed her lips into a firm line, her gaze darting all over the courtyard as though trying to find the words to say. When her gaze finally lifted to Maeve, the lines of her face were filled with hardened resolve. "I will fight alongside you through the brightest of days and the darkest of nights. I will never fail you. I will never betray you. I will never leave you."

Saoirse's words were a chord. Broken yet melodic. Devastatingly beautiful. Maeve studied her, reaching up lightly to touch the rose in her hair. "You have a poet's soul. Did you know?"

A sheen misted across Saoirse's eyes, and her smile was brittle. Pained. "So I've been told."

"Maeve."

Tiernan's voice sent a shiver of anticipation down her spine. Goosebumps prickled along her spine as she turned to face him. His gaze roved over her, slow and languid. Her soul sang before him. A flush spread across her chest, rising into her cheeks. He looked at her like she was the essence of life, with a deep and intense yearning, like she was the air he needed to breathe.

"*Astora.*" He spoke into her mind and she held her breath.

There was a gentle tug on her heart, and the witch thread marking her warmed.

She inclined her head. "*My lord.*"

"*You know my name.*" It was a statement of fact, not a question.

Maeve's eyes darted to his neck, where a golden sun tattoo spiraled down below the collar of his shirt. She looked back up at him, unable to break the spell he cast upon her. "*You are Tiernan Velless, High King of the Summer Court.*"

"*And?*" he asked mildly, his brow arching.

The thread tying her to him pulled tight. "*And you are mine.*"

Tiernan bowed before her. He rose, then rolled the cuff of his tattered shirt, displaying his forearm. There, marking his wrist, was the imprint of witch thread. It was an exact replica of her own—a star bursting between twin mountain peaks. *"My soul is yours, astora. In this life, in every life, from now until I draw my last breath."*

Maeve's bottom lip trembled, and she bit it to keep the swell of emotion at bay. *"What if my memory never comes back?"*

"Then I will wait." He moved in, close enough to touch her, yet he held back. *"For as long as it takes."*

Tiernan reached out, the tips of his fingers barely grazing her own. *"Remember me, astora."* He lowered his head, gently pressing his forehead against hers. *"Remember."*

Vague images filtered through her mind, moving in and out of focus. She grasped for them. Just like the breeze cooling her skin, they were impossible to catch, slipping between her fingers.

A broken sob escaped her.

Lir stepped up to them then, clamping a firm hand on Tiernan's shoulder. "That's enough for today, my lord."

His voice was quiet, heavy with regret.

Maeve inhaled, but it was different. A distinctive scent filled her—one of mountains and flowers. A smell she both knew and remembered. Her eyes widened.

Merrick was on the move before she could utter a word.

"To arms!" he shouted. Fae warriors sprinted along the upper walls of the courtyard, their weapons at the ready, their arrows notched. Merrick rushed to the opposite side, his sword drawn.

"Wait!" She reached out to stop him, but Lir grabbed her instead, dragging her behind him.

"Get her out of here!" Tiernan demanded, as two swords appeared in his hands.

"What? No!" Maeve struggled against Lir, fighting to maintain her ground. She didn't need to be carted away, she could fight just as well as the rest of them. Better, even. "Lir, let me go!"

He stared down at her, hesitating.

"You *know* me." She jerked her arm again, a silent demand for him to release her.

"My lady, I—"

"Please," she begged, pleading with him.

His silver gaze stole to Tiernan, who was halfway across the courtyard. "Fine. But at least promise you'll stay by my side."

She nodded sharply. "I promise."

Lir surged toward the chaos, then came up short. Maeve catapulted forward but he shot one arm out, catching her.

Before their eyes, plumes of shadows emerged from the center of the courtyard. They swirled like flames of night, expanding and unfurling into the eternal darkness of destruction. From beside her, Lir stiffened, raising both of his curved swords. Ready to defend.

"Steady," Tiernan commanded, his voice low and thunderous.

The shadows billowed, and a figure strolled out from the darkness. Beams of sunlight splintered off of him, illuminating his swath of dark teal hair. He lifted his head, and from across the courtyard, a pair of striking lavender eyes found her.

"Hey, Princess." Rowan shoved his hands into the pockets of his pants. "Long time no see."

"Rowan!"

Maeve's squeal caught Tiernan off guard, and he watched in shock as she sprinted toward Rowan, then launched herself into his arms.

Envy sank its covetous claws into Tiernan's back, scarring him.

"Holy shit." Merrick lowered his weapon, staring at Maeve, who was still held in Rowan's embrace. "He's back."

Rowan glanced over the top of Maeve's head, the corner of his mouth curving into a deliberate smirk. "In the flesh."

That fucking fae.

Tiernan fisted his hands at his sides, enraged. For weeks he'd waited for Maeve to come back to Niahvess, back to him. He'd longed for her. Ached for her. He brought the full force of his magic down upon his city when her fear of whatever she faced in the Ether had ravaged him like his own affliction. Countless nights had been spent lying awake, wondering if he'd ever see her again. Hell, he'd even made that damned journey all the way to Maghmell just to find a way to bring her back home, back to him. All of it, only to stand here now, and see her in the arms of another.

Thunder echoed in the distance, the promise of a storm of his making.

Lir came to stand beside him, sheathing both of his swords.

"Another time, my lord." He nodded to where Maeve and Rowan were encircled with shadows. "He is all she knows."

Godsdamnit.

"You're here." Maeve leaned back, her gaze searching for something beyond Rowan. "But how are you here?"

"It would appear my fate has been decided." Rowan's shadows drew back, gradually dwindling. "I've come to help you fight the war against Parisa."

Tiernan took note of the poignancy of his words. To fight, not to win.

Maeve stepped back and Tiernan relaxed slightly.

She peered up at him, through the swirl of shadows. "Aed sent you back?"

"He did." Rowan glanced behind him. "I brought you something."

He let out a low whistle and all of a sudden a white *faolan* darted from out of the shadows.

"The fuck." Tiernan instantly reached for his sword as flashbacks of his near death experience in the Kethwyn Woods slammed into him, stealing his breath.

The beast rushed Maeve, and he readied to pierce the white ball of fur through the heart, hesitating only when he saw Maeve drop to her knees and cuddle the wolfling.

"Cahira!" Maeve cried as the pup bounded into her lap. She ran her fingers over the *faolan*'s fur, smiling brightly up at Rowan. "Thank you."

Again, Tiernan's gut twisted with resentment.

At once, Ceridwen, Brynn, and Saoirse were all clamoring around the *faolan* with the vivid blue jewel glowing on its forehead. A frost *faolan*, then. The females practically melted as though they'd never seen a pet before, cooing over the pup, ruffling its fur, their voices far more high-pitched than usual.

"Oh, isn't she just beautiful?" Ceridwen crooned.

"The prettiest little wolfling I ever did see," Saoirse agreed.

Tiernan silenced his groan. Unbelievable.

"Well." Ceridwen stood, attempting to regain her composure, her face beaming. She looked over at Rowan. "This is unexpected."

He offered her a small bow. "It's good to see you again, my lady."

She curtsied in kind, demure and once more the epitome of an Archfae. "And you, my lord."

Merrick and Rowan clasped forearms in greeting, the hunter nodding in a show of respect. "How was it in the Ether, Rowan?"

Rowan remained focused on Maeve, his eyes never leaving her. "Delightfully informative."

It was then Tiernan saw it, the Astralstone glinting from Rowan's waist.

"So," he drawled, "you're the Nightweaver."

Rowan straightened, his hand gliding lightly over the hilt where the dagger gleamed like midnight and thousands of stars. His smile was slow and precise. "At your service."

Tiernan's chest hollowed out. Maeve and Rowan. The Dawnbringer and the Nightweaver. He couldn't help it, uncertainty carved its way deep inside of him. He told himself Maeve would never do anything to betray his trust, just as he would always remain faithful to her...but she and Rowan shared a very particular past. They'd been intimate with one another, to an extent, and it was the combining of their power, the sacrifice of their ancient love for one another, that created the first fae to walk the realm.

Maeve had spent all that time in the Ether, with no recollection of him. If her thoughts were only of Rowan, then perhaps he filled the emptiness in her heart as well.

The torment of even considering it, of entertaining those thoughts, left him gutted. He turned away from them and tried to focus on anything else, only to find Ceridwen watching him.

"*Let it be,*" her voice whispered into his mind, sensing the disquiet.

"*How can I?*" he countered. "*She's right here, right in front of me, and I can't even touch her. She barely looks at me. Her heart is no longer mine.*"

Ceridwen shook her head. "*You must give her time. She needs your help now more than ever, Tier. Her memories will return, and when they do, the witch thread bonding the two of you together will be unbreakable. She's your mate, Tiernan. Your sirra. She is fated to you. No one else. Just you.*"

He scrubbed his hands over his face, then pinched the bridge of his nose. *"It's not that easy. Don't you remember? She has to choose me."*

"She already has."

Gods, this was like some kind of fresh hell.

"My lord?"

Rowan's voice pulled Tiernan from his conversation with Ceridwen. He faced the Nightweaver, shuttering away his emotions, his insecurities, his dread. He kept his voice even and cool. "Rowan."

"Might I have a word?"

Tiernan stole a glance at Maeve, who was playing with her pet *faolan,* while Brynn and Saoirse fawned over the pup. Lir stood off to the side, standing guard, while Merrick struggled in vain to keep from laughing when the wolfling emptied its bladder on the studded toe of Lir's boot.

The commander glowered, muttering a few choice words under his breath.

"This way." Tiernan strode to the opposite side of the courtyard, where the shade from the palm trees stretched as the sun made its descent into the sky. At least over here, they would be out of earshot of the ladies, should the conversation become...intense. "What is it?"

Rowan rocked back onto his heels, taking stock of him. "I'm taking Maeve to the memory keeper."

"Absolutely not." Tiernan crossed his arms over his chest, refusing to be swayed. The irony of the situation was not lost on him. Not so long ago, Maeve had considered having her memories of Rowan wiped from her mind. Unfortunately, it was Tiernan who had been erased instead. "I'll not have that wretch of a fae picking through her mind, determining which recollections of hers are worth keeping and which ones are not."

"Would you rather her have no memories of you at all?" Rowan squared off, leveling him with an indignant glare. His shadows crawled, his eyes flashed. "Check your selfish agenda, High King. Because trust me, I have no problem making sure the only male she remembers of the two of us is me."

Thunder cracked overhead as Tiernan's magic broke loose. Dark clouds rolled overhead, cloaking the sky, diminishing the sun.

Everyone in the courtyard turned to stare at him.

Everyone except Maeve.

She looked up, as though a storm might be coming.

Goddess save him, not even his magic was enough to bring her back to him.

"Why should I believe you're doing this to help her?" Tiernan's harsh words scraped between them, forging a bridge of mistrust. "How do I know you won't convince the memory keeper to steal her memories of me, of all of us, completely?"

There was a glimmer of power, a force Tiernan recognized. He sensed the darkness then, the cool shift in the air, the ever-present threat it promised. Once, not so long ago, it had been a part of him. Before Aed had taken it back.

"Because I fucking love her." Destruction settled around Rowan's shoulders and his magic flared. "And because my soul already knows that she can never be mine."

Chapter Three

A sinewy shadow curled around Maeve's braid, tugging it gently.

She looked up to see Rowan standing over her. She still couldn't believe he'd come back from the Ether, and she certainly hadn't expected him to be so...pleasant considering her abrupt departure. She'd left him there in the library with Laurel, without even bothering to say goodbye.

He extended his hand to her and she accepted, allowing him to pull her to her feet. Cahira bounded around her in a circle, then darted across the courtyard to Tiernan, who looked more than a little displeased to have the wolfling in his general vicinity. But she plopped down next to him, waiting patiently for him to pet her.

Tiernan's gaze lifted, finding Maeve's, and without taking his eyes off of her, he slowly reached out and ran his fingers lightly across the top of Cahira's head. Obedient to a fault, Cahira nuzzled him, then promptly curled into a ball to nap. Right next to him. Tiernan's face was unreadable, stony even. But Maeve's heart warmed at the sight.

"Maeve."

She glanced over at Rowan, belatedly realizing he still held her hand. Easing out of his grip, she wrapped her arms around herself, then pulled in her wings until they vanished completely. An emotion clouded his eyes, one Maeve recognized. He blinked, but the hurt remained.

"Come with me," he said, his voice soft.

"Where are we going?" she asked, unable to disguise the wariness creeping into her tone.

He angled his head toward the gates. "To visit an old friend of mine."

She knew everyone watched her with weighted expectations. It didn't matter if they were pretending to carry on with conversations of their own, or if they acted as though they weren't keenly aware of the fact that Rowan wanted to take her away from them. She knew they listened, hearing every word, their unspoken discomfort pinning her beneath a boulder of guilt.

Again, Maeve looked in Tiernan's direction. Not for permission or approval, but for something she couldn't quite name.

He nodded once. Solemn and resolute.

"Okay," she agreed, but hesitation tugged at her. Trepidation coated her skin like ice, chilling her. It was an unnerving sensation, like standing at a crossroads and realizing she would have to make a choice. As though she knew that going with Rowan to wherever he was taking her would somehow change things. Permanently.

He headed for the gates and she followed, unable to bring herself to look back at Tiernan for fear of what she would see reflected in his eyes.

Anger? Betrayal? Despair?

Maeve didn't know how she would respond if faced with

those sentiments, especially if they came from him. It was bad enough she couldn't remember him, and though he put up a strong front, it belied the truth of his torment. Perhaps he'd forgotten how profoundly the witch thread connected them to one another. She'd been keenly aware of his feelings, all of them, despite how well he'd attempted to disguise them under the appearance of understanding. The depth of love he felt for her. The rush of stinging jealousy when Rowan arrived. The buried fear that he would lose her again. Forever.

The last thing she wanted to do was to cause him any more pain, so she kept her head down as she walked alongside Rowan out the gates and into the city below.

Eventually, the dazzling beauty of Niahvess captured her full attention, and the pang of remorse ebbed away.

The Crown City of the Summer Court was glorious. Flowers of every color bloomed from baskets, overflowing across the foot bridges like a rainbow of blossoms. Faerie fire flickered to life in the many lanterns, illuminating the walkways so the canals gleamed as though they'd been doused with golden ink. Even though the sun was dipping far into the western sky, and nightfall was gradually approaching, the floating city came alive. Summer fae spilled out of shops and cafes, mingling in groups as the soothing notes of a flute filled the air.

Together, Maeve and Rowan crossed the bridge leading into the city, and the path before them split into three directions. She came to an abrupt halt, trepidation sinking deep into the pit of her stomach. Rowan headed off to the right, where there was no music, no echoes of laughter, and only scant slivers of light.

It wasn't fear that kept her rooted in place, but something else entirely.

Up ahead, Rowan realized Maeve was no longer with him

and paused, turning back to face her. "Is something wrong?"

"No." Maeve shook her head and hurried to catch up with him. "Of course not."

But that persistent sense of foreboding poked along her spine.

"What is this place?" she asked, her voice barely above a whisper.

It was nothing at all like the vibrancy she'd just witnessed. Here, the fae kept their heads ducked low, casting hasty glances over their shoulders. Their footfalls were quickened as they moved without speaking, avoiding eye contact with anyone who passed them at all costs.

Rowan strolled down the stone path as though he hadn't a care in the world. "This is the Shadow District."

This time, Maeve reached for his hand.

He interlaced their fingers, continuing his easy pace. His relaxed confidence gradually loosened the knot of tension in her stomach.

"Are you back for good?" She hoped conversation would distract her from the fact he had yet to explain who they were going to see and why.

"Of course, Princess."

"What about Laurel?"

"She remains in the Ether."

At that, her gaze swung up to him. There was something about his tone that seemed off. But in the teeming darkness of the Shadow District, she couldn't get a good read on him, and his expression remained shuttered.

Sensing his discomfort, Maeve changed the subject.

"You told Tiernan you're here to help us fight a war." There was a tingling in the back of her mind, like this was something she should already know and understand. It should be important to her, significant. "Do you think we'll win?"

Rowan squeezed her hand. "I hope so."

He stopped in front of a shop with battered shutters and windows that were covered in grime. A wooden sign hung loose in the breeze, creaking with each slight gust. The faded lettering read the name Recollections.

"I feel like I've been here before," Maeve murmured, but Rowan said nothing.

He simply opened the door and led her inside.

Instantly, Maeve was assaulted by the musty scent of old books and weathered papers. On the far wall, a small fire was stoked to life, filling the shop with carved shadows and shreds of light. There was a shelf full of odd baubles—paintings within wooden frames that shifted and blurred so the image was never quite clear, hourglasses with sand floating upward instead of pouring down, interesting trinkets, and jars filled with questionable contents.

A fae ambled forward from the back of the shop, the clicking of his cane the only sound in the silence between them. His eyes were bright but his face was weary. Heavy lines sank deep across his forehead, disappearing beneath his long, graying hair. When he smiled, Maeve almost caught the dimming remnants of his youth.

He propped his cane in front of him, grasping it with both hands. "I was wondering when I'd see the two of you together again."

Rowan dropped Maeve's hand. "Hello, Cormac."

"Nightweaver." Cormac inclined his head. "Dawnbringer."

Maeve inched closer, curiosity drawing her in to the elder fae male. "How is it you age?"

Cormac stared at her, then laughed. Full and crackling. "My sort of magic takes a toll on the soul, Dawnbringer. Every memory, every recollection I take, is years off of my own life. And for each one I give, time works in reverse, restoring me."

Maeve gaped at him. "You're a memory keeper."

"Indeed I am." He bowed slowly, and Maeve thought for certain she could hear his bones groan in protest.

She made to step back, to put distance between herself and the fae who collected the past the way others accumulated books or treasures. But Rowan's palm moved to the small of her back, grounding her in place.

"Maeve needs her memory restored." The pads of his fingers casually tapped along her spine. "She was in the Ether with me, but everything from her life before her time there is gone."

Cormac eyed them speculatively, the lines forming shallow crevices along his forehead deepened with every passing second. He gestured to the round table placed in the center of four chairs, and a worn leather book appeared. The thin parchment pages flipped of their own accord, skimming through scribbles and notes. A feathered pen hovered above the book, ink already dripping from its pointed tip, splattering onto the blank page below.

"She needs your help." There was an urgency in Rowan's voice, and Maeve wondered if perhaps the situation of her memory loss was more dire than she realized. "For Faeven."

Cormac sighed. He ran his thumb beneath his dry lips, back and forth over the coarse gray hairs sprouting from his chin. "The price will be high."

Rowan's hand stilled on her back. "I'll pay it."

"Rowan, no." Maeve whirled on him, grabbing his shirt, fisting it with both of her hands. There was no telling what the memory keeper would demand of him, of either of them, and she couldn't allow Rowan to carry a debt meant for her. "I can't let you do that, not for me."

But he glanced down at her, the corner of his mouth curving into a smirk.

"There's nothing I wouldn't do for you, Princess." Rowan's smile vanished. He smoothed some of the fallen strands of her hair back from her face, curing them behind her ear. "I thought you would have realized that by now."

"Rowan…" Maeve searched his face. Shadows of heartache haunted his lavender eyes. Everything he did for her, he did out of love. A sentiment she couldn't return, at least not in the way he wished. She faced Cormac. Bitterness swept through her. She understood nothing was ever given freely, but she would be damned if Rowan was dragged into some grievous arrangement at her expense. "What's the cost?"

"A single memory belonging to the Nightweaver." Cormac hobbled over to one of the chairs and lowered himself with painstaking slowness. He tapped his cane once, and the floating pen lowered itself to the pages of the book. "One of my choosing."

"No." Maeve shook her head, refusing to agree to such terms. Cormac would gain access to the whole of Rowan's mind, allowing him to pick through Rowan's past like he was browsing a market full of valuable wares. "This is madness. There has to be another way."

"This is the only way." Rowan clasped her hand again and tugged her toward the chairs. She dropped into one, feeling as though she was about to make a terrible mistake. Rowan seated himself next to her, his thumb tracing idle shapes on the back of her hand.

"Don't worry, Princess. Cormac won't hurt you. Because if he does…" Rowan paused. Shadows crept out from around him, slinking like veins of destruction. "I'll end him on the spot."

Maeve wasn't worried about herself.

She was worried about him.

"Well, then." Cormac eased back and nodded toward the pen. It scratched along the surface of the parchment, inking letters along in elaborate script. The words Dawnbringer and Nightweaver appeared, entwined together with ink of black and gold. "Shall we begin?"

Maeve sank further into her seat, unable to move. She rubbed her lips together, sending Rowan a hasty glance.

He squeezed her hand, then stood. "I'll go first."

Her heart skittered, pounding against the increasing tightness of her chest.

"Close your eyes, Nightweaver." Cormac's voice was calm, and Rowan did as he was instructed. "Now—"

"Wait!" Maeve jolted forward, gripped by the irrational fear that this would somehow end them both.

Rowan peeled one eye open, his brow arched in question. "Yes?"

"Is it going to be painful?" The question spilled from her.

"Not in the least." Rowan offered her a reassuring smile. "Completely harmless."

"Have you done this before?" she asked, trying to delay the inevitable.

"A time or two."

Maeve opened her mouth to ask another question, but Rowan bent down and pressed one finger to her lips.

"The sooner we get this over with," he said, his voice cloaking her like velvet, "the sooner you can go home."

Unsettled and slightly defeated, Maeve sat back. "Okay."

Cormac cleared his throat, his brown gaze fixated on her. "Are we ready?"

Rowan straightened and closed his eyes again. "Yes."

Magic spread through the small space, the heady scent of orange blossom and cedarwood expelling the damp, stale smell of the shop. Cormac closed his eyes as well, and a strange, blue hue floated around him, almost like an aura. Tendrils of the glowing light danced toward Rowan, encircling his head.

Maeve grabbed the cushion of her seat, her nails digging into the aged leather to keep herself from grabbing him and running out of there. Rowan remained utterly still as the luminescent magic washed over him.

Her gaze slid to Cormac, his brows furrowing, then lifting as he searched through the memories of Rowan's mind.

"That's the one," he mumbled, and the feathered pen swiftly scrawled something across the pages of the open book.

Maeve peered over, anxious for a glimpse of what was being written, of which memory Cormac had decided to take. But the inked words were unintelligible. Nothing more than a series of lines and strange shapes that reminded her of runes.

Suddenly, a blot of ink bled onto the parchment. The pen stopped moving and the light faded away. Cormac's magic withdrew.

Maeve stared at the book, her gaze finally sliding to Rowan, only to find him staring down at her.

She searched his face, her eyes sweeping over him rapidly for any sign of injury. But he appeared fine. Perfectly normal, even.

"Your turn, Princess."

Maeve stood, the pitch of nervousness causing her palms to sweat. She scrubbed them hastily against the leather of her armor.

"Which memory did he take?" she whispered, knowing full well Cormac could hear.

"I don't know." Rowan shrugged, a small laugh escaping him. "I suppose it doesn't really matter."

"There's nothing to fear, Dawnbringer." Cormac tried to calm her, but the creaking of his voice reminded her of groaning ancient oak trees and the snapping of branches. "Now, it will take some time for you, since we're restoring the vast majority of your memories. I should warn you, this will not be a quick process. You will *feel*. You will experience. You will live every moment of your life in its entirety all over again. Do you understand?"

Maeve nodded, but her mouth was dry. Papery and sticky. A tremble of doubt slicked down her spine.

Rowan shifted closer to her. "I'm right here."

Maeve swallowed down the knot of trepidation clogging the back of her throat and closed her eyes.

"On your word, Dawnbringer." Cormac's craggy voice drifted over to her.

She sucked in a shaking breath. "I'm ready."

At first there was nothing, just the agonizing expectation of waiting. On the next inhale, the scent of magic filled her, accompanied by the lightest of touches across her forehead and around her ears. It was as though a soft cloth of silk had been draped across her eyes, and the hairs along the back of her neck stood on end.

Then, all that was forgotten poured into her.

Maeve stood within a glimmering orb of pale blue light. Papers with images swirled all around her, like pages ripped from a storybook. She snagged one between her fingers, plucking it out of the air, and she was in Kells.

The roughened material of her bedding snagged against the fabric of her leggings as she curled her legs underneath her. She kept her head down, unable to keep the tears of betrayal away. Her cheek stung, the imprints of Carman's hand lingering against her skin. She opened her impossibly small hands, like that of a child, channeling the magic budding inside of her. A teddy bear took form, created from scraps of cotton and bits of thread, with buttons for eyes. Maeve clutched it to her, already knowing the makeshift stuffed animal would be ripped away from her the moment it was discovered.

Dropping the piece of paper, she staggered back, reaching

for a different one.

She was in a training field, fighting alongside a girl with silver hair. They sparred with wooden swords as a man with a hood thrown over his head watched them, calling out instructions and correcting them on their form. In a blink, the wood morphed into steel, and she and Saoirse were no longer young girls practicing the art of war, but skilled warriors bred to kill.

Saoirse yanked a daisy out of the ground and tucked it behind her ear. "It will help cover the stench of blood."

Her smile was radiant, her piercing blue eyes alight with confidence.

But a strong, masculine voice cut through Saoirse's charm, and this time, Maeve was matched against Casimir.

"Ready your weapon," he demanded.

Maeve followed his order, and when she raised the sword in her hands, metal cuffs with intricate whorls were bound to her wrists.

The memory fluttered to the ground and the whirlwind of pages whipping around her intensified. Image after image slammed into her, assaulting her mind. She gasped against the onslaught, swayed as the story of her life bound itself together.

Slanting rain pelted her as the cold bite of the cage burned against her back, ready to dump her into the angry ocean below. Courage fueled her as the earth split open and dark fae attacked Kells, the Scathing opening its wide mouth, spreading decay across her homeland. The Autumn Ceilie burned before her eyes, Rowan's touch almost a promise, yet cloyed by uncertainty.

The pages of her mind sewed themselves into a leather binding, flipping faster, and stealing her breath. Every moment, every glimpse of who she was, of who she became, forged together. Pieces of her past overwhelmed her. Flooded her. She struggled to maintain control against the emotions ravaging her, but each one snagged upon the strings of her heart, tearing through her from the inside out. Anguish. Suffering. Despair. The strength of them caused her nose to tingle and her eyes to burn as unbidden tears escaped her.

Casimir's betrayal opened a gaping wound inside of Maeve, worsened by Saoirse falling beneath the crush of Carman's guards. Then Fearghal's hot breath slid along Maeve's neck while his blade dipped in nightshade hissed across her flesh. Carving her. Breaking her. A moonless night shattered her senses as Rowan towered over her, protecting her from the rain of swords falling from the sky.

"Don't cry for me, Princess."

This was her tragic ballad. A tale woven from heartbreak and pain. Chapters of loss and trauma, inked with enduring agony.

Then she felt it, that warming ember of love.

Slight to start, nothing more than a spark as faces and names, as the family of her choosing, rewrote her new beginning. They ignited a fire within her, one she was willing to fight for until her death.

Eyes of twilight met hers.

Tiernan.

He uttered a single word. *"Astora."*

Pulse of my heart.

A spring of eternal love welled inside of Maeve, and she choked back a sob. The last few pages of her story settled into place with a thousand blank ones ready to be filled.

Her vision blurred, her chest heaved.

Night jasmine, wooded moss, and mountain sage cocooned her, welcomed her.

"I've got you."

Those were the last words Maeve heard before she sank into the darkness.

Chapter Four

It wasn't very often Tiernan found himself in his throne room. In fact, he rarely spent any time in the outdoor space at all unless absolutely necessary. Mostly because it reminded him of his parents. His mother had planted the plumeria trees herself. She would collect all the fallen petals, then crush them and combine them with scented oils—usually rose, or lily, or lemon—to create an elixir for her hair. Sometimes, it lingered on the faintest of breezes.

The gilded throne stood watch behind him, poised like a shrine to the sun, to the magic of Summer. Tiernan had lost count of the number of times he'd witnessed his father sitting there, positioned upon the dais, pretending to punish him for some recklessly foolish incident from his youth.

But on this night, the solitude and emptiness of the throne room was a welcome comfort. His only company was the rustling of swaying palms and the distant crash of the sea upon the shoreline. He paced in silence, his footfalls following the path of golden stones inlaid in the ground to resemble a swirling sun.

The last time he'd come to the throne room, he'd been left feeling helpless. Maeve had been traded to Garvan in exchange for Ceridwen, and all Tiernan could do was wait for the merrows to help her escape. It was eerily similar to the situation he found himself in now. This constant waiting.

"He'll bring her back." Lir's voice sounded from the shadows creeping along the wall. Ever watchful. Ever vigilant.

"I know." Tiernan ran a hand through his hair and gazed up at the night sky. Lazy clouds rolled across the darkened heavens, blotting out the beams of moonlight. He liked to think Lir was right, and that Rowan would hold true to his word.

He reached for Maeve's emotions through the witch thread, knowing better than to disturb her if she was indeed in the midst of her memory restoration. She seemed calm and unbothered, as though nothing was out of the ordinary.

It set Tiernan's nerves on edge.

Lir shifted beneath one of the looming palm trees, the silver hoops climbing up his ears glinting in the pale light. He crossed his arms over his chest, lounging against the uneven surface of the tree's trunk. "You should have seen her."

Confusion drew Tiernan's brows together. "When?"

"When she found out you were gone." Lir shook his head. There was the slightest upturn of his lips and something akin to awe shone bright in his silver eyes. "I've never seen anything like it. Her magic, the sheer *power* of her, was astonishing."

Except Tiernan had seen her, or at least he thought as much. He'd been chained in iron, busted and bleeding, when he sensed a change in the air. He looked up toward the mountain peaks and there, exploding between them, looked what he could only describe as a dazzling starburst.

Maeve had landed on the ground before him a moment later.

He glanced down at his wrist, tracing the witch thread with

his finger. Perhaps it was no coincidence that what he witnessed and what marked his skin were nearly identical images.

Lir shoved off the tree, a look of grave concern haunted his face. "She would have torn open the realms for you."

He didn't doubt it.

Tiernan rubbed his thumb along the glittering back ink. "I worry for her."

"These things take time, Your Highness." Lir skimmed the heavens, searching. "Returning one's memory is no easy feat."

"No, I'm not concerned about how long it takes." Tiernan shook his head and took to pacing once more, the clicking of his boots echoing softly in the night. "But..."

He paused. Hesitated.

Lir watched him with quiet understanding.

"This will change her, Lir." Tiernan spread his arms wide, the ache in his heart expanding, because he knew, he *knew* she would hurt even though the transfer of memories was harmless. "She will relive her memories all over again. She will suffer through the trauma she worked so hard to overcome. Enduring something horrific once is terrible on its own."

He thought of his mate, of how much torment she'd faced in the short span of her life.

"But being forced to survive it twice?" Tiernan shook his head. "What if it breaks her?"

"Maeve is a survivor, my lord."

"But even the strongest of hearts will need time to heal."

The beating of wings cutting through the night air stole Tiernan's attention skyward. His gaze skimmed the black velvet sky, and just beyond a bank of gray clouds, he caught sight of a fae flying toward them. Not just any fae. Rowan.

Moonlight spilled around him, reflecting a golden pink braid.

"Fuck." Tiernan darted toward the center of the throne room just as Rowan landed, carrying a limp Maeve in his arms. "What happened?"

"She'll be okay." Rowan lifted Maeve, gently transferring her into Tiernan's hold. "She just needs to rest. It was...a lot."

Tiernan glanced over at his commander, and Lir stepped forward. "What did he take from her in exchange for her memories?"

Rowan's gaze slid to Maeve and he shoved his hands into his pockets. "I took care of it."

Lir bowed, and the tense silence evaporated between them. "We appreciate it more than you know."

He lifted his shoulders, shrugging off the gratefulness as though it was nothing. "It was the least I could do."

Maeve curled into Tiernan's hold, and he clutched her against his chest. "I'm assuming you'll stay here for the duration?"

"If you don't mind." Rowan made a little clicking noise out of the corner of his mouth. "I can't imagine Parisa would be very welcoming if I showed up again."

No. Probably not.

Lir gestured toward the main courtyard. "I'll show you to your quarters, my lord."

Rowan's entire body tensed, and for the first time Tiernan could ever recall, the fae looked painfully uncomfortable in his own skin. "I'm not—"

"You are Archfae," Tiernan interjected, keeping his voice low and firm. "Your mother was Brigid's sister. Not only that, but you're the Nightweaver. I'm fairly certain you're worthy of the title owed to you."

Rowan remained silent. He inclined his head in acknowledgement, then followed Lir out into the courtyard.

Shifting a sleeping Maeve in his arms, Tiernan carried her

to his bedroom. He laid her down, carefully removing her armor so as not to disturb her. Though her breathing was deep and he knew she slumbered, it was fitful and troubled. He glamoured her an oversized nightshirt, one of her favorites, then sat down on the edge of the bed. For a brief moment, he considered undoing the length of her braid, then thought better of it. It looked far more complicated up close and the last thing he wanted to do was startle her awake.

Tiernan tilted his head back and looked up at the glass dome ceiling, where the stars sparkled like diamonds set on fire, and the moon seemed to smile down upon them.

A gripping sensation seized his heart. It was a bone-deep ache that pulled all the air from his lungs, hollowed out his chest, and gradually, his grieving soul began to mend.

She was home.

He squeezed his eyes shut.

The last time Tiernan cried was when his parents died during the Evernight War, but he couldn't stop the single tear from sliding out of the corner of his eye.

Sun and sky, she was finally home.

He exhaled, and when he opened his eyes, he summoned his guitar.

Strumming softly, Tiernan sang for her. Only for her.

"Pulse of my heart, it beats only for thee,
 Through dreams, and realms, and centuries.
 Bound to you through night, and the in-between.
 Soul of my soul, our lives entwined by fate,
 For each breath, each sigh, I will always wait.
 My once now and forever Faerie Queen."

Warmth bathed Maeve's skin, the touch of the sun as soothing as a lover's caress.

She breathed in deeply, inhaling the scent of sun-drenched palms, warm sand, and plumeria. This place brought her comfort. This place was home.

Home.

Maeve gasped and jolted upright, her eyes flying open.

Her gaze swung wildly around the room, taking it all in, everything exactly as she remembered. A guitar propped up in the corner, a wardrobe that was partially open, and a glass domed ceiling revealing the stunning blue sky. And then she saw him.

He was leaning against the double glass doors that led out onto their shared balcony. Twilight eyes flecked with gold were focused on her, his face unreadable beneath a swath of midnight hair. He stood as though carved from stone. Unmoving. She wasn't even sure if he was breathing. His arms were folded across his bare chest and sunlight glinted off of his bronze body, each muscle seemingly crafted by a god. Even his tattoos looked sun-kissed, glittering gold displaying swirling suns and crashing waves.

Sun and sky, he was magnificent.

Surely, she had to be dreaming.

"Not a dream, *astora*."

Maeve slid out from under the comforter, her bare feet touching the wooden floor. Her knees trembled, and she took one step forward, worried that if she moved any closer, he would disappear.

Then his mouth curved into a slow smile.

She darted across the room and leapt into his waiting arms. He caught her without even stumbling, and she locked her legs around his waist, clutching him. His strong arms wrapped around her, and he tucked her head beneath his chin as her chest heaved, desperate to be as close to him as possible.

"Tiernan." His name fell from her lips on a strangled sob.

"I'm here, Maeve." He cradled her against him, pressing featherlight kisses across her temple. He bent his head low, breathing her in, like she was the very essence of his soul. "I'm here."

"I missed you." The tears came freely now, hot and fast, sliding down her cheeks. She shuddered and his grip tightened. "I missed you so much."

"I'll never lose you again," he murmured into her hair as he carried her over to the bed. He sat on the edge, positioning her in his lap.

Maeve held on, continuing to straddle him. She wove her arms around him, unable to let go. He was here, holding her, and he was real. Burying her face in his neck, she reveled in the feel of his skin, in the beating of his heart, in the way his soul reached for hers, binding them together.

"Are you alright?" he asked, his low baritone a balm to the anguish of being separated from one another.

"I will be." She didn't want to relay the experience with the memory keeper. It was awful, having to relive so much of her life all over again. It had been far more intense than she ever expected, and she hadn't realized how many times she'd been left broken.

"Do you want to talk about it?"

There was no pressure. No demand. Just a simple question. "No."

She didn't want to talk about anything. She simply wanted to be with him, to feel him, and be near him.

Maeve nuzzled her nose against the column of his neck, pressing her lips to where his pulse beat solely for her. He was all she ever needed in this life and the next, all she ever wanted.

He was her anchor. Her rock. A thousand lifetimes with him would never be enough. "I only want you."

Even as she spoke the words, her blood started to hum. Desire, a swell of longing suppressed inside her, simmered to life. It was as though she'd been woken from a centuries-long sleep, and all she craved was him filling every inch of her. She wanted his hands, his mouth, his tongue, his cock. All of it. All of *him*, touching and tasting all of her.

Tiernan's hands moved to her hips, gripping her, fastening her to where she could already feel him hardening beneath his pants.

"*Astora*," he growled, smothering a groan.

She was bare beneath the nightshirt she wore—she'd never been fond of fancy undergarments—and the friction of him pressing against her swollen flesh nearly sent her over the edge.

Maeve slid off his lap and headed toward the bathing suite.

"Where do you think you're going?" Tiernan stood, prowling toward her.

"I need a shower." She lifted one shoulder, then let it fall, as though it was the most obvious thing in the world.

Lust darkened his gaze. "You do realize I'm never letting you out of my sight again, don't you?"

She peeled off the nightshirt, shimmied a little, and tossed it to the floor. "Then I suppose you'll just have to join me."

Tiernan switched on the overhead faucet and Maeve wasted no time in reaching for the waistband of his pants. He snared both of her wrists with one hand.

"Patience." Bending down, he brushed his lips across hers. Once. Twice. "Shower first."

Disgruntled and more than a little frustrated, Maeve begrudgingly let him nudge her into the steaming water.

He removed his pants slowly, kicking them aside, then stepped into the shower after her. He was stunning. Bronze skin. Golden tattoos. Hard muscles. She drank him in, devouring every solid plane of him, her eyes lingering on the cut of his waist. She dropped her gaze to where he strained for her, and a shiver of anticipation raced down her spine.

Maeve shampooed and conditioned her hair, enjoying the way the damp ringlets fell over her wet skin, appreciating the way Tiernan's cock thickened at the sight of her. She lathered herself next, coating her body in sudsy bubbles, making sure to run her hands over every dip and curve. To cup her breasts. To glide her fingers down her stomach and then lower. The scent of the soap wasn't nearly strong enough to disguise her arousal. Yet still, he kept his hands to himself.

He leaned against the shower wall, watching her, drinking her in, as tiny rivulets of water slid down his rippled abdomen. Her nipples hardened, and delicious shivers tingled along her spine. She stood beneath the spray, the hot water rinsing away the last of the soap, every drop teasing her sensitive body until she could no longer withstand the space between them.

Tiernan crossed his arms, flexing intentionally, a wicked gleam flashing in his eyes.

Maeve reached out, running the pad of her fingers along the underside of his cock, toying with golden studs piercing the length of him. His jaw clenched.

She glared up at him. "Why won't you touch me?"

His grin only ignited the fire burning inside her. "All good things to those who wait."

"Fine," she snapped, taking a distinctive step back, and the air surrounding her cooled. "I'll just do it myself."

Without waiting for his response, Maeve delved two fingers between her slick folds. She tipped her head back, gasping as waves of self-induced pleasure coursed through her.

"Fucking gods," Tiernan growled, low and guttural. "Not here."

Maeve pouted. "Why not?"

He grabbed her by the waist, dragging her against him. "I have somewhere better in mind."

Magic crushed her, fusing her to Tiernan as they *faded*.

Warm air dried her skin and hair, and the beauty of the cove appeared before her. Soft sand cushioned her feet and she stepped back, her gaze roving over the waves lapping the shore and the gaping opening overhead where light played with shadow. She moved in a slow circle, welcoming the solace it brought to her soul.

She'd missed this place.

She'd missed him more.

Her skin prickled in a provoking sense of awareness. She turned to find Tiernan, fully nude and fully erect, stalking toward her like predator to prey.

"Tier—"

His mouth was on hers before she could finish. Every thought fled her mind as his tongue meshed with hers, as the taste of him caused her knees to buckle. One hand cupped the back of her neck, angling her to deepen the kiss, while the other stole around her waist to keep her from melting into the sand. He nipped at her, tugging her bottom lip into his mouth with his teeth, and she clutched at his shoulders, clinging with her nails.

Tiernan's hand slid from her neck to her breast, squeezing the tender flesh, his thumb grazing back and forth across her nipple until it peaked beneath his touch.

Maeve rose up on her toes, pressing all of her softness into every inch of his solid body. She wrapped one finger around a short lock of his hair, pulling him in closer for another kiss. "I went to a sex toy shop in the Ether."

He smiled against her mouth, his shoulders shuddering in a poor attempt to hide his amusement. The hand on her back floated down her spine, grabbing her ass. "Missed me that much?"

"I did."

Tiernan guided her backward, small steps at a time through the sand, until her back was flush against the cool surface of the cove's stone wall. The tips of his fingers trailed across her stomach, slinking lower, until they hovered just above her clit.

Maeve caught on fire.

She jerked her hips forward in a silent plea for him to ease the need for release. The pad of his finger rubbed the sensitive bundle of nerves in slow, tantalizing circles.

His mouth moved from her lips to her jaw, then her neck, licking and sucking as he went, while his finger continued to tease her. "And what did you buy?"

"Onyx nipple clamps and—" Maeve sucked in a breath as he ceased his torment of her clit and shoved two fingers deep inside her.

"And?" he asked, his voice thick with desire.

"And..." She couldn't think clearly. There was only Tiernan. And his hands. And his mouth.

"Focus." He whispered the word across her lips and she arched, grinding herself against him.

"An illusion elixir. It brought you to me...on the beach."

Those fingers pushing into her curled and Maeve's head fell forward, resting on his shoulder as she sucked in greedy gulps of air.

"And did I please you?" he crooned, working her harder, driving her closer to the edge.

Maeve nodded, unable to form words.

"Shall I do it again?"

Incoherency fogged Maeve's mind, then Tiernan sank into the sand on his knees before her. His tongue swirled over her clit, sending sparks of pleasure straight through her. Sliding his fingers in and out of her wet folds, he sucked her delicate bud into the hot confines of his mouth. One firm hand gripped her ass, holding her in place as she fisted her trembling hands into his hair. She cried out as the orgasm tore through her and she spiraled into oblivion.

But Tiernan wasn't done with her yet.

He stood, hooked one hand under her knee and lifted her leg. The tip of his cock prodded lightly at the apex of her thighs, nudging her open for him. Anticipation caused her toes to curl. Already her breathing was ragged once again, her heart still thundering wildly since she'd yet to come down off her post-release high. Bending forward, he lightly pressed his forehead against hers. She looked up, ready to drown in the twilight pools of his eyes.

"Can you come for me again, *astora?*" he whispered.

Again, Maeve nodded furiously.

He made a kind of *tsk*ing noise out of the corner of his mouth. "Use your words, I want to hear that pretty voice of yours."

"Yes, my lord." Her words came out husky and harsh.

He chuckled, a low rumble reverberating through his chest. *"That's my girl."*

The witch thread shivered, and he surged into her.

Maeve writhed in his arms, clenching him with every thrust as he stretched her wider, filling her until she couldn't take anymore.

"Fuck," Tiernan growled, his free arm snaking around her waist. "Always so tight for me."

"Only for you," she breathed, her nails scouring his back. "Only ever for you."

Over and over he drove into her, lifting her higher, sending her soaring. The studs along his hardened length sent waves of ecstasy pulsing through her core, and she threw her arms around his neck, desperate for him to lose himself inside of her.

"More," she begged, even as he pinned her against the cold wall of the cave. "Show me how much you missed me."

"With pleasure."

He grabbed her other leg, hoisting her up as he plunged further into her. She dug her heels into his back, urging him closer, wanting everything, willing to take it all. His hands molded to her thighs, his breathing growing ragged.

"I love you." Tiernan groaned, his rough voice scraping past her ear. "Infinitely."

"I love you." She sucked in a breath, quaking as her climax rocked through her and stars danced in front of her eyes. "Eternally."

Tiernan roared, emptying himself inside her, filling her with his seed.

A tiny, insignificant voice flitted through the back of her mind.

Maybe. One day.

Maeve smiled to herself and then a rush of magic surrounded her as they *faded* once more, back to the Summer Court. She found herself beneath the spray of a lukewarm shower, wrapped in Tiernan's arms.

"Are you hungry?" he asked, switching off the shower and stepping out.

Maeve gave him a once over, taking in the flush of his bronze skin.

"Get your mind out of the gutter, my lady." He smirked. "I meant, do you want some food?"

She grabbed a towel and dried off. "Do you have any of those lemon scones?"

"Anything you want."

"Then yes, I'm famished."

They dressed, Maeve opting for black leggings and a crimson jeweled corset, while Tiernan wore his signature gray pants and cobalt shirt with cuffs rolled just enough to reveal those gloriously tanned forearms.

A skitter of trepidation snaked down her spine, but Tiernan laced their fingers together, extending his calm confidence to her.

They entered the hall and Maeve saw a woman, a mortal, bustling down the other end with her graying hair pulled back into a tidy bun.

"Deirdre!" Maeve darted toward her and the older woman spun, her face alight with surprise and love.

"My lady!" Deirdre cried, gathering Maeve into her arms as tears slid down her weathered cheeks. "You've come back to us! Oh, you've come back."

Deirdre squeezed Maeve again, hugging her fiercely, then finally let her go. Her knowing gaze slid to Tiernan. "I'll make some more of that special brew of tea for you, dear heart. I've got a feeling you'll be needing it."

Maeve flushed, her skin turning a brighter shade of pink with each passing second.

Right. The tea. Something she hated, but was apparently the only way to ensure her moon cycles stayed consistent.

"Of course," Maeve ducked her head, grabbing Tiernan's hand. She could feel the weight of his gaze upon her as they bid Deirdre farewell, continuing to the verandah.

"Maybe." He repeated her words back to her, his voice soft. "One day."

She looked up at him, meeting the unasked questions lingering in his gaze. "After this is all over. After we win."

He squeezed her hands. "I would love nothing more."

Tiernan opened the door to the verandah, and everyone

turned to stare at her. They were all there. Her friends. Her family.

Lir. Merrick. Ceridwen. Saoirse. Brynn.

All of them staring at her. Watching. Waiting. Full of hope and silent expectation.

Tiernan lifted her hand and placed a kiss upon her knuckles, nodding once. "Welcome home, *astora*."

Chapter Five

Tiernan stood back and watched as Maeve was overwhelmed by the love she deserved. She was swallowed in a wave of embraces, laughter, and even a few tears. He absorbed all of it, the way she was showered with affection by those who loved her most. It felt like an eternity had passed without her.

Not only had she returned to them, but her arrival back from the Ether had fully restored Faeven. The Four Courts were no longer withering away or succumbing to decay and death. Everything was blooming, thriving, somehow even more vibrant than before. Only the Spring Court remained shrouded in its veil of gloom.

That was something they would have to discuss. But first, Tiernan was going to let his future queen eat breakfast and regain some of her composure.

Once everyone was seated around the table, a spread of food appeared before them. There were sugar dusted berries, of which Merrick dumped half onto his plate. The amount of food was enough to feed a small unit of warriors with platters of sizzling meats, bowls of biscuits, jars filled with jam, and a wide variety of baked goods. Including those lemon scones Maeve enjoyed so much.

As the final cup of coffee was poured, Tiernan sat back and settled into his chair with Maeve by his side. For a moment, all was right in his world.

And then Rowan walked out onto the verandah.

He shoved a hand through his hair, his gaze stealing around the table before landing on Maeve. "Morning."

Ceridwen scooted her chair over and motioned to him. "Come sit by me, my lord. There's plenty of room."

By the look on Merrick's face, Tiernan wasn't so sure he agreed.

Maeve leaned over, her voice hushed. "I didn't realize Rowan was Archfae. I just assumed...I mean, he never mentioned it."

"It's not something he speaks of often." Tiernan took a sip of his coffee. "I don't blame him, though. If Parisa was my cousin, I wouldn't want any—"

"What!" Maeve shrieked, and Tiernan bobbled his cup of coffee. It clattered against the table and sloshed, spilling over the rim. Silence descended all around them, and Maeve's head swiveled in Rowan's direction. "Parisa is your *cousin?*"

"She is." Rowan slathered raspberry jam onto his biscuit.

Maeve's mouth fell open. "You never told me that."

Rowan looked up, meeting her gaze, his face blank and impassive. "You never asked."

She snapped her mouth shut.

Tiernan slid his hand under the table and gave her thigh a reassuring squeeze.

"So, wait a minute." Saoirse pointed a piece of bacon at Rowan, one of her brows lifting in curiosity. "If we kill Parisa, does that mean you become the High King of Spring?"

"That is the way heirs and bloodlines usually work." Rowan took a bite of his biscuit, chewing thoughtfully. "Though I can't say I have any interest in ruling over a Crown City."

"Agreed." Merrick nodded, reaching for another helping of berries. "Fuck that shit."

Of course Merrick would agree. If anything ever happened to Ciara, he would be forced to leave Niahvess and return to Ashdara as the rightful heir.

"But what about Suvarese?" Maeve asked, turning her attention back to Rowan. "You can't just abandon your Court."

"From what I hear," Rowan mused, eyeing the biscuit in his hand. "They've already chosen a new queen."

He pinned her with a pointed look.

Tension settled in the air, thick and stifling. Maeve flushed beneath Rowan's intense gaze. Annoyance coiled around every muscle in Tiernan's body, tightening until he was ready to snap. Why Rowan felt the need to bring up something like *that*, after Maeve had only just gotten her memories back, was beyond him. It was heartless. Cruel.

"That's something we can discuss later," Tiernan interjected coldly, drawing the conversation out of the strained silence. "For now, we need to focus on winning this war."

"You should probably call another meeting, *moh Rí*." Lir spoke from the opposite end of the table, his large frame sandwiched between Saoirse and Brynn. "I'm sure High King Dorian would be very much interested in seeing his daughter."

From beside Tiernan, Maeve's breath caught. He grabbed her hand, ran his thumbs lightly upon her knuckles. "No. Maeve shouldn't have to see her father during talks of battle."

He turned to her, leaning close. "How would you like to go to Kyol tomorrow? For a surprise visit?"

"I'd love that." She kissed him soundly on the mouth. "And I love you."

"*I love you, too.*" He spoke the words into her mind, knowing Rowan was watching.

Maeve glanced around the outdoor space, looking for something. "Where's Cahira?"

"She's in the courtyard, living her best life." Brynn grinned, her eyes flashing from gold to a vivid green. "You know, turning the fountains into ice sculptures and things like that."

"Maybe after breakfast we can—" Maeve began but was cut off by the sudden shift in the air.

Shadowy masses unfurled where the balcony overlooked the sea. Hollow, sunken faces with eyes glowing like midnight fires appeared beneath black cloaks. Two forms took shape, their feet never quite touching the ground.

Tethra and Dian had arrived.

Balor was still not among them.

Maeve stood and the Furies bowed before her.

"My queen," they murmured in unison, their voices low and gravelly.

"Tethra. Dian." Maeve beamed, brilliant as the sun. But a tiny line crinkled across her brow. "Where's Balor?"

"Maeve." Tiernan pushed back from his seat and came to stand beside her. "It's time we talk about everything that happened in the Ether, and all that happened here while you were gone."

Tiernan hated to have this conversation so soon, but there was no other way. With war looming steadily on the horizon, it was best if they laid all their cards upon the table, even if some of them were the hardest of truths.

Maeve sat back down, the food she had eaten settling in her stomach like a rock. Much time had passed while she was in the Ether, too much if she was being honest. She twisted her hands in her lap, silently cursing herself for not understanding the implied meaning behind Aed's words sooner. She should've known better. She should have *listened.* If she'd only asked to come home, then he would've brought her back. They could have strategized and planned out the best way to defeat Parisa. Instead, that bitch of a fae was hidden away behind her dense wall of impenetrable magic and they were blind to her intentions.

Guilt gnawed at Maeve.

"So," Merrick drawled, leaning back in his chair and tucking his hands behind his head. "Who wants to go first?"

Tiernan clasped Maeve's hand, threading their fingers together. "I'll start."

As her *sirra's* story unfolded around her, Maeve struggled to break free from the claws of remorse latched around her heart. She heard the pain in his voice when he told her about Faeven dying, how the Four Courts seemed on the verge of utter collapse without her. Because if she had been in Niahvess where she belonged, none of that would have happened. Even though he explained they originally thought Parisa was behind the devastation, Maeve couldn't help but feel she was the one at fault.

But she sat in silence while he told her of the *Syol Lorhr,* a sentient book of ancient lore inked in runes with blood from the goddess Danua. Maeve thought about asking if she could read the book, perhaps she could make sense of these runes, but then Tiernan mentioned Maghmell and she jerked upright in her seat.

"Wait. You went to Maghmell?" Maeve stared at him, fully aware of the dangers behind such an errand. Tiernan had almost died there once, he told her as much. To think he went back *again*, Maeve couldn't comprehend such madness.

"I did." Tiernan nodded. "With Aran."

Maeve's heart tumbled from her chest, her breathing grew shallow.

"They fought off a pack of cursed *faolan* and a sea serpent." Merrick winked, as though it was a joke of some kind.

"Barely," Tiernan muttered, his tone darkening. But then his gaze slid to Maeve and the lines of his face softened. "Your wolfling can stay so long as she doesn't try to kill me."

Maeve gave him a weak smile. "How did you survive?"

He paled.

Panic spiked through her, swift as a blade. Her blood ran cold, freezing her from the inside out. Fear strangled her. "Not Aran—"

"No! Gods, no." Tiernan grabbed her then, hauling her into his lap. He brushed her hair back from her face, soothing her. Calming her. "Aran is safe. He's currently sailing to Wenfyre to ask the druid queen there for assistance in the war against Parisa."

"It was Balor who saved us, Maeve." Tiernan spoke softly but she heard the harbored regret that clung to every word. "Without him, Aran and I would have died in the Kethwyn Woods."

"I see." Maeve stared at the toes of her boots, unable to meet anyone's gaze. She already knew what Tiernan would say next, but she asked anyway. "And where is Balor now?"

"There's been no sign of him since."

Her shoulders dropped and she slumped against Tiernan's chest. She'd thought the Furies to be incapable of dying, though she supposed everyone, otherworldly being or not, had their limits. The war hadn't even begun and already she'd lost so much. So many. How many more would die at her command?

She stole a hasty glance around the table, daring a look at each one of them from beneath her lashes. These were her friends, her family. She would fight with them. For them. But Maeve was no fool. Death never played favorites. Her nose tingled, and she pressed her lips together in a firm line. She would not cry here. Tears would only cut open a weakness, a wound of the heart for all to see.

She ducked her head, letting her curtain of hair block her face from view. But even through the golden pink strands, she spied a pair of lavender eyes watching her every move.

Tethra knelt before her, drawing her attention back to the Furies. His wraith-like body expanded in long shadows, never quite touching the ground. He reached out, placing one chilling finger beneath her chin, and tilted her head up to meet his blazing eyes. "He followed them of his own accord, my queen. He did only what he knew you would have asked of him. If he is indeed no longer with us, then his death was one of great honor."

The Fury fell back and stood, stepping next to his brother.

Clearing her throat, she forced herself to sit up straight, to roll her shoulders back, and project the embodiment of a queen. "Where is Wenfyre and who rules it?"

"You can reach Wenfyre by sailing to the southeast across the Gaelsong Sea." It was Lir who answered her. He kept his hands folded in his lap, his elbows braced on the arms of the wooden chair. His face remained impassive as he spoke, the epitome of a commanding general. "It is the home of the druid queen, Ariawyn Pethorn."

"Aran thought it best we seek her assistance and form an alliance against Parisa," Ceridwen added, tugging lightly at the sheer indigo sleeve of her gown. Her ruby lips curved into a small smile, and the lightest traces of serenity cocooned Maeve like a comforting embrace. "The druids of Wenfyre control a powerful naval fleet, and Aran seemed to think Queen Ariawyn would be more inclined to help us as opposed to some of the other less than generous fae realms."

Maeve rolled the new information over in her mind. From what she recalled about druids in many of the books she'd read, they possessed an earthbound magic, a kind of power that tied them to the land. They used spells and incantations, worked with crystals and runes, and some of them wielded staffs. If they also had a fleet of ships at their disposal, then that alone would make them a rather formidable ally.

"And Ciara is calling in a favor." Tiernan shifted in his seat. His fingers tapped a restless rhythm across the top of the table, but his gaze was focused on Merrick. "Apparently Prince Drake Kalstrand of Brackroth owes her a debt."

At the mention of his sister and this Prince of Brackroth, Merrick scowled. His mouth twisted into a sneer, and he folded his arms across his chest. "I still think it's a terrible idea. Nothing about Prince Drake is trustworthy. He has a blackened soul and lacks any morals."

Maeve's brow quirked. It was obvious Merrick had an aversion to this prince, but he sounded exactly like the kind of person they wanted on their side. At least when it came down to fighting Parisa. "And Prince Drake is...who, exactly?"

Lir opened his mouth to respond but Merrick was faster. He leaned forward, his cerulean eyes flashing with contempt. "He's an assassin, my lady. A bloodthirsty, expertly trained killer. Dead bodies are his calling card."

At that revelation, Maeve blanched, easing back a little.

"An assassin with a legion of dragons at his back," Brynn added. She rolled a toothpick between her lips, her gaze narrowing when she faced Merrick. Her golden brown eyes turned nearly black. "Not even you can deny we could use them on our side."

The line across Merrick's forehead deepened, and he shoved his hair back from his face. "Sure, but at what expense?"

"I suggest you leave that matter to your sister," Tiernan answered coolly.

Tempers and tensions hung heavy in the air, so dense, Maeve thought for sure she could cut through the animosity with a blade.

Strained seconds slowly ticked by and Maeve was about to suggest they adjourn this unpleasant meeting completely, when Cahira bounded onto the balcony in a flurry of white fur and ice crystals. Beside her, Tiernan visibly stiffened, and Maeve would've smiled were it not for the fact he had only recently admitted that he and Aran had been attacked by a pack of cursed *faolan* on their way to Maghmell.

The mere thought of it made her stomach twist into unforgiving knots.

Reaching down, Maeve ran her fingers through Cahira's downy fur, ruffling the spot just between her ears. The leather collar she wore—the one Rowan had given to her as a gift for the wolfling and *not* as a necklace—glimmered in the sunlight. Cahira licked Maeve's hand, then padded around in a small circle twice before curling up into a fluffy ball at Tiernan's feet.

He inhaled sharply, and Maeve peered up at him. "So, you and Aran made it to Maghmell?"

"We did." He pressed a kiss to her temple, running his hand gently up and down her spine. "We thought Danua could help us bring the life back to Faeven. We didn't realize it was dying because you were in the Ether. It made no difference though, because when we arrived, she was gone."

"Because she was with me." Something splintered inside Maeve, cracking straight through to her soul.

Tiernan and Aran had gone to Maghmell thinking they could save Faeven. But their journey was for nothing, because

Danua had come to find *her* instead. They'd almost died. And it would have been all her fault.

She glanced down at her lap, where her hands were clenched tightly into fists. She uncurled them slowly, opening her palms, imagined them dripping crimson with the blood of her *sirra* and her brother.

There was a gentle push of magic, a nudge of compassion, and Maeve let the balm of Ceridwen's grace roll over her.

"Danua was with you?" she asked softly, sending tiny waves of soothing energy that rippled around Maeve.

"Yes. She came looking for me." Maeve was fully aware she was once again the center of attention. Even Tiernan's hand remained motionless on her back. "She found me in the Stygian Spine."

Rowan raked a hand through his hair and blew out a harsh breath.

Saoirse took notice. Her brows furrowed, her gaze darting from Maeve to Rowan then back again. "What's the Stygian Spine?"

Maeve sighed. "Perhaps I should start at the beginning."

So she told them about the Ether, capturing their undivided attention. She mentioned training with Rowan and pretended to ignore the way Tiernan's entire body tensed, his grip on her waist tightening. Maeve continued on about the encounter with Queen Marella when she gifted Rowan the Astralstone. It never occurred to her that merrows could pass between the realms beneath the surface of the sea. Though maybe that was another kind of magic entirely, one she knew nothing about. Perhaps she could find a book on the subject once the war was over. Maeve shook her head lightly, relaying only the important pieces of information from her time in the Ether. She glossed over the attack by the dire wolves, and didn't mention Laurel at all. She considered it, especially when she got to the part about the wandering souls, but that part of her story in particular seemed to set Tiernan off, and the might of his power cracked overhead as lightning streaked across the sky.

She opted to end that part quickly, finishing with, "And then I shattered the realms."

Saoirse choked on her coffee.

Ceridwen gasped.

And Merrick, who was casually leaning back in his seat, toppled out of it, landing hard on the stone floor.

Lir slammed both of his hands upon the table and lurched forward. "You *what?*"

It was the most emotion she'd ever seen from him. She reared back, and Tiernan's arms came swiftly around her waist.

"It was an accident." She swallowed down the knot of guilt clogging her throat. "I lost control."

"I'm not mad, my lady." Lir ran a hand over his face, easing back into his chair. "I'm fucking impressed."

"Is that when you went into the Stygian Spine? When the goddess of life found you?" Brynn asked, hooking an arm under Merrick and heaving him from off the floor.

"No." Maeve shook her head, preparing for the inevitable. "I went into the Stygian Spine later. To get to Diamarvh."

"Seven hells," Brynn muttered, her toothpick dangling from her bottom lip.

Saoirse's scowl only deepened, confusion clouding the blue of her eyes. "Diamarvh?"

"The home of the Wild Hunt," Lir clarified.

Saoirse's mouth fell open.

Merrick dropped back into his seat, scrubbing both hands over his face. "Sun and sky, Maeve."

She tried to smile but it was strained. Unnatural. "I spoke to Dubhan, the Lord of the Wild Hunt."

Rowan bowed his head, already knowing what was coming.

"They will not aid us." As soon as she said it, her mouth ran dry, like it was filled with ash and dust. "The tides of fate are not in our favor."

If she could erase the grave looks of despondency from their faces, she would. If there had been a single spark of hope among them, she'd smothered it. Extinguished it completely. She was supposed to be the strong one, the brave one. Full of resilience and fire. But she didn't even have the courage to look in the faces of those she loved most because she knew what she would see reflected back at her. Disappointment. Dread. Defeat.

"We will win." Tiernan cut through the uncertainty, his resolve unyielding. "We are reaching beyond the borders of Faeven for assistance. We will not fall. Not again. Not so long as I breathe."

Murmurs of assent circulated but they lacked vigor. Doubt plagued them all.

Brynn rapped her knuckles on the table. "I'm confused. Did Danua help you reach Diamarvh?"

Maeve shook her head. "No."

"Did Rowan?" Saoirse asked.

"No," Maeve repeated the word, quieter this time.

"Maeve is more than capable of handling things on her own." Rowan toyed idly with the cuffs of his sleeve.

"Maeve." Ceridwen tilted her head, her hair falling around her like liquid sunlight. "What exactly did the goddess of life say to you?"

"Very little." She remembered the encounter clearly. Danua spoke in riddles. She gave no direction. No encouragement. "It wasn't so much as what she said to me, but what she showed me."

"A vision, then," Ceridwen confirmed.

Vision. Illusion. They were one and the same. But Maeve

knew what she saw, what fate awaited her, all of them, even if the goddess of life claimed it could still be altered.

"*Astora.*" Tiernan's voice whispered past her ear. "What did you see?"

"I saw death." She didn't want to describe it, didn't want to relive that harrowing experience ever again. But she could not allow any of them to think this war would be without sacrifice. "I saw a battlefield littered with bodies, where blood soaked the spongy earth. Where ash fell from the sky like rain and the smoke from dying fires hung thick in the air. I saw all of your deaths." Her voice broke then, cracking beneath the emotion crushing her chest like a boulder. "I saw the end."

Tiernan's arm fell from her waist, and Ceridwen gasped.

"What?" Maeve looked between them, terrified of what she would find. "What is it?"

"I had the same vision." Ceridwen's face grew pallid, stealing the blush of her cheeks. "But in mine, there were two survivors."

"Who?" Rowan croaked.

"The Dawnbringer." Her gaze roved over each one of them before finally settling on Rowan. "And the Nightweaver."

Rowan's head fell back and he groaned. "Shit."

"Well, this is one hell of a way to start the day." Merrick waved his hand and a decanter of amber liquid appeared. "Who wants a shot?"

"Me." Saoirse held out her empty coffee cup. "Fill it up."

"She said I could change it," Maeve murmured, accepting the shot of whiskey Merrick handed her.

"And you will. We all will." Tiernan clinked his glass against hers and downed his shot in one gulp. "Together."

"That's right." Ceridwen sniffed her glass. Her nose twitched and she set it back down, a serene smile gracing her ruby lips. "Especially since we know how and where to invade the Spring Court."

Lir's silver eyes widened. "We do?"

"It's through the Pass of Veils." Maeve finally swallowed her own whiskey, wishing it burned more than just the back of her throat.

Tiernan shifted, angling her in his lap so she looked up at him. "How did you know? I've only told Ceridwen."

"I saw it." Maeve reached for another lemon scone, even though she wasn't hungry. "When I came for you and Merrick."

"Good eye, my lady." Merrick flashed her a wink. "I wish the rest of us had been informed."

"It was my intention to tell all of you." Tiernan tapped his fingers along Maeve's thigh in a rhythmic pattern. "Unfortunately, you and I were detained by a group of trooping fae."

"Oh." Brynn drew the word out. "Right."

Tiernan chuckled. "Right."

There was a flutter of wings and a blur of white fur, as Cahira bounded onto the verandah, then plopped down at Maeve's feet.

"Well, at least we have a frost *faolan* on our side." Tiernan bent over and ruffled Cahira's fur. "Where did you find her, anyway?"

"She was a gift from the god of death." Maeve smiled down at the wolfling. "For my birthday."

"Oh, your birthday!" Ceridwen squealed with excitement, and then her face fell. "We missed it."

Saoirse stole one of Lir's biscuits off his plate. "That just means she finally figured out the date."

"It's Samhwyn," Rowan said softly.

Maeve looked over at him, but he refused to meet her gaze.

"Of course it is," Tiernan said, placing a kiss on her jaw.

Ceridwen sighed. "How fitting."

Merrick stood, stretching his arms overhead. "Looks like we've got a war to train for."

He pinned Maeve with his cerulean gaze. "How about it, my lady?" He wiggled his brows for effect. "I'll go easy on you."

Maeve stood, shoving down the pangs of guilt into the darkest part of her heart. There would be time to reflect on self-reproach and all she could have done differently later. She forced herself to smile. "You're on."

Chapter Six

Everyone was on the stretch of beach where the turquoise waves of the Lismore Marin crested and crashed, leaving behind a trail of bubbly foam. The sun heated Tiernan's skin, and beads of sweat to slid down his back. It had been some time since they'd conducted a training session on the sandy shoreline, even longer since they had all done so together.

"Alright, listen up." Lir stood in the center, one curved sword in his grip. "Just so everyone knows the rules. Blades only. No magic. No wings." He shot a pointed look at Tiernan, Maeve, and Ceridwen. "And try not to injure one another too severely."

Lir stalked over to Saoirse, kicking up sand in his wake. "I challenge Saoirse, everyone else, pair off."

Merrick moved in front of Maeve, grinning. He tipped his blade toward her, his eyes dancing. "You're mine, Dawnbringer."

She smirked, glamouring a sword and twirling it with one hand. "Bring it on, little hunter."

Brynn trotted over to Ceridwen, her burgundy curls bouncing. She flourished one of her many daggers, then bowed excessively. "My lady, would you do me the honor?"

Ceridwen pulled one of her own. The sunlight glinted off the rubies lining its hilt like drops of blood. She placed a slender hand over her heart. "I thought you'd never ask."

Tiernan stepped back, thinking he'd wait until one of them conceded, but then a shadow emerged, and Rowan stepped into the haze of Summer.

He inclined his head. "Looks like it's you and me, High King."

Shit.

From the corner of Tiernan's eye, he caught Maeve watching them. It might take some self-control, but he could temper his jealousy for Maeve's benefit, and act as though he didn't care if the male standing across from him was in love with her. He would be the epitome of an esteemed warrior for his mate. He would play by the rules, he would fight fairly. And no matter what, he wouldn't give into the urge to cut off Rowan's hands for ever touching Maeve.

His shirt clung to him, sticking to his back, hindering his movements. Annoyed, he yanked it off and tossed it to the ground. Lir and Merrick followed suit, and Rowan removed his as well, though his chest was battered with vicious scars.

Tiernan hadn't realized how severely he'd been tortured in Kells while chained in Carman's dungeon.

"Oh, what the fuck." Saoirse crossed her arms, glaring at them. But her face betrayed her as she scraped her teeth along her bottom lip. "How come all the boys get to take off their shirts and we don't?"

"Trust me." Merrick laughed, lifting one brow in provocation. "No one will stop you if you want to join us."

"What say you, Lir?" Saoirse spun to face the commander,

her silver braid whipping, the plumeria tucked behind her ear fluttering in the breeze. "Do you think you'll still be able to best me if I take off my shirt?"

"Sun and sky." He pressed his thumb and middle finger to his temples, squeezing. A dark rose colored his cheeks. "On your mark!"

"I'll take that as a no," Saoirse taunted, readying her weapon.

Lir rolled his eyes to the cloudless sky. "Begin!"

Chaos erupted along the beach as the violent clang of metal shattered the air.

Rowan was on Tiernan in record time, his movements swift and agile. Their blades clashed, the sound near deafening, as Rowan swung hard and Tiernan blocked the first strike. He spun away, moving through the sand with ease, and Rowan stepped into the next attack.

"Tell me, Your Highness." Rowan's voice was low, barely loud enough to hear over the call of the sea. He lunged, the brunt of his assault causing Tiernan to grit his teeth. "How long have you wanted to run a blade through my heart?"

Tiernan planted his boot in the sand and shoved him backward. "Longer than I care to admit."

"Good." Rowan kept his sword raised, walking in a slow circle around him. "Because the feeling is mutual."

Again, the Nightweaver came at him in a series of rapid assaults. Tiernan met each one of them. Dodging. Parrying. Refusing to give in to Rowan's taunts.

The Nightweaver shoved his hair back from his face, glaring, his pale purple eyes firing with the heat of suppressed loathing. "I could have made her mine, you know."

"Yet you did not." Tiernan blew out a steadying breath. He would not cave to Rowan's goading, though the sting of envy burned in his gut. His attempt to dampen it was fleeting. He was well aware of every moment Rowan had shared with Maeve.

"I know more about her than you ever will. I was there when Carman threw her into that damned cage, when she drugged her with tea to encourage memory loss so the fear was always fresh." Rowan launched himself at Tiernan, his attacks growing more volatile. Tiernan ducked, just missing a blow, as Rowan's sword sailed through the air above his head. "I know the innermost workings of her mind. I know when she lies, when she masks the threat of tears."

He smiled, ruthless. "Just like I know how she smells. How she tastes."

The bindings of Tiernan's control snapped.

The fucking fae had gone one step too far.

"She made her choice," Tiernan growled, his blood raging. He swung with blinding fury, ready to cut Rowan down.

The Nightweaver's laughter was mocking. "Who says I can't change her mind?"

Tiernan roared. He slammed into Rowan with the magnitude of a thousand boulders tumbling down a cliffside, knocking him backward. Baring his teeth, Tiernan assailed upon him again. "If you dare lay a single finger on her, I'll destroy you."

"Interesting." Rowan sneered, malice dripping from his tone. "That power belongs to *me* now."

A cacophony of noise rang in Tiernan's ears, but all he could see was the bloody, pulpy mess he wanted to make of Rowan's face.

Suddenly Lir was between them, throwing his arms out to either side. The force of his magic sent Tiernan staggering back while Rowan stumbled away from him.

"I said *draw*," Lir bellowed. His glare cut from Tiernan to Rowan, then back again. "That's enough."

Tiernan sucked in a breath. His muscles screamed at him, ached from exertion. Sweat poured from every surface of his body. He glowered, pissed at Rowan for not knowing how to keep his fucking mouth shut, and furious at himself for losing his composure.

He couldn't bring himself to look at Maeve, even though he knew she stood nearby. She'd likely watched their entire fight unfold.

Rowan scoffed, tossed his sword onto the sand, then sauntered off back toward the palace.

Merrick loosed a whistle, appearing by Tiernan's side a moment later. He ducked his head, angling himself so his back faced Maeve, and kept his voice quiet. "What was all that about?"

Tiernan's back spasmed as the muscles there tensed. "Take a guess."

A beat of silence passed between them.

"You need to get your shit together, my lord. I know he gets under your skin, and for good reason, but whether you like it or not, we need him to win this war. Bury the past." Merrick clamped one hand on Tiernan's shoulder. "Mind yourself, my lord. Your mate is watching."

Lanced with regret, Tiernan slowly allowed his gaze to travel over to Maeve.

She stood a few feet from him, her sword dangling loosely in her hand. Her skin was flushed, her curls were wild, and tiny beads of sweat slid from her forehead to her cheeks. But there was an emotion banked deep in her eyes. Something powerful, yet unreadable.

"Let's go," Lir announced, motioning to the palace. He nodded once, stiffly, and gradually everyone trudged back up the hill, their hushed conversations disappearing on the warm breeze.

Tiernan walked over to Maeve, rubbing the back of his neck as though he could somehow dissolve his shame, disgruntled by his own actions. "I'm sorry."

She dropped her sword, cupping his face with both hands. Her eyes sought his own.

"You were right." Rising on her toes, she kissed him softly on the mouth. "I chose *you*."

Then her nose crinkled. "You need a shower."

He chuckled, smacking her on the butt. "I could say the same to you."

She blinked, the mirth in her eyes warming into longing. "Meet you there?"

Tiernan moved closer, towering over her, enjoying the way her mouth parted in surprise. "I have a better idea."

"Is that so?" she asked, wrapping her arms around his neck.

He grinned, pressing a kiss to her forehead. "We can go there now, if you'd like."

"Yes, please."

Tiernan slid his arm around her waist, pulling her flush against him. She gazed up at him, and he knew if he stared for too long into those sea-mist eyes of hers, he'd drown.

"Who won?" he asked, his voice hoarse.

Maeve's smile left him breathless. "Me."

"That's my girl."

Tiernan tucked her head beneath her chin, holding her close, and *faded* them to the Vista.

MAEVE STOOD on the small balcony of the Vista, overlooking the border of Summer, the jeweled forests of Autumn, and in the far distance, the rugged snow-capped mountains of Winter. Afternoon sunlight dripped over every surface of Faeven, dousing the land in a wash of gold. The Vista was perched on one of the Summer Court's outlying mountains, and here there was a distinctive chill in the air as the falling leaves beckoned her, whispering her name.

She tugged her satin robe around her, shivering.

Freshly showered, she inched further out onto the balcony and inhaled, breathing in the faint scent of the sea as it mingled with aged oak and damp earth.

She felt Tiernan's presence the moment before his arms came around her waist. Tipping her head back, she rested against the length of his body, content with the solace of his embrace.

Maeve glanced down to her left hand, where the ring she wore glinted a deep blue, then flashed to a cool violet, twinkling in the sun. She ran her thumb beneath the solid gold band, remembering the moment Tiernan asked her to be his wife, right before Parisa attacked them. A wedding seemed like such an insignificant celebration when their very lives were at stake.

"I don't want my own Court," she announced softly.

"What do you mean?" Tiernan nuzzled her neck, pressing his lips to where her pulse beat solely for him. "There's plenty of space to build—"

"No," Maeve interrupted, turning in his arms so she faced him. She looked up at him, admiring the strong line of jaw, his prominent cheekbones, his broad, bronze chest. "I mean, I don't want to be separated from you. I want to live in Niahvess. With you. I don't want my own palace or throne. I want us to build a life together, assuming we ever get the chance."

She hadn't intended to say those last few thoughts out loud, but it was too late to take them back. They hung in the air between them, floating on everything else that was left unsaid.

Tiernan ran his thumb along her bottom lip, gliding his hand beneath her chin. In his eyes, she saw everything she ever wanted.

"You are not alone in your fear, and if you feel that you are, then give it to me. I will take all of it. Your worries, your despair, your suffering. I will be the boulder upon which you place your burdens."

He kissed her, speaking his next words against her mouth. "Let me carry them for you."

The familiar sting of tears pricked at the corner of her eyes. She hastily blinked them away, willing them not to fall. Not here. Not now. "It's more than that."

"Then tell me," he urged, threading his fingers through her loose curls.

"What if we lose this?" Maeve looked away from him, staring out over the vast expanse of Faeven, where wonder and magic lived and breathed. "What if we lose all of it? Us. The war. Niahvess. Everyone who holds a piece of our heart."

Tiernan watched her carefully, his brow knitting in concern. "Where is this coming from, Maeve?"

She opened her mouth to respond, but a breath shuddered out of her instead. The Lord of the Wild Hunt was right, the odds were stacked against them. In the game of fate, they held the losing hand. The illusion from the Stygian Spine haunted her. Each time she closed her eyes, she saw the vision more clearly, the death of those she loved spread over the ruins of a battlefield. The end of her world as she knew it. She could smell the stench of fresh blood, the sooty odor of dwindling fires. But the pang of agony, the grief...tortured her soul.

Danua had told her it could be changed, that Maeve could alter this disastrous predetermination. But she didn't know *how*. Considering how long it took her to figure out how to get home from the Ether, finding a way to save everyone she loved would be nearly impossible. There simply wasn't enough time.

Tiernan cupped her cheek, and she leaned into his touch.

"You know I love you, *astora*. Just as you know I respect

you. I will not delve into your mind to discover what troubles you." He bent forward, resting his forehead against hers. "I trust you will tell me when you are ready."

Maeve nodded, and her lips found his, soft and warm. The kiss was gentle, a mere brushing of the lips.

"What if we lose?" she whispered again, her fear lingering in the space between them.

Tiernan grasped both of her hands, clutching them to his heart.

"Then we go together." Determination hardened the beautiful planes of his face. "Knowing we fought for everything we love."

But it wouldn't be so easy. Not with Parisa as their enemy. She didn't want Maeve dead, she wanted her as a weapon. She wanted to control the power of creation, the lifeblood of magic, and she would kill anyone who stood in her way. No, Parisa wouldn't kill Maeve on a battlefield. That duty would have to fall to someone else.

"Tier?" Maeve's voice was hoarse. Her heart wrenched inside of her, knowing the severity of what she was about to ask of him. Knowing it would break him.

"Yes?"

"I need you to promise me something."

He sensed it.

She felt the shift in his demeanor. The way his muscles tensed beneath her touch. Wariness darkened his eyes. But still, he nodded once. "Alright."

"If we fall, if Faeven falls to Parisa, I need you to promise me right now that you won't let her take me." Maeve searched his eyes, silently imploring him to understand. She wasn't asking for protection or safe-keeping, she was asking something more. Something crucial.

But the corners of Tiernan's mouth lifted into a small smile. "You know I will never let that happen."

Maeve shook her head. "No. That's not what I mean."

"*Astora—*"

"Swear it to me." She spoke in earnest, steeling her purpose. Once, not so long ago, she'd welcomed death, waited for it like an old friend. This would be no different. She would not be afraid, but she would be damned if she was ever used against her own free will. Stepping back, she faced the High King of Summer in his entirety. In this, she would remain unbreakable. She would not falter.

Tiernan's eyes widened in understanding. Devastation crashed through him, and the solid weight of his anguish ripped right into her.

"Vow to me on this day that you will be the one to take my life. The moment you know, the second you realize we stand no chance against her, take your blade and end me. I would rather die knowing I love you, then have her use me against all that we love."

"No." Tiernan choked the word out, his complexion turning ashen. "No. I cannot."

The witch thread binding them scoured her wrist, pulsing.

"You must," she demanded. "I will not be her weapon."

He squeezed his eyes shut, turning away from her.

"Tiernan." Maeve reached out, grabbing his arm, forcing him to look at her. When he opened his eyes again, the twilight had dimmed, the flecks of sunlight diminished completely. "You know it is my power she seeks. Coupled with the *virdis lepatite*, she will be unstoppable."

He paled. "Maeve..."

His heart fractured, shattering her own into a thousand pieces. But Faeven's survival couldn't depend upon broken hearts and anguished souls. Duty would prevail above love. Always.

"A queen worthy of her name would make such a sacrifice, my lord." Maeve rolled her shoulders back, lifting her chin. Power throbbed around her, raising her hair from her shoulders, casting the Vista in a rosy gold hue. Her magic surrounded them in a swell of intensity and the tattoos marking her skin glowed, illuminating her from within. She was not just an Archfae. She was the Dawnbringer, a demigoddess whose soul had lived a thousand lives. Maeve leveled her mate with a poignant stare. "Vow it."

Tiernan inhaled sharply, his gaze hardening, growing colder with each passing second. He dropped to his knees before her, never once looking away, and held out his hand. Standing before him, they clasped one another's wrists.

"I, Tiernan Velless, vow on this day that if Faeven falls to the wrath of Parisa, I will be the one to end your life."

Tendrils of radiant magic flowed from Maeve toward Tiernan, binding his wrist in a Strand of golden pink roses.

He lowered his head. "I will die without you."

Maeve helped him rise to his feet as her magic ebbed, as she sought the threads of their love through the bond, channeling all of her affection, her devotion, into him. She stepped into him, placing her hand over his heart. "I will forever live in your soul."

"It won't be enough," Tiernan muttered. "It will never be enough."

"Then make it enough." Maeve rose up on her toes, locking her arms around his neck and pulling him close. His hands remained on her waist, unmoving. "Kiss me, my lord. Do not allow her to steal these moments from us."

Not when they might be our last, she wanted to say.

Tiernan obliged her at first, pressing his mouth to hers. The muscles of his shoulders bunched beneath her palms, the tension rolling off of him in waves of pained remorse.

"Claim me," she whispered, running the tip of her tongue along the seam of his lips. Coaxing him.

Finally, he yielded, allowing her entry. He slanted his mouth across hers, exploring. Tasting. Their tongues slid over one another in a long, languid kiss. Slow and deliberate. As though he meant to cherish her. To worship her.

His hands tugged gently on the sash at her waist, so the satin fell open, and the cool rush of air assaulted her bare flesh. The pads of his fingers slid beneath her robe, skimming from her thighs, to her hips, to the underside of her breasts, then back down again. He repeated the motion, this time with his roughened palms, taking his time to enjoy every inch of her. His fingers strummed along her spine, dipping low to the curve of her bottom, then glided up and around her to cup her breasts. Lazily, he stroked his thumb back and forth across her nipples, until they hardened into swollen peaks.

She arched into him, desire burning low in her belly.

Tiernan's mouth moved to her neck, scraping his teeth, nipping, then laving his tongue over each spot to soften the sting.

Maeve melted against him, sinking her nails into his shoulders to hold herself upright. Her core throbbed, swollen and wet, desperate for his touch. Again, she jerked her hips forward, rubbing herself against the thick bulge in his pants. The friction of fabric against her clit caused her head to tip back, but her mate seemed all too happy to take his time with her.

Very well.

If he wanted to torment her, then she was perfectly capable of the same kind of torture.

Maeve ran her nails across Tiernan's chest, scouring him,

following the ripples of his muscles all the way to the waistband of his pants.

"Maeve..." he warned, but she smirked, unfastening them with ease so they dropped to the ground and the full and perfect length of his cock sprang free.

Gods, he was glorious.

His thumbs ceased their ministrations of her nipples, and she sank to her knees before him. Tiernan's breath quickened, and when she looked up, heat pooled between her legs as he ran his teeth along his bottom lip. Oh, but she would wipe that smug expression off his face.

Maeve's tongue darted out, swiping just the tip of his cock, and Tiernan groaned. Before he could recover, she sucked him into her mouth.

"Shit." The word hissed out of him.

She drew him deeper, sliding her tongue along the cool studs piercing his shaft. He fisted a hand in her hair, urging her to take more of him. All of him. Gripping his hips with her nails, she set the pace, licking and teasing his thickening length, while her own desire pooled between her thighs.

"Stop." Tiernan held her in place, and her gaze flicked up to him. "Fuck, you look so pretty with my cock in your mouth."

Maeve arched a brow but then he stepped back, pulling out.

"But you, *astora*, are a queen." He lifted her from off the floor. "And you kneel for no one."

Gripping her waist, he spun her so she faced away from him. He nudged her towards the bed, grabbing her breast and squeezing, while his other hand worked its way around her abdomen. Then lower still. His palm glided down her skin, sinking to where she wanted him to touch her most. His fingertips gently brushed the aching bundle of nerves at the apex of her thighs, working her, pressing firm enough for her to squirm in his hold. Maeve bit her lip, rocking her hips back into him. Her thighs bumped into the edge of the bed and she stumbled forward, gasping as he slid one finger down the seam of her core.

"I am your servant." Tiernan's breath was warm against her cheek, and she shivered. "Now, do you still want me to claim you, *moh Ríenna?*"

My queen.

Her heart thundered, wild with anticipation.

"Yes." The word left her in a rush.

His hot tongue slid from the lobe of her ear, all the way to the point. "Bend over."

Maeve did as she was told, seizing the bedding with both hands for purchase. He nudged her legs apart, spreading them so the head of his cock was poised at her entrance. She barely had time to catch her breath before he shoved deep inside of her, filling her completely.

Every stroke sent her reeling, every thrust sent her soaring. She cried out, the feel of him moving inside her, of reaching the pinnacle of desire, caused her entire body to quiver. He grabbed her hips, jerking her against him, gripping her so hard, she was sure she'd bear the marks of his fingerprints later.

He surged in and out of her, harder and faster.

A thousand sensations spiraled within her, building to the point of release.

"You are mine." The timbre of his voice trembled through her. "And I will worship you...until the stars fall from the sky."

Maeve's blood hummed with the brilliance of the dawn and the ethereal glow of twilight. The witch thread twined around her soul, binding her to Tiernan.

He groaned, his cock swelling inside of her, his release imminent.

"Eternally," she whimpered, her body spasming as the

climax stole through her, sending her tumbling headfirst into a lust-filled haze.

"Infinitely." Tiernan plunged into her one final time, emptying himself inside of her on a resounding groan as thunder rumbled in the distance.

In the moments following their passion, Maeve found herself at a loss for words. She was curled against Tiernan, her back nestled against his chest. He had one arm thrown protectively around her waist, and all she could focus on was the tattoo of roses now marking his wrist. A reminder of his vow to her. The oath she knew he would honor, no matter the cost.

At some point, they should probably return to Niahvess. It wouldn't be long before dusk blanketed the skies, before the stars winked into existence.

But for now, she was willing to lie there in the safety of his arms for as long as possible. If she closed her eyes, she could pretend the horrors they would soon face didn't exist. She could imagine a world with a wedding, and future children, and all the things she never thought possible.

Because Maeve knew the moment she opened her eyes, the dream would evaporate.

After all, nothing could last forever.

Chapter Seven

Tiernan faded back to Niahvess with Maeve sound asleep in his arms.

He tucked her into his bed and she snuggled beneath the covers, pulling them up to her chin. Her hair spilled over his pillowcase in long, loose curls as her chest rose and fell in steady, even breaths, her subconscious carrying her off into the land of dreams. In sleep, she looked peaceful. Happy. There were no lines of worry creasing her brow, no shadows of fear haunting her eyes.

She needed her rest, needed her strength.

He bent over, placing the lightest of kisses on her temple, then quietly slipped out of the bedroom, closing the door behind him. Releasing the breath he'd been holding, Tiernan looked down at his wrist.

Sun and sky, what the hell was he going to do?

The Strand emblazoned on his skin cemented his pledge to her. But the rules of vows and bargains were not the same. If a fae didn't hold true to their end of a deal, whatever was given to them in exchange was taken away. Depending on the magnitude of such an agreement, it wasn't always insufferable. But if Tiernan retracted his vow, if he broke his oath to Maeve, the punishment was severe. According to the laws written in blood by the first High Kings and Queens, he would be stripped of his title and forced into exile. He would become a Dorai, one of the banished.

He would never see Maeve or Niahvess ever again.

Tiernan headed down the open corridor to Ceridwen's room. He had to speak with his twin. It was a difficult thing to ask, as he knew Ceridwen's visions had become unpredictable and more consuming as of late, but he needed her to revisit the battlefield. Surely since Maeve's return, the vision had been altered somehow or changed for the better. His sister was a renowned seer and she'd only ever been wrong once before.

When the dark fae infiltrated the Four Courts, she'd been plagued with nightmares. She misinterpreted them, thinking it was a spell of bad dreams, not realizing it was an omen. No one had any idea Faeven would be plunged into what would become the Evernight War. Ceridwen hadn't seen it coming.

Tiernan rounded the corner, lost in thought, and shoved open the door to Ceridwen's room.

"Ah, fuck." He nearly tripped over himself and immediately stumbled backward, averting his eyes.

There was Merrick, sprawled across Ceridwen's bed, with his hands tucked behind his head, naked as the day of his birth.

"Shit!" Merrick scrambled for a blanket, grabbing the dark red comforter and draping it across his lap. "Apologies, my lord."

"Save it." Tiernan pinned his hunter with a hard look. It wasn't the first time he'd seen his best friend naked. There'd been numerous drunken stupors in their youth where Merrick's clothing had magically disappeared. But the last place he expected to find Merrick fully nude was in Ceridwen's bed.

His sister peeked her head out of the door of the bathing suite, her fluffy robe twirling around her. She stepped out, fully covered—thank the gods—her mouth turned down in displeasure.

"Honestly, Tier." Her voice was calm but a blush bled into her cheeks. "You should learn to knock first."

"You're right, of course." Tiernan grabbed the door handle and backed out. "Forgive me."

A faint line creased her brow, and she tilted her head, concerned. "Did you need something?"

"It can wait." Tiernan sent Merrick another look of warning, then closed the door.

"What the fuck," he muttered, shaking the image from his mind. He thought there might have been something going on between Merrick and Ceridwen, but he figured if his sister wanted him to be informed of her love life, then she would tell him. He would be lying if he wasn't bothered by the fact that Ceridwen's supposed *sirra* didn't want her, and if that particular male was indeed Merrick, he would have some serious explaining to do. But Tiernan knew his sister, just like he knew she preferred to keep her feelings to herself. So, he'd never questioned it. And even though he'd walked in on...whatever that was, he would still keep his opinions to himself.

It was best to let them enjoy each other's company, considering their time on this plane of existence could be coming to an end.

He strolled through his palace, with no real purpose, only to find himself standing in front of the doors of the library.

Perhaps the answers he sought were in here instead.

Tiernan opened the door slowly, worried he might accidentally walk in on another intimate encounter, then breathed a sigh a relief when nothing but ancient books and the glow of dim light greeted him.

The walls were lined with towering shelves, each one crammed with books, some of them having gone untouched for hundreds of years. There were a few rolling ladders and even an entire second level, which, much to Tiernan's dismay, he'd never even explored. Faerie fire flickered to life in hanging sconces and candles as he passed, the scent of melted wax and aged parchment lingering in the air. Instantly, his gaze was drawn to the mural in the center of the library.

He moved closer, his footfalls echoing softly in the silent space, until he stood right beneath it.

It moved with a life of its own, displaying nothing but a vast mixture of swirling grays rolling across its canvas like storm clouds.

Tiernan pulled out a chair and leaned back, gazing up at it. The last time he was here, the mural had shown him the Pass of Veils, the only entrance into the heavy mist surrounding the Spring Court. Perhaps it held other secrets, as well.

"It's a sentient object, not a crystal ball."

Tiernan jolted upright, spinning in his seat to find Rowan standing near the opposite wall with a stack of books in his hands.

"What are you doing here?" he demanded, unnerved not to have realized Rowan was even in the library at all.

Rowan lifted the books he held as though they were proof of some kind. "I've been here for hours."

Tiernan's gaze narrowed, tracking the fae as he moved closer. "I didn't sense you."

Rowan shrugged, indifferent. "Perks of being the Night-weaver, I suppose."

"Right." Tiernan huffed in annoyance, returning his attention to the mural, a stab of resentment lodging itself in his gut.

Though he remained focused on the mural, he was well aware of Rowan's every move, tracking him as he strolled around the library, humming to himself. Tiernan drummed his fingers along the table, his agitation growing.

"Is there a particular book you're looking for?" he ground out. "Maybe I can help you find it so you can leave?"

"No." Rowan drew the word out, the corner of his mouth twitching. "I just have a fondness for libraries."

"I bet you do," Tiernan muttered.

The last time Rowan was in here, he had his face buried between Maeve's legs. The memory seared across Tiernan's mind with stark clarity. All-encompassing rage followed, nearly snapping his self-control. He'd seen exactly what Rowan had done to her in Maeve's mind. Her arousal had reeked of his scent. Tiernan had known then that she was his *sirra*, but she only had eyes for Rowan, and there wasn't a damn thing he could do about it.

Rowan's low chuckle grated against the walls while he pretended to peruse the shelves.

Fucking fae.

Tiernan looked back up at the mural. Shades of gray churned across its surface and it billowed like an abyss. A chasm of beginnings. A void of endings.

He shifted, trying to disentangle himself from the trepidation tangling around him like a cluster of strangling vines.

"Maeve doesn't think we'll win," he said quietly, surprising himself.

Rowan took the seat across from him, lowering his pile of books onto the table. The titles all varied, anything from legends surrounding ancient wars to a romantic fairy tale about a mortal princess who was transformed into a siren.

Rowan watched him a moment longer, then looked away, reaching for one of his books. "And what do you think?"

"I don't know." The answer was too honest. Too real. And it troubled him. "If we don't defeat Parisa, it will be worse than before. Worse than the Evernight War."

Rowan flipped through the pages of one of the books, his eyes skimming but not quite reading. "Well, that's one thing we can agree on."

"I wonder how much the mural knows," Tiernan murmured out loud, not really expecting a response.

But Rowan answered anyway. "I think the real question is how much is it willing to show us."

"I suppose there's only one way to find out." Tiernan looked up. There were any number of questions he could ask, but there was no way of knowing if the mural would even answer another one. The first time he'd asked, he hadn't even realized the mural was sentient. He was just musing to himself, trying to make sense of all the terrible things happening around him. But this time, it was with intent. This time, it was purposeful. And there was one thing that bothered him more than anything else. "Show me what lies beyond the shrouded veil of the Spring Court."

At that, Rowan's head snapped up, his gaze fixated on the mural.

The mass of cloudy gray watercolors faded, revealing a stone oval-shaped structure. It looked like a theater of some kind, except the walls were impossibly high and there was no ceiling, leaving it exposed to the elements. But then the image blurred and another took its place—miles of cold iron and lumbering giants causing the ground to quake and the mountains to tremble. Once more, the colors bled away, this time to display the dungeon of the Spring Court. Dozens of cages were filled with fae, stretching their arms through the thin bars, all of them moaning and wailing, their eyes glazed with bloodlust. They looked fiendish. Drugged.

Again the grays of the mural roiled and Tiernan swore every hair on his body stood on end, for now he stared at a nightmare come to life.

It was the Sluagh. The damned ones.

Thousands of them.

All at Parisa's disposal.

"Oh, fuck," Rowan muttered as the mural returned to its distorted swirls of gray.

Sun and sky, it was worse than Tiernan ever thought possible. If they weren't prepared, it wouldn't be a war. It would be a massacre.

Rowan slammed his book shut, jarring Tiernan from his thoughts. "Perhaps you better call that meeting with the other Courts sooner rather than later."

Tiernan winced. "I promised Maeve a day with her father, without talks of war. She deserves that much."

Across from him, Rowan sat back. "Very well. One more day of avoiding the inevitable won't hurt...much."

Tiernan told himself it would be fine. It was just as Rowan said, one more day. Maeve needed to see Dorian, she needed that time to establish a connection with her father since she'd been taken away so quickly after their first meeting. It was the least he could do for her, given there might never be another chance.

He adjusted his sleeves, rolling them up, then glamoured a piece of parchment and pen. He would have to note everything the mural revealed to make sure everyone knew exactly what was coming. To ensure they understood that this impending war might indeed be the end.

Rowan cleared his throat, and Tiernan glanced up.

"That's new." He was staring at Tiernan's wrist, where Maeve's Strand glimmered against his skin like ribbons of rose gold silk.

"Yes." Tiernan swallowed. It wouldn't come to that. He would do whatever necessary to make sure it *never* came to that.

Rowan studied him, his face impassive. Unreadable. "A bargain or a vow?"

"A vow."

"What kind?" There was an edge in Rowan's voice now, and Tiernan was growing weary of his constant questions.

He stood, refusing to get into another fight. Because this time, Lir wasn't here to stop either of them from killing each other. "The kind that binds me to kill someone we both love...in the event that Faeven falls."

Rowan paled, but offered a weak smile. "Sounds like something she would do."

"Indeed."

Tiernan turned to go when Lir strode into the library.

He drew himself up, glancing warily between the two of them, a scowl forming across his brow. Then he met Tiernan's gaze, nodding once in greeting. "My lord, we've got company."

Chapter Eight

Maeve stirred from her sleep, stretching out her muscles. Her eyes fluttered open, and she stared up at a violet-hued sky. The stars were just beginning to peek out from behind wisps of indigo clouds as dusk settled across the glass domed ceiling.

She was no longer in the Vista, but back in Tiernan's room. Glancing down, she realized she was still in her robe from earlier. He must have *faded* them back to the palace after she fell asleep. Granted, she hadn't planned on taking a nap in the middle of the afternoon, but maybe her body was still recovering from her exchange with the memory keeper.

Yawning once, Maeve climbed out of bed, her gaze latching onto the adjoining door. The one that led to her bedroom. She had yet to step foot inside it since her return from the Ether. She padded across the hardwood floor, her hand hovering just above the handle to the door. There was no reason to be nervous or anxious, it was only a bedroom, but for some reason, she couldn't quite shake off the hesitancy rooting her in place.

Ridiculous.

Maeve pushed the door open and was met with the cool rush of familiarity.

This was where she stayed when she first arrived in Faeven, the room Tiernan had arranged just for her. On the far wall was the weapon rack Lir had constructed for her. The sword she'd crafted for Queen Marella was still there, its pearlescent blade shimmering like the sea when the waves were kissed by moonlight. Her sword of sunlight was there as well, glowing. Pulsing with power. A pile of books was stacked on her nightstand and her mother's wardrobe—a gift from Shay—was partially open, as though she'd been searching for something the last time she was in this room.

She walked over to the wardrobe, running her fingers along the smooth surface of the carved wood, admiring the abundance of decadent gowns, all the colors of Autumn, tucked neatly inside of its doors. Her gaze skimmed over the velvet lined drawers full of jewels and crowns, wondering if her mother ever wore them for special occasions, or if she decorated herself in rubies and black diamonds simply because she felt like it.

Maeve liked to imagine it was the latter.

Her stomach rumbled. If she was quick, she wouldn't miss dinner. But then one of her mother's gowns caught her eye. It was two pieces, the skirt was black silk with a strikingly high slit, and the top was cropped, covered heavily with dark purple gems and gold beads. She supposed she *could* dress as an Archfae for the evening. Besides, Ceridwen always wore her finest clothing. Maeve wasn't sure she'd ever seen the High Princess of Summer in anything other than a stunning gown.

Dressing quickly, she ran her hands through her rumpled hair, attempting to smooth the curls. She cleansed her face, brushed her teeth, then headed back into Tiernan's room and grabbed her Aurastone from beneath her pillow. Fastening it to her thigh, she gave herself a once over in the mirror.

Good enough, all things considered.

She yanked open the bedroom door and squeaked.

There was Lir, waiting for her. The same way he'd always done. Ever patient. Ever vigilant. He wore all black, except the collar and sleeves of his shirt were trimmed in tiny golden stars. Both of his curved swords were strapped to his waist, and the polished studs on the toes of his boots gleamed in the faint light of the corridor.

His silver gaze roved over her, and he inclined his head. "My lady."

Maeve lowered herself into a curtsy. "Commander."

Lir offered his arm and she accepted, allowing him to lead her to the verandah. They walked in amiable silence until she got the distinctive feeling he was watching her.

She looked over at him.

"Does this one have pockets?" he asked.

"Unfortunately, no." Maeve smiled, and the corner of his mouth lifted in return. "I suppose I'll have to see if Deirdre can remedy that for me."

They rounded the corner, and Maeve's breath caught her in chest. The library was just up ahead.

"After dinner." Lir veered them away from the engraved doors and Maeve's smile only widened.

"You should know," he continued, "we have a visitor."

Something in his voice set her on edge and her steps stuttered, but Lir kept her upright. "Who is it?"

"Casimir Vawda."

"What? Casimir is here?" Maeve whirled on him, stopping in her tracks. She clutched the sleeve of his shirt. "Why?"

He regarded her carefully, considering his next words.

"He's been supplying us with information in regards to Parisa's movements within the Spring Court."

"Has he now..." Maeve's stomach dropped, her appetite suddenly evading her. The trust she'd built with Casimir had been broken the moment he handed her over to Parisa. He'd yet to prove himself a valuable ally, and she saw no reason to rely upon anything he said. Especially not when he was still in Parisa's confidence. "And you believe him?"

He shifted on his feet, resigned. "I'm afraid we don't have much of a choice."

"How long has he been here?" she asked as he opened the door to the verandah for her.

"Two hours."

"Two hours?" Maeve's voice pitched, drawing the attention of everyone seated at the outdoor table.

Tiernan, Merrick, Rowan, and Casimir were on their feet the second she arrived. Ceridwen remained seated, sipping her tea, while Brynn and Saoirse looked to be having some kind of competition over who could flick their dagger through their fingers the fastest. Their mouths snapped shut, their contest ending, when they saw Maeve standing in the doorway.

The males bowed, and something about their extreme chivalry grated on Maeve's nerves. She lifted her chin out of spite, sending them each a cool glare, lingering a moment longer on Casimir. His hood was shoved back, his dark eyes hidden beneath a swath of brown hair.

Maeve bristled. "Is there a reason I wasn't invited to this little party?"

"You were resting." Tiernan pulled out a chair for her, but she made no move to sit.

Maeve crossed her arms. "And?"

"And you've only just gotten your memories returned to

you." He smiled, but it was contrived, and he tucked his hands behind his back. "I thought you might need—"

"Might I remind you, my lord," she interrupted, silencing him, "that I am not in need of coddling."

Tiernan stared at her, seconds of strained tension pulling taut between them. Then he arched a singular brow, his voice infiltrating her mind. *"Perhaps you're in need of something else, then?"*

Heat bled into her cheeks, but she schooled her expression into one of neutrality. *"Do not change the subject."*

The corner of his lips twitched.

Damn him.

"Forgive me, my lady." Tiernan reached for her hand, pulling her to him. He wrapped his arms around her waist, his palms skimming her flesh, and her blood hummed. "The next time something of importance comes up, I'll ensure you're informed right away."

She pressed a kiss to the underside of his jaw.

"You're looking rather pretty tonight, Maeve." Ceridwen nodded toward her gown, a smile pulling at her ruby lips. "I don't believe I've seen that one before."

Maeve softened. "It was my mother's."

"It's beautiful," Saoirse agreed, before sending a scathing look at Casimir.

Merrick nodded, leaning back in his seat. "An Archfae in every sense of the word."

Wariness slithered down Maeve's spine. Her fingers curled around the back of the chair, her nails digging into the wood. "Why do I get the feeling your compliments have an ulterior motive?"

Silence descended upon the verandah. Everyone was looking at her, but no one could quite meet her eye. Awkward tension thickened in the air, made even more uncomfortable by the fact that every one of them seemed to know something, and none of them had the decency to tell her.

"Enough!" Maeve threw her arms out to the side, exasperated. She couldn't stand it anymore. She was sick of them tiptoeing around her, of treating her like she was some delicate flower that would wither away to nothing at the slightest threat of a breeze. "Stop this. Stop acting as though I'm going to shatter at any moment. I am not fragile. I will *not* break."

She turned, her brows furrowing as she faced Tiernan. Out of everyone, she would have thought he would be the one to understand her, to never underestimate her, to believe in her. "Do you really think I'm so weak that I can't handle whatever it is you need to tell me?"

Rowan coughed, clearing his throat. "Told you we should have woken her up."

Low thunder rumbled and Tiernan's gaze darkened, his eyes swirling with the threat of an incoming storm. He glared at Rowan before returning his attention back to Maeve. "Of course not, you are far from weak. We just—"

"Then say it," Maeve demanded. "Whatever it is, say it. Now."

"Garvan escaped." Casimir's abrupt announcement cut through the stifling resentment burrowing itself inside of her.

Maeve's gut clenched, a harrowing sensation that scalded the back of her throat with hot bile. Her chest caved, hollowing out as the sickening memories haunted her and took up residence in the forefront of her mind. Garvan, who sold out the Summer Court and condemned Tiernan and Ceridwen's parents to death. Garvan, who skinned the merrows and sold their scales. Garvan, who murdered Shay, leaving him to bleed out and die in the courtyard of Niahvess. His atrocities were numerous, a list of crimes Maeve would not soon forget.

She expected to be overcome with fury, maybe even a shred

of fear, knowing that he'd somehow broken free of the iron binding him within Kyol's dungeon. But instead, cold vengeance pierced her straight through and she sharpened its blade, ready to strike.

"How?" The word croaked out of her.

"The only plausible explanation is that it was an inside job." Casimir's voice was eerily calm. He steepled his fingers together, his face a mask of untroubled indifference. "Garvan was under lock and key. His cell was guarded every hour of every day."

That seemed like a rather pertinent piece of information for someone to have, especially when that particular someone was working with the enemy.

Maeve scowled, yet she seemed to be the only one exuding any kind of caution. Even Saoirse looked as though she believed him, though her lips were pressed into a firm line. Her glare cut to Casimir, like she was ready to plunge a dagger into his chest.

"And how are you so sure he escaped?" Maeve questioned, doubt tugging steadily on her conscience.

Casimir spread his palms open and lifted his head, faerie fire burning in the lights overhead illuminating his face. It was then Maeve saw the bone-deep exhaustion, the discoloration beneath his eyes, the lines of weariness embedded into his tanned skin. He looked like a man who'd fought a thousand battles, winning none of them, even though Maeve knew that was the furthest thing from the truth.

He possessed the soul of a warrior. Bloodshed pumped through his veins. He'd seen much, lost much, and every battle, every conflict he'd ever faced, harbored itself in the depths of his dark gaze.

"I bide most of my time in the Autumn Court." He said it as though it was the only explanation he needed.

"You mean when you're not busy being Parisa's puppet?"

Saoirse countered, her knuckles whitening around the hilt of the dagger in her hand.

Casimir spared her a glance. To most, it would look dismissive, flippant even. But not to Maeve. She saw the anguish flash in his eyes, the quick burn of acceptance of one's fate.

"I will pay for my crimes in due time, Saoirse. Though as much as you want to kill me..." He paused, lowering his head once more. "I will die by someone else's hands."

Maeve imagined Parisa would be more than pleased to end his life. Especially if she ever learned he was apparently working against her.

But testing Casimir's loyalties would have to wait. Right now, there were more important matters at stake. Like the fact that Garvan was no longer in the dungeon where he belonged.

"Where is he now?" Maeve asked, determined to end him once and for all.

Casimir shook his head. "No one knows."

Murmurs of frustration and hushed whispers of unease spread among them, but Maeve would not be so easily deterred. If anyone could find Garvan, it would be her. He was her brother, after all, and the familial Strand tying them to one another would lead her right to him.

She closed her eyes, drowning out all sound around her, until the beating of her heart echoed in her ears. Searching for that buried pull, that connection she longed to sever, she waded through the swell of neglect, diving deeper into the darkest part of her soul where she found the decaying Strand bonding her to her duplicitous sibling.

Garvan's mind was a violent storm of thoughts. A descent into the madness of corruption. Chaos fabricated the extent of his damaged soul, making it impossible to determine the nature of his intent. He was suffering and rage. Bitterness and self-loathing. Yet beneath the surface of those volatile emotions was a thin layer of desolation. His heart was black, rotted from years of malevolence, but a sliver of regret had lodged itself somewhere within those putrid walls, concealed and forgotten.

He moved with stealth, a skeleton of his former self, clinging to shadows as he crept through the darkened halls of Kyol's palace.

There was another pull, but this Strand was stronger. More powerful.

It bound her to Dorian.

Maeve's eyes flew open. She sucked in a breath as all the air was pulled from her lungs, leaving her gasping. "He's going to kill my father."

Lir stood abruptly. "We need to—"

"There's no time!" Maeve would not lose her father, not to her bastard of a brother. Shay had already been taken from her. She would not fail her bloodline again. Still dressed in her overly formal attire, Maeve pulled her Aurastone. "I must stop him."

"Maeve," Tiernan warned, stepping closer.

Saoirse shoved to her feet, her silver braid whipping behind her. "You don't know how he escaped, Maeve. He might not be alone. He could have soldiers working with him. There could be dark fae."

Maeve ignored their concerns. She was already wasting too much time. "Then I'll figure that out when I get there."

"Whoa, my lady." Merrick raised both hands in an attempt to appease her. "Just hang on a second. You need a plan. You can't just barge into Kyol and take on Garvan, you have no idea what could be waiting for you."

Her lungs burned and she wanted to scream. Why didn't anyone understand her? When would they realize she could take care of herself? It was like she had those damned cuffs on her wrists all over again.

"I will not stand by and do nothing." She called upon her magic, preparing to *fade*.

Tiernan grabbed her arm, his grip almost punishing. "Be reasonable. You can't do this on your own."

Maeve yanked her arm free, the ice of her glare enough to freeze all of their hearts. "Watch me."

Chapter Nine

"Godsdamnit!" Tiernan shouted, fury ravaging him.

Why was she so fucking infuriating?

The witch thread marking his wrist seared his skin, and he clamped one hand over it to cease its burning. His magic revolted. Lightning ripped overhead, diminishing the stars and terrorizing the skies. Thunder cracked and the ground beneath his feet trembled.

"Where the hell did she go?" Saoirse demanded, darting toward the balcony. Lir flung one arm out, snagging her by the waist to keep her from flying over the edge.

"To Autumn, most likely." Casimir stood up slowly, throwing his hood over his head. "To kill her brother."

"Okay," Saoirse snapped, spinning out of Lir's hold. "But *where* in Autumn?"

"I would assume she went to the palace." Casimir kept his expression even and unbothered. "Considering Garvan is apparently planning to kill their father."

Saoirse launched herself at the drakon, her dagger aimed to strike true. "You bastard—"

But again, Lir was faster. This time he snatched her wrist, wrenching it behind her back. She yelped, her dagger clattering against the stone floor. "That's enough. He's of no use to us if he's dead."

"I'm not going to kill him." Saoirse huffed out a breath, struggling against Lir's hold. He pinned her against him, immobilizing her. "I'm just going to cut off every one of his limbs, starting with his cock, until he begs for mercy and admits all of this is his fault."

Rowan winced and Merrick reared back, cupping one hand over his dick.

"Seven hells," he muttered, "remind me to never piss her off."

"If your tongue is as sharp as your blade, I suggest you save it." Lir's tone was deadly. The cold kind of malice Tiernan had only ever seen from him in times of war. Lir shifted, tightening his grip, still holding the silver-haired warrior hostage. "Otherwise, both of them are likely to get you killed."

Soothing, gentle magic invaded the hostile space, drawing the anger and wrath.

"Tiernan can find Maeve." Ceridwen looked down into her teacup, her brow knitting when she found the contents empty. "He bears the witch thread. It is similar to a Strand, yet different. Still a bond, but witch magic can be rather potent."

Ceridwen was far too melancholy for Tiernan's liking.

Brynn tucked her dagger away, rising from her seat. "We have to go after her. If Garvan got out, then he had help. We don't know the numbers, but Maeve won't be able to stave off a small army of Autumn warriors by herself."

"Sure she can." Rowan crossed his arms and rocked back onto his heels in a silent challenge.

The verandah was hushed. Eerily quiet.

Tiernan turned to face the Nightweaver, his movements painfully slow. "What did you say?"

"In not as many words, I said you severely underestimate your betrothed. All of you do." Rowan's gaze slid to each one of them, driving his point home. "She is not the weak mortal princess from Kells. She is Archfae. A demigoddess in her own right. And far more powerful than any of you could ever imagine."

Fists clenched, Tiernan locked his jaw, inhaling sharply before speaking. But he already knew, no matter what else was said here tonight, none of it was going to end well. "Maeve may be more powerful, but that doesn't mean I have to stand by and let her fight every battle on her own."

The corner of Rowan's mouth tugged upward into a spiteful smirk. "I don't recall her asking for your help."

Tiernan's vision went red, and all he wanted was Rowan's blood on his hands.

"You fucking—"

He tore across the verandah, aiming for the Nightweaver's throat. The table flipped, scattering bowls of food across the floor as glasses and plates shattered around them. He lunged forward, grabbing the prick of a fae and slamming him onto the ground. Rage fired through him and was met with vengeful satisfaction as his fist collided with Rowan's jaw. His head snapped back and blood spurted out from his mouth, but it wasn't enough to disguise the grin peeling across the bastard's face.

Tiernan hauled his arm back to land another blow, but this time, Rowan caught his fist with one hand. His purple gaze went dark, igniting with malice.

Rowan heaved, throwing Tiernan backward. His spine hit the stone wall behind him, and bits of rock tumbled down on top of his head. Pain exploded along his shoulder, but he regained his bearing just in time to duck his head and roll right as Rowan's fist smashed into the wall, leaving a gaping hole. Tiernan leapt to his feet and swung, meeting his mark on the side of Rowan's face, the resounding crunch of flesh and bone reverberating through him.

He was vaguely aware of everyone around them, but their voices droned in and out of his mind.

"Should we intervene?" Merrick asked from somewhere off to Tiernan's right.

Lir answered with a decided, "No."

So they continued to fight, unleashing all their jealousy and anger in a battle of blood, fists, and broken bones. They were evenly matched, each striking the other before dodging the next assault. Tiernan knew at least two of his ribs were cracked. The bruises would be vicious, and his eye had already begun to swell. But at least he wasn't spitting blood. He'd decked Rowan right in his pretty face, the rush of smug triumph enough to make Tiernan forget about the fact that his lip was busted open.

Suddenly, a flash of silver tore across Tiernan's line of sight.

Saoirse had Rowan pinned against the crumbling wall, the tip of her blade poised at the base of his neck.

Brynn was in Tiernan's face, the cold bite of metal stinging his heated flesh as she pressed the flat edge of her blade to his throat. Her eyes flashed from piercing blue to dangerous red.

Ceridwen stood between them, her body trembling with outrage.

"Are you two done?" Her voice was nothing short of venomous. "Can we stop this incessant fighting?"

Tiernan pointed at Rowan. "He started it."

"Oh, real mature," Rowan drawled, wiping the back of his hand across his bloodied mouth.

"Fuck off," Tiernan spat.

"No more." Ceridwen's chest heaved with indignation. "I will tolerate no more of this."

She strode over to Rowan, her dress of sapphire swirling around her, and for a moment, Tiernan thought she might slap him across the face. But the air shifted. Where it was once charged with loathing and frustration, there were now ripples of serenity, of calming tranquility. Rowan stiffened against the soothing touch of her magic.

"I am sorry you lost her, my lord. I am sorry you've been forced to sacrifice your love for her through the centuries. I am sorry for your suffering, for the depth of your despair." Ceridwen reached up, and with almost painful tenderness, she cupped Rowan's bruised cheek. "I am *sorry*."

The apology hung between them, sucking the fight from Tiernan's lungs.

Saoirse lowered her weapon, and Rowan slumped against the wall.

"It wasn't my choice." He was thoroughly defeated. "I never would have given her up if I had known...if I had known I'd lose her forever."

Ceridwen's magic swallowed them, drowned them in relentless waves of compassion.

Brynn stepped away from Tiernan, her eyes slowly returning to a warm gold.

Rowan pushed off the wall, then rolled his shoulders back. His gaze meeting Tiernan's from across the verandah.

"I'm glad she chose you." He swiped his thumb against the corner of his mouth, glancing pointedly at Tiernan's wrist before looking back up at him. "I could never be the one to kill her."

He crossed his arms over his chest, leaving Tiernan to field the stunned silence that followed.

"What?" Saoirse stared at Rowan, then spun around to face Tiernan. "What did he just say?"

"Exactly what it sounds like," Tiernan murmured.

"Tiernan?" His name fell from his sister's lips in a hoarse whisper.

"I took an oath." He rolled the cuffs of his sleeve to display the rose gold tattoo marking his wrist. He swallowed the knot of trepidation clogging his throat. "Maeve made me vow that if Faeven falls, if it looks like all hope is lost and we stand no chance of winning, that I will take her life. To ensure Parisa cannot use her against us."

Brynn gaped at him, her mouth falling open in shock. "You can't be serious."

He looked at her, lost for words.

"But you worded it differently, right?" There was a pang of desperation in Saoirse's words. She plucked the flower that had fallen from behind her ear from off the ground and repositioned it. "I mean, you're fae. That's what you do to get out of something. You twist your words."

Merrick clutched his heart, feigning hurt. "Ouch."

But the look on Saoirse's face, the pure grief, struck Tiernan in the heart.

"My oath to Maeve stands true." He bowed his head. "I'm sorry for it."

"How could you agree to such a thing?" Saoirse pressed her fingers to her temples, exasperated. "And you're all just willing to sit here and wait for her to return just because *he* thinks she can handle herself?"

She pointed an accusatory finger in Rowan's direction.

"She's capable," he repeated, his resolve unwavering.

"We're all capable," Saoirse fired back. "Every one of us has fought and bled, but that doesn't mean we should have to fight our battles alone. Maeve is stubborn. She has fire in her soul.

But she grew up in the human lands, she was raised as a mortal."

Saoirse's blue eyes landed on Tiernan. "You of all people should know emotions can cloud her judgment. Her desire to help, to save and protect, blinds her to the manipulation and the cunning ability of the fae."

She shook her head. "Have you learned nothing?"

With that, she stalked off across the verandah, not even bothering with the door. She stomped over the debris and climbed through the hole in the wall created by Rowan's fist.

"Saoirse," Ceridwen called after her. "Where are you going?"

"To find her!"

Tiernan glanced over at Lir, jerking his head in Saoirse's direction. "Follow her. She'll get herself killed before she reaches Autumn's border."

Lir nodded, setting off after the infuriated warrior.

"If you're that worried about your mate," Rowan drawled, smoothing the wrinkles from his shirt. "Attune to her emotions. Your fancy witch marking will let you know if she's in peril. Unless you're worried that I'm right, of course, that she doesn't actually need you as much as you'd like to believe."

Tiernan's muscles seized on instinct. Again, his fists clenched in fury.

He'd felt the crushing weight of her fear more often than he cared to admit. The worst was when he could do nothing about it.

"Then go after her." Rowan headed toward the door, tossing a backward glance over his shoulder. "But don't say I didn't warn you."

Damn it.

Tiernan could take Rowan's word and let Maeve go after Garvan alone. Hell, she'd probably already found him, given how much time he'd wasted in his brawl with Rowan. But if he went after her, there was a good chance she'd be incensed, and likely take it as some kind of personal offense against her abilities. Already he'd tried to convince her not to go by herself and that had backfired in his face. But if Saoirse was right, he could be making a terrible mistake by sitting here and waiting for her to return.

Muttering a stream of vile swears, he reached to Maeve's mind through the witch thread.

"If you need me, say the word."

Silence followed, and then finally, her voice slid into his thoughts.

"I can handle my brother on my own."

Chapter Ten

Tiernan's voice echoed quietly in the back of Maeve's mind, but she remained motionless, measuring each breath until it faded completely, and she could focus on the task at hand.

Garvan crept down the hall, slinking toward her father's bedroom like a decrepit snake. His dark red hair had lost most of its luster, it was stringy and thin in most places. His skin clung to his gaunt face as though it would melt off at any second. He looked frail and weak, with his threadbare clothing barely clinging to his malnourished form. Maeve almost didn't recognize him.

From the shadows, he scarcely resembled the strong, powerful Archfae she remembered. He was a phantom, empty and withering.

"I know you're there, darling sister," he rasped, his voice gruff. "A Strand binding siblings is unbreakable. Unless one of them dies, of course."

Maeve clenched her jaw so tightly her temples started to ache. "You are no brother of mine."

She stepped from the shadows, and he turned to face her.

His peeled lips cracked open into a cruel smile. "Keep telling yourself that."

Her grip tightened around the hilt of her Aurastone, and she moved closer, her heels clicking softly against the obsidian floor. Amber light washed the corridor, just enough to see him clearly. "You cursed our father. You killed our brother. You—"

"I do not need you to recite all the crimes I have committed." Garvan's face twisted into a scowl, but the rancor hardening his tone waned. "Aran already ensured I suffered...thoroughly."

Maeve faltered.

Aran tortured Garvan?

She knew Garvan deserved every punishment bestowed upon him, but she never imagined Aran would be the one to inflict it. The thought of it made her cringe. She'd never been on the receiving end of her eldest brother's wrath.

"Come to kill me, have you, sister?" Garvan asked, withdrawn.

"Eventually." Maeve's magic flared in warning. "But not yet."

He bowed, his bones cracking. "By all means, postpone my agony. Aran was quite good at it."

Maeve's heart tumbled into the acidic pit of her churning stomach. She didn't want to think about all the ways Aran would have tormented Garvan. He could command the decay and death of any living thing, rotting any plant or creature from the inside out.

Bile coated the back of her throat, but she remained steadfast. She would not let those thoughts sway her from killing Garvan.

"You intend to end our father's life." It was a statement of fact, not a question.

He blew out a ragged breath, the greasy tendrils of his hair fluttering slightly. "I intend to have a discussion with him."

"Not tonight." She stalked toward him, but Garvan held his ground, plastering one bony hand against the smooth stone wall to keep him upright. "Why?"

He glared at her. "Why what?"

Maeve searched his emerald eyes, looking for that one shred of merit she knew resided in the darkest part of his soul. She'd seen it...once. "Why did you choose her over us?"

His mouth pressed into a firm line. "I did what I thought was best for Autumn."

"By cursing our father to remain a fox forever?" Maeve shook her head. He was unbelievable.

"He wasn't *here*." Pain lanced through Garvan and his expression changed, morphing from one of anger to harrowing grief. She saw it in his eyes, that endless sea of sorrow. Of fear. And for a moment, the male standing before her was no longer a merciless traitor, but a terrified High Prince who'd lost everything. "Our father's mind was lost to madness. When our mother vanished, it wrecked him. When she died, it ruined him. For years after her disappearance, he blamed himself. She left without a trace. We had no idea the reason she abandoned us was to keep you safe."

Regret clutched Maeve's heart, squeezing until she could barely breathe. "And you thought Parisa would help?"

Garvan shrugged, his gaze drifting to the floor. "She offered me control over Autumn. I thought I was saving our Court."

"And what did you give her in return?" Maeve asked, suddenly fearful of the answer.

"An eternity of servitude." He ducked his head. "I can never deny her. Never refuse her."

When he looked back up at her, a glassy sheen glazed his eyes and pinned her with remorse. "Use your blade against me, dear sister. For you would be doing me the greatest of favors."

Maeve stepped back. It wasn't supposed to be like this, she wasn't supposed to pity him. She wanted to feel the rush of rage, of hatred, for all the wicked things he'd done. When she killed him, she wanted to stare into his eyes and smile as the life drained from his body. She didn't want to wrap him in empathy, she wanted revenge.

She lowered her Aurastone, barely. "Let me help you."

A sad laugh escaped him. "It's too late for me, Maeve. I know where I'm going once I die, and it is not the eternal paradise of Maghmell."

The Sluagh. Even in death, he would become Parisa's slave.

Her heart fractured. "Garvan, I—"

"Do it now and do it quickly," he begged. "Before she realizes she has access to my mind again. Before she can compel me to kill anyone else."

Again, she backed away from him but he ambled toward her, desperation filling his watery gaze.

"Do not pity me, sister." His hand closed around her wrist and she struggled to wrench herself free from his hold.

From down the hall, a door burst open, the walls shuddering in the wake of the High King of Autumn. Dorian stood a few feet away, his powerful aura glowing around him. "What is the meaning of this?"

Maeve opened her mouth to explain, but there was a suck of harsh air, and she watched in horror as Garvan plunged her Aurastone into his own heart.

His slight body slumped against her and she caught him in her arms, a trail of something sticky and warm sliding down her wrist. Carefully, Maeve sank onto her knees with Garvan's head coming to rest on her lap. Blood trickled from the corner of his mouth, spilling down his chin. He gripped her hand, his fingers nearly frozen against her skin. The green of his eyes warmed one final time, and he gave her a broken smile.

"Garvan." His name slipped from her lips in a grating whisper.

A throbbing ache stole through her heart, crushing her. The fraying thread connecting her to Garvan spasmed, pulling taut. Maeve gasped, rocking back as the Strand unraveled, severing them completely.

Garvan died exactly as she planned.

Staring up into her eyes.

The thud of footfalls echoed too loudly in her ears, and there was a scrape of rough voices. Guards, maybe? She couldn't be sure. Nor could she tear her gaze away from her Aurastone, still protruding out of Garvan's chest.

She sat back on her bloodied hands, tucking them beneath her. A masculine hand wrapped around the hilt and she squeezed her eyes shut, wincing at the suctioning sound of her blade being pulled from his heart.

"It's okay, *alanuhv.*" Dorian gathered her into his arms as the Autumn guards hefted Garvan's lifeless body, carrying him away. He pulled her to her feet and handed her the Aurastone. There was no trace left of the life she'd taken.

Maeve sheathed it quickly, unable to look at its shimmering gleam. Her nose tingled, her eyes burned, and she shuddered into her father's embrace.

"He was broken, Maeve." Dorian smoothed her hair, cupping the back of her head. "No one could save him."

"I tried," Maeve choked out.

"I know." Dorian held her closer, pressing a gentle kiss to her forehead. "But you must remember, we all have our limits. Try as we might, we can't save everyone."

Her father led her further down the corridor, away from the scene of death that was already being scrubbed away as though it hadn't existed at all. She walked with him through the gilded hall, where sconces fashioned into crimson glass leaves glowed with faerie fire. Tapestries of Autumn splendor lined one wall, while arching windows soared along the other, each one coming to a definitive point.

Maeve wondered what it would have been like if her mother were still alive. She could almost hear Fianna's voice calling to her, could almost picture the stunning beauty of her mother's smile.

Emotion crashed into her, a tidal wave of shame. It pulled her beneath the surface, drowned her in guilt. So much of this was her fault. So many atrocities, so much despair, and all of it could be traced back to her.

"I'm sorry." The words fell from her before she could stop them.

Dorian glanced down at her, a line of concern crinkling across his brow. "Whatever for?"

"For taking her from you."

His expression softened into one of kindness. Of pure love. "You never took her from me. Was I lost without her for a time? Yes. Did I miss her and grieve her? Yes."

"But," he continued, tucking her arm into the crook of his elbow, "your mother and I were fated. I *knew* she carried you, blood of my blood. Just as I knew whatever reason she had for leaving must have been far greater than anything I could have imagined."

Maeve shook her head, trying to make sense of it. "Garvan said you—"

"We all deal with grief in our own ways, Maeve." He patted her hand. "Do not ever feel like this is your fault. I may have lost your mother, but she gave me you."

She threw her arms around his waist, hugging him fiercely. "Will you tell me about her?"

Dorian laughed. "Where shall I start?"

"From the beginning." Maeve looked up into his face, where she could now see remnants of herself. "I want to know everything about her. And you."

"Come with me." They turned a corner, where the palace walls were lined with fluid paintings of shifting images depicting the history of Autumn. High Kings and High Queens from before, a visual representation of Maeve's lineage. "Fianna Ruhdneah was fire and smoke. Her beauty was unrivaled, her laughter enough to make even the strongest of males drop to their knees."

He nudged open a door, revealing a study filled with shelves of books. There was a sleek wooden desk that faced a window where the moonlight dusted the tops of jeweled trees. A fire roared to life in the hearth, warming the cozy space.

"If there is one thing you should know about your mother," Dorian said, walking over to the desk. He opened the top drawer and pulled out a thick leather-bound book embossed with gold lettering. "It was that she was a reader."

He sent her a knowing look.

"A reader who also loved to write." He handed her the book.

The leather was soft against Maeve's hands and she trailed the tip of her finger over the golden letters. "She was a writer..."

"Your mother wrote this story during the Evernight War and in the months following Carman's rule." Dorian tucked his hands behind her back. "I image she wrote it for you."

Maeve opened the book, the pages of parchment velvety beneath her touch. A delicate scent floated in the air around her—apple blossoms and citrus spice. The scent of her mother.

Written at the bottom of the first page, in flowing, elegant script, was a dedication.

. . .

*T*O THE FIRE *of my soul,*

I will carry you in my heart, for now and forever, you are mine.

May you always shine brighter than the dawn.

TEARS slid down Maeve's cheek, as the words blurred before her eyes.

"You are the keeper of fate, *alanhuv*. The weaver of destiny." Her father slid one finger under her chin, tilting her face up to him. "Your story is one for the ages, older than the recording of time. The aurora never loses to the darkness, it only ever rises."

He kissed the top of her head. "If you need me, you'll know where to find me."

Dorian left her then, and Maeve lost herself in the story of her mother's life.

She devoured Fianna's handwritten words, learning all she could about the mother she never knew. Maeve read about Fianna's childhood, the moment she met Dorian, and when each High Prince of Autumn was born. Flipping through the pages, she fell into a world of dazzling Four Courts and flourishing magic, a place not yet touched by the greedy hands of darkness. Maeve's heart nearly skittered out of her chest when she realized her mother's best friend was Helena, the late High Queen of Summer—Tiernan's mother.

One day they'd hoped to unite their Courts.

The storm of Summer and the jewel of Autumn.

More tears fell, harder this time, and Maeve blinked them away as she read the inscription on the final page.

.   .   .

I KNOW my womb will swell with you soon, just as I know I will not be there to watch you fully come into your power. I will miss your first laugh, your first smile, your first steps. But know that I am always watching you, my cherished daughter. Be courageous. Be wondrous. You are magic and life, the one true faerie queen.

MAEVE CLOSED THE BOOK, clutching it to her chest, and went in search of her father. She followed the gentle tug on the Strand, winding her way through the glowing corridors of Kyol's palace, and discovered Dorian standing on one of the numerous balconies. Waterfalls rushed down from either side, their spray sparkling like tiny diamonds in the fading light of the moon. She stood beside him, silent, breathing in the life of the Autumn Court.

"When this is all over," he said, taking her hand, "I want you to rule Autumn."

"What?" Maeve startled, turning to stare up at him. "But Aran is the heir. He—"

"He doesn't want it," Dorian finished for her. "I've already spoken to him on the matter. The sea has changed him. He intends to sail after the war, though if you ask me, I think it's because he finds himself in love with someone not of our realm."

Maeve's heart sank. Aran planned to leave again. For good, this time. "What about you? Don't you like being king?"

His eyes, emerald like Aran and Garvan's, shone with a swell of sorrow. "What good am I as a king, without my queen?"

He gave her hand a reassuring squeeze. "I think it was time Autumn was ruled by the one destined for it."

Dorian released her, then turned to go.

"Papa?" Maeve called and he turned back, offering her the faintest of smiles. "I love you."

"And I love you." He bowed. "More than you will ever know."

He walked away, leaving her alone, and Maeve *faded* back to Niahvess.

She appeared in Tiernan's room, thinking she would find himself asleep, but instead, he was standing by the glass doors leading their shared balcony. His back was to her and though she knew he sensed her arrival, he didn't turn to greet her.

"Hi."

He raked a hand through his midnight hair, but still he said nothing.

"Garvan is dead." She tried again to get some kind of response out of him. Yet his emotions remained sealed off from her, locked behind a stone-cold wall. The muscles in his shoulders were tense, the energy around him crackled like a bolt of lightning ready to strike.

"Tiernan?"

Finally, he slowly turned to face her, and it was then she saw the cut on his lip, the gash and swelling beneath his eyes, and the mottled bruising around his ribs.

"Tier! What happened?"

She rushed forward but he stepped back, away from her. "It's nothing."

Maeve halted in her tracks, frozen in place by the sting of rejection. Instantly, she shielded herself in defense, shuttering herself off from him. "It's obviously something. You're bleeding."

His gaze dipped down to her skirt. "And you're covered in blood that is not your own."

Rearing back, Maeve tucked her mother's book under one

arm, then frowned. Unusual tension dampened the room, making it insufferable. "Are you mad at me?"

He laughed, harsh and grating.

"You told me some time ago to either stand behind you, stand beside you, or get out of your fucking way." He tilted his head, scrutinizing her. "Perhaps it's time I should choose the latter."

"What? Don't be ridiculous." She couldn't believe he'd throw her own words back in her face. They buried such petty altercations and left behind where they belonged. "Of course I want you to stand with me, I—"

"Do you?" he asked, storming toward her as thunder rumbled through the heavens. "Because it was very clear you didn't want nor need my help tonight."

"No." Maeve shook her head, dismissing the unfair allegation. "You told me I couldn't go by myself, so—"

"So what?" The thunder cracked louder this time, the makings of a violent storm. "You had to prove me wrong? You had to make a statement? I am aware of your greatness, Maeve, but did you ever stop to think that maybe everyone here isn't quite ready to lose you again just because you think you have to make a point?"

"I'm not making a point!" Maeve's voice pitched and a rise of anger bubbled inside of her. "I was trying to save my father's life."

"And you did. And I'm *so* fucking proud of you." It sounded like he meant it, but the words dripped with diluted sarcasm. "But you got lucky."

She staggered back. "Excuse me?"

Tiernan was closer now, crowding in on her, stealing her space. Her air. "You. Got. Lucky."

Maeve was ready to argue but he barreled on, silencing her.

"What if it had been a trap? What if some of Autumn's

soldiers were on Garvan's side and released him on purpose?" He stalked away from her, fuming, and the ground trembled beneath them. "Seven hells, Maeve. Parisa could have been there. You don't know. You didn't even think. You didn't make a plan. You just acted on your own without giving a damn about anyone or anything else."

An unwelcome sensation clenched her stomach, carving her from the inside out.

"How did he escape?" Tiernan demanded, whirling on her.

"What?"

"How did he escape, Maeve?" He threw out his arms, his magic pulsing with power. "Did you even ask him? Or were you too busy being the fucking savior?"

Maeve clamped her mouth shut. She hadn't asked how Garvan had escaped because it didn't matter. He was dead. Nothing else made a difference. And Tiernan was wrong. She wasn't *lucky*. She knew damn good and well how to handle herself. She knew a war was coming and she would win it, with or without him.

"I don't have to justify myself to you." She lifted her chin. "Or anyone."

She spun on her heel, heading for the door of her own bedroom.

"You're just going to walk away?"

Maeve didn't answer, and she didn't look back.

"Fine. You fight your battles by yourself, Dawnbringer," Tiernan retorted, vehemence laced his words. "And the rest of us will fight ours together."

She yanked open the door and slammed it shut behind her, so the hinges rattled. Explosive thunder quaked the walls of her room and she trembled, slouching against the doorframe. Maeve half expected, half hoped, Tiernan would break down the door and come after her. But only agonizing silence followed in the aftermath of their argument.

She listened for him, felt for him, but he was gone.

Maeve held her mother's book to her chest, sliding down the door until she landed on the cool ground. Her soul ached. Her heart wept. For the first time since her return to Niahvess, she felt completely alone.

Chapter Eleven

Tiernan *faded* to the Vista.

Alone.

He needed to calm down. To breathe. But damn, Maeve was so incredibly stubborn. So recklessly foolish. He never wanted to limit her, he simply wanted to help her, and it infuriated him beyond belief that she was too blind to see it.

Dropping onto the bed, he stretched out and summoned his guitar. He plucked idly at the strings, trying to strum out an evocative melody that had been stuck in his head for days, but the chords wouldn't come. Frustrated, he gripped the neck of the instrument, determined to at least get the opening chord out of his mind, but one of the strings snapped.

He tossed the guitar onto the foot of the bed. Attempting to do anything while agitated was useless. Maybe if he closed his eyes, he could recenter. Refocus. He threw his arm over his eyes, breathing deeply.

The scent of rose water and ocean mist filled the room as Ceridwen *faded* into the Vista.

"Tiernan?" Her voice was soft, lyrical.

"What is it, Ceridwen?" He kept his eyes closed.

"I take it Maeve returned from Kyol," she mused, her gentle footfalls moving toward him.

He grunted. "What gave it away?"

"Oh, I don't know. Possibly the raucous thunder and gale-force winds." The bed shifted, sinking as she sat on the edge. "I'm sure she'll come around. It was just a fight."

Something about her words triggered him, setting him off. His exasperation skyrocketed. He jolted upright, staring at his twin.

"It's not just a fight. It's her playing a dangerous game with dire consequences." Tiernan raked both hands through his hair, tucking his legs under him. "Why does she think she has to do everything on her own? Doesn't she know we love her, that we *want* to help her?"

Ceridwen's lulling magic enveloped the space, and he struggled against it. He didn't want her sympathy.

"You have to remember, Maeve has never known true love. Not of this magnitude. Not of this depth." Ceridwen angled her head so her curtain of golden hair fell around her. "She was emotionally abused most of her life. She's always had to do everything on her own."

"What about Saoirse?" Tiernan countered. The silver-haired warrior loved Maeve dearly. Would probably die for her if it came down to it. "And Casimir?"

Because even though the drakon had been the one to hand Maeve over to Parisa, his conscience had gotten the better of him. He couldn't bear to see her in pain. None of them could.

Ceridwen sighed, toying with the satin sash of her dark pink gown. "They answered to Carman. They loved her as best they knew how, but at the end of the day, their allegiance was to Carman. Not to Maeve. And she knew that, just like she knew she would never be a priority."

Tiernan groaned, scrubbing both of his hands over his face. She made a valid point. "All I want is to keep her safe. I don't want to lose her again."

"I understand. But she feels on a level you and I never will. She is powerful, more so than ever before. She is a demigoddess, Tiernan. Magic incarnate. A creator and destroyer of worlds." Ceridwen stood, smoothing her gown so it rippled around her. "I believe Saoirse was right...Maeve's emotions could be the very thing that ends us all."

Dread burrowed itself into Tiernan's heart. It froze his blood, as though shards of ice were being pumped through his veins. Alarm caused the hairs along the back of his neck to stand on end and he shifted in an attempt to ward off the harrowing sensation.

Tiernan watched his sister carefully. She didn't look troubled, her brow was smooth, but there was something in her eyes, something unsettling. His muscles tensed on instinct.

"What are you saying?" he asked.

Ceridwen remained solemn. "This war will change everything."

She bowed her head, then *faded* from the Vista.

There would be no rest for him now. Not with Ceridwen's ominous statement hanging in the air, unnerving him.

He reached for Maeve through their bond, preparing to be swept away by the flood of her emotions. There was a subtle pull down the witch thread, the remnants of dwindling frustration, hurt, anger, and...something more cavernous. Whatever this feeling was, she kept it locked away, hidden behind a wall she'd built around her heart. It was deep in her soul, festering in the darkness, untouched by the light. And worse, she was blocking him from it, keeping it concealed from his view.

If only she would talk to him, then maybe she would remember that she could trust him. With everything. Her time in the Ether had changed her, not necessarily for the better or worse, but she was not the same as when she left. She was bottling things up, shielding herself. He had to find a way to get her to open back up to him.

Determined to make things right, Tiernan *faded* back to his room.

The witch thread tugged him toward the balcony. He glanced toward the door connecting their rooms—the one Maeve had slammed shut—and found it cracked open. His heart warmed. Slightly. Quietly, he treaded across the floor and nudged open the glass doors to the balcony, only to find Maeve sound asleep on one of the outdoor chairs. Moonlight spilled over her, so her tattoos glittered, and her hair shone like pale pink diamonds.

He moved toward her and wasn't the least bit surprised to find a book splayed open in her lap.

Tiernan collected the book, closing it, and headed back into her room to place it on the nightstand. Then he went back for her, gathering her sleeping form into his arms. She snuggled against him, sighing, and all he wanted was to live in this moment. To imagine them together for an eternity with no war, no strife, no turmoil. But instead, he laid her down upon the bed, willing to give her the space she needed. Glamouring her into a nightshirt and out of the gown still stained with Garvan's dried blood, he covered her with a plush blanket, then turned to go.

He was almost to the door connecting their rooms when the faintest whisper stopped him in his tracks.

"Don't leave me."

Tiernan stilled, turning slowly back to the bed where she slept.

Her eyes were closed, but one arm was stretched out across the bed, reaching for him.

Loosing a breath, he peeled off his shirt, and climbed into the bed next to her. She snuggled into his side, clinging to him, but the gnawing ache of apprehension did not ease.

Even with Maeve safely tucked into his arms, he couldn't seem to rid himself of the emptiness spreading inside of him.

Tiernan closed his eyes, willing himself to believe that it was nothing more than a bad dream. Because a tiny, insignificant part of him knew he was losing. Not only Maeve, but also her heart.

MAEVE LOOKED AROUND HER, then squeezed her eyes shut.

She wasn't here. Not again. This wasn't real, it was a figment of her imagination. She'd already suffered through this illusion once, she refused to do so again. But when she opened her eyes, the vastness of the battlefield remained.

Blood dampened the ground, causing her nose to burn. The skies were overcast, thick with the dense haze of smoke and smoldering fires. Dozens of bodies were sprawled at her feet, all of them face down. She didn't dare turn them over, couldn't bring herself to look into the lifeless eyes of faces she knew, of names she recalled. Off to her right, indistinct shadows emerged from the fine mist crawling along the ground. There was a familiarity there.

The Nightweaver.

Maeve turned from him, searching for the glow of the dawn, but the goddess of life was nowhere to be found.

She threw her arms out, spinning in a circle. "You told me I could change this!"

There was no response.

"How?" Maeve demanded. "Please, show me how!"

"Maeve." A low voice rumbled from behind her and she whirled at the sound, a scream clogging the back of her throat.

It was Tiernan, but not. His handsome face was distorted, the flesh mangled. His cheekbones were sunken and splotched a hideous shade of bluish-black. Blood trickled from the corner of his mouth to his chin. The leather armor he wore had been shredded, and he'd suffered numerous wounds, all of them seeping crimson and staining his chest. But his eyes gave him away. They were empty pits, devoid of life. Staring through her instead of at her.

Tiernan was dead.

"Maeve." He reached for her with one gnarled hand and Maeve screamed.

She swung hard, flailing in an effort to get away from him as bile scalded the back of her throat.

But he was faster.

Tiernan grabbed her hand, and she loosed a wail of raw fear.

Maeve's heart plummeted, cold sweat licked her skin, and her eyes flew open. She jerked. Thrashed. Only to realize she was no longer on that damning battlefield but in the safety of her room. Moonlight slanted in overhead, slashing across Tiernan, who was very much alive and breathing, with her fist clutched tightly in his hand. He sat up in the bed watching her, his gaze unreadable in the dim light.

She'd almost struck him.

Her chest rose and fell in rapid succession, each breath slowly becoming easier as she became more aware of her surroundings.

A nightmare. That's all it was, a terrible, awful nightmare.

Maeve scrambled across the bed and into his lap. His arms came around her without hesitation while she straddled him, locking her hands tightly around his neck. She buried her face into his bare chest, listening for his heartbeat, matching its rhythm, letting his steady breathing guide her.

"The vision?" he asked, his voice rough with sleep.

"Yes." Maeve clutched him, fearful that if she let go, she'd fall right back into that dreadful dream. "I don't know how to change it."

"We'll find a way. I'll do whatever I can to help." Tiernan adjusted his hold on her, drawing her in closer until the warmth of his body surrounded her. "If you'll let me."

Maeve nodded, but seeds of doubt had already taken root in the back of her mind. She didn't think anyone could help her. Not anymore.

Chapter Twelve

Maeve stood in the throne room of Niahvess surrounded by members of Summer, Autumn, and Winter. Two days had passed since her fight with Tiernan, since she'd gone to Kyol on her own and taken Garvan's life. She'd spent most of them training in an effort to avoid overthinking, but now, with everyone arriving to go over the details of their battle plan, Maeve was alone with her thoughts. She stood off to the side, watching as they greeted one another like old friends, and feeling like somewhat of an outsider. As though she didn't quite belong.

A large wooden table was placed in the center of the room with enough chairs for everyone in attendance. The sun was just making its ascent into the sky, but there was no excessive spread of delicious food or boisterous laughter to lighten the ever-present weight of tension. It was solemn and morose, much like her mood. To keep herself busy, she fidgeted with the crystal beading of her violet gown while quietly observing all those around her with Cahira dozing at her feet.

Dorian was there with a handful of Autumn guards and

Aeralie, who smirked at something Brynn said before kissing her soundly on the lips.

Maeve smiled when Brynn blushed at the adorable display of affection.

There was an interesting air between Ceridwen and Merrick, an awkward tension Maeve couldn't quite pinpoint. Like an undercurrent of reservation, as though something had happened between them. The stolen glances were painfully obvious, as was the way they stood near one another, yet each refused to acknowledge the other's existence.

Maeve shook her head, reminding herself to ask Ceridwen about that later. Because right now, she was avoiding all eye contact with Ciara, the bitchy ice queen. But when Maeve caught the eye of Malachy Brannon, a flush spread into her cheeks. She clearly remembered her interaction with the Commander of the Winter Legion. He'd readily danced with her during the Sunatalis celebration, then graciously allowed her to use him as a means of making Tiernan teem with jealousy.

Not her finest hour.

Malachy strode over to her, his eyes glinting. He flashed her a dashing smile before capturing her hand and brushing a light kiss across her knuckles. "My lady, I must say, it is an absolute pleasure to see you again."

"Commander." She curtsied, grateful when he released her hand because she could feel the heat of Tiernan's gaze burning into her back. "It's good to be home."

He looked down, his lips lifting at the sight of the sleeping *faolan*. "She's cute."

"This is Cahira." At the sound of her name, the wolfling woke, sniffing the air.

Her pale blue gaze latched onto Malachy. She studied him

for a moment, as though debating whether or not he posed a threat, then curled back into a ball of white fur.

"Frost *faolan* are rare. We have a few in Ashdara, their magic is exceptionally useful." Malachy inclined his head, lifting one brow. "If you're ever interested, I'd be more than willing to help you train her."

Maeve beamed at the proposition, even though she doubted Tiernan would let her spend any time with the Winter general alone. Even if it was for training. "That's a lovely offer, Commander. I'll consider it."

He nodded, his gaze sliding to his left as Saoirse approached them. Malachy returned to his post at Ciara's side, though the Winter queen made a show of pretending she hadn't known *exactly* where he'd gone.

"Can we talk?" Saoirse jerked her head to a corner of the throne room, out of earshot of everyone else.

"Of course." Maeve nodded, following her best friend to where their conversation would be more private and not put fully on display for everyone to witness. She was mentally preparing herself to tell Saoirse everything that happened in Kyol, including Garvan's death and about the book her mother had written, when Saoirse rounded on her.

Saoirse pointed an accusing finger in her direction. "You need to stop this."

Great.

All Maeve needed was for someone else to tell her how all the events leading up to now were her fault.

"I'm aware." She rolled her shoulders back, ready to stand her ground. "I don't need a reminder that the outcome of this war lies heavily on my shoulders."

"No." Saoirse's sapphire eyes darkened. "I mean these disappearing acts. You can't keep running off to go take care of shit on your own while leaving the rest of us to wonder if you'll live or die."

A spark of annoyance simmered low in Maeve's gut. First Tiernan, now Saoirse. She bristled. "I can take care of myself."

"That's not the point," Saoirse countered, fisting her hands on her hips.

Maeve threw her arms out to the side. "Then what is?"

Because she was damn well tired of everyone within these palace walls trying to tell her what she could and could not do.

"The point is that you don't *have* to do all of it by yourself. You're not alone anymore, Maeve. You're not that scared little girl sitting in a cage over an angry ocean. Everyone here"—Saoirse gestured around the throne room—"loves you. Values you. It's not us and you. It's *all* of us. Together."

Maeve shifted on her feet. The heels she wore were pinching her toes, and she was growing weary of having this same conversation. Again. "There's more to it than that."

"Then tell me," Saoirse pleaded. The white petals of the rose tucked behind into hair fluttered in the faint breeze. "Let me help you."

Saoirse would never know the level of guilt, the compounding sense of remorse that burgeoned within Maeve's soul with each passing day. It was like she was pinned to the ground by a boulder but instead of anyone coming to her rescue and heaving the blasted thing off of her, a new one was continuously being added until her lungs caved in, and it grew more difficult to catch her breath.

Maeve shook her head. "You wouldn't understand."

"Oh, bullshit. I *know* you." Saoirse moved closer, her gaze narrowing, and Maeve realized the lines at the corner of her eyes had deepened. She was aging. But Saoirse barreled on, as though she was still as youthful and full of life as ever. "Just like

I know you continue to *feel*. You may be a badass bitch, but you're emotional and—"

Maeve reared back. "I am *not* emotional."

Cahira stirred from across the room, whining slightly.

"Yes, you are. You wear your heart on your fucking sleeve." Saoirse crossed her arms, glowering. "And until you come to terms with that, it will make it all the easier for Parisa to manipulate you."

The blow struck low.

Maeve clenched her hands at her side, her magic snapping as a swell of anger simmered to the surface. She sucked in a breath in an effort to maintain control. Her muscles tensed, the power coursing through her quivered. "I don't have time for this. The meeting is about to start, so if you'd excuse me, I need to go find a way to save us all from dying."

Saoirse rolled her eyes, but Maeve paid her no mind.

She stalked over toward the table, not allowing herself to make eye contact with any of them. She shouldn't expect any of them to understand. Parisa was after her, she intended to use Maeve like a weapon to bring Faeven to their knees. Everyone else was just a casualty, a victim of Maeve's mistakes. Sure, she could tell them she was drowning in a sea of regret, of self-loathing, but she already knew the outcome of such a statement.

No one would ever let her out of their sight. She would be coddled and protected, all while they reassured her that none of this was her fault. They would act as though what she was feeling was normal, and she would be forced to withstand their pitying glances, the sympathetic plights. But they would realize it soon enough. Eventually, once the war was underway, they would all see her for what she truly was—a plague brought down upon them in the guise of a champion.

Which was why she would have to take on Parisa by herself.

There was no other alternative.

Maeve seated herself at the table right as Tiernan said, "Let's begin, shall we?"

She didn't miss the worry in his eyes when he stole a glance in her direction. She sought solace elsewhere, looking for one person in particular, but not finding him in attendance. "Where's Rowan?"

"Right here." He appeared in a swirl of shadows, seating himself across from her. Ever calm, he ignored the way half of the group gaped at him, as though they'd just seen a spirit traverse the afterlife. His lavender eyes searched hers and his brows furrowed. "I thought you might find this useful."

Rowan slid a book across the table.

The emerald binding was faded at the edges and the pages within had yellowed. Gold letters were etched into the cover, and Maeve stared at the gift with confusion. Why in the world would Rowan give her a book on the history of the Spring Court?

She sent him a questioning look.

He lifted one shoulder, his face giving nothing away. "In case you're ever in need of some light reading."

Maeve nodded, and Tiernan's voice slipped into her mind like a gentle caress.

"Ready?"

She gave him a whisper of a smile and nodded once.

He reached over and clasped her hand, preparing to address the Courts, looking every inch a High King. She interlocked their fingers and held her breath.

"I won't start this meeting with false pretenses. I won't tell you that this war will be without challenge, and I certainly will not promise victory." Tension coiled through him, radiating down the bond, until Maeve clenched her jaw to stop it from trembling. "Because as it stands right now, the outcome is grim."

"I had a vision," Ceridwen stated, her lulling voice unnaturally calm given the circumstances. She took a sip of her tea, then set it back down on the small saucer. It rattled slightly. "One in which only the Dawnbringer and the Nightweaver survive."

Malachy leaned forward from the opposite end of the table, planting his chin on one fist. "And who, exactly, is the Nightweaver?"

"Me." Ice dripped from Rowan's tone, and Malachy sat back abruptly. No other explanation was needed.

"Unfortunately for us," Ceridwen continued as though the Winter commander hadn't interrupted her, "Maeve has witnessed the same."

Maeve would sooner condemn herself to death than have to admit the truth of Ceridwen's statement to anyone else. But Ciara left her with no choice.

The High Queen of Winter's gaze landed on Maeve, piercing her. But when she spoke, her words were hushed, edged with the fear each of them silently harbored. "Is this true?"

Maeve could only nod.

"Well." Ciara sat back, her crown of diamond snowflakes glittering in the morning sunlight. "That's unfortunate indeed."

"There is a sliver of hope." Tiernan squeezed Maeve's hand, but her grip had gone limp. "We discovered a way to access Suvarese. There's a gap in Parisa's shroud around the Spring Court, through the Pass of Veils."

"So..." Malachy drummed his fingers on the table, his growing unrest palpable. "We'll have to face the giants first?"

Lir, who'd been painfully silent since the meeting began,

cleared his throat. The silver of his eyes flared hot. "Assuming any have survived her wrath."

Tiernan turned his attention to Ciara, easily glossing over the bubbling hostility between the two commanders. "Has there been any word from Brackroth?"

Ciara dipped her head, her deep berry painted lips curving. "Prince Drake has assured me he will send reinforcements...in the form of dragons."

Maeve almost choked. "Dragons?"

Dragons. Not a drakon, like Casimir. But actual *dragons*. She hadn't even known the mythical beasts still existed and now they were supposedly coming to fight for Faeven. The thought was both exciting and absolutely terrifying. Why had no one told her they'd aligned themselves with a kingdom who had an entire force of dragons at their disposal?

Merrick's harsh laugh pulled Maeve from her thoughts.

"Are you serious?" The hunter glared at his sister. "You expect me to believe that the Prince of Brackroth is going to send his legion of dragon riders to come help us?"

Ciara remained effortlessly stoic. She was the epitome of composure despite her brother's verbal attack. The High Queen set her jaw. "I called in my favor."

Merrick shook his head, and Brynn clamped him firmly on the shoulder, muttering something into his ear. He eased back, but the stern lines hardening his expression did not ease.

"Favors aside..." Dorian casually intervened, his poised demeanor subduing the rising tempers between the siblings. "Is Prince Drake reliable?"

"Yes, Your Highness." Ciara folded her hands in her lap. "He always stays true to his word."

Frost crystallized the glass of water set before the High Queen, turning it to ice. Tiny, incandescent snowflakes fell around her, and Maeve wondered what, exactly, this supposed favor cost Ciara in return.

Tiernan, however, looked moderately relieved. Apparently, the confirmation of dragons seemed to ease the troubles of his mind and his grip on her hand slowly relaxed. He addressed Dorian next. "My lord, has there been any word from the High Prince?"

Dorian smiled, his brows lifting. Maeve felt a soft tug on the familial Strand, and her father said, "Ask him yourself."

Maeve whipped around in her chair, almost tumbling out of it and onto the ground. Sure enough, standing behind her, looking windswept and sea-worn, was Aran. His rich red hair was longer now, and he wore it pulled back in a high knot. Loose pieces fell haphazardly, framing his handsome face. The sun had kissed his skin during his travels, giving him a slightly more golden sheen. He wore a loose burnt orange shirt tucked into a pair of brown pants, and his boots had definitely seen better days. Around his neck was the compass that would always lead him home, to Autumn, and the piece of sea glass she gave him shone like a pink ruby in the sunlight.

"Aran!" She jumped out of her seat, nearly tripping over her gown, and launched herself into his arms.

He caught her easily, lifting her into the air, spinning them once.

"I missed you," she whispered, breathing in the familiar scent of him. He still smelled of amber woods and spice, but with a hint of sea spray.

Aran squeezed her once before setting her back down. "Not as much as I missed you."

She grabbed his hand, leading him back to the table so he could sit on the other side of her.

"High Prince." Tiernan smiled, nodding in Aran's direction. "Welcome back."

"It's good to be home," he said, brushing an absentminded kiss on top of Maeve's head.

Lir stood and bowed in greeting. "I take it you've brought news from Wenfyre, Your Highness?"

"Indeed I have." Aran glanced around the table, acknowledging everyone. Until he spotted Rowan. His eyes widened, then he quickly blinked, as though he wasn't quite sure he believed the sight before him. "You're...not dead."

Rowan smirked, loosening the collar of his black silk shirt. "Very much alive, actually."

Aran stared a moment longer before glancing over at Maeve, then back at Rowan. "How is that possible?"

"A story for another time, perhaps." Rowan lounged against the high-back chair, lifting one hand. "I believe you coming bearing news."

"Yes. Right." Aran shook his head, refocusing. He pulled a rolled piece of parchment bound with a red ribbon from the pocket of his shirt and handed it to Tiernan. "Queen Ariawyn has agreed to assist us in the war. As we speak, a fleet of druid vessels is on their way to Faeven's shores."

Tiernan unrolled the piece of parchment, skimming the content. Maeve peered over his shoulder and he angled it toward her, giving her a better view.

Maeve read the elegant script, following the loops and swirls of the letters. At the very bottom of the document, two signatures were inked. One in deep green, the other in bold crimson. Aran and Queen Ariawyn's names glared up at her. "This is a contract."

"Yes," Aran confirmed.

"What does it say?" Dorian asked, and Tiernan passed the parchment to him.

Aran sat back, his hands coming to rest on the arms of his

chair. "Only that we will repay the favor, should the need ever arise."

Tiernan eased back in his seat, and Maeve wished she could wipe away the shadows of worry haunting his face. She could see his mind working, calculating. His brow was furrowed and his teeth scraped along his bottom lip. "Is Queen Ariawyn worried Wenfyre may soon face a threat?"

"She mentioned something about a twin sister. From what I gathered, the sister was banished from Wenfyre a number of years ago. But rumors have begun to circulate about her dealings and the possibility of an attack. I would assume it's out of revenge, but my thoughts are my own." Aran leaned forward, his gaze snagging on Saoirse. "You were right. About the druids. The ones who were pure of heart were both striking and beautiful, their attachment to the magic of nature was astounding. But the ones who were tainted or corrupt were less than pleasing to look upon. Some of them were downright hideous."

Saoirse's answering smile illuminated her face and Maeve continued to listen, partially, as the Court members discussed more about the druids, the dragons, and all the plans they were putting into motion. Her heart swelled with pride. With affection. Even if they'd been unable to reach her in the Ether, even if they thought she might never return, it hadn't stopped them waiting around for the next attack from Parisa. They made preparations, they formed alliances, and they were willing to protect all of Faeven. Just like her.

Yet a tiny needle of doubt continued to prod at her. She'd spoken to the Wild Hunt at Diamarvh, and Dubhan had refused to aid her in her endeavor. Worrying her bottom lip between her teeth, her mind wandered listlessly, framing and reframing all she knew, all she'd learned. Even if they received help from outside of Faeven's borders, Maeve wasn't sure it would be enough to turn the tides of fate in their favor.

Besides, she'd just had that nightmarish vision again, and the ending remained unchanged. Danua claimed she could change it, but she'd failed to tell her how to do so. It was apparent she would have to figure out that much on her own.

It seemed fairly obvious to her that even with a band of dragons and a fleet of druids, it wouldn't be enough to defeat Parisa. Not so long as she retained control of the Sluagh and used them to do her bidding. There had to be something else.

Something she was missing.

"Maeve?" Tiernan's voice jarred her from her thoughts, and she glanced over at him.

"Hm?"

"What do you think?" he asked.

"Of?" she squeaked, humiliated at being caught not paying attention to anything he said.

Tiernan gestured before her. "Of Aran's battle map?"

Maeve looked down at a detailed map of the Spring Court spread before her. Encampments were set up just outside of the Pass of Veils and along the Rainbow River with each of the Courts—Summer, Autumn, and Winter— staged in various locations. The Winter Legion was to the north, near the mountains bordering their own Court. Autumn was stationed in the valley and divided by the river, in what Maeve could only assume was the fallen city of Suvarese. And Summer, well, the Summer Legion, led by Lir, Merrick, and Brynn, was at the forefront. Their forces surrounded the base of Parisa's palace. Painted blotches of black dotted the sky, taking the form of dragons while Aran's magic brought the fleet of druids to life, showing their mass of boats off the coast of the Lismore Marin while they sailed on the cresting waves.

"It looks…" Like a place where everyone she loved would die. Like a graveyard for the bravest of warriors.

"Good," she finished weakly.

Tiernan sat back, his gaze weighing heavily on her. "That's it?"

She nodded, reaching down to pet Cahira in a poor attempt to avoid the concern clouding his eyes.

"Okay." He drew the word out, shifting his focus to her father.

Maeve expelled a breath. It was too much, too many would perish, and it would all be for nothing. She had to find a way to end this, to save them. There was no way she could allow them all to sacrifice so much, not if the vision she and Ceridwen shared held any truth. She would not let them die in vain, the guilt of it would smother her soul, it would taint her conscience for an eternity.

Aran leaned over to her and whispered, "Are you alright?"

"Yes. Fine." She offered him a tight, pinched smile. "Completely fine."

He didn't believe her. Not in the slightest.

"So," Merrick drawled. "When are we doing this thing?"

Aran sat up. "Queen Ariawyn's forces will be here by week's end."

Tiernan nodded, looking at Ciara. "And Prince Drake?"

The snowflakes falling around the High Queen of Winter had vanished, but her frosty exterior remained intact. "I have his word he will arrive when summoned."

"And when, exactly, do you plan on summoning him?" Merrick asked, the rise of challenge coloring his tone.

Ciara's sharp gaze pinned her brother. "When our circumstances are dire."

Merrick rolled his cerulean eyes to the heavens. "Great."

Tiernan slammed his palm onto the table, rattling the glasses. "I believe that's enough talk of war for one day."

Thank the goddess. Maeve wasn't sure she could handle any more of it. Not of the impending battle, not of the burden of despair, not of the never-ending guilt that continued to drain her of life. She needed to get away, to go do something, anything to take her mind off of the fact that if she didn't find a way to end this soon, everyone she ever loved would die. And it would be all her fault.

Maeve stood abruptly and every male followed suit.

"If you'd excuse me," she muttered, fully aware that every pair of eyes in the throne room were focused solely on her.

"Where are you going?" Saoirse asked, her words layered with a hint of suspicion.

Maeve was suffocating. She needed to go to a place where she could breathe, where she could think. Where she could unleash all the anger and frustration mounting inside of her. "I just need to go hit something."

She stalked off toward the courtyard, with Cahira on her heels.

"Be kind to the palm trees," Merrick called out after her. "You butchered the last one."

At one point, his wonderful sense of humor would have brought her a sense of consolation, would have endeared her, and lifted her spirits.

But not anymore.

Because if Maeve was too emotional, too reckless with her feelings, then from now on she would do what was required of her. She would cease to feel anything at all.

Chapter Thirteen

Aran approached Tiernan, coming into his line of sight. "A word, Your Highness?" he asked.

Tiernan nodded, but didn't take his eyes off of Maeve's retreating form. "Of course."

The High Prince shifted on his feet as Dorian walked over to them. Standing next to one another, it was easy to see the similarities between father and son. Both possessed the same wavy, dark red hair, high cheekbones, and prominent chin. But Aran had a cleft in his chin with that distinctive scar cutting through it.

Aran tugged on the collar of his loose shirt, then adjusted the compass and piece of sea glass hanging from his neck. He was ill at ease, uncomfortable in his own skin.

"The Strand binding me to Garvan is no more." He stated it as fact, his words shallow. Empty.

Tiernan confirmed with a single nod. "Garvan escaped the dungeon in Kyol. Maeve...she killed him."

"What? How?" Stunned, Aran glanced between Tiernan and his father. "He was chained in iron. If someone let him out, that means there may be traitors in Autumn's ranks. Parisa could have infiltrated our forces and—"

"That's impossible," Dorian interrupted smoothly, tucking his hands behind him.

"How do you know?" Aran's brow knitted with concern.

"Because I'm the one who released him."

"*What?*" Aran shouted, bewildered.

Tiernan reached for his sword.

"There's no need for that, High King." Dorian remained unfazed, as though helping his treasonous son escape imprisonment was of little concern to the rest of them.

Granted, Garvan was dead. But that was entirely beside the point.

"My son was ready to die," Dorian continued, inhaling deeply. If there was any pain hidden beneath his cool façade, he kept it well hidden. "So, I gave him the chance to make amends."

Tiernan's hand hovered near the hilt of his weapon. "You mean you gave him the easy way out."

"I assure you..." Dorian's magic blazed, a baleful rush of death and decay. "Nothing about his punishment was *easy*."

Aran winced, ducking his head to disguise his shame.

Because he'd been the one to torture Garvan. Tiernan remembered Aran professing it to the will ó wisp as his darkest secret. He wielded his magic against his brother, rotting Garvan from the inside out, dragging him to the brink of death, only to let him heal for a time before repeating the process all over again.

"Garvan made a deal with Parisa. A poor one, though perhaps if I had been more present, I could have swayed him from such a decision." Dorian's mouth pressed into a firm line, masking the anguish behind his carefully crafted appearance.

"Do not blame yourself for that, father." Aran gripped Dorian's arm. "He made his choice."

"As we all do." The High King of Autumn relented, and years of weariness bled into his face, aging him. "Just as we carry guilt in our own way."

"Why did you release him?" Tiernan asked, trying to make sense of the High King's reasoning.

"Because he would rather die than be forced to do Parisa's bidding any longer. I suppose in that sense, he and Maeve are rather similar." Dorian sighed, spreading his arms. "So, I gave him an option. He could either die by my hand, or by Maeve's... he chose his sister."

Tiernan's mind emptied of all rational thought. Dorian had allowed Garvan to choose who would be the one to end his life, and he'd picked Maeve. Tiernan's resilient *sirra*, who already carried the weight of the world upon her shoulders, who'd already witnessed so much death in her life. She suffered so much, and yet her own father had unknowingly forced her hand into taking the life of one of her siblings.

He didn't know whether to be furious or dumbfounded by Dorian's complete lack of sympathy toward his daughter.

"Did she know, I mean...did she realize..." Aran stumbled through his words, unable to form a coherent thought.

Apparently, he was just as taken aback as Tiernan.

"There was no hate in Maeve's heart for Garvan when he died. In fact, I believe she felt empathy." The High King seemed to ponder this notion, as though such a thing was unthinkable for the fae. "His death brought her to tears."

Fucking gods.

Tiernan had no idea. He didn't realize Maeve had been upset over Garvan's death. But Tiernan was all too familiar with the agony experienced when the Strand tying one to a family member snapped. He'd felt it when his parents were murdered, he knew she endured the same when Shay died. And now, Garvan as well.

He raked his hands through his hair, seething. The brunt of his anger, of his frustration and misery, was directed only at himself. Because she hadn't felt like she could tell him, she hadn't come to him in her time of need.

Or perhaps it was because he'd been set on making her feel terrible for *fading* to Kyol without him.

Tiernan silenced a groan, then pinched the bridge of his nose.

Such a classic dick move on his part.

"Your sister forgave your brother in the last few moments of his life." Dorian placed a hand on Aran's shoulder, squeezing lightly. "Perhaps in time, you can do the same."

With that, the High King turned, leaving Tiernan and Aran alone in the throne room.

He wanted to go find Maeve and apologize for everything. He would beg for her forgiveness. Vow to never make such a heartless mistake again.

But then he saw the look on Aran's face.

The High Prince's eyes were vacant. He looked crestfallen. Soulless.

Tiernan inclined his head. "You look like you could use a drink."

"And then some," Aran muttered.

"I know a place."

"Say no more."

It took very little convincing to drag Aran into Niahvess. Tiernan brought him to the Merrows Lair, a tavern he frequented in his youth with Lir and Merrick. He shoved open the doors and was instantly assaulted by the smell of stale alcohol and *spraedagh* root. Puffs of pink smoke floated in the air and other than a handful of

Summer fae hunched over the bar, the place was damn near empty.

Though he shouldn't have expected much else, the sun was barely to its highest point in the sky.

Tiernan strode up to the bar. The three fae brooding over their beverages blinked at his arrival, bowed, then quickly scooted further down the bar.

"Your Highness." Eggard, the owner of the Merrows Lair, was a burly fae with a scraggly beard and eyes that twinkled. He dipped his head. "It's been some time, my lord. What'll it be?"

Tiernan glanced over at Aran, who somehow managed to look forlorn and bemused all at once, then raised two fingers. "Whiskey. Better make it a double."

Maeve stood on the shores of Niahvess, with ropes of fire and smoke swirling around her. She blasted the crashing waves, relishing the way they hissed and recoiled against the flames. Her magic swallowed her, fueled her. Sparks of fire fell around her like rain, scorching the soft pink sand. Summoning her sword of sunlight, she lunged into the first attack against her imaginary opponent. The steps replayed in her mind, skill after skill drilled into her from Casimir's relentless training.

Dodge. Attack. Parry. Attack.

Attack. Attack. Attack.

Sweat dripped from her brow into her eyes and she blinked away the sting of saltwater. Twirling her sword overhead, she reared back, the blaze of her weapon slashing through the thick humidity. She sprinted down one end of the beach, then tucked the sword behind her as she dove forward in a flip, kicking her legs through the air.

Her chest heaved with each strike.

A flurry of emotions churned through her, but she smothered them. Locked them away. She no longer had time to *feel*. She couldn't be weak. Not ever again. She refused to allow herself to be the reason they failed.

Every so often, Cahira would expel a cloud of frost or a sprinkling of snow to cool her down, but Maeve continued to push herself. Eventually, the wolfing tired of watching her cut down invisible opponents. She huffed, whined once, then sauntered back toward the palace to escape the heat, leaving Maeve to fight her own inner demons.

Picking up the pace, Maeve exerted herself with fierce accuracy until her muscles throbbed, until she thought her heart would burst. She swung and stabbed, eliminating the threats she imagined in her mind. Pain. Fear. Doubt. Guilt. She would destroy them all. Until there was nothing left.

Rowan once told her that her mortal heart would be her downfall.

Maeve laughed, a dissonant sound swallowed by the crashing waves.

Never again.

She whirled once more, kicking up sand that clung to her flushed cheeks, and came face-to-face with Ceridwen. Her golden hair spilled around her like sunlight and the sleeves of her turquoise gown rippled lightly in the warm breeze. She smiled, her ruby lips curving.

"Hey, Cer." Maeve lowered her weapon, sucking in a ragged breath of air. She shifted, planting one hand on her hip. "How long have you been standing there?"

"Long enough." She held out one hand to Maeve. "Walk with me?"

Maeve dismissed her sword, her body slowly relaxing as Ceridwen's magic floated around her. It eased the tension threatening to snap her muscles in half and soothed the swell of emotions patiently waiting to devour her. Maeve took Ceridwen's hand, and the torment agonizing her gradually ebbed into nothingness.

They strolled down the shoreline, hand in hand, the tranquility of Ceridwen's magic temporarily keeping all of Maeve's inner demons away.

"Your aura has changed." It was a casual statement, said the way one might comment on the weather.

"Has it?" Maeve asked, unsure of the direction this particular conversation was headed.

"Yes. It still retains its hues of the dawn, but it's different now." Ceridwen looked over at her, shielding her eyes from the sun.

"How?" Uncertainty twisted in Maeve's gut. If this had anything to do with her emotions...

"There's a splash of twilight there, now." Ceridwen reached over, gently tapping one finger on Maeve's heart. "I believe it has something to do with this."

Tiernan. The bond they shared had altered her aura.

"Do I color his aura, too?" It was a curious thing to consider, but for some reason Maeve couldn't explain, she desperately needed that validation.

Ceridwen nodded. "You do."

They continued to walk down the beach in amiable silence, but there was an undercurrent of something else hovering between them. Maeve knew Ceridwen hadn't sought her out to discuss the colors of her aura. "What is it you really need, Cer?"

Ceridwen stopped abruptly and turned to face her. She looked at Maeve in earnest. Though her brow remained smooth and untroubled, the depths of her eyes were searching, peering into Maeve's soul. "I need you to remember."

Maeve blinked.

"Remember what?" She'd already had her memory restored, surely she wasn't still forgetting something.

"I need you to remember what you're fighting for, Maeve." Ceridwen squeezed her hand, and her magic flowed into Maeve.

If Tiernan was the storm, Ceridwen was the solace.

"I'm fighting for Faeven. For everyone in that palace." Maeve needed her to understand. She just needed one person to believe in her, to trust that she knew what she was doing, even if she had to do it all on her own. "I'm fighting for *you*."

"And your future," Ceridwen added, lifting one brow. "I know we've shared a similar vision, but I'm a seer, Maeve. I've seen beyond this war. Beyond what you believe to be our end."

Maeve shook her head. "I don't understand."

"Do you trust me?" Ceridwen asked.

"With my life."

"Then let me show you." Ceridwen captured Maeve's other hand, clutching both of them to her chest. "Now, close your eyes."

Maeve let go of her hesitation and did as she was instructed. Magic enveloped her, gentle and soothing, wrapping her in an embrace. She inhaled the scent of orange blossom and cedarwood, and in the next breath, she was drawn into Ceridwen's vision.

They stood together in a courtyard where the brilliance of the sun warmed the air, where morning dewdrops glittered on rose petals like diamonds. Wherever they were, Maeve recognized this place as home. Her soul was happy here. Her heart was pure. There was a tug on the bond, a calling, and she knew Tiernan was near. Maeve turned to look for him, but the sound of giggles and laughter drew her attention in the other direction.

Four fae children played in the courtyard, dancing and smiling. The beauty of them stole her breath. There were three boys, all with midnight hair and grayish green eyes, and one girl whose golden pink curls tumbled down her back. She spun around, and a pair of twilight eyes flecked with gold met Maeve's gaze and lingered. Her smile was dazzling.

Mine.

The word echoed in Maeve's mind and she knew it to be true.

These were her children, the ones she would bear with Tiernan.

Delight filled her, and a rush of elation unlike anything she'd ever known swelled inside of her heart. Children. She would have *children.*

Taron. Cillian. Shay. Avalia.

Maeve swiped at her cheeks, wiping away the tears she didn't realize had fallen.

Slowly, the vision faded, and she was back on the beach with Ceridwen still holding her hands.

"You see?" she asked, pulling Maeve in close. "You will turn the tides of fate in our favor. Not only for us, but for them. For your children. For the lives of those not yet brought into this world."

Ceridwen released her and Maeve sniffed, one hand instantly going to her stomach.

"Your heart is not a weakness, it is your greatest strength." Ceridwen stepped back. "Use it."

Then the High Princess *faded* from the shore.

Maeve stood alone for a moment longer, but all she wanted to do was go find Tiernan. She wanted to feel the strength of him as he held her, she wanted to kiss him, and love him, and tell him she would find a way to save this world they loved. For them. For their future.

Following the bond of the witch thread, Maeve wandered through the winding pathways of Niahvess until she found herself standing in front of a tavern.

Her brow furrowed and she peered up at the sky. The sun was not much past midday, but then the sound of raucous male laughter filled her ears, and she shoved open the door. She walked inside and stumbled to a stop. The corner of her lips twitched.

Sitting at the bar, their eyes glazed from overindulgence, were Tiernan and Aran. They were ridiculously drunk.

Chapter Fourteen

Tiernan's head was throbbing, a consistent ache that began in his temples and spread all the way down to the base of his neck. His entire body was heavy, each limb felt as though it had been filled with compacted sand. A dead weight he could barely move of his own accord. The world was spinning beyond his control, and he swore he was stuck in a violent whirlwind of alcohol and pink smoke. Groaning, he slowly slid his left leg off the edge of the bed to cease the dizzying momentum that left him feeling like he was going to fall over even though he was already lying down.

Never again, he warned himself.

He was far too old to partake in drinking such copious amounts of alcohol in one sitting.

At some point, Maeve had found him and Aran drinking in the Merrows Lair. He remembered dancing with her, spinning her around, and laughing until his cheeks hurt. By then, however, he'd barely been able to stand up on his own, and he was fairly certain Lir had carried his ass home. Day drinking had seemed like a good idea at the time, but now Tiernan was regretting his decision.

Mistakes had definitely been made.

All he wanted to do was try to tumble back into oblivion in an effort to sleep off this blasted hangover, but the scent of coffee, crispy bacon, and biscuits lured him awake.

Tiernan squinted his eyes open, expecting the glare of the sun to blind him, but instead, he was met with a soft, dim light. Night had already fallen, and in the hearth a fire crackled, casting his room in a wash of gold and shadows.

He rolled over and his stomach revolted.

Swallowing the burn of acid in the back of his throat, he blinked and refocused on his surroundings.

There was Maeve, sitting on the bed, with a tray of food before her. The fire behind her highlighted the golden pink of her hair as it tumbled freely down her back. But what drew his attention the most was what she was wearing. In place of a cotton nightshirt, she wore a deep red nightgown. Tiny black diamonds were scattered across the sheer material, not nearly enough of them to disguise the swell of her breasts or her nipples protruding against the delicate fabric. It barely covered her upper thighs, and the straps were so thin, he could probably snap them in half with his teeth.

His cock pulsed to life, straining against the confines of his pants, and he eased himself into a sitting position, ready to devour her. There was only one cure for a hangover, and it involved delving his tongue between her thighs, the sweet taste of her on his tongue damn near euphoric.

Maeve smiled, gesturing to the tray between them. "I thought you might wake up hungry."

He grinned in return, wolfish. "There's only one thing I want to eat right now."

Surprisingly, she blushed, and it only made him want her even more.

"Food first." She trailed one finger idly along the tops of her breasts. "Then maybe I'll let you have dessert."

It was all the motivation Tiernan needed.

He grabbed a piece of bacon. "Did Aran return to Kyol?"

"He didn't make it that far." Maeve laughed, stirring the contents of a teacup. "He's sleeping off his hangover in one of the guest rooms. I believe Brynn offered to help nurse him back to life once he wakes up."

She handed Tiernan the teacup. "She also told me to give you this."

Tiernan winced, shrinking away from the wretched concoction. It was a product of Brynn's own making, a tea that was more like a sludge. He had no idea what she tossed into the mixture. All he knew was that it was an instant remedy for overindulgence and was the most foul tasting thing he'd ever had in his life.

His lip curled. "Do I have to?"

He accepted the cup, staring down at the thick, dark brew. The putrid scent of it was enough to make his nostrils burn.

Maeve smirked. "I mean, if you don't want dessert then—"

"Fine." Tiernan bit the word out. Fuck. He downed the gross contents in one gulp, and a shudder wrecked his body. The "tea" was bitter and earthy, a horrible creation of mud and herbs.

He shoveled another piece of bacon in his mouth to rid himself of the nasty flavor, swallowing it down with some water. Then he reached for a biscuit in the hopes that it would soak up some of the alcohol sloshing around in his gut.

"I spoke with Ceridwen today." Maeve toyed with one of her curls, running the strand between two of her fingers.

"Oh?" Tiernan took a small, hesitant sip of coffee. Already the pain in his skull was easing.

"She shared a vision with me."

His head snapped up, and she added quickly, "A post-war vision. Not a bad one."

Well, that was a small and welcome relief.

"And what did you see in his vision?" he asked, setting down the coffee and opting for more water instead.

"Our children."

Tiernan choked. He pounded his chest with his fist, then coughed one more time.

Maeve smiled, amusement twinkling in her eyes. "Four of them."

"Four?" he croaked.

"Three boys and one girl."

He looked at her then, *really* looked at her. She was glowing, illuminated from within. It had nothing to do with the magic coursing through her veins and everything to do with the fact that she was envisioning their life together. Gods, he loved her so fucking much.

"Taron, Cillian, Shay, and Avalia." She counted them off on her fingers.

The witch thread marking Tiernan's wrist warmed, and a sensation wrapped around his heart, squeezing. Hope. "You already named them?"

"Not exactly." She shook her head, her lips pursing in thought. "It was more like a feeling. Like something I knew."

Tiernan lifted the tray from the bed and set it on the nightstand. "You'll be a wonderful mother. I have no doubt our children will adore you."

He grabbed her waist, dragging her against him until she straddled him. Wrapping one arm around her waist, he used his free hand to cup the back of her neck. "But only I will ever worship you."

He brushed his mouth across hers, once, twice, as her arms wove around him. She opened for him readily when he traced the seam of her lips with his tongue. He claimed her in a clash of thunder and flames. Touching her was like holding fire in his hands. Their tongues tangled in a dance, each of them wanting more, wanting all of what the other could give. Angling her head, he deepened the kiss, stoking the spark that flickered inside of her.

Maeve's hips arched forward as she rubbed herself against the stiff length of his erection. Tiernan swallowed a groan, sliding his hands to her back. He grabbed a fistful of her curls, twining them between his fingers, and tugged. Her head tipped back on a gasp, and he scraped his teeth down the column of her throat while she squirmed in his lap.

Her nails dug into his shoulders for purchase and he ventured lower, enjoying the way the tiny black diamonds sparkled across her breasts. Bending down, he sucked one into his mouth, teasing her pretty pink nipple through the soft fabric. The bud hardened into a peak and he laved his tongue around it, swirling, stroking, until her breathless pants echoed in his ears. Again, she ground herself against him, but he had every intention of taking his time, of extending the length of her pleasure for as long as possible.

Tiernan pulled back, capturing her other breast with his hand. He rolled the twin peak between his thumb and forefinger, pinching slightly. She jerked, clinging to him.

"I thought you hated frilly undergarments," he mumbled, tracing the plunging neckline of the nightgown with one finger.

"Only lacy ones." Maeve laughed, trembling in his arms. "And I'm not wearing any undergarments."

Tiernan glanced down between them.

Sure enough, he could see every beautiful inch of her beneath the fine fabric.

"Fuck," he growled, then lifted her off his lap before depositing her back onto the bed. He peeled off his shirt and tossed it aside. She scooted back against the headboard, cushioned by the small mountain of pillows. She'd drawn her knees up and he arched one brow as he settled himself before her. "Open up for me, *moh Rienna*. I'm ready for dessert."

Her eyes, already glazed with lust, widened at his command, but she obeyed. On a quick inhale, her legs fell open. He crawled closer, positioning himself between her thighs, ready to feast on his future queen.

Tiernan grabbed the hem of her nightgown and nudged it upward, so it pooled around her waist, leaving her bare for him. The scent of her arousal was ambrosia to his senses. He blew a light puff of air across her exposed flesh, then pushed two fingers deep inside of her.

Maeve's hips bucked off the bed, but Tiernan splayed one hand across her stomach, pinning her in place. His tongue flicked out, curling around her clit, circling the bundle of nerves until she was writhing beneath his hold. He worked her in steady, fluid movements, pushing his fingers in, then slowly drawing them out. The little sounds she made were like music, and he looked up at her from between her legs while continuing his sensual ministrations, only to find her eyes closed and her mouth open.

Oh, but she was beautiful when she lost herself to him.

"Tiernan," she gasped, her hands snaring the bedsheets, clenching them so her knuckles turned white. "I need more."

"Patience, *astora*," he whispered, then fused his mouth to her clit. He slipped another finger inside, stretching her, preparing her for his thick shaft.

Her stomach tensed under his hand, her legs quaked.

She was so close.

He increased his speed, sucking on her, plundering her. Finally, she cried out as the orgasm stole through, leaving her soft and pliant on the bed. Her skin was flushed, her chest heaving.

And they were only just getting started.

Tiernan withdrew, holding up two of his fingers. They were soaked with her wetness. His gaze slid to his mate. "Do you know what you taste like, Maeve?"

She shook her head, her lashes fluttering back.

He flashed her a rakish smile. "You're about to find out."

Not wanting to waste any precious second, Tiernan glamoured away his pants, taking her flimsy nightgown with them. He settled himself between her, cupping the back of her knees, and hooking them over his shoulders. The head of his pulsing cock was nestled comfortably against her slick cunt, begging to drive her over the edge once more.

"Open your mouth." He held out his fingers to her. "You're positively delicious. I could spend the rest of my days devouring your sweet cunt and never tire of it."

Her pupils dilated, and her tongue swiped hastily along her bottom lip.

Godsdamn, he *needed* her.

Tiernan thought she might lick the tips, just a mere flick of her tongue, but when she sucked both of his fingers into her warm mouth, he groaned.

His cock surged, desperate for her.

He couldn't wait any longer.

Planting both hands on either side of her, Tiernan thrusted hard, driving his aching shaft deep inside her. A cry fell from Maeve's lips and her arms flew up behind her, grabbing onto the headboard. She was so tight, so wet, every pump nearly sent him spiraling. In and out he shoved into her, the tight walls of her clenching around the full length of him, causing a fire to burn low in his gut.

"You are mine." He spoke the words through gritted teeth. "Mine to love. Mine to kiss. Mine to fuck."

"Yes," she cried, her hands holding onto the headboard as he stretched her wider. "Gods, yes."

Tiernan swelled within Maeve's heat, his cock thickening so that each time he sank further into her core, it was like entering her for the first time all over again.

Just a little longer.

A little more.

He wanted her to come one more time, then he could empty himself inside her.

Maeve lifted her hips in a silent plea, and Tiernan almost came undone. Covering her hands with his own, he fired himself into her with relentless force. He trailed his mouth across her soft flesh, scraping his teeth along her neck. He continued to pump, gliding in and out of her, angling his hips so he teased her core with the cool studs of his piercings.

She cried out, desperate for him.

Her body spasmed beneath him, her muscles squeezing his shaft. He was ready to lose his mind to the overwhelming rush of her pleasure. She was begging now, sobbing out his name like a song. Her thighs shuddered as release exploded through her, shimmering down the witch thread in a violent crash of desire.

Tiernan drove himself into her one final time, the storm of his lust spilling into her. Filling her.

Maeve's legs went limp, falling from his shoulders while she sagged against the headboard. Her cheeks were pink and her breathing was labored, the erratic beating of her heart a perfect match to his own. He eased back, gently gathering her into his arms, and adjusted her so her backside was curled against him.

She snuggled into him, and his cock twitched.

Absolutely not.

His *sirra* needed rest.

And he needed to catch his breath. At least for another hour or two.

He reached down and tugged one of the blankets over them, enjoying the contented little sigh that escaped her.

"Infinitely," he murmured, brushing some of her hair back from her cheek.

"Eternally," she whispered in return.

Minutes slowly ticked by into hours, and though Tiernan knew at some point he had fallen asleep during the night, it didn't last long.

The door to his bedroom burst open just as the first rays of sunlight speared through the balcony door. He jolted upright, instantly tossing one hand over Maeve.

Merrick stood in the doorway, eyes wide. He bowed quickly. "My lord."

"What is it?" Tiernan asked, every muscle in his body instantly on high alert.

Beside him, Maeve clutched the blanket to her chest and sat up, her gaze darting between the two of them.

"I just received word from Ciara." Merrick was ashen, and he swallowed. "Ashdara is under attack."

"Are you certain? Because last time..." Tiernan trailed off. Because the last time they'd thought the Winter Court was in peril, it was actually Niahvess that had been assaulted. And Maeve had lost Shay.

"I'm positive, my lord." He nodded, the streak of hot pink running through his hair shining brighter in the early morning light. "Giants are on the move."

Shit.

"We'll *fade* in, otherwise we'll never get there in time

before they destroy the city." Tiernan's mind shifted into battle-mode. "Put Saoirse in charge of our forces here and increase patrols at all borders. Any warrior who can *fade* comes to Winter with us."

"And the Furies," Maeve added, her back straightening. "The Furies come with us."

"Yes, my lady." Merrick inclined his head. "My lord."

Then he vanished.

Tiernan stood and glamoured himself in full armor. The leather molded to his muscles, protected his chest. Maeve did the same, her aubergine leathers shielding every inch of her.

He held out his hand to her. "Are you ready, *moh Rienna?*"

She nodded sharply, her eyes flaring with determination. "Always, *moh Rí.*"

Chapter Fifteen

Tiernan *faded* into the western edge of the Winter Court, only to find it had descended into chaos. The mass of gray clouds disguising the sun made it nearly impossible to see anything beyond a few feet in front of him.

He squinted into the snowstorm, spying Winter warriors in silver leather and fur cloaks sprinting across fields of snow as seven giants lumbered out of the thick forest bordering the Spring Court. Some carried clubs outfitted with metal spikes, while others uprooted trees, snapping the mighty trunks in half to form massive wooden weapons. Cords of black veins crawled over their mangled faces, dried blood clung to their scraggly beards. Their breastplates were tarnished, and many of the giants bore wounds that left their armor in shreds, as though something far more powerful had ripped through the dense layers of leather and bronze.

It was their eyes, however, that drew Tiernan's attention. They were glazed, possibly even entranced, and he wondered if the giants were of sound mind and body...or if they were being controlled by some other force.

Through the swirling snow, Tiernan caught sight of Malachy Brannon in the distance, his sword raised high above his head. The commander gave a sharp nod of respect before leading a charge of warriors into the fray.

"Separate them!" Malachy ordered, his call echoing across the frozen landscape. "They'll fall faster if they're not together!"

Tiernan faced the few fae he had with him—Maeve, Lir, Merrick, Brynn, Rowan, and about twenty Summer soldiers. "You heard Commander Brannon! Split them up!"

Rowan didn't even hesitate. He pulled his Astralstone, its blade capturing the essence of nightfall. Black wings erupted from his back and he shot into the winter white sky with a mass of shadows unfurling behind him. Lir and Merrick took off in separate directions—Lir to the northwest, Merrick to the southwest—a cluster of Summer warriors decked in cobalt and gold breaking away behind each of them. Brynn bolted straight ahead, her burgundy curls scattered with snowflakes as she ran, joining a group of Winter fae.

From beside him, Maeve bounced with anticipation.

"Maeve." Through their bond, her name reverberated like a warning.

She tossed a glance at him from over her shoulder, then blew him a kiss, her golden pink curls whipping in the cold breeze. *"I'll be fine."*

At least her confidence had yet to waver.

He watched as she sprinted away from him, a glimmering aura of magic cascading around her. The Furies, Tethra and Dian, swarmed at her sides, stealing through the swirl of snow like midnight wraiths. Unrelenting. Unstoppable.

She's more than competent, Tiernan reminded himself. She was a skilled warrior, expertly trained, and a master of her magic. The last thing Maeve needed was him constantly trying to look out for her because chances were, he would only get in her way.

Besides, the Furies would protect their queen with their lives, just as Balor had done for him.

Forcing himself not to glance back at her one more time, Tiernan unsheathed both of his swords, then stole into the mind of the giant nearest him. Seizing the giant's thoughts, he compelled the creature of the mountains, bending him to his will. He delved deeper into the giant's subconscious, sifting through tainted thoughts, only to discover a sickening power pulsing there. Polluted magic sullied its blood, corrupted its mind, poisoning it with the desire to kill. To destroy. The giant ambled forward, thrashing, his eyes wild. He dropped to his knees, sending a flurry of snow into the air, and a group of soldiers stumbled back. Tiernan held tight to his reins of control, his magic intensifying as the giant clawed through the increasing snow storm, unable able to defend himself from the string of attacks. Each blade met its mark and the giant bellowed.

Malachy rushed toward him in a blur of silver and navy. In one quick movement, he leapt into the air, grabbed the hilt of his sword with both hands, and plunged the blade into the back of the giant's neck.

Blood so dark it looked almost black splattered in every direction, speckling the pristine terrain with splotches of death.

Merrick led an assault against one of the other giants. The hunter utilized his esteemed prowess to ensnare the giant's ankles with vines of thistlebriar. The plant erupted from the earth in snarls of deep evergreen, coiling around the giant's legs and snatching his arms. With his already limited movement hindered by the thistlebriar, the giant bellowed before tripping and falling face first into the snowdrift. The earth trembled beneath the weight of his collapse, and the trees shuddered, their branches trembling. Surrounded by Summer and Winter warriors, he would be dead in a matter of minutes.

An ache prodded deep within Tiernan's chest. It pained him to bear witness to such an atrocity, to know he was one of the driving forces behind the demise that befell the giants. Those who inhabited the Pass of Veils kept to themselves, neutral in all things. Neither friend nor foe. For them to attack blindly, to wreak havoc without reason, could only mean one thing.

They were being controlled by Parisa. He wouldn't be at all surprised if she was using that dark venom she'd concocted to command them. If it affected the giants this severely, then the fae she'd administered the vile substance to were most likely suffering in a far worse state.

Summoning his wings, Tiernan took to the skies, circling the giants overhead. From his vantage point, his vision was slightly obscured, but he could just make out the expanse of the snow-covered field. Two giants had already fallen, so there were five left. He cut through the chilly breeze, coasting on the frozen gusts, angling himself for a better view. For a split second, Tiernan almost wished he'd stayed on the ground, as Tethra and Dian were a horrific sight to behold.

The Furies had driven one of the giants back toward the forest's edge. Its gaze was unfocused as it hoisted the club in its meaty grip, swinging blindly. He snarled, spittle flying from his mouth, turning into droplets of ice that clung to his beard. The giant lurched in the general direction of Tethra, but his movements were far too sluggish to match the speed of the Fury. Tethra lunged, snatching the giant's arm, his ghastly, skeletal hands melting the armor to the creature's flesh. An ear-splitting yowl erupted from the giant as Dian materialized on the other side, taking hold of his other arm. Tiernan thought they intended to drag him to the ground, to restrain him somehow.

But the Furies' eyes, glowing like the burning embers of a fire, reflected a ferocity of which Tiernan had never seen.

At once, both of the Furies pulled…in opposite directions.

The giant's arms were ripped off, the snapping of bones and the tearing of tendons enough to cause Tiernan's stomach to clench. Black blood oozed from the gaping holes, and the sockets of its arms revealed nothing but dangling pieces of shredded muscles. The giant bowed backward, his cavernous cry of pain more harrowing than Tiernan could handle.

Thunder exploded across the heavens in a deafening crack. Violet lightning splintered through the overcast clouds and flurries of snow, striking down the giant, ending his misery in one final blow. Tiernan turned away from the horrendous scene before him, his gut roiling.

Lir and Malachy had cornered another giant, while Rowan had taken on one by himself, vanishing them both beneath the guise of shadows and darkness. Tiernan was well-versed in the power of destruction, and he imagined it wouldn't be long before the abilities of the Nightweaver were on full display.

But Maeve…

He squinted, peering through the thin blanket of falling snow.

Maeve was nowhere to be seen.

Shit.

He knew he shouldn't have let her out of his sight.

Tiernan swooped down, tucking in his wings as he searched for any sign of her. All he needed was a small reassurance, a spark of fire, a swell of smoke, a glimpse of her glowing, rose gold tattoos.

But there was nothing.

Damn it, where was she?

He soared across the snowy field with his gaze glued to the ground, not realizing his mistake before it was too late.

There was no avoiding the collision. A giant's fist slammed into him, crushing the air from his lungs, shattering multiple ribs, the distinctive cracking of bones unmistakable. His head snapped back with so much force, he thought the impact might've broken his neck. Blood filled his mouth as he flew backward, unable to maintain control. White hot pain lanced through every muscle of his body as he spiraled towards the ground, and the world spun in a dizzying blur of colors. He squeezed his eyes shut, waiting for the moment when he struck the ground, preparing himself for the rush of agony that would follow.

But something yanked hard at the back of his neck, a vicious tug that plucked him right out of the air.

Tiernan blinked and looked up to discover Rowan flying above him, his fist clenched around the collar of Tiernan's armor. Rowan dove downward, dropped Tiernan unceremoniously onto the ground, then landed before him. His lavender eyes flashed with rage.

"Get your head in the game, High King," he spat through clenched teeth.

Tiernan shook his head as sharp pangs spasmed through him. He sucked in a ragged breath. "I can't find Maeve."

Rowan tossed out one arm, the tip of the Astralstone in his hand pointed to the north, where an inferno of fiery red flames lashed out from a fae who shimmered like the sunrise. "Your mate can handle herself. You, on the other hand, need to fucking pay attention, otherwise you're going to get yourself killed."

Tiernan opened his mouth to offer some bullshit explanation, but Rowan cut him off.

"And we both know how that story ends." The Nightweaver smirked. "With Maeve coming to me, looking for a shoulder to cry on."

Rowan spun away in a wall of shadows and was skyward a second later, heading back to the giant still engulfed in a sea of darkness.

Fucking fae.

Tiernan aimed to join him back up in the air, silently cursing the bastard for being right, when a disturbing thought jabbed at the back of his mind.

He scanned the wintry battlefield once more.

Three giants were dead. Lir and Malachy were battling a fourth while Rowan took on the fifth. If Maeve was fighting the sixth one, then where was the seventh?

The snowstorm had intensified, its strong gusts making it difficult for him to navigate. Flurries swirled around him and he veered left, quickly spying Maeve on the ground below. Her arms were raised, her palms splayed open. Magic billowed around her, carrying the scent of cinnamon woods and vanilla to him as she summoned the depth of her power. Snow gathered before her, morphing into icy shards with edges sharp enough to pierce the toughest of leather. They blasted outward in a violent attack, assailing the giant like a rain of vicious silver blades.

She flipped through the air, all stealth and grace. Her movements were fluid. She never faltered. She never missed. Again, her magic swelled and from the frozen wind beating against her, she crafted a sword of clouds and frost.

Maeve was flying toward the giant a second later, her wings of rose gold and ivory whipping behind her as she readied her weapon.

A shadow loomed, just out of her reach.

Rowan.

No, that couldn't be right.

Tiernan glanced over his shoulder and his heart sank. Rowan was behind him.

It was the seventh giant, and Maeve had no clue he was heading straight for her.

"No!" Tiernan dove toward her as the giant raised his fist, ready to crush her into nothing more than bones and dust. "Maeve!"

Her gaze swung in his direction, her eyes widening as he grabbed her by the waist, just as an iridescent bubble fell around them, shielding them both. They tumbled to the ground, Tiernan holding her tight against him as they rolled.

He was on his feet a second later.

"What are you doing?" Maeve cried, but there was anger in her voice. A tremble of resentment.

"Saving your life!"

He stalked out of her protective little bubble as magic pumped through his veins, burgeoned by fear. By panic. His magic thrummed in time to the erratic beating of his heart and the vengeful storm of Summer roiled across the heavens, darkening the skies.

"I had it under control," she snapped, her fury growing.

The witch thread marking his wrist burned hot with her rage.

No. No, she didn't have it under control. She was risking her life by taking on two giants all by herself. She had no idea about the kind of peril she faced.

Maeve marched across the snow toward him, a torrent of emotions etching into hard lines against the soft planes of her face, but Tiernan refused to let her any closer.

"Stand back!" he commanded and without thinking, his magic thieved its way into her body, throwing her backward against her own will.

Focusing on keeping Maeve safe, he unleashed the might of his wrath. Streaks of violet lightning ripped down from the tumultuous clouds, striking both of the giants at once. Their screams ruptured the heavens as their burned flesh melted from their bodies, as they jerked and flailed against the callous cruelty of his nature. He attacked them until the stench of burnt skin filled his nostrils, until their bones crumbled and turned to ash. Until he knew, without a doubt, they were both dead.

Then, only then, did his magic recede, did he release Maeve from his hold.

Tiernan stood, chest heaving from exertion, his magic nearly depleted. He'd gone too far. If Ceridwen had been here, instead of back in Niahvess helping Saoirse, she would've scolded him like a child for being so decidedly foolish.

But he'd kept Maeve out of harm's way, and that was all that mattered.

Exhaustion bled into him, stealing his strength.

Out of the corner of his eye, he knew everyone was watching him, Summer and Winter warriors alike. Lir, Merrick, Brynn, Rowan, and even Malachy stood nearby, their gazes lingering on the grotesque mess littering the fields of the Winter Court.

And he thought what the Furies had done was heinous.

"Tiernan."

At the sound of Maeve's voice, he steeled his spine. He would have to grovel for her forgiveness, but if it meant she stayed alive, then so be it.

He turned to her and was met with the biting sting of her hand against his face.

"Fuck you," she hissed, her sea-swept eyes darkening.

He staggered back a step, and she fisted her hands on her hips. Anger rolled off of her in waves so thick, he thought for sure she would smother him.

"Admit it right now," she demanded, glaring at him. "You don't trust me."

Wrong. She was so fucking wrong.

He sensed it then. The culmination of all they'd endured without one another had been steadily simmering, and now it was ready to boil over, to scald them both.

Tiernan lifted his chin, anticipating her typical mannerism. "Only if you admit you have a goddess complex."

"I *am* a goddess!" Maeve roared, her voice thunderous, and nearly every male in their general vicinity took a cautious step back. The females, however, stood their ground. "Your fear of losing me is preventing you from seeing it. You're not helping me, Tiernan. You're holding me back."

Rowan stood off to the side, casually shifting his weight, and let out a low whistle.

Tiernan tossed his hands out to the side. "Why won't you just let me help you!"

He meant it as a question, but again, it came out as more of a demand.

"Because I don't need your help!" Maeve shouted. "I don't need you at all!"

Without another word, she stormed off toward the forest, muttering a stream of foul swears. All of it directed at him.

"Damn," Merrick mumbled, then raked a hand through his hair.

Tiernan glanced around at all the fae surrounding him. Many refused to meet his gaze, save for Brynn. She stared at him. Hard. Then shook her head once.

"Fucking gods." Tiernan sought Lir in the crowd, and with less force, spoke into his commander's mind. *"Follow her. Whatever you do, don't fucking help her. But follow her."*

Lir bowed, then set off after Maeve, his footfalls the only sound echoing across the vast expanse of snow and death.

Malachy strode up, rubbed one hand along the back of his neck. "Quite the spitfire you have on your hands."

"Tell me about it." Tiernan shook off Maeve's words, ignored the severity of the hurt still pulsing in the deepest part of his heart. "Merrick, *fade* to Niahvess and return with a report as soon as possible."

The hunter nodded once, then vanished a moment later.

"We should set up camp here for the night." Tiernan looked to Malachy for confirmation. "Just in case."

Malachy dipped his head. "Agreed, my lord."

As Malachy issued orders, Tiernan's gaze slid toward the footprints in the snow that were already being covered by the steady fall of more snowflakes. If Maeve didn't need Tiernan, then fine, he would figure out where they went from here later. But Lir was sworn to protect her, and there wasn't a damn thing she could do about it.

Chapter Sixteen

Maeve stomped through the forest, agitation firing through her with each crunch of snow beneath her boots. Her hand burned from where she had slapped Tiernan across the face. But damn, that male had infuriated her more than she ever thought possible. She might've felt a tiny bit of regret at the harshness of her words, and they would definitely need to have a heavy conversation whenever she cooled off...

But he had no right.

No right to stop her from fighting. No right to tell her what to do, to try to command her like one of his soldiers. No right to take *control* of her body, all in the name of keeping her safe.

She huffed out an annoyed breath, and it misted before her.

Now that the heat of battle was fading, she realized how ridiculously cold it was in the Winter Court. But she didn't care. She didn't need any warming layers. It wasn't like she was going to stay gone for too long, but she had to walk away from Tiernan before she did something worse. Like stab him in the chest.

"Fucking fae," she muttered to herself, her pace slowing.

Maeve knew Lir trailed her. Sometimes he was like her shadow. Always there. Always watching. He stayed behind her, unspeaking, his stoic presence more a comfort than anything else, and she welcomed the quiet.

The woods here were still. Almost unnaturally quiet. There was no birdsong, no scampering of forest creatures. Perhaps it was simply too cold for them here. It was barely the afternoon, but already the sun was starting its descent into the western sky, and the hazy, overcast light narrowly splintered in through the thick canopy of trees.

"Why are you following me?" she asked, not bothering to turn around.

She could feel the shift in his demeanor, imagined his spine locking into place, preparing for some kind of confrontation.

"No reason." His deep voice was soft and Maeve frowned.

Unlikely. She had no doubt Tiernan had sent him after her.

Maeve ran her palm along the roughened bark of a tree trunk as she passed. "I'm fine, Lir."

"I'm aware, my lady."

A sigh escaped her. She continued her trek through the winter woods, wrapping her arms around herself. There was no point in being angry with Lir. He was only doing what was asked of him—well that, and he was sworn to protect her. The Strand marking his upper arm, a vow to his High King, bound him to keep her safe at all costs.

"Why don't you ever shift?" she asked suddenly, knowing he continued to lurk behind her, keeping a cautious distance between them.

Maeve sensed his trepidation on the topic, felt it with each passing second it took before he finally responded to her.

"It's not something I care to do very often, my lady."

"And why is that?" She tossed a glance back and caught sight of him of few paces back. His shoulders were dropped, as though there was some invisible weight holding them down, but his keen gaze was focused on her. She paused, turning to face him fully.

Lir hesitated, then said, "Shifting into my wolf form is... painful. Not in a physical sense, but it brings back unwanted memories."

Hurt darkened his eyes, an emotion Maeve had never seen manifest in him. Lir was always so steadfast and resilient, so effortlessly calm and composed. To witness him express such a sentiment to her...her heart ached.

"I only shift when it is absolutely necessary." Lir strolled a little closer, his studded boots crunching lightly against the frozen ground. "When I feel I can inflict more suffering with claws and fangs than I can with my swords."

Maeve nodded. There were more questions she wanted to ask, especially since Lir's past was somewhat of a mystery to her. But the look on his face told her he'd already said enough, more than he intended.

Ducking her head, she kept walking. Slower this time. Her breath misted before her and the trees bristled against the chilling breeze. The cold air seemed to cool her temper as well. It wouldn't be long before Tiernan set out to find her, or slipped into her mind, and asked her to return. He deserved nothing less than the silent treatment after that little stunt he pulled, and though she planned on forgiving him, she also knew he wasn't the only one who needed to apologize. Her words had been harsh. Unkind and cruel.

"Maybe we should—" The words died in the back of her throat when she saw drops of crimson staining the snow-covered ground. She froze. "Blood."

A trail of it.

Deep scarlet against glittering white.

Lir was beside her a second later, one curved blade drawn. His silver gaze narrowed. He stood close, and they shared a glance. He put one finger to his lips, then pointed with his sword.

She nodded.

One step at a time, they trekked forward, their footfalls as light as possible against the snowy forest floor.

Then Lir's arm shot out, holding her back.

And Maeve realized why.

Propped up against the wide trunk of a tree was a fae, a soldier of the Winter Legion. He looked like he'd been mauled by some type of animal. Slashes tore across the fine leathers of his armor, revealing deep wounds to his chest. Blood soaked his front and with every breath he took, the life shuddered out of him. His skin was ashen, sweat coated his brow despite the cold temperature, and his lips were cracked and peeling. One hand was outstretched, reaching for the fallen sword by his side.

He was dying.

"Lir." Maeve's whisper was harsh against her own ears. "We have to help him. I can help him."

She could. She could do it this time. It wouldn't be like when Shay died, she could save this male. She wouldn't fail. Not again.

The commander hesitated.

"Please, Lir." She grabbed his arm. "We can't leave him here. He'll die."

Lir's steely gaze surveyed the forest for any possible threat, but he relented. "Alright, my lady. Let's get him out of here. We'll carry him out of the woods and then you can heal him."

"Okay," Maeve agreed, inching closer. "Okay."

The fae's face twisted, contorting in agony. He opened his

mouth to speak, but the words were garbled. Blood spilled from his lips as he choked, struggling to speak to them.

"Shh." Maeve smoothed his damp hair back from his slick brow. "It's okay, we're going to help you."

The soldier jerked violently.

"Be calm." Lir wasn't nearly as reassuring in his manner. "I'll take him from under the shoulders. Grab his ankles, my lady."

Maeve bent down when the glint of something gold on the ground beside the injured soldier caught her eye. Her brows pinched together. "What's that?"

Lir knelt beside her, then shook his head, dismissive. "Looks like an amulet of some kind. Possibly a family heirloom."

An heirloom...

No, this was no ordinary necklace. It looked far too new to be an heirloom. The gold disc hanging from the chain was engraved with a bundle of springtime flowers strangled by a vine of foiled leaves.

"Why would a fae of Winter be in possession of something like this?" Maeve reached for it and the fae male thrashed.

"My lady!" Lir startled. "Wait!"

Lir grabbed Maeve's arm just as she grabbed the amulet.

Darkness swarmed them.

A pounding pressure slammed into Maeve, crushing her, stealing all the air from her lungs. She cried out as pain seared through her, piercing her from every angle. The world raged around her, a brutal force that left her disoriented and nauseous. It was like she'd been plunged beneath the surface of a turbulent sea, the volatile waves tossed her around, wrenching her back and forth until she thought her soul would be ripped from her body.

The pressure continued to build, squeezing her until she could no longer catch her breath.

On Maeve's final gasp, everything went dark.

MAEVE'S HEAD THROBBED, a constant ache that pulsed along her temples all the way to the base of her neck. Her entire body *hurt*, like she'd fought a hundred battles and lost every single one. Groaning, she rolled onto her side and shivered. Cool, damp stone pressed into her cheek, chilling her weary bones. Exhaustion tugged at her, a heavy weight that sealed the lids of her eyes closed, so all she wanted to do was drift back into a state of endless unconsciousness.

The icy hand of death squeezed her throat, the frozen touch of it burning her skin.

No, that couldn't be right.

Aed would never be so cruel, not to her.

Inhaling slowly, Maeve winced as a foul, putrid scent filled her nose. The stench of bodily fluids and sweat hung in the stale air, thick and suffocating. She shifted, and the clanking noise of chains echoed in her ears. Chains. She mulled the word over in the fog of her mind, trying to make sense of it. There was a steady dripping sound—like the *plop, plop, plop* of rainwater as it splattered against a rough surface.

Perhaps this was some sort of lucid dream, and all she had to do was wake up.

She struggled to open her eyes, squinting against the guttering amber light that barely illuminated her surroundings. Long shadows crawled across the darkened space and she eased herself up into a sitting position, bracing her hands against the slimy surface beneath her.

Maeve recoiled.

What the...

Metal bars stretched up to the ceiling like an enclosure. She blinked, and the haze of her mind cleared as her position came into terrifying focus. She was locked inside a cell.

Not just any cell. A dungeon. One she recognized, one that dragged her back to the horrific memory of a blade dipped in nightshade carving into her skin, of Fearghal's rancid breath and merciless smile.

Alarm fired through her, and by all rights, her magic should have whipped through her like a torrent in response to the panic racing through her. But there was only a dull thrum. Her power was muffled, unreachable, as though it had been stifled by something stronger than herself.

Maeve's hand floated to her neck, where the bite of cold metal held her captive, singeing the tips of her fingers. She hissed in pain.

Iron.

Her wrists and ankles were unbound, but a link of leaden chains was anchored to the stone flooring, binding the iron around her throat.

"Oh, sweet goddess," she whispered hoarsely, her throat raw.

Not again.

"My lady." A gruff male voice came from somewhere off to her left.

Lir.

She crawled across the cell, as far as she could reach without cutting off her airway. Peering into the dim light, she spied Lir in the enclosure across from her. He wore iron around his neck, same as her, and the silver glint of his eyes found her. Her gaze roved over him, searching for any kind of injury. A faint amber glow of light illuminated the space between them. It wheezed in and out, burning bright, then fading just as quickly. She couldn't detect any visible wounds on Lir, only the reflection of understanding staring back at her.

He knew as well as she did that there would be no way out.

Maeve slid her arm through the bars, stretching, straining toward him. He did the same, extending his hand toward her through his cell. Their fingers just brushed one another before the resounding click of heels against hard stone grated down the dismal hall dividing them.

She jerked her arm back, and her heart thundered.

A thousand thoughts flooded Maeve's mind. It had been careless of her to wander into those damned woods. One impulsive decision had endangered all she loved and put Lir in harm's way. Guilt slammed into her, leaving her breathless. She'd been too rash and failed to heed Tiernan's warning. All he wanted to do was protect her, love her, but she'd been bound and determined to prove she only needed to rely upon herself. It was all her fault, and now she might never see him again.

No, a steadfast voice whispered through the thickening cloud of doubt building in her mind.

No.

Maeve refused to fall to Parisa. She would never surrender to that bitch of a fae. There was too much at stake, too much worth fighting for to give up now. She had to find a way out, she had to save Lir and get them both back to the safety of the Summer Court. It would not end like this, not here. The goddess Danua had shown Maeve a battlefield, and it was on those blood-soaked grounds where her fate would be determined, not in some grotesque dungeon. And not at the mercy of a vile faerie whose greed for power threatened to destroy everything.

"Maeve." A sickeningly saccharine voice called out, and Parisa strolled into view, flanked by four guards.

At least, Maeve assumed they were guards.

Their movements were stilted and convulsive. Even when standing perfectly still, their arms twitched, their heads jerked uncontrollably. Their eyes were orbs of black, glassy and unblinking.

Just looking at them caused Maeve's skin to crawl with unease.

But it was Parisa who fared worse than all of them.

Stringy pieces of gray hair fell to her bony shoulders, and her skin was so translucent, Maeve could almost see the muscles and tendons beneath the papery layer of Parisa's flesh. She donned robes of black, but the heavy velvet did nothing to disguise the frail figure of the fae's rotting body. Her cheeks were hollow and sharply angled, so sunken, she looked almost skeletal. The crown of onyx spindles she wore was far too heavy for her head, causing her forehead to wrinkle like bulging mounds of excess flesh. Over one eye, the one that Maeve had gouged out at their last battle, was a scrap of black lace.

It fluttered lightly, revealing a crusted scar and a shoddy stitching job oozing with infection.

Maeve grit her teeth against the sight.

Dangling from Parisa's neck, on a thin chain of gold, was the *virdis lepatite.*

The source of her power.

Maeve's nails bit into the palms of her hands. She would destroy that fucking gemstone. And then she would destroy Parisa.

Parisa sauntered closer, her lips peeling back into an unnatural smile, revealing tiny, pointed teeth. "Such a pleasure to see you again."

"Really?" Maeve glared up at the vile fae. "I wouldn't imagine so, considering you're missing an eye."

"How kind of you to notice," Parisa jeered, running her

tongue along the sharpened edges of her teeth. "Especially since I've come to repay the favor."

Well, fuck.

Maeve swallowed, but it was like trying to gulp down wet sand. Suffocating. Impossible.

Across from her, Lir surged forward. He wrestled the bars, as though trying to dislocate them from the stone ceiling and floors. Bits of rock and dust tumbled around him, covering him in tiny bits of debris.

"Don't you dare lay a hand on her!" he roared, his fists clenching around the bars separating them until his knuckles whitened.

Parisa laughed, a rasping cackle. "By all means, please. Try and stop me."

She pulled a dagger from the folds of her velvet robe. Its blade captured the beauty of the world as it shimmered with vibrant iridescence. In her gangly hand, she held the glow of the dawn.

Maeve's Aurastone.

Her hand went to her thigh—the sheath was empty.

"No!" Maeve lurched toward Parisa, but the iron collar around her neck yanked her backward like a leash.

Lir was incensed, seething with fury. He bellowed Maeve's name, thrashing against the iron that bound him. Even in the pale lights, she could see his body tremble with rage. His eyes flared with a kind of wrath she had never witnessed from him.

Parisa tilted her head, her crown sagging. "How strange. The famed Commander of the Summer Legion seems quite possessive of you."

Maeve's heart tumbled from her chest, roiled in the acidic pit of her stomach. Cold swept through her, freezing her lungs, turning her blood to ice. All the color drained from her face. She saw it then, the intent, the malicious gleam in Parisa's eye.

"Leave him alone." She kept her tone even, though she wanted to rip through the dungeon and tear Parisa's heart out with her bare hands. "It's me you want, not him."

Lir's ragged breathing filled the warped space.

"Ah, so true. And it's you I shall have, of course. But his actions speak volumes." Parisa pressed the tip of the Aurastone into the flesh of her finger, twirling it idly. "How curious...it's almost as though he's sworn to protect you."

Maeve's breath hitched. Lir's Strand. The one binding him to save her, no matter the cost. That was why he was wild with panic.

"No!" She gripped the bars, desperate to regain Parisa's attention. "You want my power. You want revenge on *me*. I'm the one who gouged your eye out. It's me, not him!"

Her voice cracked on the last word.

"Such a valid point." Parisa offered another venomous smile. "But taking his eye will hurt you so much worse, won't it, my pet?"

She nodded toward one of her guards, and he removed a ring of keys.

"No!" Maeve screamed, wrenching herself forward. Iron scalded her neck, choking her. "No, please!"

The guard unlocked Lir's cell, then strode in. Two more followed in after him, forcing Lir to his knees, holding him in place.

Lir remained silent. Stoic. Unfaltering.

A broken sob escaped Maeve, shattering her resolve. "Lir."

"Be brave, my lady." The corner of his mouth lifted into one of his rare smiles.

"Please!" Maeve tried again, shoving one arm between the bars in an effort to reach him. The cold iron burned hotter against her skin. "I beg of you!"

"There will be plenty of time for begging later, Maeve."

Parisa entered Lir's cell, capturing his chin, and forcing him to look up at her. "Silver is such a pretty color. I can't wait to add it to my collection."

Maeve was unable to tear her gaze away. She couldn't bring herself to look anywhere else. She stared only at the fae who'd been sworn to protect her from anything and anyone, who was now staying true to his vow. She bit down on her tongue until the metallic tang of blood coated her mouth as Parisa used the Aurastone to carve out Lir's left eye. He tensed as the blade sank into his umber flesh, but not once did he make a sound. Not a single groan or cry of agony. Instead, he watched Maeve the entire time with his remaining eye.

Hot, silent tears fell down her cheeks as her own dagger was used against someone she loved. She cringed at the sucking sound as the blade sliced through his skin, and then there was a distinctive *pop*.

Maeve paled.

Parisa caught Lir's eye in her hand and he slumped to the ground, his handsome face etched with unimaginable pain.

"Yes," Parisa murmured. She pierced his detached eye with the Aurastone, then held it up for closer inspection. Bits of tendons still clung to it and drops of blood slid down her wrist. She swiveled it, smiling. "This will make a fine trophy indeed."

She strode out of Lir's cell, nodding once.

"Take this pathetic commander back to his Court. Dump him there." Her papery lips puckered in thought. "As a gift. A promise of things to come."

"Lir!" Maeve shouted as the guards hauled him out of the cell. Even after being brutalized, as they dragged him away, he fought. For her.

Her breathing grew shallow, her stomach heaved.

"Don't worry, my pet." Parisa flipped her spiny fingers in a little wave. "I'll be back for you later."

The click of her heels gradually faded down the corridor of the dungeon, and Maeve was all alone in the harrowing silence.

"I'm sorry." The words were gravelly and raw. Meaningless. "I'm so sorry."

Maeve's gaze slid to the cell across from her, where flies feasted on a puddle of crimson. She clutched her stomach and retched, emptying herself until bile burned the back of her throat. Until there was nothing left.

Chapter Seventeen

Tiernan stared at the thick expanse of woods bordering the Winter and Spring Courts. His gaze drifted to the overcast sky where clouds of gray blocked out the sinking sun. Random snowflakes fluttered down, collecting on the shoulders of his armor, and he brushed them off in annoyance. His patience was waning. It didn't matter if Maeve was still pissed at him, the hour was growing late and before long, darkness would descend upon the Winter Court.

Surely Lir would have convinced her to return by now.

He glanced around the field where Winter and Summer soldiers alike were burning the bodies of the fallen giants. The wind carried away the stench of burnt flesh, the snowfall lightly covered their ashes and the scarlet staining ground, erasing all traces of battle.

Three Winter warriors lost their lives during the attack. Malachy placed silver medallions upon their closed eyes, then encased each of them in a thin layer of ice. They would be transported back to Ashdara for a proper burial, where they would be mourned and remembered beneath a tree with leaves that sparkled like sapphires. Brynn was making her rounds with a few of the healers, tending to wounds and injuries, of which thankfully, there were not many.

Tethra and Dian appeared slightly restless, shifting back and forth, their odd glowing eyes focused on the outlying forest.

The crunch of snow sounded to Tiernan's left as Merrick *faded* in next to him.

He bowed. "Niahvess and Summer's borders are secure, my lord. As of now, there's no threat to us or our Court."

Tiernan's gaze remained trained on the thick expanse of trees, where it seemed no life stirred.

Merrick looked at the forest's edge, then back to Tiernan. "What is it, my lord?"

"Maeve and Lir have not yet returned from the woods." He glanced up at the sky once more. Already the sunlight was being washed away, doused in hues of faint purple and dark blue.

A line furrowed across Merrick's brow. He shook his head, then raked a hand through his silver hair, and the hot pink lock fell across his face. "No. No, that can't be right."

"What do you mean?" Tiernan demanded. "I saw them walk in there. We all saw them go in."

Rowan strode across the snow toward them, shoving his hands into his pockets. "Something wrong?"

Tiernan ignored him and stared at his hunter, whose eyes had closed.

Merrick inhaled deeply, and then he paled. When he opened his eyes, they were wide with an emotion Tiernan recognized all too well.

Fear.

"No, my lord." He swallowed, tugging on the collar of his armor. "I can't detect a trace of either of them."

Rowan reared back. "Son of a—"

"No!" Tiernan shouted, and took off toward the tree line. Panic fired through him as he raced into the forest, his heart dropping with every step. "They have to be in there!"

Merrick and Rowan sprinted after him, their footfalls clamoring in his ears.

Evergreens blurred past Tiernan, their branches reaching for him like the claws of a monster, snaring his armor in an attempt to slow him, to stop him. Terror struck him like the blade of a dagger, digging into his back, ripping through muscles and tendons. He never should have let her walk off, he never should have let her out of his sight. They were entirely too close to the Spring Court. Too close to Parisa. Spears of ice-cold fear lanced through his heart and he sucked in a breath, the frozen air freezing his lungs.

"Maeve!" His gaze swung wildly, latching onto anything that could offer a sign of their whereabouts. Snapped branches, staggered footprints, a shred of clothing.

Not again. He couldn't lose her again. Not to Parisa. That vile fae bitch would destroy her. Mind, body, and soul.

"Fuck!" Tiernan roared, his own fury damning him. He'd made such a careless mistake. They were in the midst of a war, and he'd tried to play the part of her hero. If only he'd let her fight those damn giants on her own, then she never would've stormed off. She never would have said she didn't need him. She never would have *left* him.

He grabbed his wrist, tearing at the sleeve of his leathers to reveal the witch thread marking him. The twin mountains with the star bursting between them throbbed against his flesh, but the bond tying him to his mate was silent.

There was nothing.

Maeve and Lir were gone.

"There!" Merrick called, pointing at the base of a nearby tree.

Tiernan's heart lurched in a sudden beat of hope, but the crushing weight of remorse left him hollow when he spied what Merrick had discovered.

Propped against the tree was the lifeless body of a Winter fae soldier. His chest was mangled, as though he'd been attacked by some kind of beast. The warrior's armor was in shreds, his eyes were empty, and his mouth was parted as though he'd been trying to speak or call for help before his death. From the looks of it, he'd bled out right before they'd arrived.

Merrick knelt down on the snowy forest floor. He reached out, carefully closing the fallen fae's eyes. Then he took another deep breath. Hunting. Tracking. His magic flared, the dense scent of orange blossom and cedarwood overpowering the metallic stench of fresh blood. Spreading one hand, he placed his palm against the rough bark of the tree. Still kneeling, he swiped his free hand through the snow then made a fist, so tiny droplets of water seeped out through his closed knuckles. A cold breeze sifted through the trees overhead, rustling the leaves, sending a flurry of snow scattering to the ground around them. He stood, and the brilliant blue of his eyes swirled.

"They were here."

Rowan stepped forward, his gaze focused on something deeper within the woods. Something Tiernan couldn't quite see. "Where are they now?"

"I don't know, my lord." Merrick dusted the snow from his leathers, casting one more long look at the Winter fae. He moved in a slow circle, inspecting the woods. "It's like they vanished."

Impossible.

Archfae could *fade,* but they didn't simply *disappear* without a trace.

There were only two possible explanations. Either Maeve and Lir were taken...

A sinking sensation pitched low in his gut.

Or...

"TIERNAN!" Ceridwen's voice ricocheted through his mind, and he keeled over, clutching his skull.

Merrick was by his side a second later. "My lord!"

Tiernan's chest heaved. *"What? What is it?"*

"Come home!" Fright lanced through each of her words, filling him with a sense of growing dread. *"You must come home now!"*

"Tiernan." Rowan gripped his shoulder, dragging him upright. "What's wrong?"

Maeve. Lir.

Tiernan's head snapped up and he met his hunter's fierce gaze. "Return the rest of the warriors to the Summer Court at once. If Malachy needs more help, leave only as many soldiers as we can spare. Meet me back there as soon as possible." He looked at Rowan. "You, do whatever sort of shadow magic necessary and get your ass to Niahvess."

With his orders clear, Tiernan *faded* back to his palace.

The courtyard of Niahvess was in a riot, and for one harrowing moment, Tiernan was transported back to that time not so many moons ago when he'd returned from a false alarm in the Winter Court only to find Niahvess under attack and Shay dying with his insides splayed open.

Tiernan shook the painful memory from his mind, focusing on the present.

Archers sprinted along the walls of the courtyard, firing flaming arrows that streaked overhead, illuminating the sky with fiery hues of red and orange. A dissonance of shouts and battle cries rang in his ears as groups of Summer warriors darted past him, rushing to their positions to safeguard the palace. Soldiers *faded* in from the Winter Court at random intervals, their gazes disoriented briefly before sharpening, as each of them drew a weapon, and sprang into action without hesitation. They didn't need a direct order or command. They knew their purpose, and remained unfailing to their cause— protect Niahvess at all costs.

But despite the mayhem unfolding around him, Tiernan didn't perceive any direct threat. There were no mass amounts of dark fae breaching his walls, there was no resounding clang of swords or clash of forces. He scanned the courtyard and only then did his gaze snag on Ceridwen and Saoirse. Ceridwen was on her knees next to someone, and even from the distance separating them, he could see the distinctive tremble of her hands. Power emanated from her, so her golden hair whipped around her in a flurry. There was a crescendo, an overflowing well of soothing magic, enough to quell an entire legion.

Which was exactly what Ceridwen did.

At once, the atmosphere around them changed, morphing from one of heightened awareness and defense to a placating sense of calm. The frenzied havoc of an impending conflict eased, and a composed stillness settled over the courtyard. Merrick *faded* in, looking ready to slay a dragon. He raised his sword, lunged forward, then stumbled to a stop. His fierce gaze stole around the space and he sucked in a harsh breath, an emotion banking in his eyes when he found Ceridwen among them. He lowered his weapon, his shoulders sagging.

Shadows swirled at the far end of the courtyard, a billowing rise of darkness. Rowan emerged from them, flanked by Tethra and Dian.

The Furies looked downright murderous. Violent energy crackled around them, hissing and snapping. Their sunken faces were etched with hardened resolve. Destruction and death—the power behind their namesakes—flooded the air with ruthless tension. No doubt Rowan had informed them that their queen was missing.

Again.

Tiernan looked over at the gates to the palace, and this time, Saoirse turned. She caught sight of him and rose to her feet. Tangles of silver hair had fallen loose from her braid, and she scrubbed her palms against her leggings. The dark brown fabric came smeared away with blood.

Yet Tiernan knew it did not belong to her.

He met her halfway when she held up a hand to stop him.

"Your Highness." She stole a hesitant glance over her shoulder. "I must warn you."

"Warn me," he repeated numbly. "Warn me about what? I don't see how things could possibly get any worse."

He looked past her, to where Ceridwen continued to kneel, hovering over someone. Though the fae's face was blocked from Tiernan's view, he noticed a pair of studded black boots.

Lir.

He stormed past Saoirse, avoiding her grasp as she reached out to grab him.

Lir was on the ground, his legs stretched out before him. Though his hands were pressed into the smooth stone on either side of him, it was clear the gate supported most of his weight. His leathers were covered in grime and filth, his head bent low so his twists of black hair fell in his face. His chest rose and fell in a slow rhythm, and while he looked slightly battered, for the most part he appeared to be in good health.

Ceridwen remained hunched over, her hands shaking uncontrollably. She shuddered, her breathing uneven. Like she was crying.

Tiernan placed one hand on his shoulder. "Lir."

His commander lifted his head, and a torrent of rage consumed Tiernan.

Where Lir's left eye should have been, there was nothing but a gaping wound of torn, bloody flesh. It had been gouged out completely.

"Brynn!" Tiernan whipped around, searching for his healer. "Brynn!"

He saw a tumble of burgundy curls as she shoved her way through the courtyard, her eyes shifting from gold to green to black. She darted over to them, then drew up short, the back of her hand flying to her mouth.

"Shit." She dropped down beside Lir, snapped her fingers, and a leather-stitched satchel appeared on the ground next to her. "Don't worry, Lir. I'll get you patched up in no time."

"Is that some kind of pun?" Lir grumbled.

Brynn laughed, but it was weak. "Fucking fae."

She rummaged through the satchel at her feet, pulling out glass bottles filled with questionable ointments and an assortment of jars containing some of her best homemade salves. She twisted off the lid to one of the bottles and held the amber liquid out to him. "Drink up. Let's give you something to help ease the pain."

Lir scowled as he inspected the bottle. "What is this?"

The corner of Brynn's mouth lifted. "Whiskey."

He downed it in one gulp.

"Good work, commander." Brynn opened one of the jars, revealing a thick white paste. "Now, this might sting, but I've got to heal the skin and prevent infection before I can do anything else."

She scooped a small amount onto her fingers, lightly spreading it across the wound. Lir didn't even flinch. Sitting back, Brynn blew out a small breath. "Once the flesh is no longer inflamed, then I can start work on the...repair. It might take a day or two."

Lir stared at the empty bottle in his hand, and Merrick crouched in front of him. "Can I get you another, commander?"

Lir only grunted.

Merrick grabbed the bottle and stood. "I'll take that as a yes."

Tiernan was vaguely aware of Rowan hovering near them, just outside his line of sight. Not speaking, just watching. Tiernan reached for his thoughts, just for a glimpse, to see if they coincided with his own. He didn't have to venture too far into the Nightweaver's mind to know that Rowan's primary concern aligned with his—if this was what Lir had suffered, there was no telling what Maeve would be forced to endure.

Fists coiling at his sides, Tiernan withdrew his magic.

Brynn gathered her supplies and stood, lugging the satchel over her shoulder. "We need to get him to a room so he can rest. I've got a tea I can brew for the pain, and I've got a few ideas to possibly help restore his missing eye, but I'll have to do some research first."

"Understood." Tiernan reached down and clasped Lir's hand, slowly hauling the commander to his feet.

Lir didn't release his hold on him. His good eye flared, the silver of it swirling like a cloud of storms. His voice was low as he spoke. "She's got her."

The ground beneath Tiernan gave way, rupturing out from under him. He'd been holding onto that one singular thread of hope so tightly, gripping it with every fiber of his being, but now it unraveled in his hands. Fraying. His heart plummeted into the pit of his stomach, hollowing him out completely. It was his worst fear come to life, like walking right into a nightmare and knowing there would be no way out.

Tiernan dropped back, his strength wavering.

"Tier?" Ceridwen looked up at him sharply. Her eyes were

swollen and red, her cheeks flushed. Lines of worry knitted across her brow. "What's wrong?"

There was a blur of shadows. Rowan. They swarmed him. Tiernan's gaze slid to the Nightweaver. "Parisa has Maeve."

A cry of anguish and retribution tore from Saoirse, and her blue eyes flashed with the promise of death. The Furies raged, snarling like the feral cursed *faolan* of the Kethwyn Woods. They moved in unison, shifting, pacing, ready to snap the neck of anyone who dared to look at them the wrong way.

Tiernan rolled his shoulders back, his crafted exterior of calm composure ready to crack beneath the pressure of his anger. Storm clouds brewed along the horizon, roiling like a deadly sea across the darkening sky. Lightning slashed, splintering the heavens. He would not lose Maeve. Not again. Not ever. He swore once that he would rip through the realms to find her, and he would hold true to his word. Nothing would keep him from her. He would kill every fae who stood in his path, and when he had Parisa in his clutches, he would ensure she suffered the full extent of his wrath, more severe and vengeful than even the god of death could inflict.

Images of Maeve's carved body, bloody and bruised from Fearghal's blade, slammed into him.

His magic roared with vehemence, a maelstrom of untempered fury.

He would go to the Pass of Veils himself. Once inside Parisa's shroud, he would be able to locate Maeve through the witch thread binding them. Besides, the mark had been branded onto him by that damn hag herself. Certainly her magic was far more powerful than Parisa, considering she was the one who created the *virdis lepatite*. Then he would cut down every dark fae and he would unleash the extent of his might upon the whole of the Spring Court.

Tiernan stormed toward the gates.

"Where are you going?" Ceridwen called after him, her voice pitching.

"To get her back."

Merrick jogged alongside him. "My lord, you can't go after her by yourself."

Tiernan tossed his mate's words at his hunter, biting them off in a growl. "Watch me."

He stalked forward, then halted.

Rowan stood before him, a slow swirl of shadows crawling around him.

"Move," Tiernan ground out.

The Nightweaver didn't yield. He rocked back onto his heels, lifting one brow. "You're making a mistake."

Tiernan closed the distance between them, glaring as the ferocity of their magic lashed out at one another. "I said get out of my way."

Rowan inclined his head, considering. "You don't even know where to find her."

"I'll figure that out when I get there." Tiernan reached out, ready to shove him out of the way, but Rowan caught his arm with one hand.

"Focus, High King." Rowan's lavender gaze narrowed. "Where's the one place that could tell you exactly where she's located? The one *thing* that can *show* her to you."

Tiernan went still as Rowan's words sank in, as he finally understood. "The mural."

Fuck. Again, Rowan was right. As he had been about many things. Not only the mural, but about Maeve. If Tiernan had only let her fight her own battles, then she never would have stalked off in a fit of anger.

He glanced back at the courtyard.

Merrick and Brynn had hoisted Lir's arms over their shoulders, helping him to remain upright, while Ceridwen was attempting to comfort Saoirse. The silver-haired warrior bared her teeth, looking as though she was ready to kill every single one of them.

He turned back to Rowan. "Will you help me?"

Tense beats of silence passed between them, and then Rowan bowed. "I give you my word."

Tiernan nodded. "To the library."

They set off through the open-air corridors in silence. Tiernan preferred it that way. His mind was a whirlwind of formulations and strategy. As much as he hated to admit it, he couldn't do it alone. Oh, he'd get close. Possibly within a few feet of Maeve, if he was lucky. But Parisa would set her horde of dark fae upon him, and not even his magic would be enough to fend off all of them by himself. Ciara might agree to help, and Tiernan knew Dorian would stop at nothing to save his daughter, but without Brackroth and Wenfyre's support, they'd be slaughtered. Going after Maeve wasn't a part of their plan. In fact, it was likely the one thing they'd never even considered. Her capture thwarted their agenda.

Tiernan shoved open the door to the library and strode toward the desk right below the mural. He stared up at it, set in its gilded frame, while murky colors churned in tandem, as though it was breathing of its own accord. Gripping the back of the chair in front of him, he prepared himself for the worst.

"Show us Maeve's location."

The fog-like clouds drifting across the mural eddied, revealing a palace on a cliff overlooking the Lismore Marin. Mist curled around the base of the castle, its slate walls and sweeping terraces were overgrown with ivy and wilted flowers. Bits of rock crumbled from the dingy towers, and a tarnished gate guarding the entrance groaned open on broken hinges, swaying slowly in the breeze. All around, a steady drizzle fell down from the gray skies, dampening the earth. Yet it was no longer green and lush. The land was rotting, full of decay and nearly barren. But the mural revealed nothing else, only the Crown City of Spring's once lavish palace.

Suvarese had fallen into disrepair.

Tiernan glanced down, sharing a look with Rowan.

Rowan pressed his lips into a firm line and glared up at the mural as though it had somehow personally affronted him. "Show us the Dawnbringer."

Again, the mural billowed, and this time it displayed a dungeon.

Dull amber faerie fire flickered softly, illuminating a small cell. Cast in shadows and shreds of flaxen light was Maeve. She sat on a dank stone floor, with her back against a wall and her knees pulled into her chest. Her armor was mostly intact, and her rose gold hair was shoved back from her face, soiled with sweat and filth. She'd crossed her arms and a hard line crinkled across her brow. Maeve didn't look afraid.

She looked furious.

Tiernan's blood boiled like acid when he saw the cold iron cuff clamped around her neck.

"I know where she is," Rowan murmured. "I know how to get us in undetected."

Tiernan studied him. There was something else. "But can you get us out?"

"That might be more difficult." Rowan rocked back onto his heels, his gaze scanning the mural once more before returning to Tiernan. "We don't know what Parisa is hiding behind that veil."

Tiernan shifted his weight, a pinprick of unease needling its way down his spine. He rubbed one hand along the back of his neck. "We know some things."

Rowan's brow lifted. "Is that so?"

"Casimir has been funneling us information."

"I recall as much. Though I suppose sharing such information with the likes of me is somehow beneath you." Rowan glowered at him with contempt, a smug half-smile plastered across his cocky face. "I'm assuming you struck an accord with Casimir, and if that's the case, what does he want in exchange?"

"I don't know, exactly." Tiernan shoved a hand through his hair, suddenly annoyed the drakon had been so inexplicit with his terms. "All he asked in return was that I help Maeve when the time came. He said I would know when."

"That's rather vague." Rowan ran a thumb along his chin, then folded his arms across his chest. "And what exactly did he tell you that was worth such an innocuous deal?"

"Parisa created this substance, or venom, rather. When injected into a fae, it causes them to lose control of their bodies." Tiernan inwardly cringed, remembering the night Garvan stabbed Maeve with that insignificant blade coated in the venom with the intent to steal her away to Spring. He'd almost gotten away with it, too. "It incapacitates them, and in doing so, she can control their mind and their movements."

"Your magic," Rowan interjected, his eyes widening. "She stole your magic."

"For lack of a better term, yes."

"And how many fae has she administered this supposed venom to?" Rowan asked.

"Hundreds. Maybe more, I don't know." Tiernan shifted on his feet, uncomfortable. "Casimir mentioned Parisa overestimated her abilities. The fae who have been drugged by this venom, their minds are completely gone. She can't control them, and they can't control themselves. They need more of it, they crave it. He seems to think they'll go after Maeve."

Rowan reared back. "What the fuck? What for?"

"Because Casimir thinks since she possesses the *anam ò Danua* that they'll somehow be drawn to her."

Rowan's gaze narrowed, anger ebbed around him, and his shadows swarmed like tendrils of stolen nightfall. "So, she'll either have to create more of this venom, or—"

"Or kill them," Tiernan said, already knowing his answer would only enrage the Nightweaver even more.

"Fucking gods," Rowan muttered. He paced away from the table, then raked his hands through his hair. Spinning around, he stalked back toward Tiernan, pointing one accusing finger in his direction.

"Does she know?" he demanded. "Maeve. *Does she know?*"

Tiernan stiffened, his defenses rising along with his temper. "If you're trying to imply that I withheld this information from her on purpose, you're mistaken. There were a number of more pressing matters after she got her memory back."

In truth, it had completely slipped his mind about the drugged fae beyond Spring's borders. Now, however, it seemed such a transgression would come back to haunt him. There was no doubt in his mind that Parisa would find a way to use the fae against Maeve.

They would have to be swift, whether they liked it or not. Rescuing Maeve couldn't be the onset of the war. They needed her on their side before they invaded Spring, not behind enemy lines.

"There's no telling when the Prince of Brackroth will arrive, and the Wenfyre druids won't be here for another few days." Tiernan scrubbed his hands over his face. Guilt twisted inside of him, tearing at him. He should have been more careful, more prepared. He never should have let Maeve out of his sight. "I fear we're running out of time."

Rowan nodded, more solemn than Tiernan had ever seen him. "The longer Maeve is held within the Spring Court, the worse it will be for her."

"So," Tiernan ventured, "we're in agreement?"

Rowan held his gaze. "For once."

"We'll need help."

"It's one hell of a favor to ask."

"It is, but I know someone willing to do it." Tiernan nodded toward the door of the library. "Then it's settled. When the moon is high, we'll go pay a visit to the Autumn Court."

Rowan bowed, then straightened. "Oh, and one more thing?"

Tiernan turned back to face him. "What?"

Rowan smirked. "Delve into my mind again, High King, and I'll make sure the next image you see is my head between the thighs of your future wife."

Chapter Eighteen

T he dungeon was cold.

Maeve kept her arms wrapped around herself to ward off the chill, but the damp air only seemed to worsen the situation. She clamped her jaw shut so her teeth wouldn't chatter, and she hated the rough scrape of dried skin every time she rubbed her lips together. All she had was her own body heat, which simply wasn't enough. Her fingers were like ice and she could no longer feel her toes. Minor inconveniences really, in the grand scheme of things.

Considering she was locked in a cell with a cuff of iron wrapped around her neck.

Leaning back, Maeve rested her head against the hard stone wall. She'd already lost track of time. In the belly of the dungeon where the light could not reach, time no longer mattered.

Save for the constant dripping sound of what she hoped was water, there was no other noise in the dungeon. No wails of despair or groans of agony. There were no other prisoners, and she hadn't seen a single guard stroll by on patrol. Which Maeve found oddly curious, as Parisa seemed like the type who enjoyed torturing those who disobeyed her. Surely she had an abundance of captives hidden away somewhere. Not all of them had been able to flee into the safe haven of Niahvess. There had to be thousands, if not more, who had been left behind to suffer Parisa's reign.

Yet Maeve continued to sit in the depths of the Spring Court...alone.

Perhaps Parisa intended to subject her to isolation. If that was the case, she was making a terrible mistake. Maeve's mind was quite possibly one of her greatest weapons.

Her gaze slid to the corner of the cell where there was a chunk of stale bread tossed onto a tin plate and a glass of water. If it could even be called that, as this particular substance was almost gray and had bits of dirt floating in it.

Maeve's lip curled in disgust.

In the endless silence, Maeve let her eyes drift close. Her thoughts wandered to Tiernan, and her soul ached. She didn't know how long until she would see him again, and she refused to think the worst, not allowing herself to venture down that dark and dangerous road. Instead, she focused on the warmth of his embrace, the tickle of his whispers against her cheek, the feel of his mouth taking hers. She could picture him clearly, the way he captivated her, leaving her damn near breathless just by looking at her.

Just as quickly, she saw the flash of hurt in his eyes, the way his features hardened when she lashed out at him. He hid it well in front of everyone, but she knew him better. Her words wounded him, and when she walked away from him, he let her go.

How wrong she'd been in thinking she didn't need him.

She hadn't meant it, not really, but there was no taking it

back. Now the last memory she had of them together was one of anger and heartache.

Maeve poured every piece of her soul into the witch thread connecting her to Tiernan. Love. Admiration. Trust. Respect. Her wrist warmed slightly, but if he sensed her at all, she received no response.

"Eternally," she whispered into the darkness.

The harsh sound of heels striking stone reverberated through the dungeon, and Maeve's eyes flew open.

She would be ready for whatever happened next, she would not give in to Parisa. The cost didn't matter. She would endure the pain, suffer through the torture, but she would never allow Parisa to use her against her will.

Parisa appeared in front of Maeve's cell a few moments later, still cloaked in her thick robes of black velvet to disguise her skeletal frame. Two hulking fae guards were positioned on either side of her, their movements disjointed, their eyes glazed. One of them stepped forward, unlocked Maeve's cell, then jerked back out of the way.

"Now that you'll be staying with us for the foreseeable future, I was hoping we could have a little chat."

Parisa swept into the cell, and Maeve stood, the chain of iron fastening her in place. But she refused to cower.

Maeve lifted her chin. "I have nothing to say to you."

"Really? Nothing?" Parisa cocked her head, her spindly crown slipping, compressing the extra flesh on her forehead. "You don't want to know how I found you? How I got you here?"

She gestured around the dungeon, as though Maeve's surroundings were an opulent bedroom instead of a small enclosure made of stone and metal.

"Fine," Maeve bit out. She had a feeling Parisa would tell

her either way, if anything, for the opportunity to gloat. "How?"

"It was calculated yet simple, really. A stroke of luck, if you will." Parisa's thin lips stretched across her face into a heinous smile. "You're familiar with the Puca. If I recall, you and Fearghal had a rather intimate relationship."

At the mention of Fearghal's name, Maeve recoiled. It had been in a cell just like this one where he'd carved her from ankle to cheek, taking great care to scour her breasts with his blade as slowly as possible.

She'd killed him for it.

She would do the same to anyone else who tried to touch her.

"Anyway." Parisa's bony fingers flitted through the air, the large obsidian ring she wore glinting in the pale light. "I had a Puca create that amulet into a portal for me. When I sent those stupid giants into the Winter Court, I knew you'd come running to the rescue. Always wanting to be the hero, aren't you, my pet?"

She sneered at Maeve, her pointy teeth scraping along her lips. "In the midst of the chaos, no one even noticed that the lonely Winter soldier went missing. I *had* hoped to lure you into the woods, but unfortunately, your darling High King had other plans."

Maeve stiffened, every muscle in her body tensing as though she'd been struck.

"And that's when luck favored me." She cackled, a coarse noise like nails clawing against stone. "You went into the woods on your own. Well, you and that overprotective commander. Then you waltzed your pretty little head right into my trap. Honestly, I didn't think it would work. But again..." Her thin shoulders shifted. "Luck."

"You see, Maeve," Parisa continued, moving closer. "I have

great plans for Faeven, but it seems no one shares my vision. Power is a delicious thing, as I'm sure you understand."

Her hot breath filled the lack of space between them. It was rank, as though she'd swallowed the decaying flesh of those she killed. Maeve swallowed down the burn of bile, trying not to gag.

Parisa licked her parched lips and paced in a slow circle around Maeve. "When I was blessed with the *anam ó Danua*, I—"

"You were never," Maeve spat.

Eerie silence descended upon the dungeon, somehow even quieter than before. Even that steadfast dripping sound had ceased.

Parisa faced her again, her dark, hollowed eye squinting. When she spoke, her voice was unnaturally low. "What did you say?"

"Could you restore life to a land that was dying? Could you create anything from everything around you?"

Parisa blinked, her expression blank.

Maeve smiled. "I didn't think so. You may have received a blessing from Danua, but it was not the lifeblood of magic. She would never bestow such a powerful gift on something so foul."

The back of Parisa's hand connected with Maeve's mouth, knocking her so hard, tiny stars blared across her vision. She staggered back, stunned by the force of the blow. That damn ring she wore ripped into her lip. Something warm and sticky slid down Maeve's chin.

Blood.

"Interrupt me again, and I'll ensure you suffer a punishment far worse than the sting of my hand." Parisa straightened, her lip curling in disgust. "As I was saying, there is nothing quite like the bloodlust for power. And since I'm in possession of the *virdis lepatite*, the Aurastone, and *you*, there is nothing and no one to stop me from taking all of Faeven for myself."

Maeve slid her thumb along her chin, smearing the blood there. "Aed should have killed you when he had the chance."

"Perhaps." Parisa ran her nails along the bars lining Maeve's cell, mimicking the sound of rainfall. "But even gods make mistakes."

Maeve jerked forward, the iron biting into her skin. "The Courts will never bow to you."

"Oh, but they will. And you'll be the one to punish them if they don't." She folded her arms across her chest, the sickly glow of the *virdis lepatite* pulsing at the base of her throat. "We can do this one of two ways, Maeve. You can kneel before me now, willingly, and do as I say without protest, or—"

"Never." Maeve lunged forward and spat at the bitch fae's feet.

Parisa inhaled deeply and her mouth pulled into a stern, thin line. Her gaze roved over Maeve, lingering on the tattoo of a rose marking her cheek. "It was in this very cell that Fearghal took great pleasure in breaking you."

Maeve's fists curled at her sides. She'd already overcome that once, she wouldn't be made to suffer. Her past was nothing but a page in her story, even though that particular scene was one she would gladly rip out and set on fire. "But he's not here to do your bidding anymore, is he?"

They both knew the answer.

Maeve had left Fearghal in the depths of the Scathing. He was but a pulpy mess of flesh rotting beneath the soil of Kells.

"No. Fearghal is no longer here because of you." Parisa stepped to the side, and one of the guards stepped forward. "So, allow me to introduce you to Gromede."

He was a beast of a dark fae. His angular jaw jutted forward, revealing large bottom teeth that curved upward over his wide mouth. A deep-set brow hovered above his opaque red eyes that swirled like clouds caught on fire. Where his nose should have been, there was nothing more than two slits, and his skin was freakishly gray and tinged with blue, like glaciers. Translucent even, so Maeve could see veins of black blood coursing through him. He was both terrifying and hideous.

Gromede ambled toward her, his steel armor clanking with each step of his uneven gait, made worse by the hunch protruding from his back. He reeked of damp earth and stale air, bitter, like the onset of the storms that used to lash the coast of Kells. He reminded her of the cage.

Maeve held her breath, staggering back. Away from him.

Gromede grabbed her with one meaty hand, pulling a tangle of bristly rope from his belt. He bound her wrists together, yanking tightly so the scratchy threads cut into her skin. Once he was certain she was secure, he lumbered around behind her and unlocked the chain bolted to the ground.

He wrapped the chain links around his fist, then yanked hard.

Maeve lurched forward as she stumbled to keep up. The iron gripped her throat, squeezing with each tug of Gromede's brutality.

Parisa glided ahead of them. "Come along, my pet."

"Where are you taking me?" Maeve choked out, tripping over her own feet.

"I warned you not to interrupt me again. But it seems you don't like to listen. To *anyone*. It's only fair such behavior receives a proper punishment." Parisa paused, glancing back at her, and the wash of amber light made her glow with vengeance. "It would be rude of me to show favoritism to you when there are so many others who disobeyed me as well."

Ah.

So, there were more prisoners. Just as Maeve suspected.

But if they weren't in the dungeon, then where was she keeping them?

They moved through a labyrinth of darkened corridors that seemed to wind like a serpentine maze beneath the palace of Suvarese. To Maeve, it felt like she'd been walking for hours. She was exhausted, weaker than she thought, though whether it was from the lack of nutrition or the iron diminishing her energy, she couldn't be sure. Each footfall became more of a shuffle as Gromede dragged her along like an animal on a leash. Weariness sank into her bones, her muscles ached. Rounding a corner, Maeve silenced a groan as she looked up to see a spiral staircase that seemed to go on for miles.

She trudged up each one of them, step after step. Her knees softened and her breathing grew labored. A sharp pain jabbed into her ribs, stabbing with each breath. Every so often, the guard behind her would nudge her in the back, shoving her up another few stairs. Just when she thought her lungs would give out, when she swore her body was ready to quit on her, they came to a landing.

The door before her creaked open and soft light spilled into the hall.

It wasn't bright by any means, but Maeve shielded her eyes all the same. The harsh contrast of the pitch corridors and the dim haze of the room in front of her was enough to cause her temples to throb. Her stomach revolted at the stench, the acrid smell of sweat and other pungent bodily fluids burned her nose. Her eyes watered and Maeve blinked as Gromede towed her into the space, while her vision gradually adjusted to the faint glow illuminating the chamber. Only then did she wish Parisa had taken her eye instead.

On the right side of the room, four tables were crammed side by side, each one of them showcasing a different type of weapon or device meant to inflict pain. There were grimy bottles filled with bubbling potions along with a collection of dried herbs and flowers. A petite fae with stringy hair was hunched over a mortar and pestle, grinding bits of leaves and petals into a fine paste. Next to her was a spread of various daggers, all sharpened to a gleaming point, and some other devices Maeve had never seen before. Clamps with spikes sticking out of them, metal masks with malignant faces etched onto them designed to cover someone's entire head, honed rods of birch, and whips with whetted blades poking out from the ends.

Maeve suddenly felt as though she'd swallowed an entire bag full of sand, and her heart plummeted to her stomach like a rock.

This was a torture chamber.

There was only one cell in this room, but it was vast, capable of holding a number of prisoners. Three fae were huddled near the far wall, clinging to one another. They were covered in filth, their clothing little more than ill-fitting brown tunics. Two were female, but the male crouched before them both, his arms splayed wide in a show of defense. All of them stared as Maeve entered, wary, and not one of them spoke. They didn't make a single sound.

And she knew why.

In the center of the room were four wooden posts that stretched from the floor to the beams of the ceiling. Hooks were fastened into the side of each of the beams, and two fae were hanging from them with their arms over their heads. They'd been severely beaten, whipped until their clothing stuck to their skin, until blood ran like a river beneath them, staining the stone. Both of them were males, one with sandy blond hair, the other a rich brown. Their heads were bowed, their eyes empty orbs of nothingness.

Maeve wasn't even sure they were alive.

Another Spring fae slowly approached Maeve with a pair of shears in her hand. Jagged pieces of black hair framed her oval face, and though her skin was dark bronze, the female fae blanched at the sight of Maeve. She wore the same style of tunic as the fae locked within the cage, except hers was an emerald green. The hem was frayed, and the gold stitching along the edges was worn, but for the most part, this fae looked far better off than all the rest Maeve had seen so far. There was a slight tremble in the fae's hand and her lashes fluttered down as she looked away, refusing to make eye contact.

The fae reached for her.

Maeve jerked back in surprise. "Get away from me!"

"Please, be still." Again, she made to grasp for her, wielding those shears like a blade. "I just have to—"

"Absolutely not." Maeve whipped away from the female, but this time, the solid fist of Gromede collided with her face.

Her head snapped to the side, the crunching sound of flesh and bone crackled in her ears. Pain ricocheted through her, lancing from her cheek to her head. Warm blood coated her tongue, slid from the corner of her mouth. Ribbons of darkness unfurled along the edges of her vision and she reeled backward, losing her footing. With her hands bound before her, Maeve's balance pitched, and she toppled toward the ground. The world blurred in a stream of ugly colors.

Gromede snared her by the arm, hauling her back to her feet. Waves of nausea rolled over her, and she sagged in his firm grip, dizzy and limp.

Something cool slid beneath her armor, sliding smoothly along her skin. She shuddered, helpless to fight back. Damp air assaulted her as she realized what was happening. Horrified, she blinked rapidly, desperately trying to clear her muddled thoughts, as the Spring fae cut away her leathers. Chunks of aubergine armor fell to the blood-splattered floor, and when the fae stepped back, Maeve was left naked and exposed from the waist up.

She shivered, clutching her hands to her chest in a poor attempt to cling to some shred of decency, but Gromede was having none of it. He grabbed the knot between her wrists and hoisted her arms above her head.

Then he lifted her off the ground. In one swift movement, he looped the rope binding her around a bronze hook protruding from one of the wooden beams.

Suddenly she was hanging there, just like the two half-dead fae next to her. The chain of iron fell down her front, dangling like a dead weight between her breasts.

Maeve stole a breath, but it was shallow. She couldn't see anything except the pieces of splintered wood in front of her, where likely dozens of other fae had met their end in one way or another. She focused on the whorls, where dark oak met light, where they swirled together, then peeled away. It was only physical pain, and she'd survived worse. She'd been locked into a cage over a dangerous cliff as a child, she'd been trained to fight until she was bloody and bruised, she'd been poisoned, stabbed, and had her body mutilated by a sadistic bastard.

But she'd also been loved.

Fully and completely.

So, she would endure. For her friends, for her family. For Tiernan.

She would endure.

From somewhere behind her, Parisa was humming. Maeve thought the tune was vaguely familiar, but she couldn't place it. Nor did she care enough to try.

Maeve craned her neck for a better view.

Parisa was browsing her selection of wares on one of the tables. She'd selected her whip of choice—it was long with multiple pieces of tightly bound leather, and dangling from the tip was a knot covered in silver spikes. She picked it up, lifting the ball of spikes for Maeve to see.

Gliding toward the post, Parisa peered up at her, that singular dead eye of hers glinting with malice. "This is going to hurt me more than it will hurt you."

Maeve huffed. "Unlikely."

Turning away, Parisa disappeared behind Maeve.

The whip cracked loudly, and Maeve's body involuntarily convulsed.

"Maeve." She drew out her name in her saccharine voice. "How old are you?"

"Five and twenty." Maeve forced the words out between gritted teeth.

"That's it? Such a pity. You're only a baby." It could have been awe in her tone. Or loathing. "Very well. Twenty-five lashes for each year of your miserable existence."

There was no warning, just the devastating sound of a crack, and the immense pain of spikes piercing her flesh. They ripped down her back, tearing at her skin, shredding through the scars already marking her. These would not be the pretty swirls Fearghal carved into her, they would be vicious streaks of rage. White hot pain seared through her as Parisa struck again. And again.

Six.

Maeve kept count in her mind, refusing to cry out. She would not give Parisa the satisfaction.

One particularly heinous lashing caught her shoulder, and she jerked as the sting was enough to leave her breathless. Her body was twitching on its own now, flinching as every strike of the whip scoured her, ruined her.

Fourteen.

She squeezed her eyes shut, willing away the sting of tears. Instead, she focused solely on Tiernan. She thought of his smile as the spikes snagged deeper into her skin. His caress as the warmth of her blood dripped down her spine, and the soft splatter of it filled the space between the crack of the whip and her labored breathing. She imagined he was standing right there in front of her, cupping her cheeks with both of his hands, willing her to survive for him. Even as she shivered in dread, mentally preparing for the next lashing.

But Maeve held true, she did not utter one cry of anguish. In turn, she took it all and gave Parisa nothing.

Twenty-five.

The last and, quite possibly, the worst. For this time, the spikes stuck, lodged in her back.

She swallowed down the rank air as Gromede strode over and wrenched the whip free. Her nose tingled. Her eyes flooded.

Maeve shook her head.

No. She would not cry. Not here. Not ever.

The soft click of heels sounded from somewhere off to her right.

"Take her down."

Gromede reached up and dislodged the rope from the hook. He held her by the elbows and she lolled against him, unable to keep herself upright on her own.

Parisa bent over, curving one long nail under Maeve's chin, forcing her to look up. "I know what you're thinking. You imagine yourself to be so brave by not giving me the gratification of a scream or a sob. You are strong, I'll give you that, but your weakness lies in those you hold most dear."

Her nail scraped along Maeve's jaw, drawing blood. "They will come for you. They will try and save you. Trust when I say I will kill each of them, slowly, as you look on, helpless to do anything but watch. I will break you, Maeve. Be it your mind or your heart, and when this is all over, there will be nothing left of you but the shattered remains of your soul."

Maeve slumped against Gromede, the fight draining.

"Clean her up. I can't have my most prized possession looking like such a mess when she makes her grand entrance." Parisa whirled away from her, then stalked out of the torture chamber completely.

Gromede deposited her in a chair, retreating to the opposite side of the room as the Spring fae slowly treaded toward Maeve once more. This time, she carried a salve and some ointment for healing, but there was a heavy sorrow in her eyes.

Maeve cooperated, allowing the fae to tend her devastating wounds. Her lips pressed together, and she winced as the salve was spread across the lacerations littering her back. It smelled lightly of fresh earth and rainfall, and a sigh escaped her. The fae was gentle, her small hands thorough and capable as she did her best to ease Maeve's torment. Gradually the pain ebbed, though she didn't dare ask about the state of her skin. The scarring would be horrendous, of that she had no doubt.

Fatigue tugged at Maeve. Numb to everything around her, she didn't protest when the fae dressed her in a beige linen shirt, or when she stripped her bloodied leathers from her legs, and helped her into a pair of plain brown leggings instead.

But when the Spring fae bent down to apply some of the ointment to her broken jaw, Maeve found the courage to whisper a hesitant plea.

"Help me." She swallowed, her voice hoarse. "If you can get me out of here, I can save you. I will rid this land of Parisa once and for all."

The Spring fae looked up at her then, her golden brown eyes reflecting a lifetime of suffering. She patted Maeve's hand. "It's too late for us. Just as it's too late for you."

Maeve sagged in the chair.

The fae's spirit was broken. There would be no saving her unless Maeve could save herself.

Gromede's giant frame came into focus. Bending down, he scooped Maeve up and tossed her over his shoulder.

Maeve didn't fight the dark fae. She was too tired, too weary, and the last thing she wanted was for him to punch her in the face again. So, she remained compliant, allowing him to carry her all the way back to her cell, deep within the mountain below the palace of Suvarese.

He dumped her unceremoniously onto the ground, then secured the locks of her chain.

She watched his uneven gait slowly disappear down the corridor of the dungeon until the amber faerie fire in the lantern sputtered out completely.

At once, the cell was engulfed in a swath of all-encompassing darkness.

Alone and cold, Maeve leaned back against the slimy wall and closed her eyes.

I will not yield.

I will not break.

Chapter Nineteen

Tiernan *faded* into the Autumn Court.

Leaves of ruby and citron fluttered around him on the cool breeze, carrying the scent of damp earth and mulled spices. Hollowed-out logs were hidden beneath thick brushes dotted with tiny berries, and woodland creatures scampered across the sodden ground. Before him was the Black Lake, its smooth surface glinting like obsidian against the slashes of moonlight breaking through the trees. Even in the pitch of night, the forest looked set on fire with its shimmering jeweled hues.

He took one step forward and froze, a barely detectable undercurrent of pain sweeping through him, pulsing from the witch thread marking him.

Tiernan clutched his wrist, wincing.

Sinewy shadows churned to his left, building to a mass of darkness before fanning out to reveal Rowan. The Nightweaver took one look at him, and his brow furrowed. "Hurt yourself already?"

"No. Something happened." Tiernan peeled back the

leather of his armor, staring down at his wrist. The witch thread was still there, but a dull ache throbbed just beneath the surface of his skin. He tugged the sleeve down. "She's hurt."

Rowan flinched, his gaze sharpening. "How bad?"

"I don't know, but she's not afraid..." There was a ripple of something else coursing through the witch thread, almost untraceable. A tendril of resolution. Of tenacity. "She's unyielding. Refusing to break."

"Of course she is," Rowan scoffed, glancing around the forest. He shoved his hands into the pockets of his pants, his lavender gaze scanning the dense woods. "Alright, High King, we're here. Now what?"

"I imagine you're here to see me." A rough voice scraped through the night air, and Casimir emerged from the edge of the tree line, his hood drawn low over his head. "For why else would the High King of Summer and the Nightweaver be deep within the Autumn Court and not at the palace?"

Tiernan strolled over to him, offering his hand in greeting. They grasped each other's wrists, and when they released, Tiernan leveled the drakon with a solemn look. "You saved Maeve from Parisa once, I need your assistance in doing so again."

Casimir shoved his hood back, blanching. He looked between Tiernan and Rowan, his dark gaze flashing in a play of light and shadow. "Parisa has Maeve."

Rowan nodded. "She does."

Casimir blew out a low breath, then turned away from them both. He faced the Black Lake, his shoulders dropping slightly. "It will not be easy."

"I wouldn't expect anything less." Tiernan's gaze slid to Rowan, and he nodded in return. "But we cannot leave Maeve there."

Casimir bowed his head then looked up at the sky, where

the stars took the form of constellations older than even the Ancient Ones, where secrets of the before were kept and treasured. "Entering the Spring Court will be easy, getting out will prove far more difficult. I should be able to hold a fair amount of the dark fae at bay in my drakon form. Like other fae I have encountered in the past, they are no match for fire."

Tiernan wasn't entirely sure there was any fae alive that could withstand the strength of drakon fire, but he kept that to himself.

"You understand that once we get Maeve out of Suvarese, we must be ready to attack. There will be no time to wait, no time to celebrate a reunion. Everything must be in place." Casimir turned back to them, and remorse fell around him like a cloak. "Parisa will not hesitate. Maeve has slipped from her clutches twice already."

Tiernan steeled his spine into place. Nothing would stop him, nothing would stand in his way. "Then we will prepare for our assault, with or without Brackroth and Wenfyre."

The druids were still days away with their naval fleet, and he could only pray to the Mother Goddess herself that they would arrive in time. As for Brackroth, Ciara's promise of their assistance had been rather vague. There was no guarantee they would show, no matter how dire the situation, no matter how desperately Faeven could use a horde of dragons on their side.

Rowan nodded once, his gaze sliding to Casimir. "For Maeve."

Casimir bowed. "For Maeve."

Tiernan appreciated them both on a level he couldn't quite articulate. Perhaps the words would come to him later, perhaps he'd take his final breath before ever speaking them. "I'll have Merrick inform Ciara and Dorian of our strategy. We will need their forces ready sooner than expected. But in the meantime, I have to return to Niahvess and check on Lir."

"What happened to your commander?" Casimir asked, pulling his hood back up over his head.

Rowan ran his hand along the back of his neck, toeing his boot through the dirt at their feet. "Parisa took his eye with the intent to hurt Maeve further."

"Her vengeance knows no bounds," Casimir mumbled, and though his face was partially visible from beneath his hood, the angular lines of his jaw hardened. "Her quest for power has darkened her soul. She's a monster now, tainted by the foulness of greed. There was a time, though, when her heart was pure. When love was enough for her."

"I remember." Rowan's voice was quiet, scarcely more than a whisper. "But that was long ago."

"Indeed," Casimir agreed. "Long, long ago."

Silence descended upon them, accompanied only by the breeze sifting through the trees and the occasional call of an owl.

Tiernan cleared his throat. "We meet at dawn."

"I'll be there." Casimir lifted his head and stepped back.

Then Tiernan *faded* back to the courtyard of Niahvess as Rowan was engulfed in a surge of shadows.

Tiernan assumed Rowan would retire to his room for the remainder of the night. After all, there were only a few more hours until the sun rose above the mountains to the east. But he found the Nightweaver standing a few feet from him, his gaze focused on the west.

To Suvarese.

He eyed the heir to the Spring Court, and spoke the first thought that entered his mind. "You can't *fade*."

Rowan shifted, stiffening under the scrutiny of his gaze. "No."

"What happened?" Tiernan asked. "An Archfae doesn't simply lose that ability overnight."

"I traded it. For something better." Rowan glanced over at him, and though his face was a mask of disinterest, his eyes told another story. One of sacrifice and loss.

He hadn't traded his ability to *fade* for something. He bartered it for someone.

Maeve.

"That night in Spring, when Casimir handed her off to you." It seemed the Nightweaver had given up a number of things for the Dawnbringer.

"I made a deal with the god of death. Same as you." Rowan shrugged, as though it made no difference. "Her life in exchange for *fading* seemed fair enough. I figured I'd be stuck flying or walking everywhere for the rest of my life. But when Aed gifted me the power of destruction..."

He spread his arms, and shadows danced between his open palms. "The shadows came with it."

Interesting. That dark magic had been part of Tiernan as well, yet not once had he ever been able to move between the shadows. He cocked his head, suddenly curious. "What else did he give you?"

Orange blossom and cedarwood flooded the air as Rowan's magic expanded, shifting the courtyard, morphing it into another place entirely. Misty rain fell from the sky, dampening Tiernan's hair and chilling his hands. Fog crept along the ground, almost obscuring the path of uneven cobblestone that stretched out before him. Buildings appeared on either side of him—shops, cafes, and other various storefronts—all of them washed in muted shades of gray and blue. Only one of them drew Tiernan's attention because a steady stream of golden light spilled from its rain-splattered window.

He moved closer, entranced by the glowing aura the way one might follow the glimmering of faerie lights. Up close, he peered inside the building, and his breath caught tight in his lungs. He held fast to the sight unfolding before him.

It was a library, with dozens of floor to ceiling shelves crammed with books. There was a spiral staircase in the back of the room leading to another level, and a fire sparked to life in the hearth. But the glow didn't come from the crackling flames —it came from the fae curled into a leather chair, her head bowed as she read the book cradled in her hands. Maeve's golden pink curls tumbled loosely down her shoulders, the crimson sweater she wore a perfect match to the color painting her lips. Each time she turned the page, the rustling of parchment sounded softly in Tiernan's ears, as though he sat right beside her.

Shadows formed by the hearth, and then Rowan appeared. He lounged against the wall with his arms crossed, the power of destruction rippling around him while he watched Maeve from across the room. She didn't look up, oblivious to his presence, though Tiernan imagined she knew he was there. Waiting.

The Nightweaver's gaze flicked to his through the window, and when Rowan stepped forward, the illusion vanished.

Tiernan stood in his courtyard once more, keenly aware that they might have just stumbled upon the key to rescuing Maeve from the Spring Court. The idea slammed into him, jumbling his thoughts. It was slightly unhinged, not at all strategic, and while he wasn't certain about the complexities involving illusion magic, he knew it would work. "That's it. That's how we'll do it."

Rowan arched a brow in question.

"We'll go into Suvarese under the guise of illusion." Tiernan waved his hand through the air, gesturing to where Maeve had been seated in a library. "What are your limits?"

Rowan's harsh laugh echoed up into the swaying palm trees overhead. "I have no limits."

"Don't be a dick," Tiernan countered, his patience waning. "You might be a demigod, but that power only extends to the magic of destruction, nothing else. Illusion is fae, and you know as well as I do that it comes with a price."

At the mention of the word price, Rowan instantly sobered.

"Best-case scenario, it will hold up for a few hours, assuming it's nothing too outlandish in design. We might be noticed upon closer inspection. The edges of the trees may blur, the illusion might waver if I expend too much energy." Rowan shifted his weight, running his thumb along his jaw. "Worst-case scenario...exhaustion. The magic will vanish completely, revealing us."

Tiernan nodded. It would be worth the risk. "Can you do it?"

"Yes." Rowan didn't even hesitate.

"We'll tell Casimir of our plan when he arrives." Tiernan lifted his gaze to the sky. It was still inky with the promise of night, but in a matter of hours, dawn would be on the horizon. "Get some rest, Nightweaver. You'll need it."

With that, he turned and walked away, heading through the open air corridors to the living quarters. His heart only stuttered for a moment when he passed by his and Maeve's adjoining rooms. Their scents mingled in the air, layered on top of one another, like intricately woven threads of shared time and space. Fueled with a greater determination, he kept going, knowing he would find Lir in Brynn's room. Since it housed an arsenal of healing potions and ointments, it was the most ideal location for his recovery.

He paused outside of Brynn's door, listening. Lir's deep breathing was accompanied by the hushed murmurs of Brynn's voice and her feather-like footfalls. Slowly, he nudged the door open.

Brynn glanced over, motioning for him to come inside.

Instantly, he was assaulted with the smell of crushed herbs —lavender petals, valerian root, and something minty. Shelves lined the walls of her room, each one filled with vials and glass jars. Dried flowers with twine wrapped around their stems hung from her windows. Stacks of books littered a long table, many of the pages were marked in ink by Brynn's careful hand. She stood by the bed where Lir rested, leaning over the nightstand where she ground a brown paste together with her mortar and pestle.

Tiernan slowly walked over to join her, keeping his voice low. "How is he?"

He glanced down at his commander. The wound looked better, as though it had already begun to heal. Brynn's magic had repaired most of Lir's flesh, sealing the gaping hole left behind, fusing the skin together in a faint scar that resembled a sun.

"Resting." Brynn set the mortar and pestle down, blowing out a soft breath. She tucked an errant curl behind one ear, her gaze roving over Lir's prone form, then darting up to Tiernan. "I don't think it is the injury that plagues him."

Concern cemented a line across Tiernan's brow.

"He feels like he failed Maeve. And you, my lord." Brynn shook her head lightly. "He couldn't protect her."

"He lost his eye for her." Tiernan gently placed his hand on Lir's shoulder. "That's more than most would be willing to give."

"It was either mine or hers," Lir rasped, his hand flexing, then coiling into a fist. His one good eye blinked open, the silver of it shining like the moon in the dead of night. "Parisa was going to extract her eye as repayment for the one Maeve carved out of her. But she took mine instead. She used me against her."

He turned his head away from them. "She'll use all of us against her."

"We won't allow it," Tiernan countered. Resolve hardened inside of him like the stone face of a mountain's cliff. "You did everything that was asked of you, commander."

"It wasn't enough."

"You kept her from losing an eye." Brynn reached down and squeeze his wrist. "That's more than enough."

To this, Lir said nothing.

Brynn glanced up at Tiernan, offering him a small smile that didn't quite reach her eyes. "Don't worry, my lord. I'll get him back to his usual grumpy self in no time."

"Please do." Tiernan released Lir and nodded once. "We'll need him."

Only when he was back in the quiet of the courtyard did he drop to his knees. Pressing his thumb to the witch thread, he tilted his face to the collection of stars, and whispered through the bond to Maeve.

"*Infinitely.*"

Chapter Twenty

Maeve's heart fluttered, the blood coursing through her stirred to life, and the bond shivered.

"Infinitely."

She heard Tiernan's voice clearly, as though he'd whispered the word against her cheek, the warmth of his breath tickling her ear. If she closed her eyes, she could almost feel the caress of his fingers swiping along her jaw, tilting her face up to him. She could imagine losing herself in the depths of his twilight eyes, where the flecks of gold sparkled around her like sundrops.

But Tiernan wasn't here with her.

She was still in the dungeon below Suvarese's palace.

Alone.

Minutes drifted into hours, and she gazed mindlessly into the all-encompassing darkness. There was no way to determine the time down here. No windows. No light. Just a swath of pitch that bored into her from every angle, surrounding her until she could no longer determine if her eyes were open or closed.

So, she remained seated on the cold stone floor, while she focused on every inhale and exhale in an effort to keep herself distracted from the aching whip marks lancing across her back. Even though the Spring fae from the torture room covered them in a healing salve, the sting had yet to ease.

Suddenly, a dim amber light sputtered to life at the end of the dungeon's lengthy corridor. Heavy footfalls scraped against the hard stone, like something or someone was being dragged.

Maeve held her breath, blinking harshly against the abrupt brightness, and wondered if Parisa was adding to her collection of prisoners.

But only the hulking outline of Gromede appeared. He lumbered toward her cell, a ring of keys jangling in time to his uneven gait. Maeve didn't move when he unlocked the door of her cell and stepped inside, grumbling to himself in a language she didn't understand. The monstrous guard bent down, released the latch to the chain of iron fastened to the ground, and hauled her to her feet.

For a brief moment, Maeve worried Gromede was taking her back to that awful room to be whipped again, but this time, they were going in a different direction. He led her through the cavernous maze of the dungeon, and with each step, the air grew warm and thick. A sickly sweet aroma wafted through the corridor, assaulting her senses. It reminded her of overripe cherries, tainted with bitter orange blossom, a stomach-turning syrupy scent.

She grimaced, gritting her teeth as Gromede shoved open a large wooden door and dragged her through it. Gray light enveloped her and Maeve squinted against it, gradually taking in her surroundings. She was on the main level of Suvarese's palace.

It was a dining hall, and before her was an exceedingly long table. Parisa sat at one end, her mouth peeling back in a wicked smile to reveal her pointy teeth. Huddled together was a group of about nine or ten Spring fae, their heads hung low, their bodies twitching slightly. All of them were dressed in decadent finery. The females wore gowns of silk and lace, and the males donned expertly tailored suits, their shoes polished until they gleamed. But none of the fae looked at Maeve when she entered. They didn't look at anyone. Other than the Spring fae, there were only guards in the dining hall. Four were stationed at every exit, each of them armed with swords whose blades were serrated along both sides.

She didn't want to think about how severely a weapon like that could mutilate a body.

Maeve forced herself to look away from them. Her gaze swung wildly around the space, noting every detail. Six arching windows lined the wall across from her, their dreary panes splattered with raindrops. A blanket of dense fog shrouded whatever lay beyond the palace, making it difficult to discern the time of day. Brilliant green vines curled around sparkling ivory pillars, the lush leaves bursting with blossoms of fuchsia and gold. Dark oak beams stretched across the ceiling overhead where a chandelier extended like tree limbs. Emerald leaves unfurled from its branches, and tiny flowers with pale pink petals floated just beneath it, fluttering softly like butterflies.

By all rights, it should have been lovely, but pinpricks of unease prodded down Maeve's spine.

It was all too bright, too perfect.

She glanced back up at the floating flowers above the table, and—there. The faintest of shimmers winked back at her.

Glamour.

If she didn't have this damned iron collar around her neck, she would have noticed it sooner. But at least now she knew for certain that Parisa had glamoured the entire space. Maeve didn't know what true horrors were hidden behind the overly sumptuous façade, but she somehow thought it wouldn't be long before she found out.

"Maeve, I'm so glad you could join me." Parisa gestured toward the other end of the table with her bony fingers. "Come. Sit."

Maeve didn't move. She remained as still as a corpse, a kind of knowing dread kept her rooted in place.

Parisa's brow pulled together, collecting across her forehead in ripples of extra skin. Her lips pinched and she snapped her fingers.

Gromede snatched Maeve by the shoulders, lifting her from the ground completely. She tensed under his hold, wincing slightly as he dumped her into the chair.

"Eat, Maeve," Parisa commanded, and a bowl filled with a rich brown broth and stewed vegetables appeared before her.

When she hesitated, Parisa only loosed a dramatic sigh, and rolled her eyes toward the chandelier. "It's only soup. I have no need to poison you. In fact, I can think of far better ways I'd prefer to see your demise."

She slammed the tip of the Aurastone into the table's wooden surface. "Now. Eat."

Maeve grabbed the spoon, worried that if she hesitated again, Parisa would use the Aurastone against her. Gingerly, she scooped up a small helping of the soup, and without taking her eyes off Parisa, she ate.

It was bland but not atrocious, tasting lightly of herbs, and Maeve rolled the flavors around on her tongue before finally swallowing it down. Her stomach almost revolted, it had been so long since she'd eaten. The stale bread and murky water in the dungeon hardly counted as legit sustenance. Those had likely only been offered to her just to keep her alive. She had a few more bites of the soup, glad to wash it down with the glass of clean water she'd been given.

"Good," Parisa crooned, taking dainty spoonfuls of her broth as well. "You're going to need your energy."

Still, Maeve said nothing, but the flesh along the back of her neck pebbled.

There was a shift, an unsettling sensation she couldn't quite shake, and the *virdis lepatite* dangling from Parisa's neck glowed, burning a hideous shade of green.

Music floated through the dining hall, a discordant and grieving melody. It was a harrowing tune set to the beat of a waltz, as though only the minor chords were being played. The sound of it caused her nerves to fray.

"Oh, look." Parisa eased back in her chair and folded her hands in her lap. Her eyes glinted with a kind of ravenous hunger. "It's time for the entertainment."

Maeve stared in shock as the Spring fae who'd gathered in the far corner of the hall filed into the center of the room and started dancing. They paired off in precise uniformity, moving about the space in slow circles. On any other occasion, dancing would have been fluid, a gentle ebb and flow of movement. Yet this seemed compulsory, stilted, as though some kind of outside force was compelling them. Each fae wore an expression of vacancy, an empty mask devoid of life. Save for their eyes. Their eyes told another story entirely. One of fear. Of panic.

"What game are you playing?" Maeve demanded.

She only knew of one fae who could command others through their minds. One fae whose magic was so strong, so powerful, that he could control movements, could make others bend to his will.

Tiernan.

"No game, my pet." Parisa tapped her long nails against the table, the noise clicking in time to the haunting melody. "Members of the Dark Court love to perform for their queen."

This was wrong. All of this was wrong. Parisa shouldn't

have this kind of power, she shouldn't possess such an ability. Maeve had to find a way to save these fae, to free them from Parisa's grip on their minds.

Anger coursed through her, and she clutched the spoon in her hands, bending it in half.

One of the Spring fae, a male, strode up to her. He jerked forward into a hasty bow and held out his hand.

"He only wants to dance," Parisa chided, motioning for Maeve to accept his hand.

She tried to swallow the knot of trepidation clogging the back of her throat and glanced up at the fae in question. Sandy blond hair fell across half of his face, and there was what looked like the remnants of a bruise alongside his jaw. The skin there was sallow and slightly swollen. But what drew her in were his eyes. They were the color of honey, framed with dark lashes, and *pleading*. As though begging for her help.

A breath shuddered out of her. "I..."

Gromede took one step toward her, and she bolted out of her seat.

"Of course," she muttered quickly, dropping into a clumsy curtsy. "I'd love to dance."

She allowed the male to lead her onto the floor, and as he clasped her hand, she bit back a gasp. His skin was damn near frozen. She wasn't even sure how it was possible for him to still be breathing. One hand came to rest on her waist, and even then the frigid feel of his flesh bit through the loose blouse she wore. He guided her into a steady waltz, and not once did she take her eyes off his face. His lips twitched, as though he was trying to speak, to communicate with her, but his mouth never opened. But as he stared down at her, she couldn't help but think his mind was still intact, that he was very much aware of what he was being forced to do. Or worse, that he possibly knew what was going to happen next.

The soup curdled in her stomach, causing her insides to sour.

"Now, you may be wondering how I acquired such lovely dancers, considering most of these abhorrent creatures are practically peasants." The legs of Parisa's chair grated against the gilded tile floor and she stood. Maeve glanced over her shoulder as the fae who healed her in the torture room entered the dining hall, rolling a silver cart. A white cloth was spread over the top of the cart, and five tiny daggers were laid out in a row. Next to them was a bottle with a cork stopper, the insides swirling with an inky potion. "These fae fancy themselves to be artisans, shop owners, and crafters. But their magic is mundane, just like their pathetic lives. For example, your dance partner is the son of a winemaker."

Parisa cackled and Maeve's heart stilled.

She looked up into the face of the male once more, searching, until the faint traces of familiarity stole the air from her lungs. His features were similar, but less pronounced by his youth. She'd rescued his father and younger brother from the Hagla when the Summer Court had been overrun by Spring fae desperate to escape Parisa's clutches.

A pang lodged deep inside of her, filling her with a tumultuous ache.

He hadn't been able to escape with his family.

"What are they doing here?" Maeve asked, already dreading the answer.

"I'm so glad you asked." Parisa glided over toward the silver cart, the sharp angles of her face illuminated by the glow of the *virdis lepatite*. "You might remember a little substance I've been working on. I believe your brother used it on you some time ago, yes?"

Maeve blanched.

Garvan.

He'd stabbed her with that seemingly insignificant blade, yet it had been potent enough to render her absolutely useless against him.

The fae spun her around, edging her closer to Parisa.

"Ever since then," Parisa continued, her voice becoming more gravelly, "I've been working on perfecting it. There's been a little trial and error, and unfortunately some rather severe side effects. But I believe I'd nearly got the right dosage for the desired effect."

"What are you talking about?"

The male tightened his hold on Maeve, and she glanced back up at him. His eyes were coated with a misty sheen. Tears.

"The potion I created was intended to control both the body and mind, much like the magic of your beloved High King." Her lips pursed as she pulled out the cork stopper from the bottle on the tray. She lifted one dagger, then slid the blade into the potion, giving it a little swirl. "It seems, however, not all fae are able to tolerate the injection. Some of them maintain control of their minds, like your dancing partner, but most of them...well, let's just say they've gone a bit mad."

"Mad?" Maeve repeated numbly. "Mad, how?"

She tried to disentangle herself from the dance, but the fae's grip locked around her with unmatched strength, as though his hands were fused to her. She stumbled as he hauled her into another spin, unable to break free from his grasp. Panic bubbled to the surface, and she fought to get away from him. But his fingers dug deep into her waist, bruising her. Tears slipped from the corners of his honeyed eyes.

"Crazed, my pet. Their minds are empty voids, they lack any form of self control." Parisa eyed the blade in her hand, inspecting its grayish gleam. The air was once again heavy with the suffocating scent of nearly rotten cherries, and Maeve tried not to gag. "I know it sounds wonderful, considering they're all under my control, but they've become addicted to this new substance, and I simply can't produce it fast enough to appease them."

Maeve was reeling, valiantly attempting to process everything Parisa had unloaded upon her. She'd experimented on the fae of her own court, on innocent lives. And she'd *ruined* them. She'd turned them into mindless addicts of something beyond her control, and the fae who managed to stay strong enough were trapped here in the palace to do her bidding. All while being aware that their bodies were no longer their own.

"Where are they?" Fury enraged Maeve and she whipped her head around to face Parisa. "These fae you've poisoned? What have you done with them?"

"That's for me to know, and you to find out." Parisa spread her palms wide. The dagger was gone. "It is too bad so much potential was wasted, but in reality, I only need one good batch."

There was a violent tug on the iron cuff encircling Maeve's neck and she was yanked backward. She clawed at it, gasping as the cold metal cut off her air supply.

Something sharp and painful lodged itself in Maeve's back and she yelped, her spine arching. She'd been stabbed. No, that wasn't right. *Injected.*

Maeve whirled around, the colors smearing together as her vision blurred. Gromede was there, the edges of his hideous face distorted, and in his hand was the blade Parisa had dipped into her bottle of poison. She swayed on her feet, losing feeling in her arms and legs. Her tongue felt thick, her eyelids heavy. An icy sensation flooded her veins, cold and slinking. It slithered through her, seizing her muscles, coiling around her like a vise.

Her magic hissed in return, lashing out at the intrusion, a violent clash of dark and light. Flames roared to life, plumes of smoke gathered in reckless abandon, and the lifeblood of creation clawed its way to the surface, scouring past the cold metal holding her power hostage. The iron around her neck clamped even tighter and Maeve convulsed, her body and her magic victim to the darkness owning her, burrowing deeper inside of her with every passing second.

The frozen dark magic sluiced its way into her mind, searching for any opening, any way to breach the wall Maeve had constructed around her thoughts. To protect herself from Parisa's assault.

"How does it feel?" Parisa's voice echoed, jarring. It was as though Maeve could feel the length of her nails scraping along the wall, looking for a sign of weakness, any possible flaw or break. *"Knowing that there's nothing you can do to stop me? Knowing that I can control your every move, your every thought?"*

"Not my thoughts." Maeve fought back, she would not fall to Parisa. Not here. Not ever. She would fight every hour of every day, until she died, before she ever gave up.

"No matter," Parisa waved one hand through the air in dismissal. "You'll just be fully aware of everything you do instead."

Maeve stumbled forward, her body moving according to Parisa's will. Again, she fought. She clenched her muscles, grappling for control, and locking them in place. Her legs convulsed, her arms flung out to the sides, then dropped. The dark magic grew colder, churning her blood, turning it into slivers of ice. She dug her heels in, refusing to yield. Her head snapped to the right as though she'd been slapped, her back arched with brutal force.

"I am not your puppet," she ground out, her jaw aching with each word. "You will not break me."

Blood pooled in her mouth, and she spat.

Parisa's gaunt face had hardened into stone. Irritation caused her eyes to flare with rage. She raised one hand, her knobby fingers flitting through the air in a dismissive wave. "Kill him."

Gromede grabbed Maeve's wrist and pressed the solid hilt of a dagger with a curved blade into her palm. Her hand closed around it uncontrollably.

"Kill him," Parisa repeated, her gaze latching onto the son of the winemaker, the innocent fae who'd been forced to dance with Maeve. "Carve out his heart."

"No." Maeve's grip tightened on the dagger. Parisa's magic consumed her, flooding her like the hand of death. Her arm trembled as she raised it higher. Higher. The tip of the blade aimed straight for the fae's heart. She grit her teeth.

He stood there, unable to move. Unable to flee. Tears streamed down his face, and he trembled in the knowledge his fate was nearly sealed. She could almost hear him. Praying, begging to any god or goddess to rescue him. His sorrowful eyes, so much like honey, met hers, imploring her. Willing her to fight. To save him. To save herself. To save them all.

"KILL HIM!" Parisa shrieked, her dark magic surging into Maeve.

"Never!" Maeve spun around just as her blade slashed through the air. The sound of metal sliding through flesh echoed through the dining hall, and Maeve knew she met her mark. With one yank, she ripped the dagger from Gromede's throat. Gurgling black blood spurted from the wound like a fountain, splattering on her face and clothes. The wretched fae staggered once, then toppled to the ground. Lifeless.

"Sorry," Maeve muttered, clutching the dagger in her fist. "You didn't specify *who*."

Parisa's howl was deafening. Then she lunged forward across the table, tossing one arm out in front of her.

Maeve flew backward, colliding into half of the dancing fae and knocking them down, before slamming into the wall behind her. Her head hit hard, cracking loudly, as splintering pain reverberated through her skull and down her neck. She blinked, her vision swimming against the throbbing anguish. Maeve loosed a startled cry as an invisible force dragged her away from the wall, only to toss her into it again with more force. This time, it was the breaking of her bones that ricocheted through her ears. She spasmed. Gasping. Wheezing. Icy cold blood slid from her mouth down to her chin. Agonizing torment ripped through her, and she crumpled to the ground, her back thoroughly broken.

Parisa's wails had grown dull. Distant.

Or perhaps it was Maeve who was fading away into nothingness.

"Get that bitch out of my sight," Parisa snarled.

Maeve's breathing grew shallow. Slowly, her palm opened, and the dagger tumbled soundlessly from her hand. She didn't know if Parisa still had control of her body, and she didn't care. She couldn't feel anything, anyway. Just a stark, terrifying numbness. Darkness lined the outskirts of her vision, weaving closer together with every painfully slow blink until the light was no more.

Until she was no more.

Despair swept through her. Death called to her like an old friend.

His voice was low, and velvety when he said, *"Not today, Dawnbringer."*

Chapter Twenty-One

awn crested over the horizon, and Tiernan did not sleep.

The witch thread burned like fire, searing his skin, and through the bond he felt indistinct waves of agony. Of pain. Of suffering. Maeve was injured again, yet somehow this was worse than before. More severe. It fueled him with indescribable rage, with a fury unlike anything he'd ever known. Tumultuous clouds churned over head, shuttering out the early morning light. Thunder cracked, a deafening noise, as the twin mountains trembled before his wrath. Lightning shattered the sky, illuminating the darkened heavens with violent magic. Punishing gusts of wind barreled into him, through him, as the catastrophic storm intensified.

Tiernan clenched his jaw, the last fibers of his control wavering.

Godsdammit, he should be there with her. He should have done more to protect her, to keep her from falling into Parisa's clutches.

This was all his fault.

He jerked his arm back, then whipped around, slamming his fist into the nearest palm tree. It bowed against the brute force, then snapped completely, its mighty crown of fronds tumbling to the ground in defeat.

Tiernan sensed Merrick's presence a second later.

"What is it with you and your mate beating up on these innocent palm trees?" he asked through a stifled yawn.

Tiernan faced his hunter.

Merrick leaned against the far wall of the courtyard, and though his words hinted at the promise of a taunt, all traces of humor had vanished from his face. His hair was a mess, the single streak of hot pink tangled with strands of white, as though he'd just rolled out of bed. He stood with his arms crossed, easily taking the assault of the storm that continued to rage, his expression unreadable.

A rush of magic confronted Tiernan, a great calm that soothed the volatile chaos threatening to consume him, as Ceridwen *faded* into the courtyard with Brynn right behind her.

Ceridwen slowly approached him, folding her feathery robe around her as the wind assailed them both.

"It's a bit early for a storm, is it not?" she asked quietly, her gentle voice carrying to him. She glamoured herself a steaming cup of tea, frowning as she looked up to the roiling sky. Then her gaze found him, her eyes narrowing. "Tier, have you even slept?"

"I have not." He bit the words out through gritted teeth. How could he sleep while Maeve was being tortured? The thought of rest, while knowing his *sirra* was suffering, caused bile to scald his stomach. "I will not."

Ceridwen tilted her head, studying him. She took a small sip of tea. "You'll be of no use to anyone if you're exhausted. What good is magic if it's depleted?"

Her words, always so clever, gave Tiernan pause. Gradually, the storm waned, the angry clouds rolling back to reveal slivers of golden sunlight.

From the corner of his eye, he saw the shadows arrive. They crawled across the courtyard, scaling the walls and sliding from behind the palms, before gathering a few feet from him. Rowan stepped from them, clad in black armor, looking as though he, too, had not slept.

Not that Tiernan could blame him.

Ceridwen's gaze sharpened, flicking between them both. "What's going on? What are you planning?"

Tiernan rolled his shoulders back, knowing that whatever he said next was either going to fill his sister with dread or spark her own temper. "We're going into Suvarese to retrieve Maeve."

"What?" An emotion banked in her eyes, but she blinked and it was gone.

Merrick strode up, his arms still crossed, a hard line etched into his brow. "Who's *we*?"

"Myself, Rowan, and Casimir." Tiernan didn't miss the shared looks between his twin, his hunter, and his healer. "I know it sounds like a risk—"

"That's an understatement," Merrick muttered.

"But," Tiernan continued, "both Rowan and Casimir are familiar with the Spring Court. As well as its dungeon. They've rescued Maeve once before, and they're our best chance at doing so again."

Merrick cocked a brow.

"What," he said, gesturing between Tiernan and Rowan, "are you two friends now?"

"Not friends," Rowan murmured, adjusting the chest piece of his armor.

"But also not enemies," Tiernan added, and Rowan offered him a slight nod in agreement.

Brynn moved closer, concern knitting across her brow as the heavens lightened even further. "How are you going to get in undetected?"

Rowan stepped forward, tucking his hands behind his back. "With illusion, my lady."

She balked, her eyes widening. "Illusion? That power belonged to Parisa."

He bowed regally. "And now it belongs to me."

"Since when?" Merrick countered cooly.

The corner of Rowan's mouth lifted into his usual mocking smirk. "Since Aed saw fit to give it to me."

"Wait a minute." Brynn stomped forward and jabbed Rowan squarely in the chest. "If you can cast illusions, then that night in Spring, when..."

"When swords fell from the sky like rain?" Rowan supplied for her.

Brynn lowered her arm. "Was that real?"

"Yes. Very real." While Rowan's face remained impassive at the mention of the memory, a deep pain diminished some of the light from his eyes. "That was Parisa's magic, not mine."

"Okay, so you three go into the Spring Court under an illusion." Merrick scrubbed a hand over his face, his shoulders slumping. "Then what?"

Tiernan opened his mouth, then shut it. Unfortunately, he hadn't considered what they would do next. He assumed they would just figure it out once they got there.

"And what about Casimir?" Ceridwen sipped her tea, eyeing him over its floral porcelain rim. "Will he be in drakon form?"

"Ah..." Damn it. They hadn't discussed when Casimir would shift.

Brynn glanced quickly over her shoulder, scouring the general vicinity. When she spoke, her voice was lower. "And what do we tell Saoirse?"

Fuck.

Perhaps they didn't have a plan after all.

Rowan pressed the tips of his fingers to his temples. "So many questions."

"And yet, not enough answers," Ceridwen replied smoothly, the corners of her lips curving into an impish smile.

"Alright, I understand our plan is rudimentary at best. Parisa is still in control of the Sluagh, not to mention she has a multitude of mindless drugged fae, though there's no way of knowing what she's planning to do with them. As for the Spring Court itself, we'll be lucky if anything remains." Tiernan roughed a hand along his jaw. "We're going in blind."

"But?" Ceridwen prompted.

Rowan cut in. "But the longer Maeve is with Parisa, the more of a liability she becomes."

"Not to mention she's being tortured," Tiernan muttered. Just speaking the words out loud gutted him.

Every pair of eyes landed on him.

"It's the witch thread." Tiernan meant to sound firm, but his voice was barely a hoarse whisper. "I can still feel her through the bond. It's faint, but it's there. Her pain. Her suffering. I know Parisa is tormenting her, and I cannot...I cannot stand by and do nothing."

Guilt ravaged him. Every minute, every hour that crept by carved out a piece of his soul. He would never forgive himself for letting her storm off into those godsforsaken woods. Not when he could have prevented it, when he could have saved her.

"I can't leave her there, Cer." He met his twin's sorrowful eyes. "It's not like when she was in the Ether."

He stole a glance at Rowan, who lowered his gaze.

"If we wait until Wenfyre and Brackroth arrive..." Tiernan swallowed, and a stabbing pain pierced his heart. "There may not be anything left of her to save."

Rowan stepped up next to him, placing one hand on Tiernan's shoulder. "We don't have a defined plan. But we're going in to get her, and we're not leaving without her."

A swift shadow cut across the sky, and the shape of a dragon took form, soaring through the wisps of clouds. It circled overhead, then swooped low, its massive wings beating back the palm trees and kicking up bits of sand and debris as it landed within the courtyard. Mist swirled around the beast in a flurry of magic as it shifted from dragon to human.

Casimir appeared a moment later with two swords strapped to his waist. His hood was pulled low, concealing most of his face, and he stepped toward them, his footfalls echoing quietly in the stillness of the early hour.

"My ladies." He bowed to Ceridwen and Brynn, then turned to Tiernan and Merrick. "My lords."

Casimir adjusted his hood, pushing it back slightly. His dark gaze snagged on Rowan. He eyed the Nightweaver with interest, his brows lifting slightly. "You're not bringing a weapon?"

Rowan shoved his hands into the pockets of his leather pants and rocked back on his heels, an arrogant smirk tugging at the corner of his mouth. "I am the weapon."

Fucking fae.

That kind of cocky attitude was going to get him killed—again—if he wasn't careful.

Brynn again looked to the sky, where splashes of pink and gold were bleeding into a slate blue. "Aren't you worried about trying to get inside Suvarese during the day?"

"The sun no longer shines in the Spring Court." Casimir's

tone was flat, lacking any real emotion, as though he knew there was nothing left for him there. Not even a fallen faerie princess. "The constant rain, mist, and generally abysmal weather will work in our favor."

Brynn nodded, but worried her bottom lip anyway.

Something cold and wet brushed against Tiernan's palm, and he glanced down to find Cahira, Maeve's *faolan* pup, staring up at him with crystal blue eyes. The wolfling whined, nuzzling against him once more.

"I know." Tiernan hesitated, then reached down and ruffled a hand through Cahira's soft, white fur. "I'll bring her home."

Cahira loosed a woeful howl, and Brynn crouched down to comfort the wolfling.

"When are you leaving?" Merrick asked.

Tiernan glanced over at Rowan and Casimir, then looked back at his hunter. "Now."

Ceridwen's teacup vanished, and she blew out a shuddering breath. Merrick absently reached for her hand, drawing her into his side.

"Merrick, keep your scouts vigilant. Protect the borders, and utilize the Furies...if you can find them." Tiernan hadn't seen either of them since Maeve was taken. "Brynn, you're in charge of the archers and the entire legion until Lir returns to full health."

"You make it sound like that might take longer than expected." Ceridwen wrapped her free hand around Merrick's wrist.

Tiernan nodded. "It might."

"And if you're not back by the time the druids of Wenfyre arrive?" she asked, worry clouding her twilight eyes. "What then? What do I tell Dorian and Ciara?"

It was the outcome he feared above all the rest.

He held his twin's gaze as he said, "Carry on without us, and assume the worst."

Brynn shoved to her feet and went to Ceridwen's other side. Though she was smiling, her eyes were changing colors far too quickly—blue, to gold, to deep brown, and then red—a testament to the emotions firing through her. "Fear not, my lady. He's always this downhearted before the start of battle."

Suddenly, Merrick straightened, morphing back into the role of esteemed warrior. The air was charged with energy, an understanding. He bowed stiffly. "Fair winds, *moh Rí*."

Tiernan couldn't bring himself to stay any longer, to look at them, to draw out the goodbye.

Without another word, Rowan dissolved into the shadows, Casimir shifted back into his drakon form, and Tiernan *faded* away to the Pass of Veils.

THE OUTSKIRTS of the Pass of Veils had not changed.

Situated between the Spring and Summer Courts, the entrance was nestled at the base of the mountains, just along the outer edge of Summer's most northern reaching forest. To the west was Spring, still covered with the veil of impenetrable magic Parisa had put in place. Just as the mural had shown Tiernan, there was a break in the shroud. A fissure. A weakness cutting directly through the mountain pass itself, which would hopefully allow them to enter the Spring Court undetected.

The Pass of Veils was eerily silent.

Despite being brought back to life with Maeve's return to Faeven, it seemed no creatures had ventured here. There was no birdsong, no scurrying of animals, not even a whisper of the wind. Only a stoic kind of silence, as though the mountains and trees were watching, keeping their secrets of the land closely guarded.

Tiernan found his gaze drawn to a patch of earth not far from him, where the ground still looked fresh with overturned dirt. Where Maeve had buried a trooping fae alive with nothing more than a flick of her hand.

"What's the plan, High King?"

He turned to see Casimir stalking out of the wooded forest, Rowan following in his wake with a trail of shadows behind him.

Tiernan addressed them both.

"Rowan will cast an illusion around us, so any who pass by will see nothing out of the ordinary. Just the drab façade of Suvarese." He stole a hasty glance at the Nightweaver. "No offense."

Rowan lifted both hands. "None taken."

"And then?" Casimir asked, his dark gaze scanning the silent forest and the rugged mountains towering above them.

"Once we're safely within the shroud, I'll locate Maeve through the bond of witch thread." Tiernan looked to the Pass of Veils, where the mist seemed to move and breathe of its own accord. "Though I have a feeling we already know where to find her."

"The dungeon," Rowan confirmed, nodding to Casimir. "I know the way in, as I'm sure you do as well."

Casimir tightened the belt at his waist, ensuring each of his swords was easily accessible. "I'll get us out, same as I did with Maeve the last time."

Tiernan wasn't foolish enough to believe it had been easy the first time. He knew Casimir had paid a steep price for getting Maeve out of the dungeon, even if he was the reason she'd been there in the first place. Parisa had likely brought her wrath upon the drakon for his betrayal, and knowing her, she'd shown no mercy. This time would be far more difficult. They would have to tread with extreme caution—one misstep, one wrong move, and all would be lost.

"Rowan," Tiernan regarded the Nightweaver with valid concern, "can your magic shift and alter to our surroundings?"

Rowan ran one thumb along his jaw, angling his head. "There's only one way to find out."

That was not quite the answer Tiernan had been hoping for, but it would have to suffice.

He had to remain calm and keep a clear mind. It was the only way to guarantee Maeve's safety.

"We will get to the dungeon under Rowan's illusion. Once we have Maeve, there will be no time to waste." Tiernan's heart hollowed out. He knew the risks, understood them, welcomed them. Just as he knew he was going after Maeve for a cause greater than his love for her. There was more at stake than their chance at a happy ending. "If we're discovered, the goal remains the same. Rescue Maeve and get her back to Niahvess, no matter the cost."

"I cannot *fade* and Parisa would like nothing better than to see my head on a spike." Casimir stood tall, his face impassive, like that of a battle-hardened warrior. "My fate was written in the stars long ago. If the worst happens, I will stay behind, and fight until my death."

"As will I." Tiernan knew it would come down to this. He realized what he was doing, what he *would* do, the second he asked Rowan for his help. Faeven stood a better chance at survival with the Nightweaver at the helm of the impending war than with him. It was the only way. He met Rowan's gaze then, and the gravity of the situation pulled taut between them. "If we fail, take Maeve into the shadows. Get her as far away from here as possible. Do you understand?"

Rowan bowed his head. "On my honor, my lord."

Tiernan turned, facing the Pass of Veils. Maeve was somewhere within that damned Court, and he would ruin everything in his path to find her.

Glancing over his shoulder, he nodded to Rowan and Casimir.

Magic amplified, the dense scent of orange blossom and cedarwood hung heavy in the air. Tiernan glamoured his armor, strengthening it, fortifying it. Two swords appeared by his side, the crest of Niahvess—twin mountain peaks with the sun rising between them—was emblazoned upon the cobalt blue leather covering his chest. Casimir ducked his head, his shoulders bunching in preparation for whatever they would face, and in Rowan's hand, glowing with enough force to shatter the moonlight, was the Astralstone.

The Nightweaver's illusion descended upon them, ensconcing them. The world shimmered as it disguised them, as they bled into the emptiness of slate mountains, sodden footpaths, and the curl of pulsing mist.

At once, they started their trek into the Pass of Veils.

Tiernan led the way, calm and steady, ready to make the ultimate sacrifice for his *sirra*. For his mate. For his queen.

Chapter Twenty-Two

Maeve was lost to delirium, trapped in a dream-like state, somewhere between life and death.

She wondered if perhaps this was how Ceridwen felt whenever she had one of her visions, alive, yet not quite coherent. On the brink of something altogether...*other*. Something not quite of this world.

"Maeve."

The masculine voice resonated through the fog clouding her mind. It was vaguely familiar, one she recognized. Soothing, like a dark lullaby. It made her want to curl beneath a blanket and fall asleep, drift off into an oblivion where there was nothing and no one, save for the solace of her dreams.

"Maeve." The disembodied voice called to her again, firmer this time.

She groaned, slowly blinking her eyes open.

Prone on her back, she stared up at the figure hovering above her until he became clear. Silver eyes swirling with power gazed down at her. Long black hair tipped with white framed a handsome face and a strong jawline. A line of concern furrowed across his brow and he bent closer to her, gently cupping her cheek with his smooth palm.

She squinted up at the god of death. "Am I dead?"

"Not yet." His eyes flashed. "Though why is that always the first question you ask me?"

Arching one brow, she pierced him with a knowing look, and his hand fell away. "I can think of one good reason."

He offered her a smile, but there was no humor behind it.

Maeve eased herself up onto her elbows, glancing around her. This place was unlike any she had ever seen, if it could even be called a place at all. There was nothing but low-lying mist as far as the eye could see. There were no trees, no mountains, no buildings, just a vast expanse of nothingness. Clouds swirled across the sky in shades of gray, reminding her vaguely of the mural in Tiernan's library. They moved in an almost reckless manner, coiling and unfurling without reason.

Her gaze slid back to the god of death. "Where am I?"

"Somewhere safe." His expression shifted then, more severe than she'd ever seen it, as though he was holding back the full wrath of his power from her. "Where she cannot reach you."

Maeve peered into the endless abyss of mist again. Nothing was recognizable. "But, where?"

Aed bent down, sliding two hands under her arms, and slowly lifted her to a standing position. Her knees quaked, and a tremble raced down her spine, but there was no pain.

"Easy," he murmured, locking one arm around her waist to keep her upright. "You're in between worlds, in a place of my creation. Your body is still in the palace of Suvarese, but here you only see me. You will only hear me. But more than that, you will not *feel*."

Confusion left her disoriented. How was it he could prevent her from feeling? Coolness radiated from him, and she was certain that was not a figment of her imagination. She could move her arms and legs, and knew her heart continued to beat. And she could definitely feel the weight of his hand pressed to her waist.

Then she remembered.

Parisa had been furious because Maeve had killed Gromede. She'd attacked her brutally. Her back had been broken, her spine shattered. The pain had been unimaginable. Like being set on fire and being drowned all at once. It had stolen both her breath and her will to survive.

Oh.

Clarity struck her like a chord, and she looked up at Aed. He did not meet her gaze, but his hand moved from her waist to her arm, looping them together as he started to walk. She realized it then. He was saving her from suffering, he was taking away all the pain she would feel were she still conscious.

"How long do I have?" she asked quietly. "Before I have to go back?"

"Not long, I'm afraid." He continued to stare straight ahead, and the mist at their feet moved for him as they walked. "These types of interferences aren't made to last."

They walked on in companionable silence. But with every step, the mist seemed to thicken until it was almost impenetrable. Aed continued to guide her, weaving them through the dense fog as though he knew exactly where they were going. She would never have thought to call the god of death her friend, yet now she supposed that was the exact sort of relationship that was developing between them. He'd never been her enemy, not truly, though calling him her ally seemed too bold. After all, gods and goddesses never gave anything freely.

Surely he would expect something in return.

"Why?" Maeve asked suddenly.

Again, he didn't look at her. "Why what?"

She hesitated, worried she might offend him, but knew she would have to ask lest she be bound to some unknown bargain with him. "Why are you...helping me?"

This time, Aed stopped in his tracks. He turned to face her, gathering both of her hands in his large grasp. His silver eyes burned bright with an emotion she didn't understand. "There comes a time when even the boldest of us cower. When the strongest of us break. A soul can only take so much. So much anger, pain, sorrow, and regret, before there is nothing left."

He let go of her hands, then stepped back from her.

"Find the good pieces. The joy and pleasure of life, the love and forgiveness." He smiled, his face devastatingly handsome once more. "Find the good, Maeve. And never bow. Never break."

The edges of him began to blur, fading in and out of focus. Maeve's vision grew fuzzy and she reached for him, grabbing nothing but mist. "Aed?"

"Never bow." His smooth baritone was a cold whisper against her cheek. "Never break."

"Aed!" she cried out, flinching as the strange dream world evaporated around her awoke to find herself lying flat on her stomach. Her body ached, her bones heavy with exhaustion, but the excruciating pain had subsided. The iron cuff was still snug around her neck, an uncomfortable reminder that she remained a prisoner in Parisa's Court, her freedom far from reach.

It appeared as though she was on a mattress, but it was incredibly hard like stone, and not at all comfortable. Her bleary gaze trekked around the room while she tried to discern where she was now. Soft light flickered from the dozens of candles clustered together on small wooden shelves, their drips of wax melting into puddles on each surface. Bundles of dried yarrow and willow hung along the wall across from her, and just beneath was a table piled with medicinal ointments and jars of herbal salves. The scent of lavender and mint coated the air, so heavy she could almost taste it.

Maeve groaned, struggling to push herself off the solid mattress, when a gentle feminine voice came from somewhere above her.

"Be still." Warm, weathered fingers lightly brushed her hair back from her face. "We're almost done."

Straining to see, Maeve caught a glimpse of a dingy emerald tunic from the corner of her eye. Another Spring fae, and given her current surroundings, possibly a healer.

"There we go." A new voice, male this time, a rich tenor with the faintest of lilts. "Let's get her up and see how she feels."

Maeve felt like she'd been buried beneath a pile of boulders.

They helped her into a sitting position, and Maeve squeezed her eyes shut to quell the rush of nausea. When she finally opened her eyes again, she came face-to-face with two fae. The female had kind eyes that crinkled around the edges when she smiled, and her long onyx hair was twisted back into a low ponytail at the nape of her neck. Her deep tan skin was flushed, and a dark rosy hue colored her high cheekbones. The male, however, looked as though he had never even seen the sun. His skin was pasty and ashen, but his green eyes were bright. He wore his dark brown hair tugged into a lopsided knot on the top of his head, and was dressed in a similar green tunic as the female.

"Goodness." The female swiped the back of her hand across her forehead and sucked in a deep breath. "I wasn't sure you were ever going to regain consciousness."

Maeve opened her mouth to thank them, but her words came out as more of a croak.

"Easy does it, love." The male shuffled over to the table behind him, grabbing a pitcher and a small glass, then poured it full of water. "You must be dying of thirst. You've been unconscious for a few hours."

He brought the glass back to her, carefully lifting it to her lips to help her drink.

Cool, refreshing water slid down Maeve's throat.

"I appreciate your kindness." She paused, waiting for that terrifying, slimy sensation of dark magic to fill her once more. When it failed to return, she glanced up at the fae. "But...the venom?"

"It was a necessary extraction to heal you in time," the female stated, folding her arms around her. "The Dark Queen's potion has a bad habit of inhibiting healing magic."

"I must say, your back was some of my best work." The male returned the glass to the table, worrying his bottom lip between his teeth. "I was able to repair your spine and heal the wounds from your lashing. Now, there shouldn't be any scarring. At least, not physically. But mentally..."

His voice trailed off and Maeve was grateful for it.

She held out both of her arms, inspecting herself. The pain in her back had diminished almost completely, and it looked as though the Spring healers had seen fit to clean her up as well. She was in a pair of brown leather leggings with boots that strapped up to her knees, and a loose-fitting white blouse that laced down the back.

Seconds ticked by and she silently debated seeing if she'd be able to glean any kind of information from them, when something the female said prodded at the back of her mind.

"I'm sorry." Maeve shook her head and her golden pink hair tumbled forward. "You mentioned I needed to be healed in time...for what, exactly?"

A look of caution passed between the two fae.

"We've said too much," the male grunted, and started gathering up his supplies.

"No, wait." Maeve stood abruptly, then swayed. "Please."

The female took hold of her wrist, leading her to a small wooden stool in the center of the room. Maeve grabbed her hand, she wasn't above begging. "Surely you can give me something, anything, to help me prepare."

The male simply shook his head and headed for the door. The female, however, lingered. She placed a hand on Maeve's shoulder, gently encouraging her to sit. Resigned, Maeve lowered herself onto the stool.

"Heed my words, Dawnbringer. There is nothing I can give you that will ever prepare you for what you are about to face." The female lowered her gaze to the stone floor and backed away. "Rest now, for you will need all of your strength."

Suddenly, there was a loud clanking noise, like the grinding of metal. Grit and dust rose from the ground in a cloud of debris. Maeve's lungs seized, and she coughed against the assault. She covered her nose and mouth with her blouse, tugging it upward to shield her face, and then she caught sight of the floor.

It was *moving*.

The large stone square beneath her feet was inching upward, rising from the base of the room. Higher and higher it lifted up from the floor while the light from the small room slowly diminished. The horrible noise continued, grating against her ears as the ceiling drew closer. Panicked, she slid off of the stool, knocking it from the raised stone. She cowered down on her hands and knees, peering over the edge as her heart leapt into the back of her throat.

"What are you doing?" Maeve's gaze shot to the ceiling, where she was certain to be crushed. "What's happening?"

But she could no longer see the room or the fae, and soon she imagined she wouldn't see anything ever again.

Crouching as low as possible, she held her breath and shielded her arms over her head, waiting for impact.

The cool rush of air greeted her instead.

Maeve glanced up to see the ceiling had opened as well. There was another deafening clang. The ground came to a jarring stop, and she found herself surrounded by mist. She was...outside.

"What the..."

Walking in a small circle, she took stock of her surroundings. Much like the dream world with Aed, the heavy mist impaired most of her vision. The skies were barely visible, gray and overcast by a thick blanket of clouds. A steady mist drizzled down, dampening her clothes and hair. There were no signs of life—no rustling of leaves or scurrying of wildlife, not even the familiar song of the breeze. Just an all-encompassing silence.

Chills raked across her flesh.

She took a wary step forward, and a shiver of warning raced down her spine. Mindful of what little she *could* see, Maeve edged her way through the mist, and walked right into a metal bar.

Wincing, she rubbed her fingers over her forehead.

"No," she whispered, her voice harsh. She stumbled back, swallowing the rise of anxiety threatening to consume her. Slowly raising one hand, she cut back and forth through the thick mist, the tinkling of metal echoing against the tips of her nails.

Alarm caused her heart to hammer, and her chest caved inward.

"No!" she shouted, louder this time.

The metal bars curved upward, and she darted in the other

direction, away from them. Only to find the same bars mocking her, holding her hostage. Surrounding her on all sides.

She was locked in a cage.

"No!" Dread coiled inside of her, and she grabbed the bars with both hands. "Don't leave me here!"

Rattling them, she screamed into the void. "Let me out! Someone! Anyone! Please, let me out!"

Maeve raked her fingers through her hair, wild with panic. Not again. Sun and sky, she could not live through this again. She stepped back a few paces, then surged forward, ramming her shoulder into the metal. "Not a cage! Not a cage!"

But there was no sound, save for the erratic beating of her heart, and the echo of her shallow breathing. This wasn't like the dungeon beneath the palace of Spring, this was like that awful memory from her past. The one she tried so hard to overcome.

This was like back in Kells, like the cage dangling over the Cliffs of Morrigan where Carman left her as punishment. It was too much. She stumbled backward, padding lightly across the slab of stone. It may as well have been planks of rotted wood, for the trauma of her past crawled around her like the dense wall of mist, consuming her completely.

"Please, not a cage! Anywhere else, please!" Her voice was gravel, she couldn't get air. "*I beg of you!*"

Tiny beads of cool sweat slid down her neck, and Maeve dropped to the ground, curling her knees into her chest. She wrapped her arms around her legs, clinging to any shred of warmth, to the dying flicker of hope that burned inside her.

"Not the cage," she mumbled.

Find the good.

Aed's words echoed in her mind.

Do not bow. Do not break.

"Not the cage," she repeated to herself, over and over. Her

inner terror was louder than the god of death's reassuring voice. "Not the cage."

Maeve tipped her head back, allowing the sprinkle of rain to soothe her agony. But no matter how much she struggled to find the good, she couldn't drown out the groan of wind through cliffside trees, the snapping of an aged oak branch, or the roar of an angry ocean.

Chapter Twenty-Three

The veil shrouding the Spring Court was unlike anything Tiernan had ever encountered. Not mist, yet not fog, it was almost like walking through clouds. It was impossible to see beyond a few feet in front of him, and though the heady scent of magic lingered in the air, it was tainted. Pungent almost. Burnt cedarwood and rotten orange blossom melded together in a rancid stench. Dark magic throbbed against Rowan's illusion, pulsing as though it had a heartbeat of its own.

He could barely see them, but he knew sloping mountains rose up on either side of him. The Pass of Veils was nothing more than a worn footpath with a moderate incline that cut through the upper valley. Smaller trails veered off in other directions, many of them leading to the caves that housed sleeping giants, and he silently whispered his gratitude when he, Rowan, and Casimir traveled past them undetected.

Despite making it through without incident, the Pass of Veils itself was a grueling endeavor. Loose gravel coupled with damp earth caused their footing to slip, forcing them to slow their trek and take care. The poor visibility only impeded the journey, made worse by the constant shroud inhibiting their vision. Tiernan knew the trail was treacherous even on a good day. Ledges randomly dropped off, rockslides and poor weather conditions were a continuous threat. The last thing he wanted was for one of them to tumble accidentally off the side of a cliff and plummet to their death.

By the time they reached the end of the Pass of Veils, Tiernan's muscles ached. Tension coiled along his shoulders and down his back, a grueling kind of agony from sustaining a heightened sense of relentless vigilance.

The moment they entered the Spring Court, the shroud of dark magic lifted. The late afternoon sun was hidden behind a wall of dense clouds. A low-lying mist remained, crawling along the ground, and a steady drizzle of cold rain fell from the leaden sky. Tiernan raked a hand through his hair, sending droplets flying, as his gaze quickly scanned the forest to his left. The expanse of the woods was empty. Desolate. No living creatures thrived within the fallen Spring Court, no flowers bloomed beneath the dreary heavens. Even the trees looked to be in despair—their branches drooped, leaves falling from them slowly like broken emerald tears.

Tiernan stole a glance over his shoulder at Rowan. "How long has it been since you've been back?"

Rowan was silent for a moment. He inhaled, absently running a hand over his chest. "Since I helped rescue Maeve the last time she was captured."

"What about when I sent you away from Niahvess after removing your cuffs?" He'd told him to leave, he'd wanted Rowan as far away from Maeve as possible. "Where did you go then?"

Rowan's face shuttered, a hard line forming across his brow. "Not back here. I went to Ashdara. The Spring Court will always have my loyalty, as I swore my allegiance to it years ago. But Parisa...never again will I bow to her."

Casimir came around on Tiernan's other side, both of his swords firm in his grasp. "I'll take point from here. If we keep to the southwest, we should be able to make it safely to the palace and avoid the city altogether. There's a series of tunnels beneath the dungeon, and only one that leads from the base of the mountain to the outside."

Tiernan focused on the witch thread, on the bond tying him to Maeve. He could sense her, still alive, still breathing. There was a faint tug, but it wasn't in the direction of the palace like he'd expected. He shook his head. "No, that's not right."

"What do you mean?" Casimir studied him, his brown eyes darkening with concern. "It's the only way for us to get into the dungeon unnoticed."

"Casimir is right, my lord." Rowan nodded stiffly. "The dungeon is—"

Tiernan spoke before he could finish. "She isn't in the dungeon."

"What?" Casimir asked, brows lifting slightly.

Rowan edged closer, tossing a hasty glance behind him. "If she's not in the dungeon, then where is she?"

"Somewhere else..." Tiernan reached through the bond, searching for her. His blood hummed, her dull magic calling back to him like a lost melody. "She's near the palace, but not inside of it. And she is definitely no longer in the dungeon."

"This changes things." Rowan roughed a hand over his face, his mouth pressing into a thin line.

"Indeed," Casimir agreed. He blew out a breath, turning to face the direction of the palace. "We'd been planning for an escape from the dungeon because we assumed that's where she was being held."

"It's what the mural showed us." Angry shadows rippled around Rowan, and he quickly called them back.

"Parisa must have moved Maeve to another location." Tiernan wanted to punch something. Frustration wedged itself between them. He should have accounted for this, he should have known better than to assume he understood the workings of Parisa's mind. "She probably expected me, if not all of us, to come for her at some point."

Rowan sauntered over to the edge of the illusion, and the sphere of magic surrounding them shimmered. "You think we need to watch for traps."

It wasn't a question, but a statement of fact, and Tiernan was more than inclined to agree. "I think caution is our strongest ally."

"Then we should stick to the outer edge of Suvarese, along the forest." Casimir gestured to the dismal woods off to their left. "To be safe."

Following Casimir's direction, they maneuvered their way around the outlying buildings of the city. It was a far cry from the vibrancy of Niahvess. For what should've been a city teeming with life, Suvarese was abandoned, a wasteland caught in the trenches of war and despair. Not so long ago, the Crown City of the Spring Court was a thing of beauty. Homes and shops were painted in striking hues of jade, teal, and gold. Shimmering white rooftops curved like vines, and flowers of every color of the rainbow bloomed, overflowing from window boxes and along the numerous cobblestone roads. It was like looking at a diamond beneath a grimy layer of muck. The luster of Suvarese had simply faded away.

Storefronts were boarded up with their busted doors leaning awkwardly on broken hinges. All the homes were dark, many of them victims of decaying overgrowth and crumbling stone walls. From Tiernan's vantage point, it looked as though the city had been empty for quite some time.

"Where is everyone?" he asked, his voice barely above a whisper. "Surely not everyone was able to escape into Summer."

Rowan moved closer to the deserted city, his footfalls silent against the damp grass. "I've got a bad feeling about this."

Casimir threw his arm out, halting Rowan's progression. Soundlessly, he held one finger to his lips.

A moment later, a wolf trotted out from behind one of the buildings. Its mangy black fur was matted and covered in filth, but its yellow eyes were exceptionally keen. The wolf padded past them, sniffing the air, ears twitching. The scruff along the back of its neck rose slightly, and it loosed a low, guttural snarl. Yet the beast's gaze did not focus on them, instead it looked toward the tree line, to something else beyond sight.

Cautiously, Tiernan slipped into Rowan's mind. *"Can it sense us?"*

Rowan didn't move, he didn't even appear to acknowledge the fact that Tiernan had intruded upon his thoughts. But then his brow furrowed and Tiernan heard, *"I don't think so, my lord."*

There was a flutter in the air, the beating of wings, and a midnight raven circled overhead. It let out a jarring squawk before settling on one of the decrepit rooftops.

Rowan moved one hand through the air, amplifying his magic. The illusion intensified, masking their movements, muffling their voices.

Casimir jerked his head to the left, moving with stealth to the forest for cover, when another wolf appeared between the shadows of the trees.

Shit. This was not looking good.

Casimir backed up, one step at a time.

More squawking filled the unnatural silence, and Tiernan tore his gaze away from the second wolf only to discover more ravens had descended upon the roofs of the buildings. They flapped their wings in agitation, angling their heads so that their beady little eyes seemed to stare right through the illusion. A howl pierced the air, and Tiernan turned toward it. Apprehension twisted through him, squeezing like a vise, when he noticed a third wolf slinking along the outer edges of the ruined city.

"You don't find it odd," Tiernan muttered, fixated on the approaching wolf, "that there was not a single creature alive in the pass or the forest, and now there's more than a dozen."

Rowan's fingers hovered over the hilt of his Astralstone, tapping restlessly. His gaze darted to the city, the forest, and then back again. "Not as odd as the way those ravens up there act like they can see through my magic."

"You mean the ones that look like they're tracking our every move?" Tiernan unsheathed both of his swords in one fluid motion, and the hiss of metal sliding against leather echoed in his ears.

"The very ones," Rowan confirmed as another flock of ravens arrived. They moved together as one, circling and swooping, like a cloud of darkness.

"That's because they are," Casimir murmured, jerking his head toward the swarm of birds. He pulled his hood low, glancing over at Tiernan and Rowan. "Tracking us, that is."

He readied both of his weapons.

Fuck.

Without warning, another wolf emerged from further up the trail. This one snapped its vicious jaws, its growl reverberating all the way through to Tiernan's bones. He stole a hasty look over his shoulder to confirm what he'd already suspected—the other wolves had followed them. They must have been in a pack, there were at least six of them, and Tiernan realized they weren't being tracked.

They were being herded.

Leaning forward, he kept his voice barely above a whisper, so only Rowan and Casimir could hear him when he spoke. "We've got a problem."

"Yeah, we do." A scowl creased across Rowan's brow, and he withdrew the Astralstone.

Casimir crouched, lowering himself into an attack stance.

"Steady." Tiernan watched as Rowan's magic shimmered around them, ready to crash beneath the impending threat at any moment. "On my count."

The wolves inched closer.

"One."

Those fucking ravens wouldn't shut up.

"Two."

The wolf nearest them reared back on its haunches, preparing to lunge.

"Three!"

Rowan's illusion fell, and the three of them launched into the fray. Except it was worse than anything Tiernan could have expected. He wasn't prepared for it. None of them had been prepared.

The pack of wolves shifted at once, transforming from feral beasts into Puca, those bastard fae that crafted weapons and created portals. It was one thing to fight off a band of wolves. It was something else entirely to go up against well-trained fae who were more than capable of holding their own. The one closest to Tiernan growled, and curved horns appeared, protruding from the top of his head. Black veins bulged against his tanned flesh, and his mouth twisted into a ferocious snarl, revealing a set of uneven, jagged teeth. His clothing was shredded and singed, as though it'd been burnt.

Scars littered the Puca's arms, and he stalked toward Tiernan, twirling a sword whose blade glinted with the sheen of nightshade.

Lovely.

The clash of swords drowned out the noise from those insufferable birds. There was a rush of foul magic, so wretched it caused Tiernan's stomach to heave. He bit back the burn of bile and spun away from the Puca on his left as his blades cut through the air. From his other side, Rowan loosed a few choice words, calling upon a swell of shadows, while Casimir rolled across the ground to avoid a dagger to the heart. Tiernan dodged the next strike, stepping into the turn, so his sword sliced the Puca from his shoulder to his gut.

The Puca didn't appear at all bothered by the blood soaking his shirt, or that he'd been carved across his chest. He showed no signs of injury or fatigue, despite the gaping wound marring him. Instead, he lurched toward Tiernan once more, with an evil gleam in his eye. Violet lightning splintered through the tumultuous clouds as Tiernan's storm erupted. His blood pumped as his power collided with the crush of stifling dark magic.

At once, the flock of ravens took to the sky. Tiernan tried to avoid getting himself killed while being distracted by the peculiar spectacle taking place above him. The ravens flew in a pattern, circling around and around over Suvarese, soaring through the clouds and mist. Suddenly, their annoying squawks morphed into screeches of rage. Gangly limbs and dagger-like claws ripped free from their wings, their bodies elongated, and a violent throng of dark fae blocked out the remaining shreds of dim light.

"Look out!" Casimir shouted, as the dark fae ambushed them from all sides.

Diving downward, the dark fae split off in different directions, enclosing Tiernan, Rowan, and Casimir each in a chaotic whirlwind of frenzied magic, separating them.

"No!" Tiernan lurched toward Rowan, but he vanished behind a wall of feathers and darkness.

Struggling to regain his bearings, Tiernan swung at anything and everything. They were too fast, too quick for him to catch. Wings scraped against the leather of his armor as they flew around him at a dizzying speed. Claws snared in his hair, tugged on his legs, disorienting him. All he could see was an endless pitch as the dark fae swarmed him. His blade slashed through the air, tearing into battered wings and flesh. He squinted against the onslaught, staggering backward as sharp claws scratched at his face and ears.

But they weren't attacking with intent to harm.

They were taunting him. Toying with him.

Distracting him.

Something cold clamped around his wrists, draining him. His magic slipped from his grasp, waning, like he was being smothered by some unseen force. Tiernan jerked sideways, pulling away from the strange sensation, but his movements were dulled, and a metallic scent hung heavy in the air.

A smell he recognized all too well.

Iron.

Godsdammit.

It couldn't end like this, not with him being chained in iron. There had to be another way. Another possibility of escape. He would never bow before Parisa, he would never surrender his Court, he would never give up Maeve. Rage and renewed determination fired through him. Tiernan charged forward, despite the fact that the bite of iron was like fire against his flesh. He hoisted his swords, ready to demolish every fae, every creature that stood in his way.

But they vanished.

Evaporating in a flurry of feathers and smoke, as though they hadn't even existed.

Dark clouds continued to roil overhead and raindrops fell from the sky like ice. Through the rising mist, he saw Casimir across from him. His lips were busted and bleeding, crimson against the bronze of his skin. The fabric of his hood was torn and the pupils of his eye were vertical slits. It looked like he'd been attempting to shift into his dragon form before they snared him in iron. Behind him stood another Puca, his lips twisted into a sneer. By the looks of it, Casimir had gotten a few good hits on him. The skin beneath his eye was swollen, already turning a hideous shade of greenish-blue, and blood mottled his shirt and pants.

Rowan was off to the right, not a cut on the bastard. But a female Puca held him prisoner. She'd grabbed a fistful of his hair and yanked his head back, exposing his throat. The flat edge of her blade was pressed firmly against his flesh, and Tiernan caught the quick glint of silver on Rowan's wrists. He, too, had been bound in iron.

The female whispered something into Rowan's ear, and he jerked violently, his lavender gaze turning volatile. She cackled loudly, then choked, cowering slightly behind his frame.

"Well, well..."

Tiernan went completely still, his swords sliding from his grip.

Casimir paled, as though he'd just lost his soul.

And Rowan looked ready to set the world on fire.

Parisa glided through the haze of fog as the rain slashed across her features. A cape of heavy black velvet billowed around her, but even beneath its excessive frills, there was no mistaking the angular bones protruding from beneath the fabric. Her face was skeletal, gaunt and near ashen. Folds of skin seemed to slide down her face. What was left of her hair was stringy and gray, falling to her shoulders in thin wisps. Her lashes reminded him of spider legs, and she'd painted her lips a hideous bloodied shade that stretched wide when she attempted to smile.

Tiernan recoiled at the sight of her.

He should have attacked her then. He should have gathered up his swords from the ground, and plunged them right into her heart. He wanted to watch her die by his blade, he wanted to watch the life fade from her eyes as she paid retribution for all the terror she'd forced Maeve to endure. More than anything, he longed to destroy her, to cast her vile soul back into the Sluagh, to purge her from Faeven once and for all.

But the cold iron was quick to hold him in check, an unpleasant reminder that not only was he outnumbered, but now he was also outmatched.

"If it isn't three of my least favorite males." She moved slowly through the mist, the *virdis lepatite* pulsing at the base of her throat. "The treasonous ex-lover, the lovesick and fiercely loyal king, and the arrogant cousin who somehow lost his way."

Rowan laughed, but the sound of it was raw and grating. "I'll take that as a compliment."

Parisa glared at him, her lips curling in disgust. "Shut up. Before I cut out your tongue."

Tiernan had never actually witnessed Rowan back down before, but he imagined Parisa would make good on her promises.

"So, you've come to collect your precious princess, have you?" She strolled between them, her cape trailing behind her. "Isn't it curious how one female can command the love of all three of you?"

She paused in front of Casimir, tilting his chin up with the tip of her long fingernail as she inspected him. Her voice dripped with disdain as she spoke. "Redemptive love."

Parisa moved closer to Tiernan, running one finger along his jaw. He tensed and the iron clamped down, weakening him. She gave his cheek a little pat, smacking just hard enough for it to sting. "Timeless love."

She tossed Rowan a scathing look, then smirked, knowing her barb would strike true. "And the worst of all, unrequited love."

Rowan looked carved from stone but said nothing, merely watching his estranged cousin with an immense loathing.

"Such a pity you won't be able to steal her from me again," Parisa mused, moving back through the mist. She paused, then turned around to face all three of them. "But, since you're here, I may as well request the honor of your presence at the first annual BloodFest."

Tiernan's throat ran dry, and dread caused his fists to clench. "The what?"

"Never fear, Your Highness." She waved one bony hand through the air, her painted lips pulling back into a sinister smile. "You'll have a front-row seat."

Parisa nodded sharply.

The last thing Tiernan saw was the sickening gleam in her eyes before pain exploded along the side of his head, and everything went dark.

Chapter Twenty-Four

Eventually, the haunting sounds of Kells ebbed away into nothing more than a distant memory, but Maeve had yet to find the good. Or a way out. Or the way home.

She eased herself up from the ground, body trembling, aching from clutching her knees to her chest for so long. Agony swept through her, followed by a damning rush of despair.

The cage taunted her. Ridiculed her. Sent her back to those moments when she was an innocent mortal trapped in a world of hatred with a woman who would rather see her dead than alive. Maeve couldn't recall how many empty hours she'd spent alone in that cage over the Cliffs of Morrigan, praying she didn't fall to her death, crying herself to sleep until the sea spray from the ocean replaced her tears. Even the sky looked the same. Looming gray clouds blotted out the sun as it slowly crept toward the west.

"Let me out," she whispered into the mist. It churned and sifted, making it impossible to see anything. "Please, let me out."

The hairs along the back of her neck rose when an indistinct noise sounded from off to her right. She froze in place, straining to hear. Heavy footfalls were met with labored grunts and muttering. Holding her breath, she stepped closer toward the edge of the cage, her hands lightly wrapping around the cool bars as she peered into the thick haze of clouds. The resounding clank of metal echoed in her ears, and a figure emerged from the mist.

Maeve startled, backing away.

A Spring guard ambled toward her, his evergreen leathers scuffed and worn, the golden buckles at his waist tarnished. His face was lean, framed by disheveled brown hair that fell in uneven lengths to his shoulders. He looked as though he'd just returned from war, or perhaps he'd already seen too much and would not survive another. His brow was etched in a permanent line of mistrust, and there was the faintest sheen of wariness as he approached her. In one hand, he carried a sword, in the other, a dagger.

Trepidation slithered over Maeve's skin, chilling her.

The guard held out his hands, just beyond the bars of the cage.

"Choose your weapon," he stated, his voice gruff.

Maeve glanced down at the offerings in his hand, then back up at him. "What?"

"Choose now," he spat, "or I will choose for you."

"Okay, fine." Panic seized her. She had no idea what was happening, but she certainly didn't want to test this guard's seeming lack of patience. Twisting her hands together, her gaze darted between the two weapons. She knew her strengths, knew instinctively which one would serve as an extension of herself. The dagger would always win.

Maeve rolled her shoulders back. "The dagger."

The guard eyed her curiously, arching one brow. "Are you quick with it?"

She smirked. "You could say that."

"Good." He tossed the dagger in between the bars and it clattered onto the stone ground at her feet. "You'll need all the help you can get."

The guard stalked off and Maeve quickly scooped up the dagger.

It was no Aurastone.

The weight held even in her palm, and the leather was smooth in her grip, catching on the calluses of her hand. Tiny whorls were carved into the blade, and both edges were finely sharpened. She flipped it into the air, caught it, and then swung, arcing her arm through the lingering mist. It may not have had the deadly ease of the Aurastone, but it was still an expertly crafted weapon.

The only thing Maeve couldn't figure out was why it had been given to her.

Some more muffled noises drifted through the mist and she clutched the dagger to her body, tensing on instinct. Murmurs seemed to come from every angle, colliding with whispers and the shuffling of feet. She moved in a slow circle, placing one foot in front of the other, careful not to make a sound. Her gaze scanned the swirling mist, scouring the shadows for any sign of life, any kind of movement. She would fight whatever came her way.

I will not yield.

I will not break.

"Welcome, all." Parisa's piercing voice cut through her thoughts, and Maeve spun to face an unseen threat. "To the first annual BloodFest."

Maeve's grip on the dagger tightened, and her heart rate quickened. What the hell was a BloodFest?

"As many of you have heard," Parisa continued, her voice sounding nowhere and everywhere at once. "We have a special guest among us tonight, one who will serve as our first ever participant."

Cold air blasted through the cage, and Maeve threw her arms up to shield her eyes. The freezing wind bit through the thin material of her blouse, and she shuddered. Tendrils of hair whipped around her, tangling, and she clawed at the unruly strands, desperate to see what was happening.

"Presenting my pet, Maeve."

Maeve shoved her hair back from her face and lifted her chin to a severe angle. Rage caused her blood to boil. "I am Maeve Ruhdneah! High Princess of the Autumn Court, Queen of the Furies, the Dawnbringer, blessed by the soul of the goddess Danua, warrior of Kells."

Her fingers coiled tightly around the dagger in her hand. "And I show mercy to no one."

The strange mist cleared slightly, and Maeve found herself in an arena of some kind. Gray stone walls too high for her to climb encircled the vast space. But she had no idea where one wall ended and the other began. Directly across from her was a towering archway with gates made of bronze spikes that drove into the earth. Rows of seats rose up on all sides from behind the wall, forming an oval-like shape. The audience consisted of a few Spring fae, but they were too far away, and she couldn't tell if they were in the stands of their own free will or if they'd been forced to attend. What Maeve could see, however, was that the Spring fae were vastly outnumbered by the dark fae.

They were *everywhere*.

Hideous creatures of nightmarish quality, they hissed and screeched from the shadows. There must have been hundreds of them, at least.

Maeve clenched the dagger in her fist until her fingers cramped, the terrifying realization was enough to steal her breath.

There was no way she was getting out of here alive.

Parisa was seated in a box with curtains of shimmering emerald draping on either side of her. She looked like a charlatan of a queen pretending to rule over her Court, acting as though Maeve was her jester, or a puppet of some kind. Canopies of dark green stretched out over Parisa, held in place by two gold poles where twin banners of midnight rippled in the strong breeze. She wore a new crown, this one was simpler —onyx had been twisted to mimic vines and each silver leaf was embedded with black pearls. Stabbing the mantle of wood before her was the Aurastone, its gleaming iridescent hilt calling to Maeve like a beacon.

"Are you ready for the games, my pet?" Parisa asked, leaning forward and propping one elbow upon the wooden mantle. She trailed her excessively long nail down the flat edge of the Aurastone's blade.

"What games?" Maeve asked, taking a tentative step backwards.

"Originally, I meant for you to partake in the BloodFest alone. But now it appears you'll have some company." Parisa gave a sharp nod of her head, and the wind picked up once more. This time, the skies darkened and icy rain fell in slashes from the seething clouds. She stared at Maeve, the corner of her mouth curling. "I told you they'd come for you."

Maeve whipped around. Through the churning mist, she could just see three more square metal cages, enclosed on the top and bottom by long planks of wood. Each one held a figure trapped within its confines.

She shook her head.

No. This couldn't be happening. It had been be some kind of terrible dream, or horrible nightmare, one she would wake up from at any moment. This couldn't be real. Surely they hadn't been foolish enough to come after her.

But the mist evaporated completely, and revealed Tiernan, Rowan, and Casimir each locked away in a cage.

"No," Maeve breathed.

Iron was clamped around their wrists, and though each of them appeared to have taken a beating of some kind, they were alive. Disgruntled, and clearly pissed off, but alive.

"Maeve!" Tiernan rushed to the edge of his cage and shoved one arm between the bars, the tips of his fingers desperate to reach her.

Maeve sprinted toward him, stretching out her own hand, when the cage enclosing her dissolved into nothingness. It vanished completely. She tried to stop herself, but the momentum hurtled her forward and she stumbled, flailing. The tip of her boot snared in the overgrowth covering the ground, and she flung her other arm wide to keep from accidentally stabbing herself in the chest.

One strong hand snagged her shoulder, dragging her upright.

Her breath caught in her lungs and held tight as she stared up into a pair of striking twilight eyes.

"Tier." His name broke from her lips.

"*Astora*," he whispered, his voice hoarse.

He hauled her closer, trailing his hands up her neck to cup both sides of her face. One thumb ran lightly back and forth across the top of her cheek. She inhaled deeply, breathing him in, fusing every fiber of their souls together. He smelled of palm trees and warm sandalwood, he smelled like home.

"Maeve, listen to me—"

Another harsh noise filled the air, like sand grinding against stone, drowning out his words.

"I'll fix this," she promised, gazing at the strong line of his jaw, at the flecks of gold reflected in the jeweled hue of his eyes. "I promise I'll find a way to get us out of here."

But Tiernan was no longer looking at her. His gaze was focused on something beyond her, behind her, something that made his pulse jump.

"Tiernan? What's wrong?" she asked, turning slowly, mentally preparing herself for whatever monster she would face.

At first, there was nothing but an empty black pit. The gate that had once been skewered into the ground was dragged open, groaning on its slanted hinges. Then she saw them, the disjointed movements and jerky motions of figures she'd come to recognize all too well. A group of poisoned Spring fae stumbled into the arena, each of them armed with simple swords. Even from the distance spanning between them, Maeve could see their glazed, lifeless eyes. Their minds fractured by a venom meant for her, their souls lost forever because she hadn't been fast enough to save them.

"Sun and sky," Rowan murmured, his mouth falling open slightly.

Tiernan's hands slid to her shoulders, squeezing. "They haven't seen you yet. Don't move."

Maeve froze as the drugged fae lurched into one another with no sense of direction. Her hold on the dagger tightened.

"For every ten you kill, I'll release one of your would-be rescuers." Parisa's voice rang out and the fae startled, jolting violently. "Let the games begin!"

A horn blared to life and the fae took off running, straight for her.

"No!" Maeve whipped around, clutching at the front of Tiernan's armor. "I can't, I can't kill them! They're innocent!"

"If you don't kill them," Casimir called to her, his voice tainted with urgency, "they'll kill you!"

Tiernan grabbed her wrists, pressed a hasty kiss across her knuckles. "Look at me, Maeve."

She forced herself to meet the intensity of his gaze. Her bottom lip trembled, and his eyes searched through her, all the way to her soul. He stoked the fire dwindling inside her, urging her determination to burn brighter than any star in the sky.

"Just get to ten, Maeve." He pressed her fingers to his lips. "Ten and she'll free one of us to help you."

Tiernan released her, taking ahold of her shoulders, and forcing her to turn away from him. She swallowed the rise of panic as the fae charged across the arena toward her with their weapons drawn. Her heart pounded against the constricted wall of her chest, her blood pumped vigorously despite the iron locking down her magic.

"Stay focused," Tiernan whispered, his words dancing past her ear. He kept one firm hand on her shoulder. "You are a *warrior*. See every movement in your mind's eye. Do not falter. Do not hesitate."

She nodded.

The fae were closing in on her. She could almost count the heartbeats until they were face-to-face. Their soulless eyes were wild with a ravenous kind of hunger, a desire to kill. But Maeve knew she wasn't fighting them. No. This was a fight with Parisa. She was the one who ruined them, who left them with no choice but to think killing was their only way to survive. So long as Maeve stayed one move ahead of Parisa, she would win.

"*Now, astora!*" Tiernan's voice crashed into her thoughts. "*Go, now!*"

Maeve ran.

She sprinted across the small thatch of grass toward Rowan's cage. Energy pumped through her, fired through her, as she tore across the arena.

Seven of the fae followed her, their convulsive movements jarring and unnatural.

Wind slapped at her face, stinging her cheeks. "Rowan!"

Maeve jerked her head toward the roof of his cage, praying to the goddess he understood her intent. Legs pumping, chest heaving, she clamped the hilt of the dagger between her teeth and bit down.

Rowan darted toward the backside of his cage and crouched low. He shoved his arms between the bars, cupping his hands together to form a base.

Maeve jumped, stepping up into Rowan's open hands. He grabbed her foot, securing it in his hold, and heaved her upward. A second later, she was in the air, her jaw clenched tightly around the hilt of her dagger. She caught the edge of the boards covering Rowan's cage, the tips of her fingers grappling with the damp wooden surface for leverage. Hauling herself up, she pulled her dagger from her mouth, then wrapped each finger snugly around its hilt.

Do not falter.

Do not hesitate.

A warrior's cry tore from her lungs and she launched herself into the mob of mindless fae. Most of them scrambled to get out of her way, the ones who didn't met their end.

Mid-leap, Maeve swung her arm out, curving up into a devastating arc. Lightning splintered across the stormy skies as her blade ripped through the throats of two fae. The leaden thump of their lifeless bodies dropping to the ground was nothing compared to the deafening crack of her fist slamming into the earth as she landed. The ground beneath her shuddered. Her magic hovered beyond her reach, clawing at the cold iron clamped firmly around her neck, stifling her. Hindering her. Maeve's head snapped up, and she speared the next fae who rushed for her, slicing from his navel to his sternum. Blood pooled across the front of his shirt, staining it a dark red, and his eyes rolled back into his head before he toppled over.

Three.

She lurched into a standing position and spun into the next attack, taking out a female who stumbled into her dagger. The remaining fae attempted to surround her. But even if some of these fae were seasoned in combat, they would fail against the likes of her. Maeve was born with the blood of a warrior. Carman had tossed her aside like a worthless toy, and it was Casimir who forged her into a weapon of reckoning. Those strengths, those innate qualities, those instinctive skills had only amplified once Fearghal had removed those godsforsaken cuffs.

If there was one thing Maeve could do better than anyone else, it was fight.

Every action was seamless, every motion was fluid. She moved like a ribbon of silk caught on a breeze, sleek and with deadly grace. Crimson dripped from her blade, splattering across the earth like shattered rubies. She parried and dodged the way one danced, an effortless skill she'd mastered since she first learned to walk. To her, the battlefield was her ballroom. The roars of those watching her performance was the music to which she twirled, killing another each time she met her mark. Each time another partner demanded a dance.

A male reached for her and she grabbed his wrist, hauling him close. Then she rammed the hilt of her dagger along the underside of his arm, just below the joint of his elbow. Bone cracked and her gut clenched, his howl of despair almost enough to snap her out of her murderous haze. But she plunged her blade into his heart, silencing his screams.

Seven.

"Keep going, Maeve!" Casimir shouted, his voice carrying over to her above the calamitous crowd of dark fae watching from above and the growing storm circulating overhead.

She kicked high, slamming her boot into the chest of a

female, and sent her flying across the arena. Reaching behind her, she grabbed the arm of the one attempting to sneak upon her. Like she didn't know he was there, like she couldn't hear his uneven footfalls plodding across the ground, or smell the sickly sweet stench of overripe cherries. In one swift movement, she hauled him over her shoulder and tossed him to the ground. Her blade pierced his heart a moment later.

Bending down, she reached for the sword he dropped, arming herself with two weapons.

The Spring fae were wary now. Their minds might have been gone, but they were not so quick to attack.

No matter, she would be the one to offer them a waltz of death instead.

Maeve didn't look into their faces, knowing that the emptiness reflected back at her would only serve as an emotional wound to her heart. The dagger and sword became extensions of her body. She became the weapon.

Crimson coated her hands and stained her blouse. Rain soaked her through to the bone, so her hands were ice, but so was the blood coursing through her veins. Her hair clung to her cheeks and shoulders, and though her muscles ached from exertion and her chest heaved, the beating of her heart remained calm.

The only sound she focused on was the smooth rush of metal slicing through flesh.

Ten.

"Release the drakon!" Parisa cried, her tone damn near giddy.

Maeve turned to see Casimir's cage vanish.

His dark brown gaze met hers from across the grassy expanse and alarm skittered down her spine as more drugged fae emptied into the arena. Some of them darted toward her, the rest aimed for Casimir.

But he had no weapon.

"Maeve!" Tiernan yelled, and she swore if he hadn't been locked in iron, he would have destroyed the cage separating them. "Behind you!"

There was a sudden burning sensation in her back, and she arched, hissing through her teeth as the pain spread through her lower right side like wildfire.

Tiernan roared.

Rowan raged.

But Maeve...she was past the point of caring.

Rearing back, she elbowed her attacker in the face. She didn't even turn to face them, didn't bother to spare them a blade as she flipped the sword in her hand, and drove it directly into their stomach. The sucking sound it made as she withdrew it was the only confirmation she had, and it was enough.

Fury ignited inside her as she witnessed Casimir defending himself against the poisoned fae with only his bare fists. How typical of Parisa to ensure she had the advantage.

She swiped the back of her hand across her forehead, shoving her damp curls out of her face. The rain continued to pour and Maeve locked her jaw to keep her teeth from chattering. Rushing across the sodden ground, swearing each time her boots slid against the wet earth, she bolted in Casimir's direction.

Maeve became an inferno of vengeance. Slicing. Striking. Ending lives in less time than it took to breathe.

"Cas!" she cried, and tossed her sword.

He didn't even look at her, he just lifted one arm and opened his hand. In the next blink, his fist closed around the hilt as he caught it, trusting in her aim more than she trusted herself.

She pulled up short, gasping as she reached his side.

"Stay together!" Rowan shouted from somewhere behind her. "Don't let them separate you!"

Maeve winced as she spun around, pressing her back to Casimir's. She squinted through the sheets of rain as more fae ambled toward them.

"Sun and sky," she murmured. "How many lives did she ruin?"

"Too many."

Casimir would never admit it, but she knew his words were laced with a deeper implication.

Together they fought, back to back, as they had done so many times before. He hooked her arm, tossing her smoothly across his back, and she staved off an assault from the other side.

"I'm sorry," he grunted, stabbing a fae who drew too close.

"I know." Maeve ducked low, avoiding the swipe of a blade as it cut through the rain above her head.

"If I had known—"

"Let it go, Cas." Maeve mimicked the movements of her former mentor, spinning with him as they switched positions. She couldn't look at him, couldn't take her eyes off of their opponents, but if she could...she knew what she would see within the depths of his brown gaze.

Remorse.

"We've all done something we regret in the name of love." Her breath whooshed out of her as she cut down another fae. Maeve's own words were not lost on her. "Holding a grudge against you will only harden my heart."

"I should have fought for you," he countered, his sword catching the glint of lightning as it streaked across the darkened heavens.

"You're fighting for me now." She jabbed low, slicing upward across the front of the final attacker. Warm blood splattered against her cheek and she startled, sucking in a harsh gulp of stagnant air.

"Release the traitor!" Parisa called out, her saccharine voice tinged with exasperation.

Rowan's cage disappeared and he rushed over to join them.

"Your back," he demanded. "Let me see your back."

"It's nothing."

"Your shirt is soaked in blood." He grabbed her shoulders and turned her away from him, and she swore when he peeled away the section of her blouse that stuck to her skin. "Don't lie and tell me it's nothing."

Maeve swatted at him. "I'll heal eventually. I always do. But we don't have time for this..."

She stilled as more figures entered the arena.

"Seven hells, how many more are there?" Casimir muttered, raising his sword.

Dozens of dead bodies were strewn around the massive space already. Blood soaked the ground, so thick it squished beneath Maeve's boots when she moved, and not even the rain was enough to wash it away. Her stomach roiled, and she attempted to swallow the lump of dread lodged in the back of her throat.

But these fae were...different.

Maeve stared across the distance separating them, watched as they huddled together, soaked and freezing. Stepping forward, she sheathed her dagger.

"Maeve," Rowan warned, snaring her wrist. "You've done so well. I know this hasn't been easy for you, but you cannot quit. You can't give up. Not to her. Not ever."

She shook her head. "No, Rowan. Something isn't right. Look at them. They're not like the others."

His hold on her loosened as his lavender gaze scanned the group of fae standing across from them. There were approximately ten in total, and they were all clustered, clinging to one another, seemingly frozen in place. "They're not poisoned."

Maeve clamped one hand over her mouth.

"How can you tell?" Casimir asked, his sword still raised, his gaze wary.

"Their eyes." Rowan nodded his head in their direction, and droplets of water fell from his deep teal hair. He ran a hand through it, shoving it back from his face. "They're still in control of their minds."

A beat of weighted silence fill the space between them, until Rowan said, "They know they're going to die."

And he was right. These were the dancers who had been in Parisa's dining hall. She could control their bodies if she chose, but they were aware, and they were terrified.

"Ten more, Maeve." Parisa's voice rang out in a singsong manner. "Or your precious High King dies."

"What?" Maeve shrieked, and spun to where Tiernan should have been trapped in the last cage.

He was still there, but the cage was gone, and a burly dark fae with flaming eyes and jagged teeth held him hostage. Raindrops slid down the side of his face and his twilight eyes burned bright, focused solely on her. Tiernan's arms were pinned behind his back, and the horrendous fae held a dagger in one clawed hand. The gleam of the blade caught Maeve's eye. It had been dipped in nightshade and was poised right above Tiernan's heart.

"No!" Maeve started forward and Rowan caught her by the arm, holding her back.

"Careful, Princess," he whispered.

"You can't do this!" Maeve jerked away from him, glaring up at Parisa where she sat on her fraudulent throne. The fight was leaving Maeve, slipping from her, fading as quickly as night gave way to the dawn. This was one battle she could not win.

She wouldn't be able to save everyone. If she chose Tiernan, Parisa would kill all of those innocent Spring fae, including the winemaker's son. If she chose the fae, Tiernan would be stabbed in the heart with a blade of nightshade. She was going to lose.

She knew it. Tiernan knew it.

Her heart fractured as she said the next words. "You can't make me choose."

"Oh, but I can, and I will." Parisa leaned back, her smug smile peeling back to reveal her hideously pointy teeth. "Which will it be, my pet? The lives of ten innocent fae, or the life of your mate?"

Chapter Twenty-Five

"Choose them."

Tiernan was exceptionally aware of the night-shade-dipped dagger hovering above his heart as he spoke.

But then there was only Maeve.

She turned to him, her movements painfully slow as the rest of the world seemed to fade away. Her golden pink hair was plastered to her, soaked from the rain. Blood, most of it not her own save for the wound to her back, covered almost every inch of her. The blouse she wore fell off one shoulder, revealing her tattoos that shone with the faintest glow despite the iron collar tight around her neck.

The sight of it made his blood boil.

She looked at him then, those sea-swept eyes stealing into his heart, and the swell of tears clung to her lashes. She was devastating. Fiercely bold and beautiful. A demigoddess of wrath and compassion. Fucking gods, he loved her.

"I can't lose you, Tiernan." Her voice broke a little, and he steeled himself, bracing for what the sight of her tears would do to him. "I can't."

"Choose them," he repeated.

"No." She lacked conviction, and he knew the crush of devastation the choice would place upon her. Maeve's sorrowful gaze swept over the group of fae, the ones whose very souls looked terrified, and he wasn't sure he'd ever seen her more crestfallen.

Except once.

In a bathtub, covered in someone else's blood.

This would break her, of that he was sure.

"Look at me," he commanded, his tone cutting.

Her spine straightened and she jerked her head up, angling her chin in defiance. Her eyes flashed, a flicker of confusion, but she disguised it quickly.

"Choose *them*," he ordered.

Though it was weak, and he wasn't sure how much of it she would actually feel, Tiernan sent the entirety of his heart and soul to her through their bond. Adoration, love, respect, desire, loyalty—he poured the whole of everything he felt for her into the witch thread. He wanted her to know, to never have cause to doubt, that she was the center of his universe. That she was all he would ever want, that he would sacrifice his own life if it meant she would live.

Maeve bit her bottom lip, hesitating. "I've made my choice."

"Oh good," Parisa crooned from her shabby dais. "And?"

"Will you grant me one request?" Maeve asked, glancing toward Tiernan. She unsheathed her dagger and he nodded slowly.

"And what's that, my pet?" Parisa's hideous grin stretched wide, her single eye alight with the glow of victory.

Maeve swallowed. "A final kiss. Just one."

Parisa groaned then, leaning back in her makeshift throne. "Fine. But make it quick. I want to watch the life fade from the High King's eyes when his beloved finally ends him."

Nodding sharply, Maeve turned back to Tiernan and started toward him.

"Maeve." Rowan caught her hand, but she pulled away from his grasp, closing the distance between them.

Tiernan would rather die by her hand than any other.

Everyone watched as she approached him, and the dark fae had the decency to let him go, to afford him this last opportunity to say goodbye to her. She sucked in a breath, and his gaze dropped to her mouth, to those lips just waiting to be kissed. Another step and she was closer, peering up at him from beneath a set of dark lashes. Her tempting scent—cinnamon smoke, woods, and vanilla—layered with sun-drenched palms and warm sandalwood, weakened him.

A tear slipped from the corner of her misty gray-green eyes and she searched his face, pleading with him. Begging him to find some other way. But he would not allow her to change her mind.

He bent down toward her, pressing his forehead to hers. "Your soul is mine, *astora*. In this life, in every life."

She took hold of the leather armor covering his chest and yanked him forward.

"You," she whispered across his mouth. "I will *always* choose you."

"I love you, Maeve. Infinitely."

"And I love you. Eternally." She rose up on her toes and her lips slashed across his in a kiss of urgency. It was filled with fire, with passion, with the promise of a better world built on hope and dreams.

Maeve draped her arms over his shoulders, deepening the kiss. Tiernan was acutely aware of the way she melded against him. Of the hitch in her breath. Of her sporadic thoughts. Of her hesitant movements. She hoisted the dagger, positioning it behind him, so all she would have to do was plunge it quickly into the back of his neck, and end his life without suffering.

It would break her, ruin her, and therein lay the problem.

Tiernan would never again allow her to suffer alone.

"*Do you trust me?*" he whispered into her mind, and broke their kiss.

She stared up at him. "*With my life.*"

"Good."

Uncertainty gave her pause and that was all the time he needed.

Tiernan grabbed her arms, hauling them up over her head. Maeve gasped, her eyes widening as he wrenched the dagger free from her hold. Binding both of her wrists with one hand, Tiernan whipped her around, then yanked her hard against him. She stumbled backwards into him, struggling while he easily pinned her arms to her chest, pressing her tightly against him. With his free hand, he threatened the smooth flesh of her neck with the tip of her own dagger.

"What are you doing?" Parisa shrieked from her place in the stands. "Guards!"

The dark fae clamored, a swell of tainted rage and violence so strong that the rush of dark magic nearly suffocated him.

"Not so fast, Parisa." Tiernan edged the sharpened point against Maeve's throat directly above the iron collar and Parisa froze, lifting one hand, halting the assault.

"You wouldn't dare." Fumes of sickly green smoke seeped all around her. While she appeared to maintain a sense of calm, Tiernan knew she was seething, damn near foaming at the mouth with rage.

Parisa leaned forward, gripping the edge of the mantle before her where Maeve's Aurastone glittered like the dawn.

"You don't have it in you to do it because she's your *sirra*. You wouldn't touch a single hair on her pretty little head."

"You're mistaken." Tiernan eased the blade into Maeve's skin, so it nicked her flesh. She jolted in his grip, crying out, but he held firm, clutching her against him. Unease slithered through her, causing her body to tense. Her heartbeat kicked up, her pulse as familiar to him as a song. A single drop of scarlet pooled on the blade, and Parisa surged forward. "I took a vow. An oath."

He kept his gaze locked on Parisa, barely acknowledging the fact that Rowan and Casimir were slowly inching toward them. The distraction was working. Everyone was too absorbed by the spectacle of the High King holding a dagger to the throat of his mate to pay attention to anyone or anything else.

"You see, I love her so fucking much that I agreed to be the one to take her life if it meant saving her from you." Tiernan dipped his head, brushing his lips along Maeve's ear. Her answering shiver destroyed him. "And I always keep my word."

He cut the blade deeper this time, drawing more blood.

A broken sob escaped Maeve. It would haunt him for the remainder of his days, but his actions gleaned the desired effect.

"Enough!" Parisa shouted, and the green jewel she wore pulsed with dark magic. "You've made your point, High King."

"Have I?" he taunted. "I don't see how she can be of any value. You had no problem tossing her into this BloodFest. In fact, you sat there and waited for her to die."

Parisa tossed her head back, her stringy, thinning hair stuck to her frail neck, and she cackled. "Do you actually think I'd sit here and let her die? I control every dark fae—their minds, their actions, are a mere extension of my own. I merely wanted to watch her suffer, for I know how much it kills her to take the pitiful lives of the innocent. She was never in peril. But you...you are the one I wish to see dead more than all the rest. Because with you gone, she will be that much easier to break."

Tiernan grinned, applying a bit more pressure to the blade at Maeve's throat. When she cried out and thrashed against him, Parisa nearly leapt out of her squalid throne.

"What do you want?" she shouted, lunging forward. Her eye bulged so severely that for a split second, he thought it might pop out of her head.

"That's a rather vague question." He lifted the dagger, admiring the beads of crimson sliding down its sharpened edge. "You'll have to be more specific."

"Tier..." Maeve pleaded through their bond.

"Just play along."

He tapped the blade against the iron collar, and Maeve trembled. He wasn't entirely sure she was pretending.

"Very well." Parisa clasped her hands together, eyeing him coolly. "What can I give you in order to keep you from killing Maeve? I very much want her alive."

This time, Tiernan didn't hesitate.

"Release myself, Rowan, Casimir from the iron bindings and let us go. Free those Spring fae you're using as pawns. I want them guaranteed safe passage to Niahvess. No harm should come to them in any shape or form, at any time. Ever. You will also relinquish control of their minds at once."

She looked pissed. Her too-thin eyebrows pulled into a scowl and the gaunt planes of her face hollowed out in severity. "That's a rather extensive list of demands. Anything else?"

"Yes." This was it. His last chance. "Drop the veil."

Her head tilted. "Pardon?"

"Your magic," he clarified. "Whatever you're using to shroud the Spring Court, I want you to recall it immediately and vow that it will never return."

She shook her head and leaned back, her thin wisps of

graying hair tangling around her face. "No. You ask for too much."

"That's too bad." Tiernan slid the flat edge of the blade along Maeve's neck, then with his other hand, he discreetly reached around and pinched the side of her breast. Hard.

Maeve shrieked, spasming against him.

"You win!" Parisa threw up both of her hands, gesturing wildly at her guards. "Remove the iron at once and send those pathetic fae to Niahvess. I no longer require their services."

Two Puca strode up to Rowan and Casimir and removed the iron cuffs from their wrists. Neither of them moved. They didn't flinch. They didn't draw any unwanted attention. Tiernan held out one arm at a time, while the hideous dark fae hovering near him unlatched the iron that restrained his power. The moment the metal broke free, his magic surged, and his patience waned.

"The veil, Parisa," Tiernan demanded. "Or Maeve dies."

"Fine," she snapped, huffing like the selfish fallen princess he'd always known her to be. "But as soon as I do this, you better release her, or I will bring the wrath of the Sluagh upon your Court."

Tiernan inclined his head in the slightest of acknowledgements. "I wouldn't have it any other way."

Corrupted magic tainted the air. Like festering citrus and charred wood, the stench of it permeated the arena, spreading like a disease.

Maeve recoiled, and even Tiernan tried not to retch.

Slowly, the magical shroud engulfing the Spring Court fell. Though he couldn't see past the tall stone walls surrounding them, he knew Suvarese suffered. It was as though the land had been cursed by a devastating plague, one that siphoned the life force from every plant and creature trapped within its clutches. The earth shuddered, expelling a breath of release, but it would be some time before magic ever returned to this place.

Maeve stiffened in his arms, and he knew she could sense it as well.

The way the trees seemed to weep, their leaves falling like tears. The plants that withered, reaching desperately for a shred of light before turning to ash. Flowers that would never bloom, an earth with nothing left to give.

"Now"—Parisa sneered down from her extravagant seat in the stands—"hand her over, High King."

"Tiernan..." Maeve's voice cut through his mind.

"Of course." He inclined his head, then, *"I love you."*

Tiernan shoved Maeve into Rowan's arms.

A mass of impenetrable shadows swarmed, devouring them. Tiernan heard Maeve scream his name, heard the break in her voice, and then they vanished. Dissolving like the night.

"NO!" Parisa screeched, her eye bulging with such force Tiernan thought it might pop out of her face. "Traitor!"

Tiernan opened his hands, and twin swords appeared in each palm. He pointed one of them directly at her. "I did exactly as you asked. I released her." He twirled the blade so its nightshade coating glimmered like the darkest night. "Perhaps you should be more mindful of the bargains you strike."

"Bastard," she snapped.

He smirked. "Not quite."

Casimir shifted into his drakon form without hesitation, smoke unfurling around him as his mighty wings spread wide, launching him into the sky. A terrifying screech pierced the air and his rage echoed through the valley of Suvarese. His jaws opened wide, and the scorching glow of a fireball erupted from his mouth, blasting the dark fae who swarmed into the arena. The horrible scent of burnt flesh and charred bodies filled Tiernan's nose as Casimir incinerated the nightmarish creatures.

Tiernan hacked through the charge of dark fae barreling toward him. His swords arched through the air, cutting through tendons and slashing through spines. He spun into each attack, moving with ease as he slit open throats, and ripped off heads. Blood splattered his face and armor, and he grit his teeth against the onslaught.

He was the wrath and the storm.

The tempest and the fury.

Menacing clouds reached across the sky like claws, stretching and scouring. Thunder shattered through the heavens so that the ground beneath his feet trembled and quaked. Extreme gusts of wind tore through the arena, carrying the strength of Casimir's blaze so it engulfed the endless stream of dark fae hurtling toward them. Violet lightning ripped through the clouds in streaks of fury, illuminating the silhouette of a fire-breathing dragon hell-bent on revenge. A battle cry tore from the back of Tiernan's throat and he sprinted toward the mass of enemies, his magic amplified with every hastened step as Casimir set fire to the chaos.

Wave after wave, he slaughtered them all. Parisa's shouts and screams echoed all around him, but they were indistinct and muted. For Tiernan, it was life or death. Through the cloying plumes of smoke and the blood-soaked ground, he never faltered. His muscles screamed but he ignored them. Ash coated his tongue but he remained unyielding. Relentless.

All for Maeve.

He would bleed for her. Die for her.

Nothing else mattered.

He was ruthless in his assault, a High King without a heart whose blood ran cold. He showed no mercy beneath the wrath of his blade, nor the power of his magic.

Tiernan killed them all.

A swell of all-encompassing darkness overtook the skies, the pitch of it so intense it subdued even Tiernan's storm. On first glance, it looked as though night was falling, but far too rapidly. It consumed the sky, swallowing every tree, every building, every mountain in its wake.

Casimir swooped down low, landing beside him. He loosed another piercing cry, and through his rows of vicious teeth, Tiernan could see the fiery ember of a fire blast ready to wreak havoc upon the impending threat.

Whatever had come for them startled even the dark fae—the creatures born of the Sluagh and fear, the banished ones—and they scattered in every direction. They took refuge wherever they could find it, fleeing their ranks and spiraling like the threads of a web caught in a storm. This darkness, this swath of a seeming endless void, instilled a deep fear in them, and for a split second, Tiernan wondered if perhaps he and Casimir should flee as well.

But it was too late.

The darkness overcame them.

It drowned out every sound, stole every fractal of light, obscuring them in a brutal, deadly cold. Tiernan stared into the pitch, straining to see, to hear. But there was nothing, save for the faintest ripple of magic. The shadows surrounding him pulsed, beating like a heart, like they were a living, breathing thing.

Tiernan kept his swords raised and at the ready. He moved in a slow circle, cautious and vigilant. The hairs along the back of his neck stood on end, and a prickling sense of unease crawled down his spine. He spun around, knowing that *something* lurked in the darkness. Waiting. Watching.

He blinked, and could have sworn the eternal pitch winked in return.

Tiernan reared back.

Faint, glowing orbs came into focus. Two eyes caught on fire. Then a low, rumbling voice greeted him.

"Are you ready to return home, *moh Rí?*"

The last time Tiernan heard that voice, he'd almost drowned in a river of blood.

Balor.

The Fury had returned.

Chapter Twenty-Six

"Tiernan!" Maeve screamed for him, even as Rowan's shadows stole her away. Darkness surrounded her, and a numbing coldness coated her skin. She struggled, blindly reaching for the space between the shadows where the barest scrap of light was slowly disappearing from sight. "Let me go!"

But Rowan's grip remained tight around her waist as she kicked and clawed through the mass of shadows. There was a burst of raw power, of punishing magic, and she tumbled backwards into him. Her lungs squeezed, stealing her breath, and the intense jolt left her lightheaded as a rush of nausea slammed into her.

"Rowan, please," she begged, her voice cracking. She slumped in his arms, bone-deep exhaustion dragging her down, weakening her. "We can't leave him. She'll kill him, she'll kill both of them."

A strangled sob escaped her, fracturing her heart.

Rowan continued to hold her, refusing to let her go even as the shadows slowly dissipated, and the courtyard of Niahvess came into view. Warmth cradled her, welcomed her. But it wasn't the same, it would never be the same because Tiernan wasn't here. She sucked in a ragged breath, chest heaving. Hot tears spilled down her cheeks.

Maeve blinked, and a blur of gold and turquoise appeared before her.

Ceridwen sprinted toward them, her usually smooth brow creased with worry. "Maeve!"

"Ceridwen!" This time, when Maeve attempted to untangle herself from Rowan's fierce grasp, he released her.

"Sun and sky, Maeve." Ceridwen cupped her cheek, her twilight gaze roving over her face while she took in Maeve's blood-splattered clothing. Then she slowly reached down and touched the iron collar around Maeve's neck. She hissed and jerked her hand back. "We have to get this off of her."

"I know," Rowan muttered, crossing his arms.

But Maeve wouldn't be deterred. She didn't care about the iron still clamped around her throat. She only cared about Tiernan. Her *sirra*. Her mate. "Cer, you have to help me. We have to go back. Tiernan and Casimir, they're in Suvarese with Parisa. She has them in this arena, there's dark fae everywhere. They won't survive on their own. Please, we have to save them!"

"Is this true?" Ceridwen asked, glancing over at Rowan as Brynn and Merrick ran in from the opposite side of the courtyard.

Rowan nodded. "Tiernan convinced Parisa he would kill Maeve unless she brought down the veil."

He ran one finger along the skin of Maeve's neck, just above the iron cuff. The tip of it came away smeared with her blood. "He did one hell of a job, too. For a moment, I thought he'd actually go through with it."

Brynn stormed between Rowan and Maeve, her eyes

flashing from a vivid green to near red. "So, you just *left* them there?"

Rowan visibly stiffened. His jaw clenched, and tendrils of inky shadows hovered around his shoulders. "I did what I was told to do."

"Bullshit." Merrick nudged Brynn out of the way and stabbed a finger into Rowan's chest. "We all know you want Maeve for yourself. You've been pining over her for thousands of years. Just had to wait for the right opportunity to present itself, didn't you?"

Rowan knocked Merrick's arm away, closing the distance between them so they met face-to-face. The contempt between them was palpable. One loyal to his king, the other loyal to no one.

Destructive magic pulsed around Rowan, threatening as his shadows continued to amass. "What are you trying to imply, hunter?"

"Stop," Ceridwen demanded, fisting both of her hands on her hips. "Stop this at once."

Merrick matched him with a cruel smile. "You know exactly what I'm implying, Nightweaver."

"Enough!" Maeve shouted, wedging herself between the two overprotective males. "I'll hear no more of this. We don't have time to stand around arguing with each other."

The sheer command in her voice must have struck a nerve, because Merrick stepped back first, his hands clenched into fists as his sides, and the rise of darkness lingering around Rowan vanished.

"Maeve!"

She spun toward the feminine voice calling her name, and her heart shuddered. Saoirse was sprinting her direction, her silver braid whipping in the breeze behind her, as a single purple petal fell from the flower tucked behind her ear. Just beyond her, his steps slow and measured, his presence as stoic as ever, was Lir.

"Saoirse." Maeve loosed a shaky breath. "Lir."

Throwing out both of her arms, a laugh broke from inside her when Saoirse lifted her into an embrace, spinning once.

"Thank the gods, you're alive." Saoirse set her down, then planted a kiss on each of her cheeks.

Maeve squeezed her hands once and turned to the commander. The one sworn to protect her from anything and anyone, no matter the cost.

"Lir." She looked up into his face, biting her bottom lip to keep it from trembling. One silver eye gazed back at her, and where the other should've been, there was now a small golden tattoo of a sun marking his deep, umber skin.

"Oh, Lir." Maeve choked on his name and launched herself into his arms. "I'm so sorry."

He caught her without stumbling and held tight. Unbidden tears pooled at the corner of her eyes, and again her heart wrenched with guilt.

"Don't cry, little bird." Lir smoothed a hand down the back of her tangled hair. "I'm doing much better."

"All thanks to our Brynn," Saoirse added, throwing an arm around the healer's shoulders. "Your talent is incomparable."

"Speaking of incomparable abilities..." Rowan edged forward, tucking his hands into the pockets of his black armor. "Maeve suffered a wound to her back, but it will not heal unless we can get that iron collar off her neck. Brynn, can you help her?"

Brynn's eyes widened in shock. "Yes. Yes, of course."

She opened her palm and a leather sack full of supplies appeared in her hand. Peering at the cuff wrapped around Maeve's throat, she carefully guided Maeve to the ground. "Have a seat, my lady. This might take a minute."

Maeve lowered herself onto the paved stones of the courtyard, crossing her legs beneath her. Brynn knelt down beside her and opened her satchel. She pulled out a jar of salve, an assortment of ointments, and two instruments that caused Maeve's stomach to turn. One resembled a pair of pliers from the human lands, the other looked like a pair of serrated shears.

"Don't worry, I know it looks intimidating." Brynn produced a mortar and pestle from the seemingly endless bag of supplies. "But I've removed iron from many fae. I promise you're in good hands."

Of that, Maeve had no doubt, but it didn't make her any less queasy.

She watched in silence as Brynn unsheathed one of the daggers from the band at her waist. With a quick flick of her wrist, the blade sliced cleanly across her open palm, splitting the skin.

Maeve flinched. "What are you doing?"

"Sometimes..." Brynn fisted her hand and collected the tiny drops of crimson in the stone mortar. "Blood magic is required, especially when the iron is tainted."

Swallowing the lump of anxiety lodged in the back of her throat, Maeve nodded as Brynn continued to add a mix of herbs to the mortar. She uncorked some thick liquid substance that reeked of sulphur, and poured it in as well, then ground all of it together with the pestle.

Lir moved closer, his long shadow falling across Maeve. She glanced up at him, but he wasn't looking at her. He scanned the courtyard instead.

She didn't miss the distinctive way his mouth hardened into a firm line before he asked, "Did the High King not yet return?"

"No." Merrick's voice dripped with disdain. "Someone saw fit to leave him behind."

Lir's voice dropped an octave. "What?"

Ceridwen stormed forward in a flurry of rosy satin and ribbons. She barely came to Merrick's chin, but that didn't stop her from cutting the esteemed hunter down with a menacing glare. "That's not fair."

"What do you mean, it's not fair?" Merrick's cerulean eyes burned bright, and he pointed an accusing finger in Rowan's direction. "He abandoned your brother—"

"And saved our queen!"

"For himself!" he roared.

"For all of us!" Ceridwen fired back, and a strand of raging tension snapped between them.

"Easy, you two. Quarrel some other time." Saoirse positioned herself between them both in an attempt to quell the rising tempers. Though given her stance, she looked perfectly ready to protect Ceridwen and pummel Merrick to a pulp.

Maeve scooted closer to Brynn, ducking her head. When she spoke, she kept her voice low. "I've never seen them come to blows quite like that before."

"Me either." Brynn shook her head, and her burgundy curls bounced on the light breeze. She continued working the pestle until whatever murky concoction she'd created gurgled and bubbled within the mortar. Reaching into her satchel, she pulled out a pair of worn, tan leather gloves and yanked them on. Then she glanced up, her teeth scraping along her bottom lip. "Cer?"

Ceridwen turned at her name, and Brynn jerked her head in Maeve's direction. "I'll need some assistance, please."

"Anything." Ceridwen gathered up all of Maeve's knotted curls and piled them high on her head. She bound her hair in place with a satin ribbon, leaving her neck exposed. "There we go."

Brynn placed a gentle hand upon Maeve's cheek, her eyes

now a golden brown, her gaze imploring. "I need you to understand, my lady, this might hurt."

Maeve nodded, willing herself to remain calm even though her heart was suddenly hammering like it might burst from her chest at any moment.

Ceridwen crouched low, smoothing her skirts of rose around her. Then she clutched Maeve's hands in her own, squeezing tightly. "Just breathe, Maeve."

A horrible sizzling noise filled Maeve's ears and she braced herself, her muscles seizing in preparation for the pain that would undoubtedly follow. The iron heated, scalding her flesh, and she gasped, desperate for air. The burning sting intensified and Maeve's breathing grew shallow. Her blood rushed, her magic stirred, but sweet goddess, the agony was too much.

"It burns!" she cried, squeezing her eyes shut. Tears slipped out, hot and fast. She gripped Ceridwen's hands, trying but failing to steel herself against the fire scorching her skin. It was as though her flesh was melting away, and her chest hollowed out as she gasped. "Cer, it burns!"

"Fucking hell," Merrick muttered at the same time Rowan spat out the words, "I'll kill that bitch."

Maeve's body trembled, shaking uncontrollably as the searing pain continued, as the smell of charred flesh filled her nose and sweat pooled across her brow.

Two muscled arms wrapped around her from behind, supporting her, and another sob tore from some empty place inside of her.

"Just a little longer." Brynn's voice was a hoarse whisper, etched with a different kind of pain. "Almost there."

Beads of sweat slid along her spine, dampening her filthy blouse and sticking it to her skin. Waves of nausea crashed into her, drowning her. Again, she cried out, and the arms around her tightened.

"Hang in there, little bird. I've got you."

She swayed backward just as the pain ebbed.

"There." Brynn blew out a harsh breath. "All done."

Maeve collapsed against Lir, letting him take the full brunt of her weight. Her magic rushed to the surface, wild and full of life. She was free from the iron, from Parisa's clutches. It was the same invigorating sensation when Carman's cuffs had finally been removed, as though she were suddenly alive for the first time. Everything was vibrant and clear, like she was attuned to the land of Faeven itself.

There was another lulling swell of magic, the loving caress of Ceridwen's power as it coasted over her, calming her.

Slowly, Maeve opened her eyes to find Rowan staring down at her.

No, that wasn't right.

He was staring at her neck.

Strangely self-conscious, she lifted her fingers to the area when Ceridwen grabbed her wrist and shook her head.

"It will heal," Brynn said quickly, but there was a kind of lingering sadness in her eyes. "It will take time, but it will heal."

Lir helped Maeve to stand and regain her balance, and when she was certain she wouldn't topple over her, she sought Rowan.

"What did you mean earlier?" she asked, hating that his lavender eyes dipped to her neck again before he lifted his gaze to her face. "When you said you only did what you were told? By who?"

"By the High King." Rowan straightened, adjusting the matte black buckles of his armor. "Our end goal was getting you out, no matter the cost."

He inclined his head, and his swath of teal hair fell across one half of his face. "Tiernan told me that if anything happened, the second we were in trouble, I was to take you into the shadows and head to Niahvess as quickly as possible."

He gave a slight bow and emotion flickered in his gaze, but he banked it without hesitation. "Here we are."

Ceridwen stepped up beside Maeve and placed one hand on her chest. "You would know."

Right.

The witch thread.

Maeve would feel it if something happened to Tiernan. But even as she reached for him through their bond, there was no response. Only a foreboding and still silence. For now, the only thing she could assume was that he was still alive. But she couldn't very well sit around and wait for him to die.

"I just..." Maeve pressed her fingers to her temples. "I need a minute to think."

"Maeve—" Saoirse made to follow her, but Maeve waved her off.

"I'm only going for a walk. Not far." She tried to smile, but it was impossible. "I promise."

She wandered through the open-air corridors, past the shimmering fountains. All the while, her mind continued to spin, to piece together a plan to rescue Tiernan and Casimir. She would never be able to live with herself if anything happened to them, to *him*. Her heart lurched at the thought.

The late afternoon sun dipped lower in the sky, lengthening the shadows of palm trees as she passed. A chill crept over her as she approached the verandah, the very place she'd stood when she first arrived on Faeven's shores. Waves crashed against the steps descending into the ocean's frothy depths, and when she looked west, she could just see the rugged mountains and the immense gloom that still hung over the Spring Court.

Somewhere in that wretched place, waiting for her, was Tiernan.

Hardened resolve locked her spine into place, and she rolled her shoulders back.

Maeve glanced down at the witch thread marking her wrist and tried again. *"I'm coming for you."*

"I must say," a male voice responded, laced with seduction, "I wish I was hearing those words under different circumstances."

Maeve startled and spun around.

There he stood, battered and covered in blood, but alive. His hair was a mess, the midnight pieces sticking up in every direction. The armor he wore was ripped in some places, shredded in others, and a trickle of blood slid from the cut on his lip down to his chin. A bruise marred the right side of his face, but sun and sky, he was *alive.*

"Tiernan?"

"Yes, *astora?*"

A strangled wail got caught in her throat and she ran for him, jumping into his arms. She clutched at him, buried her face in his neck, and breathed him in. She reveled in his touch, his feel, his scent. All of him, for all of her. He wrapped his arms around her, crushing her against him. This male was the whole of her heart, the entirety of her soul. He loved every broken, jagged piece of her, and she would never lose him again.

"How?" She pressed herself into him, so there was no way of knowing where she ended and he began. "How did you escape?"

"You'll be pleased to know Balor has returned from the Kethwyn Woods."

"Balor?"

The Fury. The Fury of darkness had rescued Tiernan from the Spring Court. She owed Balor a great debt, for it was twice now he had saved her mate's life.

Maeve held onto Tiernan, refusing to let go. In his arms, she was safe. In his arms, she was home.

"I'm sorry." Remorse poured from her for all the hurt she'd caused him. "I'm so sorry, Tiernan. I should have listened to you. I never should've—"

"Listen to me very carefully, you owe me *nothing*. No apologies. No explanations." Gently, he set her back down on her feet and captured her chin, silencing her protest. "You are a fucking queen, do you understand? I'm the one who screwed up. I pushed you too far and overstepped my bounds."

"Out of love," Maeve countered, threading her fingers through his hair.

"Out of fear." Tiernan gently brushed his thumb along her lips. "What I did stemmed from fear of losing you. I should have proven my love by trusting you. Fully."

"And do you trust me now?" she asked, searching his face, hoping to find the answer.

"I..." His gaze dipped to her neck, and the deep blue of his eyes darkened with rage, diminishing the flecks of gold completely. "Fucking gods."

"Brynn says it will heal." Maeve grabbed his hand in an effort to distract him. "Come along, my lord, I'm sure everyone will be curious to know how you escaped the Spring Court."

"Do not think for one moment," he growled, "that I am going to forget what she's done to you."

"I wouldn't expect anything less."

Tiernan pulled her into him, inhaling deeply, then together they *faded* back to the courtyard.

But there would be no time for a joyous reunion, not when Parisa was ready to ravage the Four Courts. Not when the dark fae were teeming with insatiable bloodlust.

Casimir had returned as well, though he looked more exhausted and worn than Maeve had ever seen him. He lounged against a palm tree as Brynn tended to some of his wounds. Ceridwen stood nearby, her features icy, likely still furious at Merrick. Lir was speaking with Saoirse, whose blue eyes were once again shooting daggers at Casimir. And the Furies shifted and swarmed like clouds of impending doom.

Tiernan approached Rowan first. He said nothing, merely clamped a strong hand on his shoulder, and nodded once. Rowan bowed slightly as a look of understanding passed between them.

Rowan had told the truth. Despite the accusations Merrick had made against him, he'd done exactly as Tiernan had directed, without hesitation.

Maeve pressed her lips together, and an odd twinge tugged on her heart.

Merrick strode up to Tiernan, his smile brief and fleeting. He bowed stiffly before both of them. "I've been in touch with High Queen Ciara and High King Dorian, as you requested, my lord. They are aware of our plans to move quickly into the Spring Court and will offer all of their support."

Tiernan nodded, giving Maeve's hand a light squeeze. She laced their fingers together tightly.

"Parisa dropped the veil of dark magic she was using to shroud the Spring Court." Tiernan glanced over at Maeve, then addressed everyone. "But I have no doubt she won't hold true to her word much longer."

If that was the case, they would need to protect Niahvess.

"Tethra and Dian will secure Summer's borders," Maeve announced, nodding toward two of the Furies.

They bowed in unison. "Yes, my queen."

"Balor." She motioned for him to come forward. The Fury glided closer, and the air around them cooled. His glowing eyes illuminated the hollowed skeleton of his face. "Welcome home.

I offer you my deepest appreciation for all you've done for myself and my family."

He dipped his head, and threads of darkness unfurled around him. "It was my honor, my queen."

Maeve looked toward the western sky, to where the fates of all those she loved would be determined. "If we don't attack her first, she'll come for us."

She didn't want to think about the ruination Parisa would wreak upon Niahvess. That bitch of a fae would destroy all that was good and beautiful. She would slaughter, wreck, and ruin. Maeve would not stand for it. She would not see her city fall to the likes of such vile magic, nor would she allow her people to suffer at the hands of a heinous monster.

Tiernan lifted their joined hands and pressed a kiss to her knuckles. "The decision is yours, *astora*."

She blinked and shook her head. "Mine?"

"You are just as much a part of this Court, as it is a part of you."

Maeve glanced around the courtyard, looking into the eyes of her friends. Of her family. A familiar sensation clutched at her, and the boulders of guilt piled upon her once more. This was no easy feat, no selfless task. Whatever choice she made, their blood would be on her hands.

Parisa would know they were coming to deliver defeat.

She turned to Tiernan, gripping his hand. "Together?"

His eyes swept through her soul as he said, "Together."

Maeve lifted her chin, and the cold hand of fear caressed her mottled neck. "Send word to all three legions of Faeven, we move into position tonight."

Chapter Twenty-Seven

Niahvess descended into a kind of organized chaos. Tiernan watched as groups of warriors bustled back and forth across the courtyard, hauling packs of supplies and bundles of weapons. The siphoning devices to withdraw the venom Parisa created were distributed among the ranks. Swords with nightshade-dipped blades were sharpened and ready, shields gleaming with the Summer Court's crest lined the far stone wall, and there was nothing but an ocean of cobalt and gold armor as far as the eye could see.

The archers were all armed with iron-tipped arrows. Lethal and deadly, they were strong enough to vanquish a dark fae with one well-aimed mark. Brynn inspected the archers, sweeping across the courtyard in long strides. Every so often she paused to disperse a jar of salve or ointment to the healers who were sorting their arsenal of medicinal wares.

Ceridwen stood like a beacon through the trenches of warfare preparation. Her hair was twisted back into a snug plait and bound with golden ribbons. Though she was silent, she tracked every move, carefully watching each warrior's expression. Any time there was a shift in demeanor—a spark of worry or apprehension—the gentle rush of her magic infiltrated the courtyard, soothing nerves and calming minds. There was one in particular, however, she seemed intent on excluding.

Every so often, she sent a scathing look of reproach in Merrick's direction, undoubtedly still pissed at the hunter from their earlier quarrel. But Merrick was no fool. He didn't dare meet her gaze in return, carefully avoiding any eye contact, while pretending to peruse the battle map Aran had given them.

Smart move.

Ceridwen was a force of reckoning all her own.

Tiernan maneuvered through the courtyard in search of his commander. He discovered Lir standing near a fountain, still as stone, his gaze locked onto Maeve. She'd glamoured herself fresh clothing, simple leggings and a blue beaded corset, and her golden pink curls were wild and unbound. She was working with Cahira, training the *faolan* to obey her commands, and a small murmur of awe erupted from those watching her as Cahira froze fronds of a palm tree swaying overhead.

"Lir." Tiernan approached, and his commander stiffened.

"I'm fine, my lord." His one silver eye remained focused on Maeve.

Tiernan crossed his arms, rocking back lightly onto his heels. "I'm sure you are."

"The wound to my eye has healed, thanks to Brynn's efforts." Lir's stoic composure only intensified. His fists clenched at his sides. "I will be ready to lead the Summer Legion into Spring at dawn."

"Of that, I have no doubt," Tiernan agreed calmly.

Lir turned on him, and the silver of his eye flashed. "Then why do I get the feeling that you're waiting for me to crack beneath the pressure? I will not step down from my position, Your Highness. I took a vow to fight alongside you until death. I swore my loyalty to you, and I have no plans of letting an injury—"

Tiernan raised one hand, silencing him. "I do not care about your injury, Commander."

A crease formed across his brow. "Sorry, my lord?"

"It's healed, as you have said. What I worry about is what's in here." Tiernan tapped Lir's armor just above his heart.

Lir glanced down, then slowly met his gaze.

"You did not fail her." It needed to be stated. Again. Tiernan would continue to reiterate the fact that Lir had not failed Maeve for however long it took, until the cold-blooded warrior understood.

Lir moved closer and lowered his head. "I could not save her."

Tiernan gripped Lir's shoulders in a firm grasp. "Listen to me. She will need you now more than ever. You know as well as I do that there is a very real chance not all of us will survive this war."

Silently, Lir nodded once.

"But she *must*." Tiernan released him, punching each of his words with urgency. "Do you understand? She *must* survive. No matter the cost."

Lir offered him a small bow. "I understand, my lord."

Long shadows stretched across the courtyard as the sun sank further into the western sky. Hues of twilight were already beginning to emerge, but Tiernan wouldn't order his army into formation until they could move with stealth under the cover of nightfall.

He stole a glance over at Maeve, at the bruised, burnt flesh of her neck. Thunder rattled the heavens, and everyone froze, turning to cast a wary gaze over at him. Rubbing the back of his neck, Tiernan ducked his head, struggling to maintain control of his temper.

"How?" Lir asked suddenly, his voice so low, Tiernan wasn't sure he'd actually spoken. Lir raked a hand through his dark twists of hair, shoving them back from his face. "How do we kill her for what she has done to our queen?"

"The same way we would anyone else." Tiernan's blood heated with vengeance, the promise of a rising storm. "Slowly."

From the corner of his eye, he spotted Merrick sifting through the clusters of warriors and archers, heading toward them with Aran's map in his hand.

He bowed quickly, then tucked his hands behind his back. "High King Dorian and High Queen Ciara are moving forces as we speak. Ciara will take the mountains to the north of Suvarese then move in. Dorian has agreed to flank both sides of the Rainbow River, which puts us at the forefront. We'll have to cross the river as well if we intend to take the high ground."

"Excellent." Tiernan waited a moment, then added, "Any word from Wenfyre or Brackroth?"

Merrick's face instantly shuttered. "Nothing yet, my lord."

Damn.

It wasn't the news Tiernan expected, but that didn't mean he would give up yet. There was still hope, however small, that one of their allies might arrive in time to help them defeat Parisa.

Maeve strode over to them with Cahira on her heels. She ruffled the *faolan*'s white fur, then took her place by Tiernan's side.

Merrick immediately lowered his gaze.

"I must apologize, my lady." He shifted on his feet, unease pouring from him in tense waves. "I should not have jumped to conclusions about Rowan. I didn't realize the High King had given him such explicit instructions."

Maeve arched one brow. Then she leaned forward and planted a featherlight kiss upon his cheek. "Then perhaps I am not the one in need of an apology."

Merrick's cheeks colored to a vivid pink, much like the streak in his hair. He muttered a few choice words, then shuffled over to where Rowan appeared to be in a deep discussion with the Furies.

Tiernan debated speaking with Ceridwen, whose eyes had frosted over at the sight of Merrick crossing her path, when Maeve launched herself into Lir's arms.

Tiernan blinked in surprise, and Lir didn't move a muscle.

"I'm sorry," she whispered as she wrapped her arms around his neck. Her eyes squeezed shut and pain lanced through her features.

Lir met Tiernan's concerned gaze over the top of her head, cautiously returning her hug. "What for now, little bird?"

She pulled back, searching his face. "For stomping off into those woods. For putting both of us at risk. For your eye, and for—"

Lir lifted a single finger to his lips and she quieted. "*Fieahr craie.*"

Confusion caused a line to crinkle across her forehead, but Tiernan knew the Old Laic phrase well. *True heart.*

Then Lir gave her something rare. One of his smiles.

"You'll figure it out," he murmured softly, before walking away.

Something cool and wet brushed along Tiernan's hand. At his feet sat Cahira, with her fluffy tail wagging and wings fluttering, waiting patiently for him to pet her.

Begrudgingly, he obliged the wolfling, reaching down to scratch her just behind her ear.

"She seems quite taken with you." A smirk tugged on the corner of Maeve's mouth.

Tiernan flashed her his most charming grin. "Would you expect anything less?"

She rolled her eyes to the sunset skies and laughed.

His heart soared at the sound of it. How long had it been since he'd last heard her laugh? Too long, considering he'd almost forgotten the beautiful sound.

But as quickly as it came, it faded.

Her brows pulled together, and a sharp inhale slipped through her lips. She winced, grabbing her hand and clutching it to her chest.

"Maeve?" Tiernan pulled her to him, gathering her in his arms. "What's wrong?"

Cahira crouched low, a feral growl erupting from her as she bared her fangs. White fur stood up on end, and her piercing blue eyes scanned the courtyard for any immediate threat.

"It's..." Maeve opened her hand, and the thread of black wrapped around her thumb sparked like a constellation caught on fire. "Oh no."

The Strand from the will ó wisp.

Tiernan cupped her face with both hands, forcing her to look up at him. Her sea-swept eyes clouded with panic. "Tell me. Tell me right now. What was your bargain? What do you owe her?"

She trembled in his hold. "I'm supposed to—"

Orange blossom and cedarwood permeated the air as ancient magic swept through the courtyard. A dazzling bird of diamonds and sapphires soared over the top of palm trees, a tail of glittering gemstones shimmering in its wake. Faerie lights flickered all around the base of the tree, illuminating the glow of dusk. Every warrior in the vicinity took a step back. No one moved. No one breathed. The bird swept downward, landing upon the smooth ledge of a fountain. Magic exploded in a rush of stardust and when the glamour finally cleared, the tiny will ó wisp sat perched before them.

She stood, her dainty, translucent wings fluttering. Then she curtsied.

"Hello, High King. Such a pleasure to see you again."

Tiernan returned the show of respect with a curt bow. "Lianan."

The wisp's opaque gaze fell on Maeve.

"Dawnbringer." She tilted her head, and a tinkling sound filled the stillness of the air, echoing softly. "Lianan has come to call in her favor. For the stars have aligned."

Tiernan looked up. The sky was a wash of blue and lavender, the sun was gone, but the stars had not yet revealed themselves.

The wisp continued to stare at Maeve, whose complexion had paled. "Are you ready?"

Maeve stole a fleeting glance at Tiernan, alarm reflected in her eyes. She faced the will ó wisp. "Yes...do we have to go somewhere?"

Tiernan reached out on instinct, grabbing her hand. He had no idea what sort of bargain Maeve had struck with Lianan, but he'd be damned if he was going to let her out of his sight again.

The wisp chuckled, though it lacked any humor. In fact, she lacked any emotion at all. "No, no. Travel is not necessary. Lianan will seek her vengeance here."

"Vengeance?" Tiernan repeated, a knot of dread taking form in his gut. "Maeve, what sort of bargain did you strike with her?"

She looked over her shoulder at him, and regret haunted the soft planes of her face.

"Only that I would kill the one responsible for destroying

all of the will ó wisp." Her teeth sank into her bottom lip. "I was desperate, Tier."

"I know." He lifted her hand to his lips, kissed it firmly. That was the night he'd found her at the Autumn Ceilie. The same night she'd run into Garvan and Shay. The same night Rowan had abandoned her in a forest teeming with trooping fae. The same night Tiernan had marked her with a mating dance. Of course she'd been desperate, she'd been terrified as well.

"I know," he whispered again, squeezing her hand.

"I don't understand." Maeve shook her head, her curls tumbling down her back. "You've come to ask me to hold up my end of our bargain. I know what's expected of me, but that must mean the one who obliterated the very existence of the will ó wisp is—"

"Here." A masculine voice cut through the strained silence.

Maeve's entire body went still, her hand turned to ice in Tiernan's grasp.

Shock reverberated through the courtyard, spreading like a turbulent tidal wave.

"Oh shit," Merrick muttered, and when Tiernan turned around, he echoed his hunter's sentiment.

Standing behind Tiernan was the one whose life Maeve would have to take in order to uphold her bargain with Lianan.

Casimir.

Chapter Twenty-Eight

"No." The word slipped out of Maeve before she could stop herself. "Cas."

It was impossible. He couldn't have been the one to do it, to wipe out almost an entire kind of fae. He wouldn't...except he would, if Parisa had demanded it of him.

She took a step toward him, and Tiernan released her hand, letting her go. But she couldn't bring herself to move any closer, she couldn't believe any of this was true. Yet, she'd taken a vow, and the Strand imprinted upon her thumb burned hot in a fiery reminder of her past agreement.

Casimir stood before her, then spread his arms wide. He wore the same black vest knotted with bands of tan leather, and the same loose pants, just like he had in Kells when they trained together. Before the Scathing ripped apart their kingdom. Before Faeven. Before now. What was only months prior seemed like a lifetime ago.

Lines of exhaustion slanted across his face, aging him. His youth had been stolen long ago. He'd traded his soul to save a faerie princess once, but his love for her hadn't been enough.

By the time his soul had been returned to him, he was already empty on the inside. The years had worn him down, this esteemed warrior whose heart was too broken to ever be repaired.

"I've done many things that I regret, Maeve. Many awful things." His dark brown eyes sought hers, and the sharp blade of regret chipped away at her heart. "But I will never show remorse for helping to shape you into the warrior you've become."

Maeve shuddered as pinpricks of anxiety crawled up her spine. Goosebumps rose on her flesh. "Tell me it isn't true, Cas. Tell me you didn't do such a horrible thing."

He shifted his weight, tugging his hood back so she could see the whole of his face. The remnants of his soul lay bare before her. "We've all done something we regret in the name of love."

The same words she'd spoken to him in that damned arena.

Something inside Maeve fractured.

He'd known.

He'd known all along.

All this time, Casimir knew she would be the one to kill him. She could see it in his eyes, the depth of understanding. Of knowledge. There was a deep sadness there, a lingering exhaustion like that of a dim flame ready to be snuffed out completely. Sun and sky, he'd even *told* her. When she'd *faded* for the first time out of anger and found herself on the banks of the Black Lake in the Autumn Court, Casimir had been the one to find her.

His words replayed in her mind. Not a farewell, but a warning.

"I'll see you again, Maeve. When the stars align."

When the stars align.

He continued to watch her with pained eyes, this weary warrior she had known for the whole of her life.

A blur of silver appeared on the outskirts of Maeve's vision, and Saoirse came into view. She was decked all in black, the sheen of her leather armor glinting like polished onyx. There was a sword sheathed at her waist, and two daggers strapped to each thigh. Her braid of moonlight was twisted back, and tiny wisps fell from the plait, framing her face. Tucked behind her ear was a blossom of lilac.

"If you can't do it," she said, her voice soft and even, "I will."

It was a burden no one should have to bear, to kill a friend. Even if Casimir had betrayed Maeve, he'd made every effort to redeem himself since, and she'd forgiven him. She couldn't hold his transgressions against him, not when he'd mistakenly thought he was doing what was right.

Maeve shook her head, running her finger along the Strand of black stars marring her skin. "It has to be me."

This was her bargain.

Her obligation to uphold.

She looked to Tiernan, to her rock, to the one who held her up and kept her steady when the world crumbled beneath her feet. He moved toward her slowly, anchoring her, willing to take all of her pain, all of her heartbreak.

"Whatever you need from me." The deep blue of his eyes shone with fervent affection, the gold flecks a gentle reminder he would catch her when she fell. "I'm here."

Maeve blew out a harsh breath.

Shadows loomed before her, and for a split second she thought it was Rowan, but it was Balor. His ethereal form glided over to her, never quite touching the ground. Power emanated from him, a ruthless darkness that diminished the light like a void.

"My queen." Balor bowed before her.

Maeve locked her spine into place. "Balor."

"I believe this belongs to you." He opened his skeletal hand, and hovering over above his palm was the Aurastone.

It shimmered with otherworldly brilliance, reflecting the hues of the dawn. Blush, lavender, pale blue, and gold.

Maeve's eyes widened as she reached for it. "How did you..."

"She cannot keep what was never hers."

Her hand closed around the hilt of the Aurastone, comfortable and familiar. Like an extension of herself. But it was heavier than usual, a dead weight in her hands. She'd ended many a life with this dagger, and it was likely many more would feel the cold slice of its wrath upon their flesh. Not once, though, had she ever been forced to use it against someone she cared about. Until now.

Maeve's gaze slid to the will ó wisp. She didn't look delighted, nor did she appear angry. Instead, her countenance was one of despondency. As though she was fully aware of the price Maeve was about to pay, and though it must be done, it would bring her no joy. It was simply a matter of being. Of existing in this world of magical covenants.

"Maeve."

Casimir's hushed voice cut through her thoughts, and when she turned back to face him, terror rooted her in place.

Carefully, he lowered himself to the ground, kneeling before her. "It's time."

"Cas." His name sounded strangled, and her stomach twisted into unforgiving knots. Her palms grew clammy, dampened by fear.

She was fully aware that every pair of eyes in the courtyard watched her, that every soul in attendance would witness the harsh and brutal truth of what it truly meant to be a fae. After all, the rules of magic were ingrained in the land. Like calls to like. Where something is given, something else must be taken. For even magic has a price.

Compassion draped across her shoulders, sympathy grazed her cheek, and the tranquil gentleness that was Ceridwen's magic helped Maeve remember to breathe.

Tiernan moved closer, gripping her elbow firmly. He would not let her fall this time. Or ever.

Casimir bent his head, and his dark brown hair tumbled forward, blocking his face from her view. With painstaking slowness, he unbuttoned the top four buttons of his vest, exposing his tanned chest. She swore she could hear the beating of his heart, the rushing of his blood, in her ears.

He looked up at her then, and in the deep brown of his eyes, she could see the memories they shared as clearly as if they were in her own mind. The first time he handed her a sword. The first time she made him smile after she nicked his shoulder with a blade. The first time she made him laugh when she punched him in the face. All those recollections from her mortal life flooded through her, making it almost impossible to catch her breath.

Casimir sighed, and when he spoke again, the words were a mantra. The same ones she'd repeated to him, over and over, as a warrior of Kells.

His golden gaze ripped through to her soul. "Aim for the heart and aim true. Do not hesitate. Be swift. Keep it clean. And when you walk away, no matter what—"

"Don't look back," she finished for him, her voice hoarse.

Casimir nodded, and then he smiled, breaking her heart.

Mentor. Friend. Traitor. Survivor. Warrior.

He was all those things, and more.

And then he closed his eyes, waiting.

Maeve's heart pounded, racing against the constricted walls

of her chest. All she was doing was prolonging the inevitable, but goddess help her, if she followed through with this, she would never recover.

She gripped the Aurastone, readying the blade to strike, and her hand trembled uncontrollably. Tears blurred her vision, and Casimir's face swam before her eyes.

Then a strong arm wrapped around her waist, a sure hand covered her own, helping her to keep the Aurastone steady.

Tiernan.

Her breath hitched. She couldn't do this. She couldn't kill him. Not Casimir.

Tiernan's grip tightened on her waist, and he pulled her in close.

Maeve's stomach heaved.

"On three," he murmured.

Her knees buckled. "No."

"Three."

With Tiernan guiding her hand, Maeve plunged the Aurastone into Casimir's heart. Magic surrounded them, pouring over them from every direction. Ceridwen's wrapped around her like a tender embrace, calming her agony. A new magic, one she'd never sensed before, swept in. The scent of it reminded her of winter pine and cold mountains, and it gradually slowed the flow of Casimir's blood, stopped the beating of his heart to spare him from suffering. Rowan's shadows emerged, collecting Casimir's body so he never touched the ground. They rose around him like a wall, shielding his lifeless body from her view.

It was Tiernan who removed the Aurastone.

And when all the magic receded, when it finally faded away, Maeve was empty. Numb. She knew tears spilled down her cheeks, but she couldn't feel them. She couldn't feel anything. Something was broken inside of her. It was deep and cavernous, and it carved her from the inside out, leaving her hollow. A shell of who she was supposed to be, a wraith of whatever she was to become.

Tiernan lifted her into his arms, cradling her against his chest. He carried her through the courtyard, his voice rumbling past her cheek, but he spoke in Old Laic. The words were laced with a thick accent, and she was too crestfallen to try to understand.

But she let him take her away, she let him carry her like a child incapable of taking care of herself. Once more, she was back in that cage over the Cliffs of Morrigan, with the angry sea waiting to swallow her whole. Except this time, a pair of golden brown eyes looked up at her from the dark depths of the ocean.

A sob broke free from where it had been lodged inside of her chest, and Tiernan held her tightly, a silent vow to never let her go.

She could only hope it would be enough.

Maeve closed her eyes. In the far off distance, she could almost hear the cries of a fallen faerie princess echoing through the misty mountains.

Chapter Twenty-Nine

Maeve sat on the edge of the bed she shared with Tiernan, vaguely aware of the sound of rushing water coming from the bathing suite.

At some point, she'd stopped crying, but the salt from her tears left stains on her cheeks. She didn't bother scrubbing them away.

There was a gentle knock on the door, and her heavy gaze lifted to see Deirdre slip quietly into the room. In her arms was a tray with a bowl of dried flowers and a bottle containing some type of milky substance. Maeve watched in silence as she tapped lightly on the partially open door of the bathing suite, then handed the tray off to Tiernan.

Deirdre's footfalls scraped softly against the hardwood floor as she shuffled over to where Maeve sat. The old woman wrung her dry, weathered hands together in her pale blue apron, twisting the fabric together so it wrinkled.

"Oh, dear heart," Deirdre murmured, shaking her head. She still wore her hair back in a tidy bun at her neck, but the strands of gray were more prominent now, stealing away most of the brown. Deep-set lines brought on by age and stress were etched into her plump face, and when she reached out to cup Maeve's cheek, it was as though the line between mortality and immortality had been drawn between them. "You've endured so much in the shortness of your life."

So much, indeed.

Now, Maeve had an eternity to withstand the consequences of her own actions, of her decisions. Assuming she lived past tomorrow.

Deirdre brushed her callused thumb across Maeve's cheek. "Eventually, the sharp edges of all this pain will dull, and time will slowly stitch together the wounds on your heart. But until then, you must persevere. If you give up now, if you quit on yourself, you won't ever recover."

Maeve blinked, staring into Deirdre's kind eyes.

She'd more or less used those exact words on herself. Perhaps they both had a point. Deirdre gave Maeve a peck on the cheek, winked, then took her leave.

Sighing, she unlaced her boots and tugged them off, discarding them on the floor. She padded barefoot across the hardwood to her vanity and peered at the reflection of herself in the gilded mirror. The warrior, the powerful female she used to know, was slipping from her grasp. If she wasn't careful, she would lose herself completely.

She peeled off her blouse next and sensed him watching her a second later.

"Maeve."

Just hearing her name roll off of Tiernan's tongue set fire to the coldest part of her soul. She looked over to find him lounging against the doorframe, his arms folded across his bare chest. Somehow the sight of him, of knowing he was hers until the very end, would always be enough. He approached her slowly, his hands tenderly coasting up and down her waist.

"Are you alright?" he asked quietly, her flesh pebbling beneath his touch.

"I will be." She stared at the tattoos marking his chest, the swirls of waves and suns. "Eventually."

Tiernan slid two fingers beneath her chin, tilting her face up to him. His thumb traced her bottom lip as he whispered, "Stay with me."

She searched his eyes, wanting nothing more than to lose herself in them, if only for a night. Carefully, she draped one arm over his shoulder and ran her fingers through his dark hair. "I'm right here."

Tiernan slid one hand lower and hooked his finger in the belt loop of her leggings, tugging her closer to him. He bent his head and lowered his lips to hers. It wasn't a kiss, he wasn't asking for anything. A gentle press and nothing more. A reminder. His words were a whisper against her mouth. "Stay with me."

Maeve inhaled deeply, breathing in the scent of him, attempting to ground herself.

Aed's words tickled the back of her mind.

Find the good.

She'd found Tiernan. He was good. And wonderful. And he loved her. Infinitely.

Maeve leaned in close, moving her lips over his. "I'm here."

He smiled against her mouth. "That's my girl."

Then he lifted her into his arms, carrying her across the room into the bathing suite. Gold light flickered from dozens of candles illuminated with faerie fire. The gilded vanity glittered like broken shards of sunlight while the ornate mirror reflected the two of them together. Battered. Bruised. Recklessly in love. He gently set her down, and it was then she noticed the tub was filled with creamy water—a milk bath—and its surface was scattered with flower petals. The lulling aroma of sweet summer roses filled her, nearly bringing her to tears again as Tiernan carefully helped her to finish undressing.

There was no hungry desire piercing his gaze, no raw lust while he took in every inch of her naked form. All she saw when she looked up into his eyes was the endless depth of a bond forged between two souls that had chosen one another.

Tiernan offered her his hand, and she stepped into the tub, sinking low into the warm, milky water as he settled in behind her.

With a tenderness that melted away the anguish tormenting her, he cleansed her body. Her spirit. Her soul. He lathered her hair, working his way through the knots and tangles of her curls, rinsing away the remnants of all she longed to forget. His hands slid over her shoulders and down to her arms, pulling her against him, and she leaned into the embrace, nestling herself against his pure strength.

"You should know..." Maeve closed her eyes, letting her head come to rest against his solid chest. "That while I was in the Spring Court, I was tortured in more ways than I thought possible."

For a moment, Tiernan was silent. There was only the pull of his breath, the steady beat of his heart. But his muscles tensed beneath her touch, fraught with tempered violence. Maeve laced their fingers together, wrapping his arms around her tightly.

"Do you wish to tell me about it?" he asked, his tone strained with fury and pain.

She nodded, sinking into him, into the comfort only he could give her.

And then she told him everything.

She told him about the bone-chilling cold of the dungeon, and the darkness that seemed to live and breathe. She told him about the torture room, the whipping, and the horrid way

Parisa's magic stole into her mind. With each word she spoke, Tiernan's hold on her tightened, and the bond pulsed between them. So she continued, the terrors she endured pouring from her. The dancers. The winemaker's son. The attack that shattered Maeve's spine, leaving her a bloodied, broken mess.

Tiernan's harsh breath floated past her ear and cheek.

"What can I do?" he asked, holding her as though he was afraid to let go. "Tell me, *astora*. Ask anything of me, and I will give it to you. There is nothing I wouldn't do for you. I will slay every last one of your enemies. I will carve Parisa's flesh from her body, crush her bones to ash and dust, if it would bring you the smallest sliver of peace."

He pressed a kiss to the horrific mark sealing her neck.

Maeve curled into him. "What I want right now is for you to kiss all the hurt away."

"And where does it hurt, *astora*?"

"Everywhere."

IF HIS FUTURE High Queen desired to be kissed everywhere, then Tiernan was more than willing to oblige.

He lifted her from the tub with ease, carrying her soft, supple body back to the bedroom. A warm breeze drifted in through the partially open glass doors leading to the balcony, and Maeve snuggled into him. The heat of her body coupled with the slick glide of her still-damp skin sent a bolt of arousal coursing through him. His blood stirred and his shaft thickened, throbbing with the need to bury himself deep inside of her.

But Tiernan was determined to take his time. To savor and explore her like it was the first time. To taste every delectable inch of her.

He laid her down upon their shared bed, pressing his palms into the mattress as he hovered above her. Wet curls splayed over the pillowcase, spilling around her like ribbons of glossy pink silk. Her skin was flushed from the bath and the rose gold tattoos covering her shimmered softly in the faint light. She lowered her gaze, her lashes casting tiny shadows across the tops of her cheeks while her eyes burned down the length of him.

Her teeth sank into her bottom lip, and he'd never seen anything more seductive in his life. It took every last ounce of his self control not to fill her right then and there.

Maeve's fingertips coasted along his abdomen, teasing him as she reached even lower.

He smirked, snaring her wrist right before she took him in her hand. "I believe you requested kisses first."

That bottom lip of hers, now slightly swollen from the bite of her teeth, stuck out in a pout. "But I—"

Tiernan kissed the tip of her nose. "Patience, *astora*."

He started at the sensitive spot just below her ear, featherlight as he moved to the scorched skin on her throat. Adjusting his weight, he repositioned himself to plant a series of kisses along her collarbone, dragging his mouth over the swell of each of her breasts. She shivered, a breath quaking from deep inside her as goosebumps pebbled all over her flesh, and her nipples hardened into tiny peaks.

Inching lower, he laved his tongue over one of the perky buds, swirling and sucking at her heated flesh until she arched against him. Her hips lifted, grinding against his hardened cock, and he bit back a groan as she squirmed beneath him. Sea-swept eyes glazed with lust, and he abandoned her full breasts for a more noble pursuit. Trailing his lips down her stomach, his mouth pressed kisses to her thigh, the back of her knee, and calf, then he worked his way back up, repeating the process on her other leg.

Maeve gripped the sheets beneath her, writhing like she was on fire, and he was the only one worthy of smothering the flames of her desire.

But he would do no such thing.

Tiernan had every intention of coaxing that spark to life. He wanted her to burn for him.

Settling himself between the apex of her thighs, he slipped two fingers into her slick entrance. Gods, she was so fucking wet for him.

Maeve jerked her hips and gasped, "You said kisses!"

He worked her in slow, languid movements, a smile pulling at the corner of his lips. "I lied."

Not bothering to wait for her response, Tiernan lowered his mouth to where he knew she wanted him most. Her precious clit had waited long enough for his attention.

Worshipping her with his tongue, he continued to taste and suck, luring her closer to that moment where she would unravel beneath him. Their bond crackled like kindling, the magic between them building to a crescendo, pitched with feverish desperation and longing. Her breathing hitched as she thrashed against the mattress, her hips arching as she demanded more from him.

His name escaped her on a moan, the sound of it enough to heighten his own hunger for her. He pushed his fingers further inside of her sweet heat, curling them, and when the scent of cinnamon woods and vanilla overwhelmed him, he nipped ever so slightly at her clit, driving her over the edge completely.

She was panting now, clawing at him. So wet and needy.

Tiernan covered her body with his own, moving up over her, his cock primed and ready to delve into her throbbing, sweet heat.

But then he saw the look in her eyes. They were greenish gray, crystal clear, and she was staring at him like she was trying to commit him to memory. Like this would be the last time she ever saw him.

He stilled, and she asked, "What if this is it?"

There was no hidden implication behind her words, he knew what she was asking. Understood the worry underneath each breath.

Maeve reached up and cupped his cheek, searching his face. "What if this is all that's left of us?"

He leaned into her touch. "Tell me your fears, *astora*."

She swallowed before speaking. "I fear that after tomorrow, there will be nothing left. That all of this, all of us, will be gone."

Tiernan nodded once, never taking his eyes off of hers. "And do you want to know my fears?"

A single tear escaped from the corner of her eye and he gently wiped it away.

"I fear I will never stop loving you. I fear all it will take is one errant spark, and you will set fire to this world." He eased onto the bed, pulling her against him, rolling her on top of him. "And I will stand with you through it all. Through the smoke and flame, through the dust and ash. I will remain by your side as you burn it all down. I fear you will become something wondrous, a true faerie queen. And that fear, *astora*, is power."

Her bottom lip quivered. "But—"

He pressed a finger to her lips.

"We are only given moments, Maeve. Glimpses in time. Take this moment with me." He ran his hands along her back, over her waist, and hips. She shuddered, adjusting herself, opening for him. "Live this moment with me."

Maeve rose slowly, then lowered herself onto his shaft. He groaned, grabbing her hips to seat himself deeper inside of her.

The walls of her tight cunt gripped his cock, clenching around him, soaking him. Each thrust brought the gentle crash of distant thunder. Each time she rocked her hips against him, the storm inside him raged.

At one point, he might've prided himself on being able to fuck her from dusk until dawn.

But not tonight.

Tonight, she was the maelstrom, and he was at her mercy.

She rode him with urgency, a demanding pace that stole the air from his lungs, until he was consumed by her completely.

"I will never pray to another god or goddess, so long as I have you." Tiernan ground the words out as he pumped himself into her. His fingers dug into her hips, bruising her. "I will worship you until the stars fall from the sky, *astora*. You are my temple."

Maeve splayed her hands on his bare chest. "You are my home."

With those words, he carried them both into the star-dusted heavens. She cried out as the orgasm speared her, as he emptied himself in one final, devastating thrust.

She collapsed on top of him, and Tiernan rolled, tucking her into his side. He pulled a satin blanket over them, cradling her against him. He wanted it to stay like this forever, with her in his arms. But each second that passed only led them closer to their fate.

Maeve snuggled into him, burying her face in his chest, and Tiernan froze.

A moment passed.

Another.

And he braced himself.

Then a quiet knock sounded on the other side of his bedroom door.

He sat up, and Maeve came with him, tugging the blanket up over her body. She knew just as well as he did that their time together was up.

"Come in," Tiernan called.

The door slowly opened, and Merrick stepped into the room in full armor.

"My lord." He ducked his head. "My lady. The Summer Legion is ready and awaiting your orders."

Beneath the covers, Maeve reached for his hand, interlacing their fingers together.

Tiernan nodded and Merrick retreated, closing the door soundly behind him.

Maeve slipped from the bed, a soft sigh escaping her. Tiernan followed, then pulled her into his arms one more time. He kissed her then. Soft. Like a promise. He grabbed her hand and placed it on top of his heart.

"Armor up, *moh Rienna*." Tiernan removed her hand, then placed another kiss in the center of her palm. "It's time to save the world."

Chapter Thirty

Midnight cloaked everything.

Maeve caught herself looking up at the stars peeking out from behind wisps of inky clouds, wondering if Casimir was up there, and hoping he found his way. Perhaps Dubhan would come to collect him, and then Casimir could join the ranks of the Wild Hunt as one of their esteemed eternal warriors.

If he belonged anywhere, it was among them.

By the time Maeve *faded* into the foothills of the Pass of Veils, just within the Spring Court, the war camp was nearly ready for the night. Tents were set up in orderly rows and small fires burned to stave off the chill lingering in the air. Warriors of the Summer Legion milled about the camp. Some of them shared rations of dried meat and fruits, while others sat in small groups, honing the blades of their weapons.

Brynn and Saoirse stood with a group of archers, their faint laughter quietly drowning out the murmured conversations echoing through the camp. Ceridwen was seated outside of one of the tents, her hair braided into a crown of gold, her gaze trained on the nearly moonless sky. Tiernan was with Lir and Merrick, surrounded by at least fifty warriors, each of them with their swords hoisted above their heads. She watched as Tiernan moved into the center of the circle, power emanating from him.

He was shirtless, his golden tattoos swirled from his neck, across his carved body, then dipped beneath the band of leather armor pants slung low across his waist. The corner of her mouth curved. She knew where those tattoos ended.

Tiernan raised his arm high, his hand splayed open. Violet lightning ricocheted down from the dark sky as energy and magic collided. The hypnotizing bolts crackled around his body, intensifying and illuminating the bronze of his skin. She stared in awe as he wielded the storm, as streaks of lightning splintered from him, imbuing the lifted swords with the strength of his magic. Each blade burned bright with a rich purple hue, charged with the storm of their king.

Tiernan was magnificent, and he was hers.

Her *sirra*.

Her mate.

Her High King.

A rousing cheer exploded from the warriors with their newly crafted weapons, drawing the gaze of everyone in the war camp.

Except for one.

Rowan sat on an overturned log in front of one of the fires, his back to Tiernan's powerful display. He held the Astralstone in his hand and ran one finger down its seamlessly sharpened edge.

Maeve glanced back over at Tiernan. He was still engulfed in the fervor of his warriors, of Summer Court fae who would undoubtedly lay down their lives for him—and her—tomorrow. So, she walked over and joined Rowan by the fire.

Half of his face was highlighted by the flickering flames, the rest of him was doused in shadows. Though whether or not they were of his own making, she couldn't be sure.

He didn't look up when she sat down beside him.

"Hey, Princess." His voice was softer than she expected, lacking its usual charm and arrogance.

She crossed her arms and leaned over, propping her elbows up on her knees. "Rowan."

He stole a glance at her then, his eyes tracking to her neck. His jaw ticked, but he said nothing.

She rubbed her lips together as the preparations continued around them, and for a fleeting moment, she felt slightly useless. "I feel like I should be doing something to help."

Rowan flipped the black blade of the Astralstone between his fingers with ease. "There will be plenty to do tomorrow."

Her gut seized, and she sat back, blowing out a rough breath. "Are you nervous?"

His lavender gaze slid to hers, one brow arched in question. "Are you?"

"Yes." Maeve blurted out the raw, honest answer before she could think better of it. "I never thought—that is, I never imagined..."

"That you'd be on the brink of war in a faerie realm?" he suggested.

"Exactly." She stretched out her hands towards the flames of the fire, coaxing them to life. To burn brighter. All in the false hope that the warmth they offered would erase the permanent coldness running through her veins. "In Kells, I always assumed I would be leading battles against other kingdoms."

She shrugged, dismissive. "I figured I would die there."

Images of the Moors drifted through her mind, of its enchanting trees, and a secluded pool of crystalline water. Of flowers and beauty. That place she'd once called home. She'd saved it, but not before Parisa had attempted to destroy it with the Scathing. With the *virdis lepatite* hanging around her neck, the dark magic she possessed seemed endless. Already Maeve had witnessed what she was capable of, but she wasn't foolish enough to think that there wasn't more danger and devastation lurking behind those decrepit palace walls.

An icy shudder pricked along her spine.

"I'm afraid," she whispered.

Rowan shifted, facing her, a swath of teal hair covering one eye. "Of death?"

"Yes. But I don't fear dying." That was something she'd been taught to expect at a young age. In fact, not so long ago, she would've welcomed death like an old friend. The irony was not lost on her that she was in Aed's good favor. "I fear the death of those I...love."

Again, he fell silent.

She wished he would say something, anything. Even if it was smug or brash. At least then, his cocksure comments would help distract her from the burdening weight of guilt harboring in her conscience. "I can't save everyone."

The truth of it was like taking a nightshade blade to the heart.

"Nor should you, that's not your purpose." Rowan sheathed the Astralstone, sliding it into a swell of shadows. "You are meant to save this *land*."

He reached down, digging his fingers into the earth. Gathering a clump of the damp soil, he turned, grabbed her wrist, and placed it in her hand. One by one, he closed her fingers over it.

"The Four Courts live and breathe because of you. Even when you were in Kells, Faeven sustained because you lived. Magic exists here because of you." He stood, wiping his hands off on his pants. "You are a creator of worlds, Maeve. When this is over, and the smoke clears, and if there is nothing left, then you will breathe life into this world once more. Because *that* is your purpose. If not, then the sacrifice we made all those thousands of years before will be in vain."

He was speaking of their souls, of the Dawnbringer and the Nightweaver.

Maeve shook her head. "I can't create a new world if I'm not alive, Rowan."

The corner of his mouth tugged into an all too familiar smirk. "You won't die."

"How can you be sure?"

"Because I won't let you." With that, Rowan walked away.

Maeve watched him go as he vanished into the shadows, like he'd never been there at all.

She gazed into the fire, watching the flames spark and dance up into the darkness pressing in on her. Part of her wished she could believe Rowan, that she could trust he'd hold true to his word. But he'd abandoned her before, and she wouldn't be surprised if he did so again.

Not that she was relying on him to keep her alive.

For that, she would rely only on herself.

"My lady." Lir approached her and bowed. The cobalt and gold of his armor glinted like the deepest part of the sea and incandescent beams of sunlight.

Maeve stood, dusted off her hands, and faced the commander. "What is it, Lir?"

"Your brother, Aran, sends word." He straightened, tucking his hands behind his back. "The Autumn Legion is in place. High Queen Ciara has taken the mountains."

Maeve looked around and spied Tiernan off to her right, watching her from a distance. He was dressed in full armor now, with his arms crossed over his chest, his face masking his emotions.

She tilted her head, curious, then cocked one hip to the side. "Lir, why are you telling me all of this and not Tiernan?"

His one silver eye flicked to the High King in question, then back to her. "I report only to my queen."

Lir bowed again, then strode away, leaving Maeve more confused than ever.

A second later, Tiernan took his place, offering his arm. "It's getting late. We should try to rest."

She tucked her hand into the crook of his elbow, leaning into him. "Did you tell Lir to report to me?"

"The Commander of the Summer Legion is capable of making his own decisions." A ghost of a smile played across his lips. "I trust his judgment."

"Tier," Maeve chided, swatting at him. "That's not an answer."

His response was nothing but a halfhearted shrug meant to silence her as he pulled open the cloth covering the entrance to their tent. A cushioned mattress was already unrolled on the ground and piled with a gray fur blanket and two pillows. Other than that, it was fairly empty, save for some rations of food and a few other necessities. Tiernan stretched out on the makeshift bed, decked in his full armor for convenience. The second his head hit the pillow, he closed his eyes.

"You should come lie down," he murmured.

"I will," she whispered back, "in just a moment."

Tiernan's breathing had already grown easy and deep. His chest rose and fell in slow succession, and he had one hand tucked behind his head, the other flat over the hilt of one of his swords. War or not, it honestly amazed her he was able to fall asleep so quickly.

If only she could be so lucky.

Though exhaustion tugged at her, she imagined it would be

some time before she succumbed to a dreamless sleep again. If ever.

Unable to rest, Maeve slipped out of the tent, back into the chilly night. A handful of guards patrolled the war camp, their gazes vigilant, their faces hardened to chiseled stone. They nodded to her as she passed. She debated sitting near one of the dying fires when a glint of silver caught her eye.

And a tiny, almost insignificant ember ignited in the shadows.

Maeve stalked over to her closest friend on the other side of the camp.

"Saoirse," she admonished, her gaze flicking to the tightly rolled papers pinched between her fingers. "I didn't know you smoked."

Saoirse was dressed in black and silver leathers, her braid of moonlight bound tightly with a midnight velvet ribbon. Two daggers were strapped to each thigh, and twin swords were sheathed at her waist. She'd lined her startling blue eyes with kohl, so they glittered like orbs of sapphire. A rosy pink orchid with golden tips was tucked behind her ear. Feminine yet lethal, she leaned back against a tree, and gazed up at the cloudy night sky through the overhang of sprawling branches. Taking another long drag, she inhaled, then blew out a puff of smoke. "Only before a fight."

Maeve propped herself up against the tree beside her.

"Can't sleep?" Saoirse asked.

"It's impossible." She picked at some of the rough bark digging into her back.

Saoirse brought the cigarette up to her lips once more, and the ember at its tip burned bright. "I know."

Maeve dug the toe of her boot into the soft earth, tracing the shape of a sun. "Do you think we'll win?"

Saoirse flicked the cigarette to the ground and snuffed it out with her heel. "I think we stand a fair enough chance."

That wasn't quite an encouraging response, but Saoirse had never been one to sugarcoat the truth.

"When I was a little girl, my mother would tell me stories about the faeries to the north. Their epic battles always blurred the lines between history and legend." Saoirse crossed her arms, angling herself against the tree's trunk once more. "There was one story in particular that I'll never forget."

"Oh?" The only stories Maeve knew of were the ones written in books, the ones she would read while staying awake into the early hours of the morning at the library in Kells. "Which one is that?"

"It was a story about a faerie queen with a human heart. She was valiant. Otherworldly. And loved fearlessly. It was rumored she fought in the deepest part of the ocean, through the darkest of forests, and the pitch of night. Her love for her kingdom was unfailing, and even when she thought all hope was lost, when she was sure her enemy would emerge victorious, her heart continued to beat. Strong and true. Out of love."

Saoirse pushed off the tree and wandered over to a nearby evergreen bush where a lone orchid bloomed, as though the lifeblood of magic was slowly trying to return to Suvarese. The flower was a brilliant blue, almost an exact match to the color of Saoirse's eyes.

"What happened?" Maeve asked as Saoirse plucked the blossom off the plant. "How did the story end?"

"I don't know." Saoirse stepped up to her and gently tucked the orchid behind her ear. "I suppose that part has yet to be written."

Maeve kissed her lightly on the cheek. "Poet."

Saoirse's smile was like moonbeams as she bowed and said, "Queen."

They joined hands, lacing their fingers together. Seconds ticked by, filled with all the things neither of them could say. Saoirse, because she didn't care for emotions. Maeve, because no words would ever be enough. They'd grown up on the training fields of Kells, side by side. They'd sparred with one another. Bled for one another. If they met their end tomorrow, at least they would go together.

Saoirse squeezed Maeve's hand firmly, then let her go. And when she walked away, her braid glinting in the fading light of a fire, she didn't look back.

Maeve stared up at the night sky until the stars faded from view, and a swarm of menacing clouds rolled in.

Tingles of dread trickled down her spine.

The pungent stench of death filled the air.

It wasn't clouds at all.

It was dark fae.

Chapter Thirty-One

"*Tiernan!*"

Maeve's scream pierced Tiernan's heart, sending a spear of terror straight through him.

He bolted out of the bed with both swords drawn, slashing through the tent to get to her. His blood pumped hard and fast as panic spurned him forward. "Maeve!"

Tiernan drew up short.

There she was, brighter than he'd ever seen her. Arms raised over her head, she gleamed with the brilliance of a thousand stars. Her rose gold tattoos glowed against her skin as the scent of orange blossom and cedarwood saturated the air. Magic seemed to suspend the space between them, lifting her hair from her shoulders so it floated around her like spiraling ribbons of satin. Lines of concentration crinkled across her brow, and she held strong while her shimmering bubble of protection covered the war camp.

Tiernan tracked her fierce gaze.

Hundreds of dark fae snarled and raged against the

strength of her protective sphere. They came in droves, in masses. He'd never seen so many nightmarish creatures all at once. It was as though the whole of the Sluagh had been unleashed upon them.

They attacked from every angle, attempting to claw their way through her magic. Some of them had long, spindly bodies with talon-like claws and empty pits for eyes. Others had elongated jaws with rows of jagged teeth capable of grinding bones to dust. He'd seen some of them before, when Niahvess came under siege months ago, and he'd heard stories about the dark fae who poured from the Scathing in Kells. Though most of those monstrous beings were glamoured mortals at the time of the attack, he doubted they'd been any less terrifying. Now, the dark fae led their assault from the ground, but many of them assailed from the sky. Their tattered wings were just enough to grant them flight, and they cut through the air in sporadic patterns, shrieking and raging. All of them were armed with some kind of weapon—swords, daggers, axes—and each of them was out for blood.

A tiny bead of sweat slid from Maeve's forehead down to her cheek.

She couldn't hold them off forever.

Warriors and archers, healers and hunters, rushed through the camp, stumbling over one another to stop and gaze at her. To stare at the terror she kept at bay. Whispers of awe spread through the legion, and murmurs of shock kept them rooted in place. There wasn't a soul within Maeve's sphere of protection who wasn't frozen in wonder and astonishment at the mere sight of her.

"To arms!" Maeve shouted, her voice ripping through the camp, shattering the dazed looks on their faces.

Thunder crashed, a deafening crack that rattled the ground and caused the trees to tremble.

"You heard your queen!" Tiernan bellowed, his magic a torrent of explosive rage. "To arms!"

He stalked over to her as every warrior in the general vicinity rushed to answer Maeve's call. Brynn moved to the back with the archers. They would need as much distance as possible to fire their arrows. Merrick took to the west with his hunters, for it would be easier for them to meet their mark under the guise of the outlying forest. Lir stood just behind him, the Summer Legion at his back, armed and ready.

Ceridwen *faded* in on his other side. She wore her cobalt leathers, their Court's crest stitched into her left sleeve. A band of jeweled daggers fell across her waist, and each one had been dipped in nightshade. The deadly gleam of the blades was unmistakable. Her long blonde hair was braided into a crown around her head, and she wore no jewelry. She'd lined her eyes heavily with kohl, and the black lines fanned out from the edge of her lashes into fine points. Just as their mother had done during the first battle of the Evernight War.

His twin straightened, her chest heaving. "To the end of the world."

Tiernan nodded once. "And back again."

He turned to Maeve, to his mate, in all of her unrivaled magnificence. Fucking gods, he loved her. If fate was not in his favor, then he would either die with her. Or for her. And so help him, he would find her again.

"*Infinitely,*" he whispered into her mind.

She did not falter as she answered, "*Eternally.*"

"Drop your shield, *astora.*" He steeled himself, knowing that all they loved, all they longed to save, would come down to this moment, this time. "We're ready."

Maeve kept her gaze on the throng of dark fae in the graying skies. With one hand raised, she lowered her other arm and opened her palm. Instantly, her sword of sunlight appeared, a beacon of light ready to cut through the darkest of nights. Majestic wings rippled from her back, ivory tipped in rose gold.

"Tonight, we take back the skies!" Maeve commanded. "We take back the land! We take back our *home!*"

Tiernan's wings ripped from his back, as did Ceridwen's beside him, and the bubble wavered.

He reached out, cupping the back of Maeve's neck, and kissed her hard. He broke it a second later and stared into those fiery sea-swept eyes. Pressing his forehead to hers, he gave an almost imperceptible nod.

Then Tiernan let her go.

"For Faeven!" The battle cry tore from her, echoing through the Summer Legion with a vengeance, and a rise of voices clamored in unison behind her.

And then the shimmering bubble fell.

Maeve was bound for the sky in the next instant.

Tiernan tore through the air as the clash and screams of battle reverberated around him. Rain slashed into him, and gusts of bone-chilling wind launched him into the fray. He cut through the air, severing the bodies of repulsive dark fae who bared their fangs and roared with bloodlust. With each strike, his sword sliced through muscle and tendon, through rotten bones and gurgling throats. He dove downward into a spiral, hacking as he went, ignoring the splatter of crimson that smeared his weapons and stuck to his face.

Through the low-lying clouds, he caught the barest hint of cinnamon smoke.

Orbs of fire exploded all around him as fire rained down from the sky. The stench of charred flesh filled his nose, and screams drowned out the chaos erupting below him as his *sirra* wrecked and ruined.

He knew he couldn't worry about her. He had to trust that she could handle herself. So long as he felt her through the witch thread, then she was safe.

A grotesque creature with bulging eyes that hung from their sockets lunged for him. He dipped back and shoved his sword upward, shredding the fae across its bulging chest, tearing through its vile flesh. Stretching his wings, Tiernan soared higher, killing three more as he flew through the clouds.

Tendrils of shadows spanned out in every direction, and a familiar feral magic unraveled before him.

Wings of midnight stole across his vision in a blur of eternal darkness. All around him, dark fae tumbled from the skies, their screams silent, their eyes empty, as the ruthless power of destruction descended upon the heavens.

The Nightweaver.

Rowan decimated everything in his path.

Tiernan slashed through more dark fae, then glanced down, his gaze scanning the ground forces. Bursts of gold and ruby shone through the disarray of battle—Autumn. Shards of silver and navy crashed into the conflict like a rogue wave—Winter. He could only hope the might of all three Courts would be enough to withstand the onslaught.

Continuing through the motions, he battled his way to the ground, taking another dark fae with each swipe of his blade. The rain was ebbing, becoming nothing more than an annoying drizzle, but at least it gave him a clear view of Suvarese.

Winding through the valley was the murky glint of what should've been the Rainbow River. The Autumn Legion, led by Aran, was on both sides of its banks, having secured the vicinity, but they weren't gaining any ground in the fight. Even with Malachy and the Winter Legion at their backs as reinforcements, it wasn't enough to take Parisa's stronghold. Balor,

Tethra, and Dian were malice incarnate. They tore limbs from bodies, ripped heads from shoulders, and for a split second, Tiernan remembered what it was like when the Furies of darkness, destruction, and death yielded to Carman's demands.

Dark fae continued to pour from the trenches of Parisa's encampment located on a hill just outside that godsdamned arena. Something glowed in the distance as though it was on fire, but through the haze of rain and smoke, it was too difficult to discern. They had to find a way up that fucking hill. *Fading* was out of the question, it expelled too much magic, too much energy, strength they would need to preserve if they wanted to ensure victory. Worse, they didn't have nearly enough fae with wings to fly across the river and take Parisa down, not with the hordes of dark fae converging around her like a swarm of festering darkness.

Tiernan attacked again, piercing his swords through creatures with empty pits for eyes, vicious claws, and rows of fangs. Stretching his wings, he soared higher. Below him, Suvarese was in ruins. Dark fae fell from the sky, their bloodied bodies littering the streets. Shops and homes were reduced to piles of rubble and smoldering cinders as Summer warriors and dark fae alike ravaged their way across the deserted Crown City. Howls of torment echoed over the battlefield. One voice rose above them all.

It was Ceridwen.

His gut clenched, and a wave of nausea slammed into him, causing his knees to weaken. He spun through the air toward the cacophony of noise.

His sister was screaming Merrick's name, her wails caught somewhere between outrage and fright. He watched, dread curdling in his stomach, as she sprinted across the expanse, leaping over dead bodies with lethal grace, aiming for a pile of ravenous dark fae. She threw both arms out in front of her, and that heap of creatures with snapping jaws and grotesque limbs writhed in pain.

Ceridwen inflicted the full extent of her suffering upon them. And the magic she rarely used, the power that caused her victims to feel as though their souls were being torn from their bodies, was unleashed.

From beneath the purge of dark fae, there was a slash of snowy white and startling hot pink. Merrick and a group of his hunters emerged from the throes of thrashing creatures smothering them—stabbing, cleaving, and obliterating their way to the surface. Many of them stood battered, bruised, and bleeding, but all of them were alive. They formed a circle, facing outward, each hunter ready to protect and die for the one beside him.

Suddenly, Rowan dove into the fray. His shadows devoured the Sluagh-born fiends surrounding Merrick and the hunters, demolishing them so only a mound of bones and dust remained in the wake of his power.

Tiernan swore to the gods, as soon as he got Parisa in his clutches, he would slice off every inch of flesh from her bones, force her to feast on her own rotted body, then cut off her damn head. And even that death would still be too kind.

"Behind you!" A feminine voice cried out.

Spears of sunlight streaked overhead, laying waste to a nearly a dozen dark fae buzzing through the sky above him. He tried to spin, to dodge the impending attack, but it was too late.

Claws shredded through his leather armor, sinking deep into his flesh. A guttural roar of agony tore from somewhere deep inside him, as the sensation of a hundred daggers scoured the center of his back. He lurched forward and a sudden force yanked him backward so violently, with so much vengeance, it felt as though his spine were being ripped from his body.

Except it wasn't his spine.

It was his wings.

Searing pain stole the air from his lungs, and a swell of nausea caused his head to spin. His swords slipped from his grip, his magic swam, struggling to heal him. Heat scoured him, ravaged him. The agony of it was unbearable. Warmth spread down his spine, tainted with a strong metallic scent. Blood. His blood. It gushed from the wound at his back, soaking his armor as he plummeted from the sky.

"TIERNAN!"

Maeve's scream sounded from somewhere above him.

Colors whirled past him as he fell, and that damned fae was still attached to him. Despite the torment raging through him, he twisted hard, reaching over his right shoulder to rip the fucking fae off of him. Rancid breath clogged his lungs, and Tiernan grabbed the creature's throat, crushing it with his bare hand. The dark fae gurgled, and blood trickled out from its mouth as Tiernan squeezed, wrenching it to the side, snapping its neck.

Then he let go.

His vision blurred, his heartbeat slowed.

"Tiernan!"

Suddenly, Maeve was there, diving toward him, her hand outstretched. Her eyes were wide with terror. She was screaming something, probably his name, but he couldn't hear it over the roar of wind echoing in his ears. Even with her wings tucked back behind her, he knew it wouldn't be enough. He tried to reach her, gods how he tried, but the momentum of the fall pulled him further from her grasp. She strained for him, her fingers mere inches from his own. But she grabbed only air.

What a bullshit way to die.

Darkness overtook him. Cold seeped into his skin, chilling him until his teeth chattered. Here, there was nothing. No sounds of battle, no cries of anguish and despair. He couldn't see anything, either. Not Maeve, or the war, or any sliver of light. Just a vast swath of endless pitch with no beginning and no end. Perhaps he was already dead. After all, he should've hit the ground by now. The impact alone would have killed him. Maybe this was the place in between worlds, the one nobody ever talked about, where one simply ceased to exist.

Something damp and solid cradled him, and the shadows dispersed.

Rowan dropped down onto the ground beside him, his midnight wings outstretched.

He owed the Nightweaver a life debt. Assuming he didn't die from blood loss first.

Tiernan struggled to sit up, but Rowan grabbed his shoulder, pressing him back down. "Don't move."

A flurry of gold and pink slammed into him.

"Fuck," Tiernan groaned, as Maeve's face faded in and out of focus.

"Tiernan." She choked on his name. Her hands coasted over his face and chest. "Oh, Tiernan. Your wings. Your *wings.*"

"He's losing too much blood, Princess." Shadows obscured the Nightweaver. "He needs a healer. Fast."

"But—"

"You can't save everyone, you told me so yourself." Rowan's disembodied voice seemed to hover from somewhere above Tiernan. "Now, focus. Call to Brynn, trust him to her care, then get your ass back in this fight where you belong."

Screeches and snarls reverberated across the battlefield, drowning out their voices. The vicious clang of swords, grunts, and peals of distress sounded closer. The press of battle was closing in on them, smothering them. Devouring them.

His eyes closed.

"No! Tier, no!" Maeve's cry, her devastating keen of despair, was the last thing he heard before everything fell silent around him.

This is it.

They would lose this war.

Chapter Thirty-Two

Maeve's knees struck the ground as she covered Tiernan's body with her own. Blood soaked the ground beneath him, flowing from his back where his wings had been ripped from him. His breathing was too shallow, his pulse was painfully slow. The bronze of his skin had lost all its luster. Now, it was pallid, leached of all color.

He was dying.

Her heart severed.

The witch thread ached as the strain of death threatened to steal him from her. It burned her skin, and her breath caught in her lungs, making it impossible to breathe. Her wrist pulsed in agony, and without warning, the searing heat from the mark binding them turned cold.

Maeve whispered a prayer to the god of death, begging him for mercy.

If you take him, take me. For if he goes, I may live, but my soul will die.

She waited for a response, but Aed did not answer her plea.

A white and gray wolf raced toward her, with about fifty

Summer warriors chasing behind him. His fangs were stained crimson, his fur was matted around his vicious jaws. He loosed a deafening howl lanced with heartache. One silver eye flashed at her. The other was missing.

Lir shifted into his fae form a moment later, pulling both of his curved swords at once. He'd suffered a wound to his shoulder and back, but neither stopped him from defending her. From protecting them both. His gaze flicked to Tiernan's near-lifeless body sprawled on the ground. Then he spun away.

"Take up arms!" he shouted, and in unison, a clamor of swords and shields answered the deep command in his voice. "Fight unto death for your king and queen! Danua favors the bold, the realm of paradise awaits all those who die a hero's death!"

At once, the warriors charged toward the horde of dark fae assailing them.

"Commander!" Rowan shouted above the fray, spreading his wings wide to shield Maeve and Tiernan. "Where is the rest of your legion?"

"This is all that remains!" Lir glanced over his shoulder, the planes of his face were etched with unyielding determination. "Get her out of here!"

"No!" Maeve shrieked as Rowan's arms locked around her waist, hauling her away from Tiernan's body. "No!"

She struggled, kicking and flailing, but he dragged her against him, and shot into the sky.

"Tiernan!"

The wind swallowed her scream.

"Rowan, you fucking bastard!" She twisted in his grasp, fought to get away from him even as she saw Brynn rushing to Tiernan's side. "Put me down!"

"Be still," he grunted as her elbow jammed into his hard stomach.

"Put me down!" she cried, tears burning in her eyes. "Put me down now!"

Maeve twisted, then slipped, and she was certain he'd let her go. But then he snared her arm, yanking her closer so this time she faced him. She cocked her arm back, clenched her hand tight, and swung.

Rowan grabbed her fist before it collided with the side of his face.

His lavender eyes burned hot, boring into her.

"He needs me," she choked out, unable to stop the tears from sliding down her cheeks.

"Look around you, Maeve." He showed her no pity. Not an ounce of sympathy. "Faeven *needs* you."

Hating him in that moment, hating herself even more, she did as she was told.

She looked.

And the end of the world stared back at her.

Their numbers had depleted. All across Suvarese, the legions of the three remaining Courts were being over-whelmed. Summer had suffered significant losses, the dead outnumbering the living. Autumn, separated by the river, had been pushed back into the mountains. Winter still held the ground there, but the dark fae had them surrounded. There was no way out. They were losing.

Fate was not on their side.

"I could tell you that he will live, but I find it difficult to lie." Rowan's voice softened. Not by much, but at least some of his anger had ebbed. Wet, dark teal hair was plastered to the side of his face, and a long gash cut across his cheek. "But on this I can swear—if you die, this world dies with you."

Maeve opened her mouth, but he silenced her with a shake of his head, spraying droplets of rainwater on her.

"We're going to cross that river. We're going to rip that

gemstone off her fucking neck and then kill that bitch." He snared her chin, forcing her to look into his eyes. "Do you understand?"

Shaken, Maeve nodded.

The witch thread continued to thrum. Faint and barely there. It was as though the cool hand of death had wrapped around her wrist and was threatening to release her at any moment.

But so long as she could feel it, Tiernan lived.

Rowan dove to the ground, moving through the air with immeasurable speed, then deposited her as close as possible to the river's blood-soaked banks as possible. Parisa's encampment was more visible now on the other side of the Rainbow River, but a few scattered trees and those damn hills kept her just out of reach. From Maeve's current vantage point, she could see something glowing beyond Parisa. It was hideously green and pulsed with tainted magic. Whatever it was, it was dangerous and not of this world. Dark fae surrounded Maeve and Rowan on all sides, but they had to find a way to get the rest of the Summer Legion across the river, otherwise they would be fighting Parisa on their own.

"Maeve!" Rowan shouted over the chaos of battle, stealing her attention. "Are you ready?"

Their gazes met.

He grabbed her hand.

And the Nightweaver and Dawnbringer collided.

Time slowed as sinewy shadows unraveled, and the darkness unfurled around them. Prisms of fractured sunlight morphed into beams of radiance, wrapping around the shadows, merging into one force of reckoning. The tendrils of power, the convergence of light and dark, of life and death, crawled over every surface, diminishing every vile being in its path to dust. On a breath, Maeve inhaled, drawing upon the deep well of magic coursing through her veins. The faint scent of Spring—bergamot, jasmine, and fresh rain—filled her senses. The land whispered to her of its lore, of its hopes and dreams, of its secrets as a cool breeze caressed her cheek.

In the next beat, the dawn and the night wove together in a seamless expanse of otherworldly decadence.

Then Rowan released her.

He pulled his Astralstone, she pulled her Aurastone, and together the forces of destruction and creation, the sacrifice from centuries ago, was untethered.

Maeve lunged into the turmoil, fighting with the valiance of one who knew the life of every remaining soul depended upon her.

The Aurastone cut through the air like a song, a crescendo of lethal grace whose tune she recognized in her soul. She twirled and spun, each strike becoming another chord in the symphony of her ruination. The war became a dance, one where she knew every move, every step, as though she had done it all before.

In another life.

Rowan surged forward, his movements calculated and precise. The Astralstone plunged and impaled with wicked satisfaction, a vigorous display of ferocious revenge. He stalked through the wreckage like a predator, waves of aggression rippling around him. Methodical, exacting, and brutal. With each fall of his blade, another enemy was annihilated.

Whereas Maeve was the ballad, Rowan was the cataclysm.

Exhaustion tugged at her, ready to drag her into the emptiness of misery. Her muscles burned, screamed at her for reprieve. Something silver flashed across the pale gray skies as dawn approached, like a streak of fading moonlight. Maeve shook her head once, then stumbled slightly, losing her balance.

"Don't you dare quit on me, Princess." Rowan took hold of her arm, yanking her upright. "Not today."

Together they stood their ground, their combined magic leaving a trail of death as they cleared a path for the Summer Legion. From the other side of the river, warriors donning scarlet and gold, silver and navy, clashed with the swarming darkness.

Autumn and Winter.

She blinked as Aran raced across her line of sight, his sword wreaking havoc, leaving a trail of devastation in his wake. Their gazes locked from across that godsdamned river, and in his eyes she saw the reflection of all she stood to lose. Her family. Her home. Malachy joined him, blood and filth coating nearly every inch of his armor. They fought against a slew of creatures, each one more terrifying than the last. Beasts with mangy black fur and curved horns protruding from their disfigured heads.

Puca.

Blind rage consumed her.

She would not fail them.

Maeve lurched toward the edge of the river, her Aurastone gleaming with the promise of victory.

Something sharp snapped inside of her heart, splitting her open. She gasped, the pain splicing through all the pieces she'd tried so desperately to repair. The ache was too cavernous. Too familiar.

A Strand, the familial bond tying her to another, had broken.

Maeve flung her hand out, clutching Rowan's arm.

"Maeve!" He pulled her close, searching her eyes. Worry harbored in the lines of his face. "What is it? Is it Tiernan?"

No.

It wasn't Tiernan.

Her gaze swung to the northwest, to the opposite side of the

Rainbow River. Where the dark fae surrounded the Autumn and Winter legions, where the horde of monsters crowded them back into the mountains.

His body lay motionless on the ground, his empty gaze staring up at the gloomy skies. Blood trickled from the corner of his mouth, oozed from the wound to his head.

In the recesses of her mind, she heard Aran roar as the rush of magic transferred from father to son.

Dorian, their father, was dead.

Maeve's heartbeat slowed until she thought it would stop completely. He was gone, stolen from her, and she'd never been afforded the opportunity to say goodbye. There were still so many things she wanted to tell him, so many things she wanted to ask him. She wanted to hear stories about his life, about how he met her mother, about how Aran, Garvan, and Shay were in their youth. She wanted to *know* him, to forge a bond between father and daughter, like ones she'd read about in the pages of a book, but had never experienced.

Aran was all she had left.

The thought of losing him, too, caused her mind to darken.

Rowan was in front of her, shouting, shaking her. But she couldn't understand anything he was saying. It was as though he stood on the other side of a glass wall. He was screaming at her, trying to break through the imaginary barricade she'd formed around herself.

But his efforts were in vain.

Suddenly, everything blurred out of focus. Colors bled into one another, a smear among the canvas of the battlefield. They churned and toiled, much like the mural in the library of Niahvess. Obscure shapes took form, blending together like muddled watercolors. She blinked away the haphazard tears. When the world around Maeve became sharp and distinct once more, panic sluiced through her as she watched her worst nightmare come to life.

Everything was drawn out, as though lost to the concept of time.

Echoing screams filled her ears, ringing with the clang of swords, the clash of metal, the sound of death.

She found Tiernan first.

His midnight hair was plastered to the side of his head, soaked with rain. Blood speckled his face, drenched his armor, and stained his hands. But he was alive. He was standing, fighting, and...yelling.

The icy cold fingers of desolation slid around Maeve's neck and squeezed as Brynn collapsed in front of him, taking a blade to the heart. A dagger intended for Tiernan. She'd healed him, shielding him from the assault, sacrificing her life so that he would live. He caught her right before she hit the ground, her burgundy curls falling limp as her head lolled against his outstretched arm.

Everywhere Maeve looked, the harrowing vision of death continued to unfold.

Merrick and Ceridwen were hedged in by a pack of nightmarish fae with black veins that bulged from their nearly translucent skin. Ceridwen was tucked in close to Merrick's side, his arm wrapped tightly around her waist. Blood spilled through his fingers while he pressed firmly against the wound to her abdomen. Her leathers were torn into pieces, revealing the swath of shredded golden flesh beneath. She clung to Merrick, her skin growing paler by the second, as he fought off the dark fae closing in on them with one hand.

They were going to die.

Maeve had to stop this, she had to save them. She couldn't bear to lose any more of her family.

She lurched forward, but something in Merrick's expression kept her frozen in place. His blue eyes widened, his jaw went slack, and for one terrifying moment, Maeve thought he'd been killed. His face reddened, heating with untempered vehemence. Veins pulsed along his neck and he bellowed one name.

"Ciara!"

The hot pink streak in his hair vanished, replaced with strands of snowy white.

His gaze latched on to something behind Maeve and she turned, tracking his line of sight.

She clamped one hand over her mouth as Ciara swayed, her body buckling on the opposite bank of the river. One of the Puca had run her clean through with a sword, twisting it, wrenching it from her stomach to her heart, while a sadistic cackle erupted from his driveling mouth. He ripped his weapon free with barbaric vigor, then lifted his leg, kicking her square in the chest. Ciara staggered backward, her crown tumbling to the ground. It bounced once. Twice. Diamonds scattered like drops of crystal and ice. Blood seeped through the silver of her armor, so vivid and bright it was as though Maeve could see Ciara's magic draining from her body.

Malachy moved with unrivaled speed, diving to catch his queen before her body toppled into the river's current. She crumpled, lifeless, into his arms.

Winter and Autumn's legions shuddered, splintering and cracking beneath the pressure of battle. Their lines would not hold for long, not with both the High King of Autumn and the High Queen of Winter now dead.

"Maeve!"

She whipped around at the sound of her name and found Tiernan sprinting toward her, the hard lines of his face set with determination. He struck down every dark fae in his path, slashing and scouring, destroying anything that stood in his way. Beads of rainwater and drops of blood sprayed from his armor and sword as he tore through death and mist to reach her. He impaled, he razed, he demolished for her, leaving a trail of dead bodies behind him as his magic amplified and the storm of Summer rained down upon them.

The second he was within arm's reach, Maeve grabbed him. Her fingers curled into the leather armor covering his chest, and she dragged him against her. Pinning him in place with a furious scowl, she glared up at him. "Don't you *ever* scare me like that again."

Tiernan winced. "Apologies, *astora*."

Even covered in blood, soaked from rain, and caked in mud, he was still so godsdamned beautiful. So much so that she could've kissed him.

Then Lir was screaming. Howling. Raging. He was running toward the river's edge, vaulting over the dead, his arm reaching out for something on the other side.

Maeve turned, her boots sliding against the sodden earth as she sought out the cause of his fury. Her heart stilled. That slash of moonlight from before hadn't been lightning. On the hilltop, where Parisa maintained the high ground and her stronghold, was a warrior dressed in all black, with a braid of silver that shone with the glow of midnight moonbeams.

"Saoirse," Maeve breathed, disbelieving.

She'd been captured.

Maeve couldn't move, couldn't think. All thought emptied from her mind as she stood frozen with fear. It kept her rooted in place, filled her with irrepressible panic. She was trapped, locked in that horrid cage once more, unable to break free as the world around her fell apart. Soon enough, the branch supporting her would snap, and the cage would fall into the ocean, taking Maeve with it. Those angry waves of damning guilt, of excruciating trauma, would pull her down into the darkest depths of an unforgiving sea, and she would drown.

Parisa stood on the damp ground, a sickly green glow emanating from her. The *virdis lepatite* hung from her neck, swinging like a pendulum against her black velvet robes. A portal of darkness churned behind her, flaring with flames from the innermost circle of hell. Horrid screams pierced the air, nightmares seethed and clawed their way through the blackened fires. It was a gateway to the Sluagh. The purgatory. The realm where the most malevolent of creatures were banished.

More terrifying, however, wasn't the portal from which the dark fae continued to emerge and wreak havoc upon the Spring Court.

No, it was the fact that Parisa's hand was twisted into Saoirse's braid, and she jerked her closer to that blazing entrance. She raised one of her dagger-like nails, slicing from the apple of Saoirse's cheek all the way to her chin. Crimson spilled down her pale skin, running over her mouth, dripping down her neck.

Saoirse didn't flinch, but her sapphire eyes burned hot with hatred.

Parisa's lips curled back into a sinister smile as she licked the tip of her nail, swallowing Saoirse's blood.

Maeve's stomach convulsed, bile scalding the back of her throat.

"Mm." Parisa's voice echoed across the battlefield. Her sneer widened. "Tastes like victory."

A plume of hideous green vapors swirled at her feet, and Parisa pushed Saoirse into the scorching portal of the Sluagh.

"NO!" Maeve screamed, flinging one arm out. "Saoirse!"

Her magic roared, frenzied and frantic.

Don't you dare! Maeve issued her command to the god of death. *Don't you dare take her from me!*

Aed's rich voice infiltrated her mind. *I can only do so much, Dawnbringer. I can't give her back.*

A wail, a grievous keen of sorrow ripped from some broken place inside of her. She reached out, willing her power to her control, summoning the full wrath of creation. Vengeful and snarling magic rose within her, rattling her bones like a caged beast. It tore through her, unhinged and ravenous, desperate for release.

Threads of power siphoned from her, flares of blinding sunlight skittered across the expanse, crackling and hissing as they neared the portal. Her body trembled as her magic delved into the pitch of dark flames, searching for a warrior with the heart of a poet, whose braid was a beam of incandescent moonlight.

She would pull her back.

She would bring her *back*.

Beads of sweat trickled along Maeve's brow as the lifeblood of magic coursed through her, amplifying with each passing second. Her knees trembled. Her breath left her in a cold shudder.

There was a loud crack, so deafening it caused Maeve's ears to ring.

Power exploded from her soul, a blast of such magnitude, it tore through the fabric of the worlds.

Maeve shattered the realms.

And then, everything fell silent.

Chapter Thirty-Three

Maeve expelled ancient magic in a force so powerful, it blasted Tiernan away from her.

He landed hard on his back, and pain splintered up and down his spine. Glaring light left him blinded as he struggled to get back on his feet and regain his bearings. He stumbled in a daze, blinking against the harsh outburst of radiance. His body continued to throb from the loss of his wings, and even though Brynn had saved him—died for him—he'd lost a significant amount of blood. He was weak, his magic nearly depleted. But nothing would stop him from returning to Maeve's side.

Nothing, perhaps, except the void looming before her.

She'd ripped apart the fabric of space and time, and a gaping chasm extending from the bloodied earth to the churning sky fractured the heavens. Veins of darkness eddied from the tear in the realm. The sinewy shadows fanned out like strands of midnight silk, twisting around the radiance emitting from her, extinguishing the light. The seam stretched wider, opening like a gaping mouth of impenetrable dark, ready to devour the world.

Ready to devour her.

Maeve faced the abyss of her creation, where the threads binding the separation of worlds had been severed. Rowan stood next to her, the Astralstone gripped tightly in one hand, staring up at the swirling mass of endlessness before them.

Deafening silence befell the battlefield, as though the void had absorbed all sound. Tiernan called out, shouting their names, but his voice was swallowed by the unnatural quiet. His warning would never reach them.

Tiernan lunged forward, but it was like moving through a dream. He swore he was running, racing to her, but he wasn't covering any ground. He was too slow, his movements sluggish.

"Save her!" he implored, forcing his thoughts into the Nightweaver's mind.

Rowan flinched like he'd finally been pulled from the trance that kept him locked in place. He reached for Maeve with his free hand. Tiernan expelled a sign of relief. Rowan would do it. He would save her. Even if it meant dragging her away to safety against her own will. She might hate them both for it, but that was something they would deal with later. Assuming they survived.

"Fuck." Rowan spat the word out, and then he did the unthinkable.

He shoved Maeve into the void.

"No!" Tiernan shouted, horrified as she was consumed by the darkness. One moment she was there, and in the next, she was gone. Untraceable. Unreachable.

Shock slammed into him, and he sank to his knees in despair. His chest caved, his breathing hollowed out as the cold rush of anguish swept through him. It was as though the god of death himself had reached into his chest and ripped out his heart. His soul wept. She was his song. His beginning and his end. His blood and tears. She was his eternity.

And she was taken from him. Forever.

Tiernan glanced down, ripping at the armor covering his wrist.

The witch thread remained, imprinted upon his flesh. But the bond was silent. He couldn't feel her, he couldn't feel anything. It was simply a tattoo upon his skin, a reminder of what was, a connection to nothingness.

Time ceased to exist.

Chapter Thirty-Four

Maeve screamed.

At least, she thought she was screaming. She could no longer be sure. Sound was distorted, a cacophony of heartbeats, rushing blood, and the ticking of what reminded her of a clock.

One moment, she'd been on the battlefield of the Spring Court, watching her best friend die. And in the next, she was... somewhere else.

Her gaze scanned her new surroundings.

The sky was a piercing blue, too vibrant to be real. Wispy, white velvet clouds floated through a sea of aquamarine, drifting aimlessly across the broad expanse. She stood in a field of emerald, the long blades of grass swaying back and forth, stirred only by the gentle breeze. The dazzling landscape stretched out before her. It was picturesque, an endless horizon of beauty. She glanced behind her, hoping Rowan might have followed her through after shoving her into the void, but she was entirely alone.

Some part of her wanted to be furious with him for

throwing her into this place, but in truth, she no longer cared. She was empty. Emotionless. There was nothing left inside of her. She'd given everything, all of her love and hope, every last broken piece of her heart to protect the ones she cared for most. She'd given her soul. And it had not been enough.

The loss was too much, the trauma too great.

She was barren of feeling—everything that made her fae, everything that had once made her human, was gone. Her Aurastone was still in her hand and she sheathed it, unable to look at the blood staining its iridescent blade.

Maeve lowered herself into the soft green grass, pulling her knees to her chest. For a moment, she simply breathed.

Blood soaked her armor, stained her hands. The metallic stench of it clung to her, and she supposed she would never be able to wash it all away. So she sat, filthy and damaged, a blemish upon the splendor of this world.

Again, she inhaled, picking up the faintest trace of smoke and amber.

"Hello, little wild one."

It was a voice she never expected to hear again.

Shay.

Maeve looked up sharply, disbelieving.

Gradually, a tall fae male came into focus. His golden hair was swept to the side, and a pair of eyes, a perfect match to her own, twinkled back at her. He smiled, broad and full, and as handsome as ever.

"Shay." Her voice broke.

She reached up for him, and he grabbed her, pulling her into his arms.

Maeve melted into his embrace, hot tears spilling down her cheeks before she could stop them. He eased back, smoothing her hair from her face, and her bottom lip quivered.

She sniffled, swiping at the errant tears. "You're alive."

"Not alive, darling sister." Shay cupped her cheek, and his eyes reflected the well of sadness brimming in her heart. "I reside in Maghmell. But it seems Danua thought you were in need of my assistance."

Maeve's brow furrowed, and she tried to ignore the tiny bubble of hope taking form in her chest. "The goddess of life wants to help me?"

"Correction," Shay countered. "She sent me to help you."

As much as she loved her brother, she wasn't entirely sure what he meant. "Help me do what, exactly?"

"*Heal.*" He draped one arm casually around her shoulders, gesturing vaguely to the spacious field. "Walk with me."

He took one step, guiding her along with him, and the world blurred into a haze of melding colors. It was like walking through realms.

Orange blossom and cedarwood surrounded her. Magic filled her. Renewed her.

Shay waved his hand before them, shifting the colors, drawing them back into focus. "Let me show you what you're fighting for."

Maeve saw a world where the mountains were so high, they almost touched a starlit sky. A place where carriages were pulled by flying stallions, where magic thrived in a way she never thought possible, where a family of stars owned the night. It was lovely. Dazzling. She'd never seen anything so wondrous.

"You're fighting for worlds not your own," Shay whispered, his voice carrying through the heavens.

Another wave of his hand, and the colors morphed before her, blending and fading to show her someplace new. This time, Maeve gazed upon a golden city dripping with sparkling grandeur. Life filled this place, but never in her wildest dreams would she have imagined a world where mortals and immortals lived among one another peacefully. Yet here, such harmony existed. The rich city sat at the edge of a magnificent harbor, where ships of all sizes docked in its bustling port. One in particular looked oddly familiar, but before she had time to place where she'd seen it before, Shay took her hand, and whisked her away into another whirl of magic as the golden city faded from sight.

He gave her hand a reaffirming squeeze. "You're fighting for those who cannot fight their battles alone."

They continued their walk through the realms, and Maeve found herself overlooking a kingdom brimming with lush greenery, where an ivory castle was situated upon a hill surrounded by an enchanting forest. She witnessed a mortal girl running barefoot through trees, her lacy white dress hoisted with both hands as she splashed through a crystal clear stream, aiming straight for a faerie ring of flowers and mushrooms. Wherever she was running to, or whoever she was running from, didn't seem to matter. For the girl did not look afraid. Her youthful face was set with fierce determination.

Shay stepped again, and she went with him. His voice was low, almost ominous, when he said, "You're fighting for those who will answer your plea for help, for the ones who will claim your enemies as their own."

The world darkened and together they stood on a frozen cliff, where gray clouds loomed, and rain fell in a steady drizzle. It looked as though it had never felt the warmth of the sun. A sense of foreboding washed over Maeve as a piercing shriek echoed through the steep, frostbitten mountains. Dragons soared overhead, their majestic wings slicing through the dense mist the same way a blade would cut through silk.

"But most importantly," Shay said, softer now, "you're fighting for your future. For those who will come after you."

Maeve saw them.

Three boys and one girl.

Her children.

Shay took her by the shoulders, turning her to face him. "Because you see, Parisa will not stop with Faeven. Greed taints her heart, the lust for power has destroyed her soul. You must be the one to end her, to cease this war before it spreads beyond Faeven's shores."

Magic cocooned her. It coasted over her skin, tickling her cheek, slowly mending all the broken pieces of who she was, of who she would become.

The air around her sifted and billowed, a golden shimmer, and then she and Shay were standing in the empty field once more.

Maeve shook her head. She knew he'd shown her other worlds, other realms. But these were all places that somehow felt dependent on her. She couldn't bear to have this rest upon her shoulders alone. "I don't know how to do that, Shay. We've already lost so many, and our father..."

She couldn't even speak the words.

Shay released her shoulders, understanding. "He waits for me in Maghmell."

A breath shuddered out of her, and she released the fear. "What if I'm not enough?"

"You have always been enough." He smiled, his eyes softening. "The love you carry in your heart makes you more than enough."

"Love," Maeve repeated numbly. It hardly seemed like such an emotion would make any sort of difference.

"Love is no match against the corruption of hate." Shay bent down, pressing a kiss to the top of her head. "Love always wins."

Then he stepped back, away from her.

"Shay?" Her breath hitched and she reached for him. He was leaving her. Again. "Shay, wait!"

"It's time for me to go, little wild one." He winked. "I'll see you again."

He *faded*, and Maeve grasped only air.

Before she could recover, Rowan tumbled into the void, and he almost fell on top of her.

"Rowan!" She grabbed his arm, hauling him to his feet. He looked just as wretched as she did, perhaps even worse. "What are you doing here?"

He crossed his arms, lightly rocking back on his heels. "I feel like it's fairly obvious. I came to bring you back."

Maeve huffed, jabbing him in the chest with an accusing finger. "But you're the one who pushed me in here!"

"And for good reason." Rowan moved closer, his gaze narrowing. "You destroyed that portal to the Sluagh. How did you do it?"

"I...I don't know." She'd only been trying to get Saoirse back. In that moment, it was all she wanted, her sole intention. But if the portal was gone, that could only mean one thing. Saoirse was gone, as well. Forever. Maeve shook her head, dismissive. "It doesn't matter how I did it."

"Oh, it fucking matters." He pointed behind him to where the void was already closed. "You're the Dawnbringer. You create, you don't destroy."

"That's not true," Maeve countered, planting both hands on her hips. "Aed told us in the Ether that I could create and destroy worlds."

"Worlds," Rowan reiterated. "Not sinister portals opened by the use of dark magic."

"What difference does that make?" Maeve glanced down at her hands. The blood covering them had dried, and she scrubbed them against her leather pants. "It's not like I was trying to close the portal. I was trying to pull Saoirse out of it."

"Sun and sky," a feminine voice drawled with contempt. "Would the two of you quit bickering? It's exhausting."

Maeve whirled around to see Laurel standing across the field, a bored expression gracing her beautiful face.

She was decked in her sleek black regalia, the same stunning leather armor she wore the night she saved Maeve from the wandering souls in the Ether. Her amethyst hair was twisted back into a high ponytail that fell to the middle of her back. Her eyes sparkled like black diamonds, and in one hand, she carried the Key to Oblivion. She twirled it idly, and its terrifying blade stole every shred of light it touched.

A shiver streaked down Maeve's spine.

Laurel stalked toward them, then stopped, cocking one hip to the side, as though she'd rather be anywhere else.

Rowan muttered something about fate, and Maeve was about to ask him what he meant when Laurel tossed a hasty glance over her shoulder.

"Time to go." She spun, raising the Key to Oblivion. It arched through the air, reopening the void.

Dark tendrils curled outward from the widening chasm like the fingers of death.

"Go? But I just got here." Rowan nodded toward the field. "Maeve has to—"

"Maeve already knows what she has to do," Laurel snapped, annoyed. Then her black gaze raked over Maeve, her brows lifting with suggestion. "Time works differently when one shatters the realms."

Maeve bristled, unsure if it was merely a statement of fact or a blatant insult.

"What was seconds for you, Rowan, was far longer for Maeve." Laurel glanced over at her, and for a brief second, her icy exterior melted. "Have no fear, that which awaits you on the other side has not changed. Everything is as you left it."

Confusion left Maeve dumbfounded. Had time stopped within the Spring Court? She opened her mouth to ask when Laurel shook her head.

"Really though." Laurel nudged her closer to the void. "You have to return. Now."

"But..."

"Go quickly!" Laurel rolled her eyes to the blue heavens, then looked back over her shoulder again. "Before we piss him off further."

"Piss who off?" Maeve demanded.

Laurel groaned, her aggravation palpable. "Someone you'll have the pleasure of meeting in another time."

Perhaps it was the urgency in Laurel's tone, or that Maeve simply didn't want to miss her opportunity to return to Faeven, to Tiernan, to try her damndest to win the war. But she nodded, then turned, staring headlong into the shadowy void.

"Rowan?" Maeve looked over at him. "Are you coming with me?"

He smiled, but it didn't reach his eyes. "I'm right behind you, Princess."

"Good luck, Dawnbringer," Laurel called out to her. "May the tides of fate be in your favor."

Maeve blinked. She'd heard that before.

Without thinking, and revived with fresh determination, she leapt into the void. But then a hand grabbed hers and held tight.

Maeve twisted against the shadows, fought as they tugged her. She kicked hard, her free arm flailing as she turned. There was Rowan, reaching through the void, straining to hold on to her hand.

"Rowan?" Apprehension caused her brow to furrow, and something akin to trepidation lanced through her heart. "Come on, you have to hurry. The void is closing."

His expression shuttered, but she saw it before he could hide it away—his intent to stay behind. He wasn't coming back with her.

"I told you already, my fate has been decided." Dark teal hair fell over half of his face, shielding his eyes. But even through the damp strands, she saw the lavender hue of them burn bright with one emotion meant solely for her. Love. "You don't need me anymore."

"What?" Maeve croaked, and the shadows holding her tugged again. She was losing her grip. Losing him, too. "But what will happen to you? Where will you go?"

"To another lifetime." He squeezed her hand, but their fingers were slipping. "To another realm."

Unexpected tears caused her vision to blur. They were cold as they slid from the corner of her eyes.

Rowan flashed his signature smirk. The one that was always so infuriating. So endearing. "Don't cry for me, Princess."

And then he let go.

Magic swelled around her, engulfing her. Stealing her vision, swallowing all sound. She drifted through the void, floating through the unraveled threads of space and time.

Rowan and Laurel were gone.

Chapter Thirty-Five

Rain continued to fall in the Spring Court, but it wasn't enough to wash away the blood soaking the ground. Shreds of sunlight tore through the ominous sky, igniting a spark of hope.

Disoriented, Maeve expelled the breath she'd been holding.

She was back on the battlefield, deposited into the chaos of death once more. But there was no time to recover, no time to replay everything she'd just experienced with Shay, Rowan, and Laurel.

She had to fight, had to win, had to live.

"Maeve!" Tiernan swept her up into his arms, crushing her against him. His scent of warm sandalwood, palms, and plumeria washed over her, becoming part of her. "I thought I lost you."

Raw agony haunted his voice, and she threw her arms around his neck, relishing the feel of him. His heart beat in time with her own, and their uneven breathing matched one another, so the rise and fall of their chests became synchronous. She buried her face in his neck, reveling in him.

"Never."

Tiernan captured both sides of her face, running his thumbs across the tops of her cheeks. His eyes harbored every emotion she thought she'd never feel again. Sadness and pain. Anger and worry. Fear and love.

"We have to get out of here. We need to fall back and regroup before we lose anymore lives, before it gets worse. Before we lose everything and everyone."

"No." Maeve held firm against his plan.

"What?" He shook his head, then shoved his wet hair back from his face. "But, Maeve—"

"Marry me, Tiernan." Her heart swelled as soon as she spoke the words.

He stared at her like she'd just invited him to sit down for a cup of coffee in the middle of a war.

"I plan on it." The corner of his mouth twitched. "As soon as this is over, I have every intention of making you my wife."

"I don't want to wait." She'd never been more sure of anything in her life. "You told me before to live the moments I'm given, and I want to live every moment with you. From now until forever."

She opened one hand, summoning her sword of sunlight. Then she raised her arm, drawing the dark, tumultuous clouds roiling overhead. She pulled them, beckoning them to her, and the lifeblood of magic coursed through her in a volatile current. The clouds spiraled toward her, forging a weapon in her opened palm, one crafted of biting wind and stinging rain, imbued with the wrath of distant thunder. A sword of storms.

Maeve handed it to Tiernan, smiling. "It's now or never."

Together, they slashed through the next tide of dark fae. Maeve moved with newfound energy, clinging desperately to that spark of hope igniting inside of her. She coaxed it to light with love, willing it to burn as bright as the dawn. The sun danced with the storm, a tantalizing display of magic, of brilliant light and ominous clouds, melding together to extinguish the dark.

Spinning on one heel, she turned to where Merrick and Ceridwen were surrounded.

No more.

Bolts of fire and iridescent streaks erupted from the tips of her fingers. Her magic ravaged the earth, scorching a path straight to them as the ground split open like the angry jaws of a raging beast, devouring the dark fae on either side. Burying them alive.

With the portal gone, all that was left to do was kill the dark fae who stood in their way of Parisa.

This time when Maeve smiled, it was with pure vengeance.

Merrick and Ceridwen rushed to them. Ceridwen was still bleeding from the wound to her side, though not as profusely, thank the gods. Merrick, however, wasted no time launching back into the fray, keeping Ceridwen safely behind him while he cut down every monster that so much as snarled in his direction.

"Merrick!" Maeve shouted. She lunged into her next attack, ducking low to avoid a blade, slicing the vile creature in half.

His sword lanced through the air, cutting off the head of a fae with gangly limbs and hideous yellow teeth. The severed head rolled by Merrick's feet, and he sneered down at it in disgust. "Yes, my lady?"

"We have to get married!" Maeve's gaze flicked to Tiernan, and the barest of smiles graced his full lips.

"As much as I love you, Maeve, my High King would have my head, if I so much as dared to try and steal you away from him." He swung his leg out and kicked hard, launching the grotesque head into the sky. "Much like this poor fellow."

"Not me and you." She laughed, the sound nearly foreign to her. "Marry me to your High King."

With Ciara gone, he was the rightful High King of Winter, which granted him the authority to conduct the binding ceremony.

Merrick reeled around, a bewildered expression plastered to his face. "Right *now*?"

"I can't think of a better time." Maeve rolled through the muck to avoid an outstretched claw of a grotesque dark fae. She pierced it through the heart, then yanked her blade free. A strong hand clasped her elbow, hauling her to her feet. Tiernan's smile was breathtaking. She gazed up into his eyes and asked, "Can you?"

"I'm a little indisposed at the moment," Merrick grunted, staving off another attack. "And besides, where the hell am I supposed to find a ribbon for the binding?"

"Right here." Ceridwen ambled forward and shoved a golden ribbon into his hand.

He glanced down at it, then stared back at her. She'd taken the ribbon from her braid, and her hair fell down around her like a waterfall of golden silk. Her face was expressionless, her ruby lips set into a hard line. An unreadable emotion flared to life in Merrick's eyes, but he quickly shuttered it away.

"Very well." Merrick dodged to the left, striking down another dark fae. His hand clenched around the ribbon, then he handed it back to Ceridwen. "Bind their left hands."

Ceridwen worked quickly, tying the strand of gold silk around both Maeve and Tiernan's wrists, weaving it between their fingers. The fabric was soft and cool and against Maeve's skin as Tiernan grabbed her hand, gripping it firmly.

Side by side they fought, never letting go of one another. They moved in unison, anticipating every parry, strike, and attack. Magic flowed through them freely, ebbing and breaking like the tide. It rose in cresting waves, crashing around them in a swell of undeniable power and strength.

"Now, Merrick!" Ceridwen shouted, calling out above the calamity of dark fae closing in on them.

Merrick's sword glinted as it cut through the swarm of darkness. He shoved Ceridwen behind him, keeping her far from their reach. "Blood of their blood, I call unto thee, Mother Goddess who commands the earth, air, and sea."

Gripping his weapon with both hands, he swung wide, slashing through the terror. "Born of one breath, one heart, and one ember, take these two souls and bind them together."

His fierce gaze cut to Maeve, and then his dimples flashed. "Say your vows."

Tiernan dragged Maeve close, lifting their joined hands above their heads, just as he would if they were dancing. His eyes were startling, clearer than she'd ever seen them. Deep blue, dark violet, flecked with mesmerizing gold. He grinned down at her, gorgeous and devastating all at once. "Maeve Ruhdneah, for as long as we walk these planes of existence, my soul will never know another. I will live for you. Breathe for you. Die for you."

Maeve had never considered wedding vows. She'd never thought about what she'd say to him in this moment, but they spilled from that broken place inside of her. That place made whole because of him. "I choose you, Tiernan Velless. And I would choose you again. In this lifetime, in every lifetime. From now until the stars burn out of the night sky, until worlds collide, you are mine."

He pressed his forehead to hers, and she swore then and there to give him everything. Every shattered, damaged piece of her.

"Infinitely," he murmured.

"Eternally," she whispered.

"Fucking kiss already," Merrick demanded.

Tiernan's smile widened, and then his mouth was on hers. Warm and inviting. He was the summer and the storm, the wicked, the wild, and the wonderful. A fairy tale come to life. He was every hope and dream, every wish and fantasy. And he was *hers*.

Maeve's arm warmed, and she glanced up to see the gold ribbon evaporate completely. The witch thread faded from her skin, and in its place, a tattoo took shape. Deep blue waves encircled her wrist, and at its center, on the inside, was a golden sun. The same one imprinted upon Tiernan's flesh as well. The new Strand bound their souls, bound their love.

A rush of arcane magic crackled in the air between them, swelling with ancient power. Fusing with intensity, it continued to build, as though it was absorbing every fiber of her. She shuddered, and pinpricks of anxiety crawled along her spine.

"*Relax, astora,*" Tiernan whispered into her mind. "*It's part of the union.*"

But there was a distinctive waver to his voice, as though not even he was entirely certain of what was happening.

The pressure continued to grow while the heady scent of orange blossom and cedarwood overwhelmed them.

When Maeve thought she couldn't take any more, when she thought for certain this surge of archaic power would end them both, an earth-shattering blast erupted from between them. Beams of iridescent light scattered across the expanse of the battlefield like the shards of a thousand broken rainbows.

When it finally cleared, Maeve saw Lir bounding over to them, his curved swords swinging through the air. He drew up short, chest heaving, a line marring his stern brow. "What in the seven hells was that?"

Merrick snorted, rolling his head from side to side. "These two decided to get married."

Lir's scowl deepened. "And I wasn't invited?"

"We'll celebrate another time, commander." Tiernan clapped him on the back. "First, we have to save our Court."

He was right, of course. Even though Maeve had somehow closed that damned portal, thousands of dark fae continued to wreak havoc on all that remained of the three legions.

With Tiernan by her side, Maeve prepared to cross the Rainbow River. The grassy knoll of its bank was slick with rainwater and blood. Her boots slid at its edge, and she grappled for purchase. Tiernan caught hold of her arm, keeping her steady. The water flowing through it was a murky gray color, its beauty long since diminished. Its current was swift, and if she recalled correctly, its riverbed was incredibly deep. Gods, she *hated* the water. At least water where she couldn't see the bottom, or when it moved with enough speed to drown her. Many of the Summer warriors would have to swim, as the nearest bridges were to the northwest and southeast. She could fly, but she refused to leave Tiernan behind.

"Ready?" he asked, lacing his fingers with hers, preparing to jump.

Maeve loosed a breath.

For Faeven, she reminded herself, refusing to think of the angry ocean.

She reared back, preparing to make the leap, when a loud rushing noise filled her ears. The tides parted, sweeping up and cleaving the river in half, revealing its sandy, pebbled bottom. Giant walls of dark water formed, so high Maeve thought they might cave in at any second.

Tiernan dragged her back a step, and then she saw a pair of black, fathomless eyes that never blinked. Shimmery scales appeared, and long, inky hair fanned out to reveal a crown of seashells and crushed pearls. Two hands with webbed fingers dug into the wet banks, and the merrow queen heaved herself into an upright position, her gaze locking onto Maeve.

"Queen Marella!" She hadn't seen the merrow queen since the Ether, and she'd assumed the merrows chose to remain neutral in the war.

"Dawnbringer." Queen Marella inclined her head in greeting. "Your reinforcements have arrived."

An almost feral-sounding battle cry echoed across the Spring Court.

Maeve sucked in a breath as hundreds, if not thousands, of druids stormed the western front. Their ships must've landed along Suvarese's shores, and they moved with exceptional speed, assailing every remaining dark fae in their path. They donned armor of twisted vines, multi-colored leaves, and gilded leather. All of them, males and females alike, had long hair woven into intricate braids. Moss or flowers decorated the striking antlers protruding from their heads. Some carried staffs, summoning the magic of the earth. Others wielded spears and battle-axes. White, brown, and green paint marked their faces with runes and whorls. They charged forward like an unstoppable force.

"Wenfyre." Disbelief shaded Tiernan's tone.

An ear-splitting shriek reverberated through the skies.

Maeve looked to the heavens, where broad shadows massed, circling like a tempest.

Her heart skipped.

Rowan.

But it wasn't the Nightweaver. It was...

"Dragons," she breathed.

"Sun and sky." Ceridwen's voice floated from somewhere behind her.

Riders sat atop their backs, steering them through the

gloom and haze. They dove through the thick clouds, their outstretched wings cutting through the mountains like blades of obsidian, scarlet, and moonstone. The beasts roared, streaks of fire emitting from their vicious jaws, scorching the hordes of dark fae threatening to end the Autumn and Winter legions.

The stench of tainted magic and charred flesh filled the air.

Maeve tried not to retch.

"Ciara was right." Merrick stepped up to her other side, his cerulean gaze focused on the dragon-riders. "The Prince of Brackroth came in our most dire of moments."

The prince was easy to spot. His dragon was the largest beast she'd ever seen, with claws rippling down its back and wings, and a tail capable of destroying castles. More interesting, however, was the way he seemed to move with the shadows.

But there would be time to admire the impressive dragons later. Right now, Maeve was going to kill Parisa.

"Let's go!" she cried, vaulting off the grassy bank and across the muddy riverbed while Queen Marella held the walls of water.

Tiernan sprinted alongside her every step of the way, with Lir, Merrick, and Ceridwen following closely behind.

Once on the other side, Maeve led the assault against the remaining dark fae, aiming straight for the hill where green smoke curled around Parisa like a sickly bonfire. Aran and Malachy stormed in from the northwest, clashing with the Puca who were quickly losing ground. The crimson and gold of Autumn rushed to the forefront, the navy and silver of Winter closing in right behind them.

Maeve held nothing back as she tackled the hill. She slaughtered. Demolished. Destroyed every revolting creature in her path. Fresh blood sizzled against the sunlight emanating from her sword, screeches of agony rang loudly in her ears.

Smoke from the fires set by the dragons caused her eyes to

water, but still she pushed. Clawing and killing with each step, each thrust, each brutal swipe of her blade.

I show mercy to no one.

She repeated the mantra over and over. Her legs ached and her arms were heavy, but still she climbed, refusing to yield.

A loud boom vibrated throughout the heavens, as though the realms had been ripped open again, and her gaze swung to Tiernan.

He shook his head once. "It wasn't me."

She sought the darkening skies, where turbulent slate clouds seethed with retribution. The ground beneath her trembled, the trees shuddered, bowing over to the force upon them. Even the mountains seemed to quake with fear. The sound of thundering hooves, like that of a hundred wild stallions, rumbled across the battlefield.

From the turmoil of darkness, they emerged.

The Wild Hunt.

The eternal warriors rode into the fray, valiant and deadly. They careened across the skies, laying waste to those not worthy of life. At the front of their deadly siege was none other than Dubhan, the Lord of the Hunt.

His stallion of midnight galloped overhead, and his unworldly gaze met hers. "The tides of fate have turned, Dawnbringer."

Empowered by his words, Maeve tore up the hill and came face-to-face with Parisa.

Her sneer stretched across her papery thin lips. The black velvet robes she wore were pristine, and the *virdis lepatite* hung from her leathery neck, its hideous green glow pulsing with dark magic. "Well, well. I see you've finally decided to grace me with your presence."

Maeve sensed Tiernan behind her, the strong beating of his heart giving her a sense of calm. "It's over, Parisa."

"Oh, my pet." She spread her bony arms wide. "It's only just beginning."

Parisa reached for the throbbing gemstone, the source of her corrupted sorcery.

But a blur of white flew in front of Maeve, diving straight for Parisa's throat.

"Cahira!" Maeve cried, clamping one hand over her mouth.

The *faolan*, however, was faster than she anticipated. Loosing a bestial growl, the wolfling ripped the *virdis lepatite* from Parisa's neck then circled back around, dropping it right into Tiernan's outstretched hand.

"No!" Parisa shrieked, rushing forward.

"*Siocahn.*"

The corner of Maeve's mouth curved as Cahira obeyed and fired a bolt of frost at Parisa's feet. Shards of ice crawled up her robes, splintering out like fragments of glass. Her translucent skin frosted over, her lips turned blue, and icicles formed around her thin scraps of hair.

Maeve threw out both hands, fiery flames pouring from the tips of her fingers. Her magic seared the ground, enclosing Parisa in a circle of flames so high they nearly licked the sky. Offering just enough warmth to ensure the bitch's heart continued to beat when Maeve carved it out of her.

"You think some fire and ice will stop me?" Parisa cackled, her dark eyes flickering with madness. "You're pathetic, Maeve. A damaged, broken soul. Look at all who have died for you, whose lives were ended because you weren't enough to save them."

Tiernan's deep baritone filtered into Maeve's mind. "*Do not listen to her, astora.*"

Parisa's body twitched, encased in ice. "You destroy everything you touch. You were never cursed with fae blood, you were cursed for merely existing."

Maeve was vaguely aware that Merrick, Ceridwen, Lir, Aran, and even Malachy had gathered closer. Ready to jump in and protect her. Ready to save her.

But this...this was her fight.

And this time, she did not need saving.

"Your friends will come to resent you," Parisa spat, and it froze to her lips. "Your mate will come to hate you. In time, you will wish you had died here, on the bloody battlefield behind you. But not even the god of death will hear your pleas."

Maeve tilted her head to one side. Slowly, she unsheathed her Aurastone, lifting it. She ran one finger along its shimmering blade. "That's where you're wrong."

Parisa faltered, and her eyes widened, frost spreading along her spidery lashes.

"The god of death will *always* answer me." Maeve flicked her dagger in her hand, then walked through the fire. "And he is far more merciful than I."

She glanced over at Tiernan. "Destroy it."

"As you wish, *moh Rienna*." Tiernan raised his sword high, bringing it down with all the fury of a storm. Green smoke unfurled from the *virdis lepatite* before the core of it cleaved, cracking in half, and the stone went dark.

"No!" Parisa raged, only to fall silent as Maeve treaded closer.

"A good man loved you once." She poised her blade, driving it into the ice formed across Parisa's chest. "This is for him. For Garvan and Shay. For my father. For Saoirse. And for every soul you've sought to destroy."

And then, Maeve carved out Parisa's heart.

Black blood oozed from the gaping wound. The ice melted as Parisa's lifeless body shriveled, crumpling to the ground in a pile of velvet and dust. Maeve pierced the bulbous organ with her Aurastone, then yanked it free. Parisa's heart blackened and turned to ash in her hand. She opened her palm, letting the slight breeze whisk away the charred remains from her skin.

Silence befell the Spring Court.

The remaining dark fae evaporated, their screams lingering after their bodies left the world.

A strong arm wrapped around her waist, pulling her in close.

Tiernan.

He pressed a kiss to her temple, and she leaned into him.

Parisa was dead. The dark fae were banished back to the Sluagh. Though the expense was significant, the war had been won.

Faeven was safe. Her home was safe. Her family was safe. Recovery would take time, years even, but she would find a way. She would mourn, then prevail. She would live.

Maeve once thought her heart was her greatest weakness. Now she discovered it to be her greatest strength.

Love always wins.

Chapter Thirty-Six

When the next sunset painted the heavens crimson and blush pink, they buried Brynn at the base of the Vista, where she would forever have the best view of Niahvess. Palm trees swayed over her grave, and the river that spilt into dozens of canals kept the flowers fully bloomed. Aeralie stayed behind long after they sang a strain in the old language, while silent tears slipped down her cheeks.

Tiernan felt Brynn's loss keenly, though he imagined it was far worse for Aeralie.

Dorian was returned to Kyol, where they constructed a granite headstone for him and Fianna, along with matching smaller ones for Garvan and Shay. Each one was carved with an image fashioned after their likeness, the expanse of their lives engraved beneath their given names. Maeve stayed in Kyol with Aran for a few days so they could mourn and grieve their loss together. Granted, Tiernan had lost both of his parents, but Maeve had lost her two brothers as well. Though he knew the pain would never truly go away, he held onto hope that eventually she would find solace in knowing they waited for her.

Once she returned from Kyol, his wife gave the silver-haired warrior a proper burial.

Maeve gathered every log herself, and bound them with twine until her knuckles cracked and bled. She built the raft, carefully covering it with a stack of fallen palm fronds despite there being no body to burn. Tiernan watched from afar because she had not asked for help, and he supposed she didn't need it. So, he stood to the side as she placed two silver coins atop the raft, keeping watch as the scent of orange blossom and cedarwood perfumed the air. An orchid the color of Saoirse's eyes bloomed from the fronds, its petals unfurling toward the setting sun. With a flick of Maeve's wrist, tiny flames ignited, and she wrapped her arms around herself as the floating pyre drifted out to sea. It coasted on the waves of the Lismore Marin, faint plumes of smoke swirling up into a bleeding sky of orange and red.

Maeve stood on the shores of Niahvess long after the pyre vanished from sight.

They never learned who crossed Saoirse into Faeven after she fled Kells, the bargain she made had died with her. Whoever it was wanted his identity kept secret, and he'd succeeded.

Days after the war, it was just the two of them on the balcony where they dined, sitting in silence. Maeve's gaze was focused on the horizon, Tiernan's gaze was focused on her. She was stunning, beautiful and radiant in a gown of scarlet silk that draped off of her shoulders and fell around her in waves. Her golden pink hair was in long, loose curls, tumbling freely. He leaned forward in his seat, reaching out to brush a fallen strand from her face. Tucking it back behind her ear, he glamoured some flowers, weaving them into her hair, just as he'd done the first day he met her.

Tiernan leaned back in his chair and opened his arms,

summoning his guitar. He strummed a few chords, a soft and gentle melody, a tune he knew he'd written for her. Then gradually, he began to sing.

"I'll tell you a story of a warrior queen,
who won battles and hearts with her spirit.
With a palace by the sea, and a throne made of dreams,
so gather round if you long to hear it."

Maeve's gaze flicked to him, and when she smiled, it was a real one. The first one he'd seen in days. He grinned in return, continuing with the lyrics he knew would ease her heart.

"Between realms she fought through pain and strife,
she is fearless, brave, and strong.
She's the mountains and seas, the magic of life,
and her legend will carry on in song."

Her nose crinkled and she sniffled once, wiping away a single tear. "Tiernan."

"Talk to me, *astora*," he murmured, wishing she'd tell him all the thoughts weighing on her mind.

Though he hadn't expected her to go into much detail, she surprised him by telling him about the field she'd found herself in, and how Shay had appeared. She spoke of worlds not their own, of magical places, and far-off realms. He remained quiet, listening intently, absorbing everything she said. Her eyes glossed with the threat of tears.

But she didn't cry.

He strummed his fingers along the table. "Perhaps we can visit one of those places some day."

She sighed. "Perhaps, but there is much to be done here first."

This was true.

At some point, Maeve would venture back to the Spring Court and attempt to revive what was left of the land. It was still a barren wasteland after the war. Much would need to be purged, and there was plenty more that would have to be renewed.

She'd wasted no time restoring his wings, and for that gift, he would be eternally grateful. Her magic had created them to be an exact replica of how they were before, and though he wouldn't be the one to admit it, he knew her wingspan was larger. Even if she let him pretend otherwise.

Maeve sat back in her chair, fiddling with one of the flowers he'd glamoured. "I still have to figure out how I'm going to rule over three Courts."

He arched a brow, amused. "Three?"

"Yes. Summer, with you, of course. But Aran doesn't want to stay in Faeven, and my father named me as heir to Autumn. Or at least, he asked me to rule in his place." She shifted, her cheeks coloring slightly. "And I assumed I would take the Spring Court as well, since Rowan...left."

It was the first time she mentioned the Nightweaver since the war ended. Maeve had been strangely quiet after Rowan's disappearance, and he knew better than to push her about what happened within the void. All he knew was that Rowan went in after her, and never came back out.

Tiernan reached out and grabbed her hand. "I'm sure you'll manage just fine."

Lir appeared at the door a few moments later. He bowed. "Your Highness, we're ready now."

Maeve tilted her head, her brows furrowing. "Ready? For what?"

"I have a surprise for you." Tiernan led her to the outdoor throne room, then paused just outside of it. "Close your eyes."

"Tier..."

"Trust me," he whispered.

Maeve sighed, but she did as he asked. He took her hand, guiding her into the throne room, carefully leading her to the center of the space.

"Now, open."

Maeve opened her eyes and gasped.

Positioned next to his throne was one crafted especially for her. It was made to look like her Aurastone, reflecting shimmering rainbows, the beauty of the dawn. The top was curved into a sun, with two crescent moons on either side, complete with an array of glittering stars.

Ceridwen stood to the right of it, her hands clasped before her, the picture of elegance.

"Sun and sky." Maeve looked at him, her eyes filling once more. "Tiernan..."

"For you, *moh Rienna*." He bowed before her.

Her steps were slow and measured as she approached it, and he didn't miss the slight tremor in her movements. Wonder, and awe, and love reverberated down the bond between them.

Merrick, Lir, Aran, and Malachy stood before the dais, bowing as she passed.

Summer warriors, along with the fae of Niahvess and those who survived the fall of Suvarese, filled the remainder of the space. Some of them were smiling, while many of them cried, watching her every movement with bated breath. Deirdre was at the front of the crowd, her eyes watery as she dabbed at them with a swath of embroidered cotton. Balor, Tethra, and Dian were in attendance as well, positioned along the far wall. Shadows of darkness swirled around them, their glowing red eyes never leaving their queen. When Maeve glanced over in their direction, each of them lowered to one knee.

Tiernan helped her up the stairs to the dais, her hand clinging tightly to his own. Ceridwen beamed, her ruby lips lifting into a smile as she lowered herself into a curtsy.

Maeve turned to face the sea of warriors. Merrick, Lir, Aran, and Malachy left their positions and walked up to the throne in unison. All four of them kneeled before her, fisting their hand over their chests.

"*Moh Rienna*, the Faerie Queen of Faeven," Merrick began, lowering his head. "I abdicate my throne, the seat of the Winter Court, to you. I pledge my loyalty to you, vow to honor your name, and will forever remain in your service."

Maeve's bottom lip trembled and her eyes widened. "Mer..."

Surely, she had to know by now, to understand that she was the one destined for this land. Legends had been born from her promise. Songs had been written about her—after all, he'd been the one to sing them to her.

She lifted her chin.

There she is.

Tiernan took his place by her side, pressing a kiss to her knuckles. He would love her until the stars fell from the sky. He brushed one hand across the top of her head and a crown appeared, crafted from gold and rubies. A crown of jeweled roses.

"You are my queen, but make no mistake, you rule over the entirety of the Four Courts." Tiernan drew her closer, inhaling the scent of her, and the Strand between them soared to a crescendo, a song he recognized in his soul. "I will only ever kneel before you, Maeve Ruhdneah Velless. My soul is yours, infinitely."

She wrapped her arms around his neck, rising on her toes. Her kiss was soft. Intimate. The promise of a thousand lifetimes.

"And I'm yours," she whispered against his mouth. "Eternally."

Tiernan captured her cheek with one hand, looking into

those sea-swept eyes, those eyes he'd known were meant for him since the first day he saw her. "You are, and always have been, the once now and forever Faerie Queen."

Epilogue

Ash fell like snow, and fires smoldered as far as the eye could see.

Her boots were soundless as she walked across the damp ground, her gaze skimming the vicinity for the one thing she sought. She knew it had to be here, somewhere. A connection like the one she'd witnessed wouldn't dissolve without leaving any trace behind. There had to be *something*.

The guardian continued her search, annoyed by the steady drizzle of rain that did little to put out the fires and was more of a hindrance than anything.

She was about to give up, to quit this ridiculous hunt for what she *knew* was here, when the faintest glimmer of light caught her eye.

"There you are," she whispered.

Of course it would be there, where a sparse patch of grass was greener than the rest, where a tiny pink rosebud blossomed from the tip of its frail stem.

How fitting, she mused.

Carefully, she bent down to inspect it.

The tiny orb glowed with swirls of golden pink, lavender, and a little spiral of teal.

A final sacrifice.

She collected it in her palm, cradling it gently.

"Aren't you a pretty thing?" The guardian smiled, running the pads of her fingers over it lightly. The orb flared brighter. "Come on, let's go show this new world exactly who you are, little fae."

Acknowledgments

Where do I even begin?

This book, this series, has such a huge hold on my heart. It took me ten years to write Crown of Roses, and there were times I didn't think anything would ever come of it. Times when I stopped writing completely because I didn't think I was good enough. Yet here we are.

First, I need to thank my cartographer and map designer, Elayna. Dream big, darling.

I also need to thank my editor, Emily Michel, who took me on during Throne of Dreams, and helped me put out the best books possible.

To Angie and Kristin, thank you so much for beta reading this book. To Lindsay, Carrie, and Chyanne, you will forever have my endless gratitude. Thank you to Emilia for backing me off so many ledges.

Thank you to my girls who will one day read the stories mommy writes, and to my husband who probably never will ;)

And to my readers, to the ones who carry a piece of Faeven in their hearts, let me just say, I love each of you. Infinitely.

To the end of the world...

About the Author

Hillary Raymer is a fantasy romance author. She's a wanderer, a storyteller, and the founder of BohoSoul Press.

Hillary has always been a dreamer, and lucky for her, she turned those dreams into stories. She has an unfinished Bachelor's Degree in English because she ran off and married a Marine halfway through college. She has an affinity toward plants, loves the mountains, and enjoys scoping out metaphysical markets for crystals. Wanderlust comes to her naturally, and she's doing her best to instill the same wild and free values in her daughters. When not writing, Hillary can be found attempting to do yoga, buying more makeup she doesn't need, or discovering small businesses on Etsy.

Join her Court here https://discord.gg/EfHVy93Gvz

For access to her backlist, sneak peeks, and current projects, subscribe to her Ream here https://reamstories.com/hillaryraymer

Also by Hillary Raymer

The Faeven Saga

Crown of Roses

Throne of Dreams

Realm of Nightmares

Void of Endings

The Starstorm Series

All the Chaos of Constellations